A SOLDIER'S SON

JACK ESTES

A Soldier's Son is a work of fiction. None of the characters ever existed. A few passages were previously published in essays, but have been fictionalized. The names, locations, military bases and events are fiction.

Cover photo by Dale Archer
O'CALLAHAN PRESS
Copyright © 2015 Jack Estes
www.jackestes.com
jackestes@comcast.net

First edition

ISBN-13: 9780997399004
ISBN-10: 0997399007
Library of Congress Control Number: 2015918086
O'Callahan Press
Lake Oswego, Oregon

I dedicate this work to my wife and children. I know living with a marine combat veteran has not been easy.

Chapter 1

The Kelly home sits on Lake Parrish with a panoramic view of the water, boat docks, and million-dollar homes. It's November 2004. The house is dark, and the lake is flat, as Mike types in front of his computer, working on tomorrow's newspaper column. He's behind schedule again, and the night editor has e-mailed three times, cursing and pressuring him to get the damn story in. But Mike likes pressure; it makes him feel more alive and powerful, as if he *does* have control of his life. He feels satisfied as he reads his essay on the screen one last time.

> Last night, when the moon was gone and the neighborhood was quiet, I grabbed my coat and walked down the hill toward Wilderness Park. With me was my squad of young marines, dead and wounded, yet still living in my memory. The air was wet and cool as they followed me down the block, gliding under streetlights and sliding past parked cars. At the bottom of the hill, we turned silently into the thick, dark woods.
>
> As a marine in Vietnam, I hated moonless nights in the jungle. It was impossible to see. My imagination would soar; I could hear my heart beat and feel the adrenaline surge. When we were dug in on the side of a mountain, trees became moving shadows, and the wind was

the enemy brushing through the broad leaf. Back then, Jesse was in the hole next to me. Padre, Stoner, and Buddy were invisible down the line. A snap of a twig was an enemy footstep, but we had been warned, "If you throw a grenade, you best have a body in the morning."

Now, after thirty-five years, I long for moonless nights. I like walking with my squad as we edge deeper into darkness. These are gentle woods, I know, but jungle memories still hang in the chilled evening air. I can feel my brothers, frozen in time, and I imagine our younger days, when we fought in the mountains near Khe Sanh or in the rice paddies and villages near Da Nang. I remember their names and faces and the cruel, violent last moments of their lives as our chopper went down. Buddy was different. He was psychologically wounded, but it took twenty years for him to die—from a drug overdose in Boston.

I walked softly along the well-used path and tried to recall how my rifle felt, the heaviness of my pack, and what it was like to be so powerful. Stoner was huge and carried the machine gun easily, cradled in his arms like a child. Padre followed him, weighed down with extra ammo and a love for Stoner that only soldiers know.

My squad is my youth, and some of them died in my arms, like Jesse. I recall him just as clearly as my wife's sweet lips and the touch of her skin. I can tell you the color of his hair and the look in his eyes as his life faded. I've told her all the stories and written all the stories, and she has listened and pulled me close when the war was too real. I don't want my squad injured anymore. I want them standing strong, rifles ready. That comforts me.

I moved carefully through the park up a slight hill to a ridge I know, where the ground is flat and even. A deer rushed by, breaking my reverie, reminding me of something long lost. It's harder going down the hill now that I am almost sixty. I moved slowly, grabbing on branches, bracing for a fall. Then I thought about another war, where our soldiers fight in a country full of sand and suicide. They are coming home in silver boxes draped with flags, surrounded by stiff salutes. Or they stagger back to family, arms and legs missing and faces burned away. At breakfast, I read about another Oregon boy who died in Iraq. He was handsome and bright. He's living inside some other soldier now. Perhaps someday this soldier, too, will be saved by a woman's touch.

It's my autumn ache, when leaves turn and the gold and red maples are shedding. Last night, when the moon disappeared, I walked in the woods with my squad, closing in on another Veterans Day.

———∞∞∞———

Mike's column flashes to the newspaper, just beating the deadline. He closes down his laptop and sits back, remembering when he was young, strong, and carried a machine gun. His eyes have adjusted to the darkness, just as they did in the war. His back is sore as he stands and begins his nightly routine, hobbling around the dark house, making sure all the doors and windows are locked. Downstairs, he checks on his teenage son, Mick. His light is off, but Mike can hear him talking on his cell...probably to his girlfriend, Cait.

Mike cracks the door and says, "Good night, Son, and get off the phone."

He climbs the stairs quietly, trying to recreate the softness of the steps he once took back in the jungle, a lifetime ago. In their bedroom, he sees that Claire's eyes are closed and her breasts are lifting and resting with each breath.

He crawls in, touches her face, and lies back, and soon he's drifted into the nightmare again.

———∞∞∞———

A red Frisbee spins slowly through a blue sky and disappears. Suddenly, the sky turns black and gray, rocked with the fury of monsoon winds and rain. Darkness crashes. In the distance, there are faint lights and the wail of a marine corps chopper, as it crosses the mountains and descends into the A Shau Valley. Waves of wind and rain pound and hammer the chopper. Lightning flashes as the Huey fires rockets and long, broken lines of red tracers into the jungle.

Inside, two pilots fight the controls, trying to keep the ship steady. The crew chief and four marines sit on webbed seats, rolling with the wind, banging back and forth against the walls. Enemy rounds smack against the chopper. The door gunner stands harnessed, his machine gun in a sling as he works it back and forth, firing a line of tracers, killing the night. Flares drop from a C-140 above, as the wet wind wails.

"Son of a bitch!" the gunner shouts as an enemy round slices through his leg. He swings the barrel of his M60 left to right and fires through the pain, sending more rattling streams of red tracers. The chopper pitches, blown by the wind and rain, while green tracers fire up from the ground.

The marines are young and strong, faces covered with camouflage paint and beads of sweat. They curse or pray silently, squeezing rifles, sleeves rolled, arms ripped. Flares and flashes light them up. The crew chief at the front of the chopper stands, stumbles, and slams against the walls. The visor on his flight helmet flips up; his mustache is soaked with spittle, and his teeth are yellow and broken. He shouts to be heard. "General's chopper went down! Your guys are getting their asses kicked! We've got to turn back."

"Bullshit!" Mike shouts. He's confident, strong, and powerfully built. He's strapped with a .45, and as he grips the stock of a sawed-off shotgun, a bulldog tattoo on his right forearm bulges.

"Your firebase is overrun! There's no place to land."

Mike jumps up and thumps his chest. "Screw you! We got our brothers down there. Take us lower, and we'll jump out of this piece of shit!" He reaches across the aisle, pulls Jesse to his feet, and shouts to the others, "Let's go. Stoner! Padre! Wake the fuck up!" Mike kicks Stoner's boots. Jesse grins while the others look stunned as more rounds riddle the chopper.

"Grab your socks and cocks, and let's kick some ass." Mike starts a loud "Haaruugah!" As the others join in, Stoner pisses himself.

A loud explosion rocks the chopper. The engine misfires. The door gunner is shot through the head. His body blows out the door and flops against the side of the chopper, hung up by his safety harness. The chopper pitches, spins, and is sucked toward the ground.

"Jesus Christ!" cries the crew chief. "We're going——"

Mike is knocked flat. He grabs the base of a webbed seat and reaches for an airborne Stoner. It's no use. Stoner grasps at Mike's shirt and then his pants, but he is ripped out the door, his face desperate, not saying a word. The chopper breaks through the trees and slams the ground, and rotors grind to a halt. Claps of thunder boom, and more lightning splits the sky, along with the hiss of white parachute flares as they glide over the jungle. What's left of the fuselage rests a few feet above the ground. Stoner is in a tree, sheared in half by the rotor. At the nose of the chopper, a fire starts. The pilot's head has shot through the glass. The copilot is strapped in, burning, mouthing blood, face destroyed, his last breath easing into the jungle.

The rain slows. The door gunner swings from his harness, his body broken, thumping against a panel. The firing has stopped. It is quiet. The wind dies. No one moans. Quiet. Rain gently taps the roof of the chopper and drips off broadleaf plants, forming puddles on the jungle floor, while the smell of burned flesh wafts through the trees. Somewhere in the dark, there is the sound of a whistle.

A group of forty North Vietnamese Army hard-core regulars gathers in a cluster, raindrops flickering on their bush covers. The soldiers are excited, looking for the chopper. They have fought days and nights and endured the terror of gunships firing, jets dropping napalm, and B-52s unloading earth-shocking five-hundred-pound bombs. Some of their comrades evaporated, some turned mad, and some, on fire, ran screaming, deep into the jungle, eardrums exploding. When the NVA finds the chopper, they will kill the marines—shoot them, shoot their dead bodies, strip them, and hack them with machetes.

An NVA captain points, his oval eyes full of hate. He blows his whistle, and his soldiers move out. Then the rain stops. In a moment, the sky is clear, and half of a moon drifts from behind a cloud and hangs in a body of stars.

Mike is alive, disoriented, swimming slowly in a tangle of jungle. His helmet is gone, his uniform shredded, and his face cut and bleeding. His shotgun is missing, and a small, broken slice of branch has pierced his left hand. He takes the Ka-bar strapped to his leg, trims the branch, and with great effort, pulls it out the other side. He takes a battle dressing from the outside pocket of his pants, tears off the plastic with his teeth, wraps his hand, and wipes blood from his broken nose. Another whistle and he feels for his .45. It's still there in its shoulder holster.

He can see the gunner swinging in the moonlight. What's left of Stoner sways in a tree as Jesse crawls slowly out of the chopper door. Mike limps to the chopper and helps Jesse out, noticing his forearm hanging in pieces. He searches Jesse's pockets and whispers, "Where's your battle dressing?"

"I forgot the sonofabitch!"

Mike looks inside the chopper, sees the last of the fire, notices the smell, the pilots, the crew chief and Padre lying lifeless. They're all dead. He hears a whistle. He has to work fast. He knows the enemy is coming. He climbs in, grabs a rifle and a bandolier of ammo, and slings it over his shoulder. He steps out through the doorway, jumps down to the ground, and wraps an arm around Jesse as they hobble from the crash site to hide in the jungle. He stops. The radio. Got to get the radio. He lays Jesse down in a thicket, picks a leech off his face, and sees a Frisbee in Jesse's hand. How can that be?

Back inside the chopper, Mike slips in a wet blanket of blood. The fire is out. In the dark, he feels the crew chief and rolls him off Padre. Padre is on his back, still wearing the radio. His legs are flopped, feet lying flat. Mike lifts him to a sitting position and works the radio pack off. A flare glides above the chopper, floats by a window, and lights their faces. Padre's eyes open.

"Help me."

⸙

Mike bolts up in bed, startled, sweating, his eyes wide open, searching. He listens. He's feeling more guilty than terrified. Moonlight crosses the lake, and shines through the French doors onto his face, as Claire sleeps next to him. The clock on the nightstand reads 3:00 a.m. He's upset: not this again. He lies back and remembers the feel of blood on his hands, the warmth, thick and sticky. He smells the jungle, the rot, the gas and oil, and sees the fire. Had life left Padre's body? What happened to him when the NVA came? He remembers Jesse—his arm hanging, bone broken. The whistle. The flares dropping. Claire reaches for him instinctively, touches him, pulls him down, and holds him until his eyes close.

Chapter 2

Mike wakes again just before the alarm clock rings and reaches out to punch it off. He turns on the lamp, and his faded bulldog tattoo is caught in the light. On the nightstand is the untitled manuscript he has just finished writing. It's a historical novel about the French Underground during World War II. It's full of Nazis, heroic French men and women, and an American soldier who falls in love with Petra, a leader of the French Resistance.

He picks up the manuscript, reads the first page, and mumbles, "Crap." The writing is sophomoric, he thinks, not nearly as good as his last book or any of his essays. Those were the essays that made him a finalist for the Pulitzer Prize for Journalism. When that happened, his agent said he'd better cash in and quick. So he wrote a war novel, which made him good money. That was two novels ago. Now, this one was full of weak characters and almost no arc. Lots of blood, though. He was good at firefights and good at describing how it feels to close off open arteries with your hands.

"Mike, the light. Please." Claire rolls over and pulls the covers.

"Sorry." Mike turns off the light and staggers toward the bathroom like a busted-up cowboy. He's fifty-eight. Nine broken bones, four knee operations, and a back full of arthritis. He's lived hard. He started knocking drunks out in bars when he was seventeen. He's been shot, stabbed, hit in the face with a brick, and he almost died from two types of malaria and amoebic dysentery.

Built like an aged athlete, he wears boxers and has a gnarled gunshot wound in his back. His chest wound looks like a handful of muscle and sinew was scooped out and covered with a flat patch of pink plastic. Mike was nineteen and crossing a rice paddy when the round hit him in the back, tumbled through his lung, broke three ribs, and made a bigger hole on its way out. With time, the lung healed fine and only started bothering him when he crossed the other side of fifty. Now, everything hurts.

In the bathroom, he flips on the light, looks in the mirror, and scratches the rash on his neck that he's had since the war; he doesn't notice the dent in his chest where his pectoral muscle used to be. The counter is full of prescription bottles, magazines, and a baseball glove. Better move it, or she'll get pissed, he reasons. His knee already hurts, and he braces his weight against the sink with one hand, swallowing pills with the other. Pills for pain, swelling, diabetes, and depression. Got to lose thirty pounds, he thinks, grabbing the fat on his belly. If I drop twenty, I won't need half of these damn pills, and she'd probably want me again.

Mike sits on the corner of the Jacuzzi and pulls on sweatpants, a Boston Red Sox T-shirt, and tennis shoes. Back in the bedroom, he picks up the remote, points it at the small plasma screen mounted above the fireplace, and pops it to cable news, where a chopper smolders in ruins. Former Marine Lieutenant Colonel Oliver North, with Fox News, is standing by the wreckage, dressed in military utilities, a flak jacket, and helmet. He is facing a camera and holding a microphone.

"This morning, another US helicopter was shot down outside of Baghdad. Sadly, the crew of four is missing. And today, November 11, is Veterans Day and marks the ninth month of the war."

This enrages Mike. He's thinking he should get the paper to send him over and have him report on this shit, and maybe he could shoot a few of those soulless Muslim bastards. He could slit a few of their throats.

"Mike, I'm trying to sleep."

Mike kills the sound and watches Iraqis gather around the chopper wreck, dancing and mugging for the camera. Mike can see the disgust on North's face. He imagines being there with his sawed-off shotgun, killing them all. Boom! He turns off the TV and glances at the single red rose he gave Claire, which is sitting on the fireplace mantle; this soothes him and makes him feel better. He puts on a Hawaiian shirt from the rocker by the dresser, walks over to the French doors, and looks out on the lake. A light fog lists across the water. It's almost dawn, boats are tied, and the docks and lake are quiet. On the other side of the lake, a few lights shine through the fog. He thinks of bloated bodies floating in a rain-filled bomb crater and then turns away.

———— ∞ ————

Mike knocks on his son's door. No answer. He knocks again.

"Mick, let's roll." A pause and silence. Another knock.

"Leave me alone. I'm tired. I want to sleep."

Mike opens the door, turns on the light, and walks inside. Pictures of baseball players and athletic awards and assorted pictures of Mick's girlfriend, Cait, plaster the walls. A life-sized cardboard cutout of Yankee old timers Maris and Mantle stands stiff on one side of the room. On the other side of the room is a long mirror hanging on the wall, a weightlifting bench in front of it, and a rack of chrome dumbbells. To the side of the bench is a desk and a laptop, with a screensaver running a picture of Mick when he was an extra in a Gus Van Sant movie. Mike and Claire brought friends and family to the opening night and cheered wildly when they saw Mick on screen, tossing a football in a park for the better part of twelve seconds.

Mick, still racked out, covers his head and grumbles.

"Your problem is you were up all night with that damn cell phone stuck in your ear." Mike smiles. He scours the room and sees clothes, comic books, and baseball gear on the floor. Jesus, what a mess. Then he glances at the picture frame above the bed. It's a photo taken more than a dozen years ago, when he took Mick to see the Vietnam Memorial. It was a powerful, life-altering trip that reached inside him and spawned the series of essays that was so well received.

He is touched when he sees the photo of Mick as a small boy, standing in front of the memorial, holding Mike's leg. It pleases him to see the photo hung up by Mick; it reminds him of a better time, when his boy thought he was a hero instead of a control freak.

"Come on, pal."

Mick throws the covers off and sits up, irritated. "You didn't even tell me about this."

"I forgot. Quit being a puss. You want to be all-state, don't you?

"No!"

Mike kicks the bed. "Let's go. I'm not spending fifty bucks an hour for you to lie in bed dreaming about Cait."

Mick rises, no shirt, wearing boxers. His shoulders are broad and thick like a steer's, and his waist is tapered with round abdominals that his buddies envy. At six foot one, he looks taller, and at two hundred pounds, he appears lighter. He's handsome, with short brown hair; a strong jawline; heavy, dark eyebrows; and blue-lilac eyes. When he smiles, his teeth are straight and white, and his eyes fire up, and people are drawn to him. He looks like Mike did when he was eighteen, without the edge and without the anguish in his eyes.

"Shit," Mick says, not wanting to be bothered.

"Watch your mouth."

Mick strides across the room slow and easy, like a stallion. He picks up a couple of fifty-pound dumbbells, stands in front of the mirror, and curls them. His biceps ball, and his triceps jump, and he smiles at his reflection and can see Mike looking at him. Mike watches him and is pleased. *He's got power,* Mike thinks, as the dumbbells swing up and down almost effortlessly. *He's coming into his body, turning into a man. Maybe that's half the problem,* Mike reasons. Mick is at that stage in life where he is separating from his parents, creating his own identity. *Individuating,* Claire calls it. But he still needs guidance and direction and discipline. Mick pumps out a couple more reps and turns to Mike.

"Don't you wish you could do this, Pops?"

"I'm starting my comeback."

"That's what you always say." Mick sets down the dumbbells and starts to hustle, his attitude changing. "I'll go, but we have to stop at the drive-through. I want to get a mocha."

"Sure, pal."

Ten years ago, when Mike and Claire bought their home, it was a beat-up foreclosure, nothing like the small mansions around it, with their private concrete docks and forty-foot yachts.

Mike and Mick built a red brick patio in the backyard a couple summers ago, and Claire furnished it with elegant, white wrought-iron furniture. They put in a well-manicured lawn that Mick and Mike and landscapers care for. Claire tends to flower beds full of white and yellow snapdragons, petunias, and red roses. In the summer, she grows a few tomatoes. It all slopes down from the house to the water. Out in front of the Kelly home is a moveable basketball hoop, in front of a three-car garage, and a front yard as flat as any putting green. In the summer, the front flower beds are full of red and pink rhododendrons and multicolored annuals.

None of this is unusual for the town of Lake Parrish, which is also the name of Mick's high school. It is a small, rolling, well-groomed burb, full of money and folks with big intentions. Located twenty minutes outside of Portland, it is often referred to as the Beverly Hills of Oregon. With little ethnic diversity, other than professional basketball players and rich Asians, it's known for its expensive homes, good schools, tony shopping, zero crime, and a pretentious white population. Mike Kelly bought here because he grew up with next to nothing, and he wanted his kids to have the best of everything—a neighborhood where he didn't have to worry about drunks blasting off shotguns at night in some alcohol-induced celebration or see neighbors fighting in their front yard. A place where the kids didn't have to pass by strip bars on the way to school like he used to do.

Dawn lifts. The lawns are moist from the fog and morning dew. The roses and rhododendrons are resting till spring. Across the street, a neighbor's engine is running, and the exhaust lifts and dissipates in the air. An early jogger runs by in shorts and gloves and a stocking cap. Mike's tired-looking SUV, with a "Veterans for Bush" bumper sticker and a marine corps decal, sits in the driveway, a dent the size of a baseball in the passenger door. Next to Mike's SUV is Claire's small, white hybrid with a simple red sticker stating, "Kindness," which Mick gave her, and it pleased her.

They leave the house. Mick has his ball cap on backward and is wearing black sweatpants and a red sweatshirt with blue Red Sox lettering. He wraps an arm around Mike's shoulder as they cross the driveway.

"You're limping, old man. You're getting soft."

"You won't think I'm getting soft when I rip off your arm and beat you over the head with it."

Mick backs off and gets in a boxing stance, does an Ali shuffle, punches Mike in the arm, and then tears off for the passenger side with a wry smile, laughing.

"Come on, Pops. You're burning light."

Mike loves being with his son. He relishes the idea of being a father and loving Mick in the way he wishes he was loved growing up. He feels good giving him opportunities, talking about baseball and school, and sharing his advice. Even though Mick rejects most of that, Mike still feels content as they climb inside and pull away, cruising through the neighborhood. It will be great to see him hit.

It's quiet as they drive; traffic is light, limited to the early commuters and other competitive parents taking their children to someone who can teach them to be better at something than their peers. But Mick's moment of frivolity, joking with his dad, turns sour. He slumps in his seat, quietly staring out the window as they drive by the baseball park and enter the freeway.

"Hope this gives you a large charge, running my life."

"What are you talking about? You love to hit."

"Not at six o'clock in the morning." Mick flips on the radio and cranks it up, tilts his seat back, and pulls his baseball hat over his eyes. Mike turns the radio down and looks at his son. Despite Mick's attitude, he's happy to be up early, driving his son to a private baseball lesson. This pushes him, Mike thinks confidently, and he'll thank me when he's older. Just considering that makes Mike feel good.

Happiness, however, can be a problem with Mike. When he's happy, he notices it. He starts picking it apart, believing it will all change. Soon his mood *does* change, and he's drifting into intrusive thoughts of violence and war, Padre and Jesse…and other young men injured and killed. That leads into concerns about Mick's well-being. What if he blows a knee working out or they get in a wreck driving down? What if some drunk coming home from an all-night bar swerves into our lane? Mick's in an ambulance and all because Mike made him get up and go hit. Jesus. That's crazy thinking. He shakes his head.

Soon, his daughter Madie is running through his brain. Just a few weeks ago she was home from school at Oregon State and on him about Mick.

"Dad, get a grip," Madie said, brushing her long wet hair after a shower. "Every year, you buy Mick hundreds of dollars of new baseball equipment and send him to special camps and brag about him all the time, and I make the dean's list, and you don't say anything!"

"I told you I was proud."

"No, you didn't. You were in your office. You told me to talk to you later. You said you were watching a tape of Mick hitting." He's too scared she's right to be able to talk about it. He doesn't want to mention that her life now seems to have nothing to do with his. Why should it? "Give me a break. I pay for your school and apartment and crap, Madie. You need to work out more. You use to be great at volleyball. Why don't you play club or something? It would be good for your attitude."

Madie shakes her head, resigned that he doesn't understand anything about her. "And you know the sad thing, Dad, is you want him to play baseball more than he does."

Mike remembers Madie's words and that memory for a moment. Claire and Madie don't understand Mike's thinking. Mick's got one shot at baseball—one opportunity to be young and strong and compete at a high level. There's nothing better than that. He'll never be eighteen again and have colleges wanting him. When Mike was young, he could have played college ball, but blew it when he got stinking drunk with his buddy Jesse and joined the marines. In some ways, it was the stupidest move he had ever made, but he knew that he'd do it again. After all the grief he went through—boot camp and then Nam—he'd do it again. It made him a man. It proved he had courage and gave him profound experiences to write from. It gave him an identity. It's different with Mick. His life is solid. No falling-down drunk for a father, showing up for ball games blasted. Or a mother who was a mental case. Once, before leaving for Vietnam, Mike stopped at Morningside Psychiatric Hospital to visit his mom. He was hoping that the fact that he was going to war would snap her back to reality for at least a moment. Maybe she would say something he could remember without flinching. Instead, she sat up in bed and stretched her arms out, screaming, "I've been through hell!" and then got up and ran to Mike and started hitting him, screaming, "I wish you were never born!" Attendants came, strapped her to the bed, and gave her a shot of something to knock her out. That was the last time he saw her before he went to war.

In twenty minutes, they turn off the freeway at Woodburn, a Hispanic community that is going through gentrification and growing pains. Off the freeway a couple miles, they pass fast food joints, grab a mocha at the drive-through, and reach the last of the old main drag.

Mike guides the SUV over railroad tracks and turns into the parking lot, just before the huge grain silo that stands vacant and for sale. Across from the silo is the Grand Slam, a rusting, gray metal warehouse with a faded painting of the great New York Yankees center fielder Mickey Mantle on the front wall, following through on his famous, furious swing. That's where Mick's name came from.

"I'm not trying to run your life. But if you don't bust ass, you'll never play college ball."

"Like I care. Dad, get a clue. You're the one who wants this, not me."

Mike sits in the car listening to talk radio while Mick is inside for some intense batting practice. He'd love to watch his son hit, and they do this twice a week, but Mike figures he's still angry, and he'll watch next time.

Soon Mick is back in the SUV. *His arms look big,* Mike thinks, but he can see that he is still fuming. Mike shrugs and pulls out of the parking lot, kicking up gravel, and then he turns onto the road. "If you want to be great, Mick, you have to work harder. Challenge yourself. Someone has to be the best; why can't it be you?"

Mick punches the dashboard. "Stop saying that crap. Stop it! Stop running my life!"

The outburst shakes Mike for a moment and makes him feel sad—then anger comes. He clenches the steering wheel hard, and the veins in his hands swell and turn blue. You ungrateful little...he catches himself, exhales, and does not respond. Just a slow nod of his head.

The SUV pulls up to the house. Mick jumps out, grabs his gear, and rushes inside, slamming the door behind him. Mike follows, feels a twinge in his knee, hesitates at the door, bends to rub it, and grimaces when it cracks.

Chapter 3

Mike walks straight to the kitchen. His blood sugar is low, and he feels the shakes coming, so he opens the fridge, grabs the orange juice, and drinks from the carton. That's better. He heads down the hall to their bedroom with its double door entry, opening into their six-hundred-square-foot room with sixteen-foot vaulted ceilings. A huge king-sized bed rests in a heavy Brazilian cherrywood frame. Across from the foot of the bed is a gas fireplace with a matching redwood surround, bookcases filled with books, and a flat-screen TV. Facing the lake is a bank of French doors with sunlight pouring in, opening to the patio, lawn, gardens, and lake. On the other side of the room are mirrored doors that open into a massive walk-in closet filled with Mike's and Claire's clothes. Much of the closet space is empty because Mike usually dresses in one of his fifty Hawaiian shirts, so there aren't a lot of suits, ties, or dress shirts. Then there is the bathroom of tile and marble, with a glass shower and large Jacuzzi, which they both use often, sometimes together. Claire is reading the newspaper in bed, and Mike walks past her quietly toward the bathroom. "Morning, baby."

"Good morning," she says pleasantly, looking up, reading glasses resting on her nose. This is the part of morning she so enjoys, reading the *New York Times,* undisturbed, a cup of coffee next to her. She reads almost every article and editorial and savors the moment. Maybe she'll get through the whole paper without the phone ringing or her husband interrupting her in the middle of the editorials.

" I'll jump in the shower."

After a quick shower and shave, Mike pulls on his blue jeans and tennis shoes and looks through his closet for the Hawaiian shirt of the day. He stands in front of the closet mirrors and straightens the black shirt with yellow, red, and green birds of paradise.

Meanwhile, Claire puts down the paper, rises, slips into leotards, and puts a CD in the stereo next to the TV. She brushes her hair a moment, places the brush on the fireplace mantle, and then feels her breasts for lumps. She is a cancer survivor. Two years ago, they found a small speck when she went in for her annual mammogram. They did a biopsy and discovered a very slow growing, noninvasive cancer. But it was cancer and a tremendous shock for the family. Together, Claire and Mike considered all the options and talked to oncologists, surgeons, and cancer survivors. They attended medical appointments together and looked through books of photos of women, showing single and double mastectomies. Finally Claire chose to have a single mastectomy and remove her left breast. Her right breast has a long scar underneath it and is quite sensitive to touch. At night in bed, Mike often touches the scar and holds the right breast in his hand. It is Claire's favorite sensation, the touching of the scar. Later, Claire had reconstructive surgery. With a blouse on, nobody can tell. But Claire can, and when she stands naked in front of the mirror, she can see the scars and new folds of skin and feel the coldness of her prosthetic.

For Mike, the ordeal triggered memories of wounded soldiers and drew him closer to Claire. And for Claire, her mastectomy looked like Mike's chest wound. When the surgery was completed, Mike gave her one of his purple hearts, and Claire cried but couldn't say why.

Claire walks to the side of the bed and lies down on a green yoga mat opposite the French doors.

When Mike walks in, Buddhist monks are chanting softly in the background. He sees Claire on the floor on all fours, letting her belly hang down and her back sag, and then she is curling up so her back looks like a startled cat. He thinks she looks so good: beautiful face, big breasts, and a nice bottom.

It's been almost two months since they've made love. He starts to feel aroused and needs to be inside her. Maybe not get down on his knees behind her, because he can't quite do that anymore, but he could stand her up naked and lean her over the bed and do her hard, like they used to when they were younger.

The years have been kind to Claire. She has always been slim and sexy, but after two kids, her body is soft with the fullness that comes with the passing years. Her face is gently lined; it gives her character and a sense of grace. When she smiles, Mike thinks she is stunning and not a woman of almost sixty.

Mike and Claire have had a good but challenging marriage. They are on the opposite sides of most political issues. He's an outgoing, shoot-from-the-hip conservative, and she's a quiet liberal. With the war in Iraq, he has become sullen and angry. They argue about the war, their kids, and politics. He feels like she is against him most of the time. She's always pushing him to see doctors about his health or his head and write a new will and plan better for the future. But that's the way Claire has been from the moment they met. She was always pushing him to be better...a better person, writer, and father. And he knows he has changed. *Certainly more than she has,* he muses.

After the war, in his wild, younger years, Mike had a lot of surface friends. there were guys that he played softball with, traveling around the state in vans and staying in hotels, or camped in tents and drinking, playing ball all week-end. Some of those same guys showed up on Harleys at his wedding party. They were just buddies he got drunk with and fought with in dingy bars—players he picked up lonely girls with, the kind of girls who would lie down if you told them they were pretty. But they were not veterans, and they're gone now. And Mike moved on with his life. And so Mike has few friends. His real friends died in the war, or he lost touch with them when he came home by himself. Mike understood that that was one of the troubling aspects of the Vietnam War. It wasn't like World War II, when soldiers went off to battle in battalions and made friends on ships as they crossed the ocean. Mike and everyone else left in small groups on airplanes and were in battle in a matter of days. If they survived, they were sent home after twelve or thirteen months, not as a unit but as individuals rotating back into the world. Then there was the shame and vitriol.

No parades for the returning soldiers; print or TV stories about how our heroic soldiers battled an evil enemy. Mike once wrote in an editorial, "Post-traumatic stress disorder had not been identified yet, so veterans were simply portrayed as psychologically damaged baby killers, devoid of respect and admiration." That period of time still lingers with Mike like an abscess on his soul.

Now Mike doesn't understand the effort people put into friendship. He's gotten close to people through need—in war, in love, in family—but he doesn't know how to do it any other way. Nothing is casual with Mike. He makes instant judgments of people and either likes them or can't stand them. He doesn't like most of Claire's friends because none of them have husbands who are veterans, so Mike and Claire don't go out much. When they do, it is usually to a writers or bookstore event, where the attention is always focused on Mike; this grates on Claire. She feels unappreciated for all the work she has done raising the children and building their estate by buying and managing rental properties. Lately, there have been more bad days than good days in their relationship.

Mike finishes putting on his belt and, except for the thickness of his belly, he is pleased at how he looks: fresh jeans, great shirt. He moves to the bookcase, turns off the music, picks up the remote, and turns on the flat-screen TV.

"Mike, I was listening to that," Claire says, lying on her back again with both feet in the air.

He sits on the corner of the bed and ignores her as he looks at the TV, flips channels, and settles on news of the war in Iraq.

"There is more bloodshed. Elements of the Third Marines attacked insurgents barricaded in a schoolhouse. A suicide bomber walked into a Shia schoolhouse and blew himself up, leaving a classroom full of dead and wounded children," the reporter says. Mike watches as marines are shown carrying children from the broken rubble while women in black burkas scream and pound their fists on their temples. Mike can tell that the marines are new in the country; fresh-faced and stunned, their eyes absorb the heinous aftermath. A dead girl here, wounded boys there, stacks of what once had been living bodies. It makes him furious.

Claire stands up and snaps off the TV. "I don't want to see this anymore. I'm sick of it."

"These murderous sons of bitches have to be stopped," Mike growls.

"I know. I know. Islamic terrorists. If we don't stop them over there, they'll be over here. Will you give it a rest? They'll still be blowing up things when you get to work."

He is unnerved by her callousness. "What's up with you? Those assholes are killing kids, for Christ's sake!" He moves to the bathroom and brushes his teeth. He knows he talks about the war too much and that it wears on Claire. He realizes he has blown her quiet time, so he takes a tube of lipstick and writes *sorry* on the mirror, not thinking about Claire having to clean the mirror.

Claire does some arm stretches with an arm behind her head and then behind her back, and then she bends over, legs spread, as her hair falls forward and nearly touches the floor. She stands erect and says, "I heard the door slam. Were you giving Mick advice again?"

He comes out of the bathroom with a towel laid across his shoulder, wiping toothpaste from his mouth. "I just told him that if he worked harder, he could play ball in college."

Claire turns to Mike; her voice raises half an octave and is filled with frustration. "Let it go. Let it be *his* dream. You have got to let him decide what he wants to be. Not you." She puts a foot on the bed and straightens her leg to stretch again. "And today, I'm going to put some money in Madie's account."

"I thought we just put money in her account."

"She needs a new battery for her laptop and has to pay for a new clutch for her Vespa. I thought it was under warranty but apparently it's not. In any case it needs replaced. And to make matters worse, she's in a huge fight with her boyfriend."

"I'd like to kick her boyfriend's ass."

Claire stops stretching, puts her hands on her hips, and says, "Show some compassion for your daughter. What would it cost for you to be nicer?"

Mike moves close and puts an arm around Claire. "I can be nice." He draws her toward him.

"Whoa, boy." Claire pushes away and pecks him on the cheek. "I'm running late." She heads to the bathroom. "I've got to see Mom this morning," she says through the door. "And talk to hospice. I've also got tenant issues, and tonight is the school board. But I'll put a nice fat chicken in the Crock-Pot."

Mike sits on the bed, discouraged. He's not thinking of her mother or fat chickens; he's thinking about having sex with his wife. Besides, her mother never did approve of him, and whenever she was around, he'd find an excuse to leave the room and take the tension with him.

Claire comes out of the bathroom dressed in nice khaki slacks and a black silk blouse. She sees Mike pouting. "Oh, don't be that way." She rubs a hand through his hair. "A woman likes a man to take his time. To think about the other person." Then she walks back into the bathroom.

She always says stuff like that. Or she'll say, *Not tonight; it's late. If you'd only come to bed earlier.*

"Well, I'm trying. I'm trying to be everything you want me to be," Mike says. Then he gets up off the bed, grabs his watch and wallet from the dresser, and follows Claire back to the bathroom. Claire is putting on makeup. Mike is behind her. He takes a breath, trying to calm down and eat his anger. He rests his hands on her shoulders and rubs them for a moment as she *oohs* and *aahs*. Then he kisses the back of her neck, reaches inside her blouse, and cups her good breast. She stirs, but only for a moment, and then she turns to Mike.

"That was nice. I told you I would be more responsive if you took medicine for your PTSD, went to therapy at the VA, and thought of my needs instead of yours all the time. I know you are in one of your anniversary dates. What did the last marriage counselor call it? Your *cycle of pain.* You have to think about how your behavior impacts me and the children. I liked it when you were on Prozac. You were mellow. More considerate of others."

"Yeah. I know. But I felt weird and couldn't get a hard-on, and it was embarrassing." Mike sulks and rests his head on her shoulder.

Claire turns back to the mirror. "I'm so rushed. We've got tenants late with their rent and maintenance issues to deal with, and I almost forgot Nancy and I have our first belly dancing class today."

"I'm going to like that," Mike says, cheering up, and then he does a little movement with his arms and hips, sliding an arm around Claire.

She smiles. "You're thinking hula, big dog."

"Right."

Claire turns back to the mirror and dabs on a touch more makeup with a brush. "Remember, I set another appointment for you at the VA today. You've got to go. Do the work. You can't just write about it."

Mike promises he'll go but feels a huge knot in his stomach as he leaves the bathroom and wanders over to the French doors. He opens them and looks at the lake, the docks and boats, and up at the blue sky. He smells the clean fall air and watches how the lake's surface ripples under the wind.

He doesn't want to go to the Veterans Medical Center. Someone will recognize him and think less of him, and it'll be all over town that he's a head case. Then nutjobs will write letters to the *Portland Reporter* saying they heard he was mentally wacked, and friends will look at him funny and say things like, "Can I help, Mike? I know what you're going through, and I know this great therapist," and shit like that. He runs that around in his mind and thinks of Claire and getting laid. It's a trade-off. Besides, he's been in marriage counseling before. He knows the frickin' head spinners. Say just enough. Let time pass and then talk about how much better he feels.

He can always use it in a column or the next book. He's always looking for material. That's how he got through going to Claire's oddball churches and weird spiritual gatherings—Church of the Universalists, Sufism, whatever. He watched as she went through rebirthing, and he tried meditation and acupuncture and several other weird things that didn't fit his comfort level. Like Sufi dancing. *Sufi dancing,* he snickers to himself, arms crossed, watching a neighbor walk down the dock toward his boat.

Put up with a lot of brain damage, he thinks. Those years when Claire began studying Sufism, she'd go to week-long retreats in Mexico or retreat centers on the California coast. She'd invite Mike, and he'd refuse, but each time she left, he'd felt jealous. Like she was making time with some bullshitting guru. But he wanted to please her and make things easier at home, so he attended a few prayer sessions, more as an observer than a participant. He'd watch them, down on their knees, heads bobbing, swaying back and forth, chanting. *Was it called Wazifa?* he wonders. They'd sing, "*Ya Shakur, Ya Shakur.*" Later, some guy with a beard and wearing a robe would be playing a guitar or a zephyr, and all the other robes would stand and twirl in circles, arms out and heads back like they were still kids at a rock festival, stoned, in the sixties. Once Mike tried it, for Claire's sake, swirling around, but he felt silly and vulnerable. Like someone could come in and drill him with a shotgun.

But Claire is a bit of a mystic, Mike reasons, and believes she can help Mike heal the pain inside. He loves her, and so for her sake he tried alternative treatments and therapies. He's already seen a dozen head shrinks for his problems with the war and their marriage. Once a therapist wanted him to stand on his head and go through past life regressions. Fuck that. Or the constellation work, where strangers stood on stage and acted out your life's problems. How stupid! Or the woman who claimed to be a world-class therapist, who stood in front of him, with her supple breasts nearly touching his chest, and panted, "Can you feel the heat? Can you feel the energy as I move my hands down your chakras?" Her hand brushed by his crotch. *Maybe she wanted to get laid by a writer...or maybe by anyone...because her husband was an androgynous geek,* Mike thought. For a long time, he did anything Claire wanted, thinking each time that it was only a few hours of misery. He shuts the French doors. Maybe if he does go to PTSD therapy at the VA, Claire might lay him more often.

Chapter 4

T oday the kitchen table is surrounded by Mick's buds Little B and Griff and his red haired girlfriend, Cait. They eat cereal and toast while Claire pours orange juice, leaving the pitcher on the table. Mike stands at the sink, observing, wanting to be liked, sucking down his third diet cola of the day.

The kids chatter away, devouring big bowls of cereal with strawberries, joking at each other's expense. "Did you ever notice how Little B's head is a bit lopsided?" Griff says. "And he's got to be an albino." Griff laughs to himself and B flips him off just as Claire turns from the stove toward the table, holding a frying pan full of little sausages. The grease is still snapping as she gives Griff a stare. "Griffen," she warns, and Griff shrinks a little and pretends to hide under the table. The truth is Little B is an unusual-looking kid in a town full of tall, blond, and handsome. He's got a mohawk, a mouth full of braces, wears saggers and a do-rag, and has a pierced ear. He bounces a basketball while he eats. His parents are divorced, and his mother lives in New York with the man who broke up the family. His dad travels, and often Little B is home alone and sometimes runs wild.

"Mrs. K," B says. "You're the best. Awesome sausage. My mom was a great cook too. Made banana pancakes. You ever make banana pancakes, Mrs. K?"

Claire smiles and adds another sausage to B's plate, skipping Griff. "Griffen, if you keep talking that way I'm going to call your mother." That has the table cracking up again.

Mike's laughing, and then he interjects, "And I'll kick your butt."

The table cools, Mick rolls his eyes, and Mike realizes he's said the wrong thing again. This is the kind of thing Mike can't quite comprehend: when to be a dad and when to be one of the guys. Like the time he caught Mick and some kids drinking beer down by the docks one night and called their parents, thinking he was doing everyone a good deed and being a solid parent. It embarrassed Mick and torqued his buddies. Maybe he should have warned them. Now he is uncomfortable and angry, and he snaps, "B, will you stop with the ball?" The way he says it makes everyone want to leave.

"I told you not to bounce the ball, dumbass," Griff says. Little B flips him some kind of hand-twisting gang sign, which Griff laughs at. Griff bumps knuckles with Mick and then leans across the table and whispers to B, "You dildo." B's face is flushing and everyone else at the table is snickering as Mike asks, "What's so funny?"

Claire pours Little B some juice and Griff blurts, "You'd better cut B off, Mrs. K, or he'll pee his pants."

Cait puts her orange juice down and says to Griff, "Do you eat with that mouth?"

"Check his Facebook," Mick says. "See what he's eating. He's got three hot dogs stuffed in his trap."

Cait laughs and says, "Check out Griff's hottie with the purple hair. She's, like, laying this lipper on Griff, and she's got a big nose ring and must be six inches taller."

"Come on, pretty boy," Mick says, bending over and picking up Griff's ball bag off the floor and tossing it to him. Mick picks up his pack and gear bag, and his group follows him to the door.

"Love you, Mom," Mick says, kissing her and ignoring Mike. As he walks out, Claire's friend Nancy walks in. She's a tiny woman in her fifties with delicate features and glasses. She wears a white visor with green frogs hopping across it.

"Wow!" Nancy says to Claire. "Things are rocking around here. At my house, about the only action going on in the morning is Randy's bowel movement." Claire laughs out loud, and Mike cracks a grin from the side of his mouth.

In the driveway at the front of the house, below the basketball hoop and next to Mike's old rig, is Cait's new white Cadillac Escalade. A "Stop the War" sticker is slapped on the back bumper and an "Impeach Bush" one on the front. The group gathers around, checking the new ride as Cait stands by, blushing and embarrassed. Her parents were antiwar hippies in the sixties, raising pot on a goat farm in Northern California. Forty years later, they own fifty coffee shops all over the West Coast and have serious money. They're easily in the top tier in a town swelling with moneyed folks. They just want Cait to be safe, so they bought her the white tank and call it a company vehicle. Cait delivers supplies to some local stores on weekends. The rest of the time, it's her ride. As if by osmosis, Cait, the student body president, turned into a demonstrator herself and is always finding some cause that needs her energy. Currently it's the Iraq war.

Little B is inspecting power doors and seats, rubbing the silver leather like it's some girl he's hooking up with. "This is so pimp city. Tinted glass. Check it out. Shit, it's got plasma," he exclaims, running his fingers over the edge of the screen bolted to the ceiling.

"This is so sick," Griff adds. "Next thing you'll be calling us white boys."

The boys laugh, and Griff grins, but Cait is annoyed. "You're both such tools."

"You think I'm a tool? Look at B. He's dressed like a jackass."

Mick turns and looks at Griff, throws an arm around his shoulders, and says, "Get in, Metro. You're the douchebag streaking his hair." B rolls into a belly laugh as they hop in, and Cait plants one on Mick's cheek. She fires the engine up, and they roll, windows down. It's sun and blue sky forever, a beautiful fall day; dew is spread across the lawns, and the trees are a wild cacophony of orange, red, and yellow colors. Mick's iPod is hooked to the stereo, blasting out, "Thank God I'm a Country Boy." They zip through the neighborhood of homes with four-car garages, filled with Jags and Mercedes Benzes. Soon they're down on LP's main street, which is brimming with new designer retail shops, and then they're past the Coffee Nook, which is one of Cait's parents' coffee shops. It's busy. A few tall, thin blondes in sweat suits and a guy in a sweater sit with their open laptops, tapping away. They honk and wave at other buds, driving in their daddies' cars. The sky is big and blue, and Mick's smiling, thinking life rocks when you're eighteen.

Little B bitches about the music, and Griff teases, "B, you're so fricking gay. If I was walking with you and dropped my wallet, I wouldn't bend over to pick it up; I'd just kick it all the way home." Everyone laughs.

"Bite me, Fandango."

"What the hell does that mean?" Griff asks.

"It means you're a cartoon," B says, and Griff shakes his head. Everyone, including B, thinks it an odd thing to say.

"That's our B," Mick interrupts. "Bringing it on with stinging verbal assaults." Another round of guffaws bounces through the car. Mick's conscience catches up with him and he says, "Sorry, B. Just messing with ya."

Cait unplugs Mick's iPod and slides in a Springsteen CD that gets groans from the back. She reaches across the seat and rests her hand on Mick's. "What's going on after baseball?"

Mick rolls up the cord of his iPod and stuffs it in his pack. "Nothing. Probably just kickin' it with Griff. Why? What's up?" He can sense Cait is going to ask him to do something.

Cait has the slightest hesitation, being careful with her words.

"After I get out of the dance team practice, I've got student council. I'm in charge of the protest committee. I thought, well, maybe you might come."

Mick doesn't want the bother. "You know I support the war. I think we need to be there."

Griff reaches over the back of the front seat and pretends to choke Mick.

"What are you protesting this time? Lesbos on the dance team?" Griff snorts as Mick fights a smile while the boys hee-haw in the back.

Trying not to laugh, Mick looks back over the seat and shoots Griff a tough stare, warning him not to be a jerk. Griff pretends to be scared but settles back in his seat, the devil in his face. "Don't be a dick brain," Mick says to Griff, winking so Cait won't see.

Cait is not happy with Griff's comment. "We're protesting the war, stupid. Mick, why are your buds so lame?"

"You're the one that's lame," Griff says. "We need to be in Iraq kicking ass," he bellows as Mick leans back over the seat again, and they bump fists.

"Tight," says Mick. They bump fists twice and twist knuckles together and say, "Lock it." And that is exactly how Mick feels—kick some ass. "Cait, love ya, but don't you remember 9/11? The towers went down, and how 'bout Saddam Hussein? He's a prick. He killed thousands of his own people, and we need to be there to straighten things out."

Cait is unfazed. "This is not about 9/11. Well, will you come or not?"

"I don't know. The old man would shit a frog." Cait tosses him pursed lips and the furled-brow look as Mick thinks about punching his dad in the mouth.

"Sorry, babe. I gotta go to the batting cages with the team."

Cait cranks the car into the parking lot of a small convenience store, shuts down, and says she's going to grab a pack of gum and a Coke. Mick gets out, and Griff shouts, "Mickr, get me a Nutter Buddy."

"Get one yourself, donkey," Mick snaps. The store is small but crowded with kids as Mick follows Cait. He grabs a couple candy bars and quickly slides them in his jean pockets, getting his adrenalin rush.

Swiping stuff is what he does on occasion. He gets a kick out of it and never gets caught. No one knows about it except Griff. Sometimes they both do it, just for fun. *If Dad found out,* Mick thinks, *I'd be hurtin' for certain. Screw it.* He slides a bag of corn nuts in his shirt. *I'm not afraid of him anymore.*

Chapter 5

Mike drives past the high school. He slows at the baseball field and remembers last summer when Mick hit three doubles and a home run over the scoreboard. From the stands behind home plate, Mike and Claire watched as the ball hung in the air against a clouded sky, disappeared over the fence, and dropped quietly on the golf course. As Mick rounded third base, the crowd roared. When Mick hit home plate, he jumped on it with both feet, grinned big, and pointed at Mike as if it were all for him. Mike was crazy proud, but that was months ago. Mick is older now, pulling away; he isn't his pal anymore.

His mood shifts as reaches the heavily wooded road that runs along the Willamette River, rolling toward Portland. On the left, it stretches for miles past firs, maples, and poplars, which hide rich-ass homes with elevators, sunrooms, and heated pools. On the right side of the road are more trees, loosely staggered, reaching down to the river. He sees a deer close to the river, head up, standing in a maze of thin maples.

He slows to a stop by the side of the road and watches the doe, alert to the sound of his car. She tilts her head and freezes. Mike remembers his father skinning deer when he was a boy. The deer was shot, gutted, its entrails steaming, and then his dad tied it to the front of his jeep. Then there was the long ride home, off the mountain, through the high desert, and back to the small farm they used to own. His dad and the other men strung the deer up in the barn, hanging it from the rafters.

"First you cut around the hooves," his father said as eight-year-old Mike sat on a stool, watching his dad work his sharp bowie knife around the deer's hoof. "Then you pull the skin down, Son."

There were always a lot of other men around, like his mean uncle Chuck, who used to twist Mike's arm around his back—to make him tough, he said. Or Marty, the fire chief, who was always drunk and falling. They'd stand around cussing and drinking whiskey. His dad did all of the cutting and butchering. Mike could see the skin being torn down the deer's legs…and the white membrane and red sinew…and how the deer's head faced the ground, with a bucket under it to catch the blood drippings, and then his mom helped wrap the meat in white paper and stored it in the freezer.

The deer dashes away, running along the side of the river. Mike shakes the memory and pulls back on the road. Soon the National Guard building comes into view. As he rounds the bend, he can see troops dressed in desert uniforms, carrying rifles and boarding canvas-covered trucks.

Deer, death, blood. He can feel his mind shifting. He's back in the world that exists parallel to this one. A world where dead marines live, strap on magazines, pick up weapons, and move out beyond the wire. It's February 14, 1968—his first patrol. Mike's squad is strung out in the rice paddies, moving slowly over the dikes. He's frightened; he doesn't want to die, and he's worried about carrying the radio. Doesn't know how to work it. Who would he call if they got hit? Then Peaches, that black kid from Georgia, blows up in front of him. Boom! He can see the smoke clear, and lying in front of him is this slab of black skin and broken bones. With each heartbeat, blood squirts from his arteries, rolls steadily across his shredded legs, and soaks the ground. Peaches rocks back and forth, pounding his fists into his temples, moaning.

The lieutenant is in Mike's face, yelling something, and then he grabs the handset, and Mike stands stunned, wiping puke off his mouth.

He tells his mind to stop it, but the intrusive thoughts continue flashing—from Peaches to the chopper going down, the crash site, and Jesse crawling out of the chopper, arm hanging. He shakes his head and tries to push the thoughts away and focus on the road. Then he glances in his rearview mirror and sees enemy soldiers disappear into the tree line.

He grips the steering wheel, confused and unsure of where he is and what he is doing. Suddenly, the tires hit the shoulder of the road and the SUV starts to plane in loose gravel. It bangs and scrapes the guardrail as Mike hits the brakes hard. He skids to a stop. The war disappears. He pounds his fist on the dashboard. "Shit!" Then it's quiet. The car engine is still running. Off to his right, sunlight breaks through the trees and cascades down the bank, over rocks, and into the river. A man is fishing on the bank, looking up at him. The current flows, and a small group of ducks drift by. As the fisherman sets down his pole and walks up the bank toward Mike, he quickly backs his SUV away from the guardrail and moves down the road.

Chapter 6

Mike drives into the underground garage at the *Portland Reporter* building and parks in his reserved spot, close to the guard shack and basement elevator. He breathes deeply, mad at himself for letting the war take hold of him again. It's pathetic. He rubs his face, looks in his rearview mirror, checks his teeth, and runs his tongue over the flatness of his lower bite. Over the years, he's ground them down worrying about money, his marriage, his job, Madie, baseball, and his boy. When the Iraq war started, he'd ground them even more intensely and noticed little cracks in his upper teeth as well. He now felt the beginning of a low-level toothache, sharpened with cold water. The teeth would need work soon.

Years ago, before Claire, he was bar hopping and chasing tail with his buddy Rick Dickings. They got into a fight with three drunks outside a sleazy night-club, underneath the neon-blue sign of the Pink Martini. He and Hardesty were kicking butt when one of the guys hit Mike in the mouth with a brick. Bam! Blood was everywhere. He caught most of his four front teeth in his hand. By the time he recovered his senses, the jerks had hauled ass. It was the only street fight he ever lost, and even today, when he drives past the Pink Martini, still open, he glances around looking for the bastards. Mike grabs his briefcase, looks at the banged-up fender, shakes his head, and mutters, "Idiot."

The thin black guard steps out of the glass shed to greet him, and Mike forces a smile.

"How's the wife, Skeeter?" Mike asks.

"Big as a damn house." He smiles. Mike nods and walks past him to the elevator.

His office is on the fourth floor of a dismal, gray concrete building in desperate need of major renovation. The building is dark and damp in the winter. When it's cold, the windows weep and the heating is uneven. In summer it's hell, so hot no one wants to be there. The newspaper is owned by a Rupert Murdoch kind of guy with old money, who is trying to buy small to midsize presses all over the country. The only problem is he also buys the real estate and runs the buildings on the cheap. This does not belie the paper's success. But it is the only daily in Portland, and it pays the best, so editors and reporters rarely leave. The joke is that they have life contracts. Built in the fifties, the building is blocks from the hub of newer high-rise buildings and throngs of renovated, old structures that form the core of the city.

Entering, he notices how drab the lobby is and thinks that the only fresh-looking thing in the vicinity is Nicole, the new receptionist on the fourth floor. He waits for the doors to spring him and is looking at Nicole: big, round eyes, full lips, and young body. *Youth is beautiful,* Mike thinks, letting his eyes linger for a second. "Glen's looking for you. He's not happy. Something about *Newsweek*." She hands Mike his mail, a puzzled look on her face.

"Great." He sorts his letters and then shoves through a swinging door into the inner offices.

It's a bullpen of desks and cubicles, surrounded by glass-walled offices. The tawdry, colorless cubicles are where most writers, assistants, and starry-eyed interns create what a local radio host calls the fish wrap. Phones always ring, and conversations are often in whispers. Mike is a big shot, which means a private office and the editor's ear. He passes desks of young reporters who look up and say, "Hi," or nod with admiration, slaps a high five to Cody, the young, tattooed Vietnamese cameraman who utters the word *Newsweek*, but Mike, in full stride, keeps moving and unlocks his door. His desk is buried in books, papers, and empty diet cola cans. On his PC, a screensaver holds a picture of Madie and

Mick. It's summer, and they are at the back of the house, standing on the dock, mugging for the viewfinder. Prestigious writing awards are stuffed in boxes, and the four novels he's written are in stacks in the corner next to a baseball bat. He gives out copies sometimes, but he keeps more than he gives away. There's something very satisfying about looking at the stacks, as if he's written not four books but twenty-four. A few copies are in Spanish—Mike still gets a kick out of picking up a book he wrote and not being able to understand more than half of it. He remembers that when Madie was in high school, she chose this edition of his book to write a book report on for Spanish class.

A small refrigerator with a photo of Claire sits by his desk. The only thing hanging on his wall is the same picture that's in Mick's bedroom: Mike and Mick at the Vietnam Memorial when Mick was just a boy. Sometimes, when his mind is resting, Mike will look up at the picture and remember how much love they once shared. How everything Mike did made Mick happy and how he wishes that those days had never ended.

Mike is still beating himself up, thinking himself a fool for smashing the SUV, as he settles into his chair. When he does anything wrong or when things are out of his control, he hates it. He used to hit himself in the face and feel such grief when he made a mistake. It reminds him of the one time he fell asleep on guard duty. Mistakes are often lethal. In his office, he's in control, comfortable, and surrounded by the clutter.

Mike picks up the morning newspaper, scans the front page, and then turns to his column. He could have changed a couple of words and made it tighter. For a moment, he feels pathetic. It's been so many years, and he keeps recycling his remorse. Maybe he'll write about baseball or boxing again or that UFC cage fighting that is so pure and violent. He folds the paper and then tosses it in a clear plastic bin with all the other papers for recycling.

Claire is on his mind—how she wants to be treated—so he calls home and leaves a "Love you, Claire" message on the recorder. It's how he reminds her that he does love her even though he doesn't always treat her like he does. He grabs a diet cola from the fridge and checks his e-mail. Before he can read one from his book publisher, he catches Glen out of the corner of his eye, talking on a cell phone, crossing the bullpen toward his office. Glen is the senior editor and runs the show. He's a big man, about six foot three, in his midsixties, with a paunch, plugged into a tight-fitting three-piece suit. As he opens Mike's door, he's still talking on his cell, wound up, and ready to explode.

"You're not listening to me!" Glen shouts, a purple vein streaking across his forehead. "It's not about truth, you idiot. It's about what you can prove. Well, screw him. Let him burn. We're not retracting anything. Get back to me." Glen snaps his cell phone shut, takes a deep breath, and strides into Mike's office.

Mike looks up, bothered by it all. "OK, what's wrong?"

"Nothing. Same old shit. Cops blowing a judge." After an awkward moment, he asks, "How's my favorite ass-kicking columnist? That was a great, great column today. Very tight. But I want to talk to you about something that's got me highly pissed off."

Mike can read Glen's face and locks on his eyes. "You didn't like my *Newsweek* piece?"

"Did I say that?"

"Didn't have to," Mike says and turns back to his screen.

"Goddammit, Mike, that's not the point. It was great too, but are you trying to make me look like an asshole?"

"My contract says I can—"

"I don't give a hot damn what your contract says. You have to talk to me first before you sell anything to anybody."

Not intimidated, Mike stands, one fist on his desk. "Glen, you told me last month you didn't want another personal bullshit column on war, so I sold it. I'm amazed you let today's fly."

"Mike!" Glen catches himself and speaks slowly and sternly. "That doesn't mean you can go to *Newsweek* without talking to me. Now sit down…please."

After decades of dealing with Glen's tantrums over everything from text and punctuation to political bent, Mike is used to his fits. He sits, shaking his head, unimpressed.

"I loved your *Newsweek* piece. Especially the chopper going down and the red Frisbee." Powerful stuff, but you can't take your work to any damn…" Glen catches his words again, takes another shallow breath, and sits down on the corner of Mike's desk. Mike gives him a look, and Glen stands up.

"Look. You almost had a Pulitzer, you've written a bestseller, and you've been here busting your balls for twenty years."

"Twenty-five."

"OK. Twenty-five. But lately you seem, uh…distracted. You're always late, and I know you have memories you're dealing with, but it's gotten in the way of your work. Why don't you take a couple weeks off? Take Claire to Mexico. Hang out at the beach. Drink some margaritas. Get a blow job. Relax."

A vacation is the last thing Mike wants to do. He hates vacations. He hates downtime. Too much thinking. He'd rather go to Iraq. The only vacations he likes are those when he's busy doing something different every day or pounding out a novel or writing a new essay. Claire can shop for hours, picking up every trinket or piece of clothing, examining each item as if it is the most unusual thing she has ever seen. She can lie by the pool reading for days, going nowhere, and doing nothing. Doing nothing makes him crazy.

"You've been talking to Claire?"

"Well, no shit. You're driving us both crazy."

" Damn, Glen. I told you not to do that shit. Maybe we'll go in July. Unless Mick is playing summer ball."

Glen fires up again. "This is not a request. I've been telling you this for weeks. You need a break. Go home! Grab your shit, and get out of here. I don't want to see you for a month."

Glen storms out of the office, looks at Cody's desk, and says, "Clean this shit up!"

Cody watches Glen exit the newsroom and whispers, "Beat off."

Mike's thinking, *What the hell is Glen talking to my wife for? What a dick.* He takes a hit of his soda, returns some e-mails, and then opens a desk drawer, shuffles some papers, and pulls out a Veterans brochure titled *Post-Traumatic Stress Disorder*. He sits back in his chair and reads.

Chapter 7

It is a beautiful fall day. The sun is out, and the air is crisp and clean. Mike edges his SUV along the winding road that leaves the city and traverses the west hills, where the homes are old and stately, on his way to the Portland Veterans Medical Center. The hospital was carved out of the side of Portland's rolling hills, and on the top floors there are sweeping, territorial views of the river and city and distant mountains. Its towering green glass walls and contemporary architecture give veterans a feeling of safety and confidence that the folks who care for them know what they're doing, unlike at the old hospital of thirty years ago. The best views are stashed in the clouds on the top floor of the cancer ward. This is where Mike's father took chemo and radiation. The view soars out over the city, down the Willamette River, and on to ruptured Mt. St. Helens with its cap blown off. On a clear day, his father could see snow-covered Mt. Hood. "It's like dying in the sky," Mike's dad used to say, hooked up with tubes in his arms and legs.

His parents divorced when he was in high school. After his mother got out of the mental hospital, she moved to Fresno, California, with little explanation. She became wealthy from the multilevel marketing of cosmetics, but she didn't call or come to see him, even after he returned from Vietnam. His father never remarried and drank himself into poverty. In his last years, he had wet brain and despair and finally cancer. On the days his dad had chemo,

Mike would stop at his father's small, dark apartment, which was cluttered with beer cans and used tissues, and the rooms smelling like cigarettes and piss. There was an old TV with rabbit ears, tinfoil wrapped around the antennas. It was always on, even as his old man lay passed out on the couch, belly swollen.

"Dad. Come on. You were supposed to be ready. Now we're going to be late."

His father would slowly sit up, head bald, stained T-shirt stretched over his bloated stomach. He'd hack and cough and spit in a brown garbage bag full of wadded up tissues. "Just a minute…Jesus Christ, let me catch my breath," his father would say. Then he'd pick up a cigarette and light it. "Whew. Help me up." Mike would lift him to his feet and watch him wobble to the bathroom, where he'd spit in the toilet and take a long pee that Mike could hear from the front room. While his father struggled with his pants and cowboy shirt, Mike emptied overflowing ashtrays, picked up used tissues, and cleared the place of beer bottles. Then he'd help him to the car.

In a way, the VA is like coming home for Mike. It's familiar and sad, because it reminds him of how he might someday hobble through the doors and never leave.

Mike pulls into the covered parking, fired up that the spaces are small and crowded. The building is always in some state of renovation. Water drips from the low ceilings throughout the dark lot, and the smell of mold is in the air.

It's a tight squeeze as he gets out of his rig and grabs his small notepad and pen. Next to the garage entrance is the smoking area, jammed with veterans, some sitting in pajamas or in wheelchairs, inhaling and exhaling long streams of smoke or selling pain pills discreetly. They're all sickly, with pasty skin, tattooed arms, and yellow nicotine-stained fingers. As Mike walks toward the entrance, he remembers his dad's thick, yellowed fingers covered in scabs and scars. He remembers the backhands he caught when his father was drunk. Then he takes notice of a vet in his seventies, Korea probably, sitting in a wheelchair, one leg missing. Tubes run from his nose to an oxygen tank but don't prevent him from drawing on a rolled cigarette. He has a hand-painted sign attached to his chair: F**king Hero.

Mike is nervous as he walks into the lobby, afraid of the emotion, worried he might talk and reveal what he fights so hard to conceal…or that he might lose it and cry. He pulls out his small notepad and pen and writes:

> The lobby is packed with damaged veterans, some in wheelchairs with full bags of urine hanging from the bottom of baggy pajamas. Others are wearing military gear, like red marine corps jackets or green army shirts from the 82nd Airborne and caps from the 101st Force Recon. A few veterans are from World War II, when society considered them heroes, some from Vietnam when they were treated with vitriol, and finally there are today's warriors, who volunteer to carry the load for the weak or the unwilling. The older soldiers' faces are thick and cracked from years of hard work or alcohol and drug abuse. The younger veterans seem startled or unsure, surrounded by men the age of their fathers or grandfathers.

Mike's eyes sweep over the room, and he thinks of a quote he just read in the *New York Times* from James Webb, the author, former senator, and Vietnam veteran. "World War II brought the Greatest Generation together. Vietnam tore it apart." *What legacy will Iraq bring?* he wonders.

And he writes.

> Many of the veterans are with women who sit patiently by their sides, comforting them with their presence or helping them pick up medication. A few push wheelchairs and many have tended to their soldier's pain for so long it has become theirs as well.

The men from his war seem older and more frail than he is. It will be years before he winds up in a chair being pushed by Claire. *What the hell am I doing here?* He takes a breath.

> In the far corner of the lobby, a woman old enough to be my mother is dressed in a vintage army uniform, playing the piano, singing World

War II–era songs, while elderly men gather around, two with canes, another braced on the piano.

It's an old movie, he thinks. A perfect glimpse into a terrible future of growing old and feeble, stuck in a wheelchair, shitting in a bag or leaning on a cane, listening to music. As he stands in the lobby, he sees an Iraq-aged soldier in a wheelchair. Both of his legs are missing, and one arm is gone at the shoulder. An attractive woman with long chestnut hair pushes the blown-up young man. A little girl skips beside his wheelchair. The wife and the veteran laugh as the child dances up to them. *The wife and the child and the soldier,* Mike thinks. And the soldier is so screwed up that his attitude doesn't make any sense. Where is the misery, the self-loathing? The, "I'm going to pick up a gun with my one goddamned hand that's left and kill somebody and then shoot myself in the fucking head." Christ! Mike freeze-frames the father and his family and puts Mick in the wheelchair—but he quickly pulls him out with a shake of his head. Screw you, Mike says to the invading image.

He puts his pad away and waits in a line at the information desk to ask for directions to group therapy. In front of him is a guy ranting and raving to himself. He turns to Mike, his long hair straggling down from a Viet Nam Vet–inscribed baseball hat. His face is beat-up, etched with wrinkles and folds, and he has a wandering glass eye. Several front teeth are broken, and his cheek is pierced with a silver ring. Might be sixty, tweaked out, spittle flying. His mouth opens wide, like a yawn, and his words come fast and overbearing.

"I been sitting on my ass for three damn hours trying to get my meds. I'm on like six kinds of psychotropic drugs, and if I don't get the right stuff, I'll Jihad all over this shit hole. Then, them assholes might pay attention. I shit you not, my brother."

"Why don't you fire up a doobie?" Mike says. "You need something to get your head straight."

The veteran laughs, not insulted, foam on his lips, face turning red. "Fucking a-a-a-! And that's not even half of it, brother."

"It sounds like you're getting the shit end of the stick."

The veteran reaches the front desk, wild and crazy as he tries to get some help from the mildly interested attendant. The attendant directs him to the pharmacy, and the madman steps away, mumbling. Mike scratches the rash on his neck and thinks maybe the guy's schizophrenic. It would be different if he could see multiple wounds, a missing arm or leg. Even the eye gone seems unimportant to him. Compassion is hard for Mike, especially when it involves mental illness. He doesn't much believe in mental illness. Not even his own.

Mike checks in at the information booth, and the attendant looks his name up on a computer screen and gives him directions to the group therapy room.

"Thanks."

He heads down the hall, past interns and orderlies, takes a crowded elevator, and gets off on the fifth floor. His throat's closing, and it's hard to swallow. He feels like he's done something wrong. That someone will discover he's troubled. Troubled like his mom when she sat up in that hospital bed after shock treatments. He isn't crazy. *She* was crazy. Just like those homeless vets who've had all the life sucked out of them. Their illnesses are like cancer of the soul, he once wrote. It eats at you for years, and then suddenly you're gone. You lose your mind and end up drunk, under a bridge, snot running down your face, no money, and no place to go.

Mike knows it's not easy ignoring his demons. Or admitting he has them. After the war, he simply thought that was unique, that the trouble he had in his mind was his alone, not shared by anyone else. It was his secret. He never once considered *not* keeping it secret. And he thinks he's hidden it pretty well all these years. Only his family really knows. Sure, he has written about his troubles and pain, but always with a sense of distance. He has learned from letters from vets and from soldiers that come up to him at readings that he seems in control and over it all. Writing eloquently is his control. But he'll work through it. Who, except another soldier, can understand what it felt like to reach into a buddy's gut wound, blinded by the night, to feel the warm blood and entrails, not sure you can stop it? How could any therapist know how it felt to have a wounded corpsman shot again and again while lying on top of you, crying, "Jesus, they're cutting me up."

What the hell do these assholes who are trying to counsel us know? Did they ever see a stack of bodies bloat and blister in the sun?

Mike stops at the door, shaking. He takes a breath and collects his composure. He thinks of Claire and all the times she said to him, "You have to go into your pain if you ever want to get beyond it."

The room looks like a college classroom—chalkboard and podium, chairs in a circle. No one speaks, and the silence is uncomfortable. Mike lingers at the edges of the circle looking for a safe place to sit, back to the wall. "Come in," a woman of about thirty tells Mike. "Any place is fine."

What the hell? She's barely out of college. The group should be led by someone who knows what they're talking about. Someone older, a veteran who's been in the shit. This is the fucking VA hospital, after all. I want to talk to a vet. This isn't right. Mike searches the room, looking to leave. Most of the veterans are older and rough-looking; some have obvious wounds and faded eyes. Two are in wheelchairs. One vet, Mike's age, is horribly burned, a tube where his nose used to be. A young black woman, barely twenty he guesses, has a hand missing and is dressed in freshly starched army fatigues. The others wear gray or black sweatshirts or red marine corps windbreakers or baseball hats from their divisions. All of them look weary.

Mike feels out of place, like he's stepped into a sacred circle of pain and suffering he is not worthy of. These soldiers are much more wounded than he is. Not just troubled. All he has are nightmares and thoughts of blowing people away.

"Welcome," the counselor says. "Let's go around the circle and introduce ourselves. Tell us where you served and maybe one word or two describing how you feel."

The burned vet speaks in a raspy whisper. "Screw this shit, lady. I want to go to Baghdad and kill somebody."

Mike's thinking, *So do I.* The room laughs; Mike nods in agreement and feels a lot better.

Chapter 8

Mick spends a long time in the shower this morning, with the lights off. It gives him time to think and consider, and if he stays in long enough he might miss his dad's morning lecture. It seems like every day his dad is on him. Either he's criticizing how he's dressed or pressing him on baseball or school. What he hates most is being warned about something his dad feels is dangerous. Mike has micromanaged him all his life, and he's sick of it.

Last summer, when he and Griff hitchhiked to California, his old man freaked out. And when he found out Mick was jumping off the abandoned train trestle into the river, Mike went ballistic. It's always something. That's why he wouldn't let Mick play football. "All you need is some jerk taking out a knee, or get a couple concussions, and your career in baseball is over," Mike used to say.

Mick soaps and lathers, thinking about college, baseball, and the war. Some days he thinks going into Iraq is stupid as shit. Maybe we should just let them kill each other. That's what the old man might say. It is their country, and do they even have the technology to launch a nuke? They're third world, man. And the guys that are getting waxed? For what? But if we do nothing, those freaks will be over here blowing themselves up. A truck bomb at the high school. Christ. Someone's got to stop them.

Besides, he and Griff could go and watch each other's backs. Come home heroes maybe and have his parents proud. He'd show his old man he could take it. And not mess up his head. He could still play baseball. He might even get on a military team. His old man couldn't bitch about that. He could go in for a couple years, that's all, and maybe end up in Hawaii or Southern California. That would be way cool. He could always go to college. Cait is going to Brown, so what the heck. That's like another world. Maybe he and Griff *could* join together. Busting caps. Killing some of those ragheads. Yeah. He can hear Mike yelling down the stairs but ignores it.

Dressed and at the kitchen table, Mick inhales some cereal covered with chocolate milk and slops down a spoonful of peanut butter. His mother has left a note that says she "cluvs" him and that she's with Nancy, so he can borrow the car. He rinses his mouth out at the kitchen sink and is out the door.

Mick walks down the crowded school hallway, back straight, shoulders square, head up, smiling, bumping fists, punching arms, high-fiving his way to class. He's wearing a white tee, cut off at the shoulders, with a small Superman insignia where a pocket might be. He likes to show off his arms. He's a big shot at Lake Parrish High School and relishes his time there, but not because it provides a fine education and produces some of the best athletes in the state. He likes it because people like him, look up to him. With a large cache of friends, he hears something new and interesting every day. LPHS also has a reputation for bright, obnoxious, rich white kids, whom he tries to steer clear of. His dad doesn't go for arrogant bastards, and neither does he. While some schools in the surrounding mid to low-income areas deal with crumbling buildings, lack of resources, poverty, violence, and high dropout rates, LPHS looks like a country club. Recently remodeled in red brick with golden domes and floor-to-ceiling windows, the school looks more like a new five-star hotel than a public high school. It has two new gyms, a state-of-the-art weight room, theaters, and classrooms wired with the latest technology. Mick's dad once observed, "Its classrooms are bulging with the leaders of tomorrow, who often are the smartasses of today." In fact, Leaders of Tomorrow is etched in stone above the school's main entrance.

Mick's pumped because today is Military Day at the school, and he finds the idea of being in the military daring and exciting, despite the brutality he has read in his dad's writing. In August, during the summer before 9/11, his dad took him to New York to watch a couple of Yankees games for his birthday. It was a big deal to tool around Central Park, zip through the neighborhoods, catch a game, and then one day they ate lunch in the Twin Towers restaurant. He remembers looking out the windows and thinking it was so far down. A few weeks later, the buildings were destroyed and many of the people he met were dead: the pretty blond girl who seated them and told them she went to NYU, the waiter who took their order, the cooks—all of them dead, and that still haunts him. It could have been him eating lunch with his dad and having a plane crash into the windows and explode. As he has grown older, he has found himself wanting to take some kind of revenge.

This morning, the marine corps recruiters have come to visit; later, after lunch, the army will show up. Their arrival is more of an anomaly than anything else. A few students are whining, some are excited; the majority just rolls with it.

Two recruiters, dressed in blue trousers with the scarlet "blood stripe," pressed, short-sleeve khaki shirts, medals in neat rows, and white dress covers, set up a table with a large foldout display in the lobby across from the cafeteria doors. The foldout is filled with photos of young, strong marines of both sexes climbing ropes, running, firing rifles, and charging through jungle or desert terrain. The words A Few Good Men in big, gold letters top the display, with neatly stacked pamphlets on courage, valor, training, and educational benefits.

Meanwhile, far-left faculty members—the kind who sport "Stop the War" bumper stickers and show up at protests—froth in the break room. Like most of society, the other teachers and administrators don't pay much attention. Even as the war in Iraq rages, sending boys home with limbs missing, no one in Lake Parrish seems overly concerned. Most of their kids are tucked safely away on college campuses.

Mick bumps into Cait as she is coming out of the school's main office. *She's got that look,* he's thinking. He can feel her buzzing, putting out attitude. A peck on the cheek, and she recoils.

"Don't patronize me."

"What? Come on, you're my girl."

She's irritated to the bone. Cait is not your typical self-consumed teenager. She refracts through the student body, bending minds to her way of thinking. She protests things like vending machines, which she was successfully able to remove from the cafeteria by lobbying the faculty, circulating petitions, and speaking in front of the school board. This did not bother the almost-anorexic girls modeling new clothes in the halls. But it bothers Mick. It's denying people the right to choose. And he likes a Snickers bar every once in a while.

As student body president, Cait helps oversee the scheduling of events. "Can't you see?" she asks. "Having a couple of marines set up a table in the lobby and pass out literature is tantamount to promoting war."

"Would you just chill? You got to pick your battles. They'll be gone in a couple of hours."

"I've been against this for weeks, Mick. You know that. I don't want the marines here, spreading their propaganda. I've talked to the school administration, pleaded with the teachers, and I even called school board members at home trying to get them canceled, but no one's listening. Hello? What's up with that?"

"Chill. What are you afraid of? You think the marines will twist some minds into joining? Here's an idea. If someone's joining, they probably thought about it a long time ago. Besides, you got the stupid table across the lobby from the marines with your antiwar bumper stickers. *Stop the War* and *Get out of Iraq Now*? Cait, that's crap! I've got class." He storms away, leaving Cait even angrier.

Mick and Griff sit bored in Spanish class, passing notes underneath their desks. Mick's arms are ripped, and every time he passes a note, his forearms and triceps flex across the aisle, and the girls sitting behind him giggle. He's still pissed with Cait and feels like she's always on him about something. Especially this war thing. Mick's writing a note. *These guys are heroes. She's so into women's lib. Doesn't she know marines are saving kids and helping out so girls can go to school?* His note slides across the aisle into Griff's hand, and he gives Mick a thumbs-up.

Class ends with the sound of a buzzer, and Mick and Griff stream through the door with the crowd, out into the packed hallway. There's a short break between classes, so they head toward the cafeteria to hang and get some juice. On the way, Griff pushes through the shoulder-to-shoulder crowd and cops a feel on a sweet freshman's butt. When she turns around, surprised, he points at Mick. The girl turns red.

"Sorry," Mick says to the girl. "My friend's a dumbass."

Griff tries for a headlock on Mick, but he's too short, and they stumble along, slap hands, and nod at a couple of buds. Little B runs up from behind, out of breath, still carrying his ball.

"What's up, dogs?"

"Griff's molesting children again."

"Sum those freshmen look tasty," B responds.

"You ever hear of jailbait?" Mick asks as they walk into the cafeteria, the crowd swelling and noise level rising.

"You're too serious, dude," Griff says.

"I've got to take a dump," says B, one hand in his pocket, scratching.

"Check your pants; it smells like you already did." Griff holds his nose. Mick smiles, shakes his head, and B shoots Griff a middle finger as they push through the noisy cafeteria, full of crowded lunch tables and bright artificial light.

Just then, the two square-jawed marine corps recruiters walk in, carrying their cardboard box and the storyboard with marine corps photos. They are polite as they clear a table and quickly set up the storyboard for the lunch crowd. They lay out some red T-shirts with gold marine corps emblems on them.

Mick watches and remembers an old photo of his dad when he was in the marines. Mike is dressed just like they are and looks strong and capable. He has the same kind of clear-eyed, clean-cut look the recruiters have. Mick likes their aura of confidence. Courage and honor are a big pull for Mick.

"They look like Mormons on 'roids," Griff jokes as one marine stands on a chair and shouts.

"Listen up, gentlemen...and ladies. Who wants to make twenty bucks in the next five minutes?"

A buzz starts, a few students shout out, and soon hands are up asking, "For what?"

"Twenty bucks." The marine pulls out a twenty-dollar bill and waves it. "Twenty bucks for the most push-ups." A bunch of boys are fired up, shoving their way toward the marines.

"Let's go, son," Griff says to Mick, throwing a forearm into his back.

Mick smiles and moves up to the recruiter with the money in his hand. *He's not as big as he looks, 'bout a buck eighty,* Mick's thinking. He sizes up his arms and can see the recruiter looking him over. Mick's sure he can beat the dude in arm wrestling.

"Screw that," mumbles Little B as Mick and Griff pass him. "Marines are a bunch of rock heads."

One recruiter explains while the other demonstrates a marine corps push-up: back straight, feet together, and head up. "Gentlemen, you must touch your chest and extend your arms."

Mick and Griff, together with a dozen other guys and a female gymnast, start out in the prone position as kids crowd around to watch and shout encouragement. They're stoked, talking loudly, letting loose with a few catcalls, "Look at that hi-ney!"

One marine counts out loud while the other checks their form and looks for cheaters and nonhacks. By the time the count reaches fifty, the girl is gone, and most of the boys have folded. Cait walks in, arms crossed, mouth tight, shaking her head and looking disgusted.

"Bust it out, Mickster," Little B shouts.

"Gentlemen, that's seventy." Now the students are going nuts, jumping on tables for a better view, stomping their feet, shouting, "Mick, Mick, Mick!" or "Griff, baaaby!" A couple of cheerleaders in uniform begin chanting, "Give it to me! Give it to me!"

They are down to Mick, Griff, and two other boys, who struggle away, their arms shaking and bellies sagging while beads of sweat drip from their foreheads to the floor. At eighty, it's just Mick and Griff in the battle. Boys are making bets, and a group of girls has joined the rally girls' chant until a teacher walks in. When they hit eighty-five, Griff looks like he's in pain. The crowd quiets. The back of his shirt has lifted and his underwear is showing. Cait looks on, not pleased.

At eighty-seven, Griff collapses. Little B bounces off the walls, cheering like it's the Super Bowl, grabbing money from the losers. Mick holds his position, and everybody waits for him to do one more push-up.

"Kick his fricking butt!" Little B screams, nearly delirious.

Mick holds for a moment longer, lifts one arm, waves to Griff, and then, to everyone's amazement, stands up. It's a tie. A groan rises from the lunchroom.

"What the hell was that?" B asks as money gets ripped back out of his hands. Mick shrugs and looks at the recruiter. "We'll split the twenty."

The marine waves the money and tells Mick, "That's some Semper Fi attitude, son," and has Mick and Griff fill out a card. He hands them each twenty bucks and a T-shirt. At about the same time, Cait stomps up to the table, fire in her eyes.

"You know you shouldn't be here. Your agreement mandated that you had to stay in the lobby."

Mick grabs Cait by the arm. "Chill. We're just having fun."

"If it was just fun, then why did they get your phone number?"

Chapter 9

Claire is preparing dinner, rinsing vegetables at the sink and moving to the cutting board to chop the carrots and golden potatoes. She switches knives and slices the early girl tomatoes, green pepper, and fat mushrooms she bought at the farmers' market in town.

In this moment, she thinks about her mother, lying in bed at assisted care, unsure of who Claire is. Most days, she drops in to massage her mother's feet and tell stories of other days, when her mother was young and danced in front of the fireplace like a schoolgirl. Or how they had the greatest time during Christmas at the farm when the family would gather around the tree and joyfully open presents. She thinks of her mother in bed, body wasting away, mind leaving.

She empties the vegetables into the silver pot and inhales the smell of her Irish stew. Cutting, cooking, and preparing bring her pleasure. In the daylight, she can stand at the sink and look out on the lake and the dock and perhaps a small boat or two churning by, pulling white waves in its wake.

Tonight, as Claire stands at the sink, the dark window reflects her image. She brushes hair from her eyes and worries that she is old. Each day, by dinnertime, her eyes are tired, and now a small pocket of skin puffs and sags beneath her left eye. She touches the spot with the back of her hand and then breaks open a head of butter lettuce and tosses it in the salad bowl. She can see in her reflection that her dead breast has dropped. She still needs plastic surgery, and this worries her. The phone rings.

"Hello."

"Mrs. Kelly, this is Chuck. I'm sorry to bother you, but we've got an issue going on at Meadow Brook Village." Chuck is her handyman.

"What's the issue? Can it wait until tomorrow? We've talked about phone calls at home in the evening unless it is something you can't handle."

"I know, I know. I'm sorry, but number eighteen, you know the Hernandez family?"

"I do."

"Well, David was drunk again, yelling and fighting with Joyce, and she threw a bottle at him and it broke a window. So I called the cops."

"Good."

"They just left and took David to jail. I'll cover the window with plywood and fix it tomorrow. I thought you should know."

"Good job. Give them a bill for your work and a written warning. I like Joyce, but she's a hothead too. Tell them this is their last chance. He's got to get into AA, and both of them into family counseling, or they're going to be evicted."

"I didn't want to bother you, but this is their second incident."

"We'll give them a week or so to get help and prove they're trying."

Claire hangs up, tired of dealing with tenants. Mike only hears the stories; he doesn't deal with any of it. He did in the beginning, but now he never has the time or inclination.

It's been lonely running the properties mostly by herself, doing the books, and being a mother all these years. She's tired of making meals and not being acknowledged for her work. Twenty-five years of cooking, cleaning, and picking up after others have given a roll to her shoulders and a weariness to her step. But it has always been important to her to have the family sit down together every night for dinner. When the kids were growing up, that was one of the things she insisted on and looked forward to. They would gather at the round oak table, hold hands, and say a blessing. "This food is the gift of God and the whole universe, the earth, the sky, and much hard work. May we live in a way to be worthy to receive it."

On occasions, when someone in the family did something to be proud of, Claire would set their place with the special red plate. It could be for Mike's books or essays. Or it could be set in front of Mick or Madie for doing well in school or sports. Sometimes the red plate would be set for sadness, for when someone needed support. It's harder now for them all to gather, with Madie in college and Mick so busy with baseball, school, his friends, and Cait.

Tonight Claire sets the red plate in front of Mike's place. She is excited but also scared that addressing his post-traumatic stress disorder symptoms at the VA will only upset him more and bring up brutal memories without any resolution. She knows from the books she's read and the spiritual classes she's attended that he has to go into the pain and not hide from it. She also doesn't want him patrolling the house at night, becoming more hyperalert than he already is. She doesn't want him angry, volatile, or remorseful—just on an even keel. She believes that psychological therapy and maybe a new medicine will help him deal with his pain. Maybe with counseling at the VA, he can be a better person, perhaps kinder and more aware of others' feelings. She knows that he *is* kind—that it's only the static of his pain getting in the way, demanding all his attention. He has to put out the fire inside before he can tend to the problems in their marriage. As they say on airplanes: attach your own oxygen mask first. But meanwhile, the problems aren't going anywhere…she's tired of his pain that doesn't seem to stop. Nobody can change that but him. If he doesn't try, she knows their marriage will not survive.

When she hears the garage door opening and closing, her body tightens. Mike enters the kitchen looking tired and vulnerable as he limps to the sink, holding a Diet Coke and a copy of the *Wall Street Journal.* He's brought the real estate edition for Claire. He stands behind her at the sink and kisses her neck.

"I love you in an apron," Mike says. Claire turns from the sink, wipes her hands on her apron, and ignores the comment. She is hopeful.

"How'd the appointment go?"

"Fine." Mike sits at the table and opens the paper to the op-ed section, looking for essays on the war, anything that supports his position on the US efforts in Iraq.

"Well?" Claire says, waiting.

"Well what?" Mike asks, sounding anxious.

Claire can tell he is annoyed, but she doesn't care. This is more important than Mike being pissed off and trying to control her with his anger.

"How was the meeting? Who was there? What did you talk about?"

"I mostly just listened," Mike answers. He sips his soda and turns a page, not looking at Claire.

Claire faces the sink, disappointed. Nothing's going to change. "Would you open some wine? The chardonnay."

Mike fumbles through a drawer looking for the corkscrew, and as he does, a bottle opener Mick bought him for Father's Day starts playing the marine corps hymn. Claire glances at Mike as the song rattles off spatulas, whisks, and wooden spoons. "We will fight for rights and freedoms and keep our honor clean." Mike locates the corkscrew just as the song turns off.

Claire takes down two wine glasses from the cupboard, sets them on the table, and says, "Tell me a good story."

Mike leans back against the counter, unemotional and disconnected from his answer.

"I don't know what to say. There was a collection of wounded and wrecked Vietnam veterans, talking bullshit, and a couple of kids just back from Iraq. Most of them were shot to shit and about all anyone talked about was Vietnam or killing Arabs."

"Sounds familiar," Claire says sarcastically.

"Christ, Claire. What do you want? I'm trying to make you happy, but I don't know if I can do this. I feel out of place. These guys are really screwed up."

"And you aren't?"

Mike tightens. "You think it's easy to spill your guts in front of strangers? It's not. Give me a break. I work hard, fifty, sixty hours a week. I'm home every night, and all I get from you is that I'm sick and need help. Jesus Christ, Claire, you don't have a fucking clue. What's inside of me is always going to be there. I can't change that. Where's Mick?"

"Stop swearing! And don't change the subject. This isn't easy on me either. It's been over twenty-five years of you avoiding help, and you make *me* out to be the bitch. Listen, buster. How you feel and behave has impacted all of us. Can't you understand that? Maybe this will help you and help our marriage." Claire takes a breath, folds her arms across her chest, and stands firm. "I want to know how it went. What did you say?"

"Will you stop this? You act like I'm a two-year-old. I'm doing this because you asked me to. Isn't that enough, for Christ's sake? I'm trying. And I told you I'm going to write about it, all right?"

"You can't write your pain away! It doesn't work. It's never worked. You've written hundreds of thousands of words on war and pain, but you refuse to really deal with your issues. You think you're addressing your pain when you're writing—all you're really doing is feeding it." Claire catches herself. It's quiet for a moment. She turns her back on Mike and tosses salad, gradually breaking apart inside. She realizes they have had this same argument for years. She gives up. She's too tired to battle. "I'm trying to help you, but I've got my own set of problems. My back hurts, and my mom is dying."

Mike listens and pours red wine in both glasses as Claire puts the salad on the table.

"I'm sorry. How's your mom?"

Claire joins Mike at the table, sits down, and is on the verge of tears. "The hospice worker came by and gave her a bath. She's so frail and thin but never complains." Mike starts to read about another attack in Iraq. "I brushed her hair, put silver sprinkles on her face, and then did her nails. Mike!"

Mike looks up. "What? What!"

"Damn it, Mike!" Claire's fork hits her plate. Her face is red and angry and then drawn. She exhales, exhausted. She takes a sip of wine, looks at Mike as if there is no hope, and says coldly, "I thought I asked you to open the chardonnay."

Mike looks like he could kill and backhands his wine glass against the wall, shattering it to pieces. Claire ducks. Guilt has already consumed him as he sees a piece of glass slice into Claire's face. He's horrified at the sight of her blood; it hits him low in the belly, as if the glass has pierced him too. At the same moment the glass hits the wall, Mick opens the kitchen door. Mike quickly gets up and grabs a dishtowel, wets it in the sink, and rushes to her side as she holds her cheek. Mick sees the wine-splattered wall and Claire in shock, bleeding just below her eye. He jerks the towel from Mike's hand, pushes him away, and starts to gently wipe the blood from Claire's face. Mike is speechless, torn inside, sickened by his actions. Mick holds the cloth to Claire's face.

"Asshole," Mick says to Mike.

"It was an accident."

"Right. It's always an accident."

"I never hurt your mother. I—"

"Stop it!" Claire shouts.

Claire and Mick sit in the backseat of the SUV as Mike drives to Providence Hospital. Mick holds his mother's hand as she presses the bloodstained cloth to her face. They are silent. Mike is consumed with remorse. He wishes he were dead. He wishes Mick had ground the broken glass into his face. There is the sound of the rain and wipers and tires turning.

The parking lot is full as they pull up under the red emergency sign. A security officer lifts a drunk out of a flower bed.

"I'll park and come in," Mike says, looking back over the seat.

Claire holds the bloody towel to her face and shows no emotion. "Please don't. You can leave; we'll take a cab home." Mick glares at his father and helps his mother out.

"Claire, I'm sorry. I'll...I'll just wait...Claire...I feel awful."

"This isn't about you," Claire says, looking back.

Mike watches them enter through the sliding glass doors and walk past an empty gurney and wheelchair up to the front desk. He stares at her, feeling helpless, and watches until an orderly guides Claire away. An ambulance pulls up behind Mike, lights flashing as he leaves the entrance and backs into a parking space. Rain pelts the windows. Mike considers the awful nature of his actions. How in one instant his life could be destroyed. Like that patrol on Mother's Ridge. His platoon was humping all day in the jungle. Hadn't been hit for almost a month. Everyone was loose as they stopped to break for water. Mike was carrying the .60 and a guy with big ears named Smitty was in front of him, laughing about something. As the patrol sucked water and pulled out smokes, Smitty chuckled to himself at some private joke floating through his brain. Then he lit a smoke and sat down on a land mine, a toe popper. Boom! Smitty's ass was an enormous hole of broken bones and ripped-open flesh. Chunks of his pelvis were turned to pulp and blood. He turned red and black as billows of smoke and dirt kicked through the air. And he was gone! Life over. Dead in an instant!

Mike's synapses fire again, and he focuses on what an awful thing he's done. Claire will hate him, divorce him, and Mick will remember this act of violence forever. Nothing he can write will repair the damage. He didn't mean to hurt her. It was an accident. But he smashed the glass with intent. He wanted to stop her from blaming him. He can't argue with her—she's better at it than he is—he can only escalate. Deep down in the furthest, rottenest part of his soul, what he really wanted was to control the moment. Control her with fear and rage. Now he would lose her. Maybe he'll go home, take off his clothes, step in the bathtub, and put a bullet in his head. No. Go away somewhere, jump off a cliff or a bridge or better yet, go to Iraq and get killed. That's better. Her pain is just a scratch, but his is so enormous for hurting her that he wants to die. She'll never understand that.

It is raining hard and after 1:00 a.m. when Mick and Claire emerge from the hospital and stand under the cover of the entryway. Claire has three stitches and a bandage over her wound the size of her thumb. Mick has an arm around her. Mike stares through the windshield. He has never felt worse. He pulls up, and they get inside. It's a long drive home. No one says a word. He spends the night in the extra bedroom but doesn't sleep. Before dawn, he's in the kitchen eating chili, drinking Diet Coke and composing a note for Claire and Mick, which he places on the kitchen table.

Claire, I am so sorry for what I did. I feel awful, and there is no excuse for losing my temper like that. I want to be OK and know I'm not. And I know I frightened you both. Mick, please forgive me. I was an idiot. I love you both and am terribly ashamed. Mike picks up the note and reads it again and then crumples it and puts it in his pocket. The note is stupid. They'd never know how bad he felt. In a fit of rage and remorse, he picks up a fork and slams it into his thigh, clenching his teeth. *This is how I feel.* He does it again, welcoming the pain. He hobbles to the kitchen sink, washes the fork, and watches the traces of blood swirl down the drain. He turns off the faucet and then limps into the hall bathroom and looks in the mirror. His pants are ruined and his leg hurts like hell. *What the hell am I doing?*

Chapter 10

Claire stands at the French doors in the bedroom, a small bandage under her eye. It has been a few days since Mike exploded. Her arms are crossed as she looks out on the lake. It's raining, and wind rocks a sailboat tied at a distant pier. Grief is etched on her face like a fine-line drawing. She is vacant inside. Drained. What remains is this hole in her heart. She's not afraid of him. She used to be; now she's just tired of it all. Tired of the pattern. It's been a long time since he last exploded but—"Shit!" she shouts. "I'm tired of his excuses, and I'm tired of him being tormented, as if his pain is more important than anyone else's."

She turns and walks toward the nightstand, lifts a suitcase, and places it on the bed next to a stack of clothes. She packs slowly, sadly, contemplating each article. She has to leave. What else is there? She has tried everything. For years, she read books on marriage and relationships and attended seminars and retreats, trying to understand him. She tried therapy and medication, yoga and meditation. She learned about post-traumatic stress disorder and depression, and she did everything from howling with the wolves to spending time in silence at a Buddhist retreat. One time Mike went along. He went because the retreat leader, who was a Zen Buddhist monk, was a former helicopter gunner in Vietnam. His chopper had been shot down, and that struck a chord of authenticity with Mike. The retreat was held at an old, run-down Catholic retreat center on the Oregon coast, just outside the tiny of town of Nestucca.

Everything they did was done in silence. Only Jermain An shin Davis and his student, Bertran, spoke. They taught a few old former soldiers and middle-aged women how to meditate, walk in silence, and eat their meals in silence. Mike mellowed. *Things were working,* Claire thinks, as she remembers walking with Mike arm and arm in silence along a path near the ocean. On the third day, a Saturday, Mike told Claire he needed to go into town and get some ant-acid and would be back shortly. He returned a few hours later during eating meditation and told her he was sorry he was late but he was sorting things out. Still, it was OK. The next day, when the retreat ended, she overheard Mike on his cell phone talking about having watched the OSU football game in a bar in Nestucca.

She blew up. She threatened to leave him again. She threatened and pleaded and begged Mike to seek help. He said he would seek help. But it was no use. Either he was too busy, too important, or too ashamed, ...and now it is too late.

The phone rings and rings and finally stops. The room feels dead. Quiet, as if no one else lives here, as if she is a stranger in her home. She stops packing and stands at the window, arms folded. The lake is churning, and the wind lifts the water in waves. The rain blows sideways. The phone rings again and again until finally Claire picks it up. She doesn't speak.

"Claire. Claire. Please don't hang up. I'm so sorry. I'm just...I...I was upset. I know I was wrong. I...I'll try Prozac. I'll get into counseling. I swear to God I will."

Claire doesn't say anything for a long time. In a way, it has been pleasant with him sleeping in the extra bedroom and leaving for work before she gets up.

"Mike...I can't take it anymore."

"I'm sorry. I won't ever get like that again. I swear to you. I'll keep going to the VA and get on medication. I'll do anything. Please don't leave me."

She's heard this before. "I don't believe you. You're a liar. I've got to go." Claire hangs up, sits on the bed, and starts to cry. Twenty-five years she has put into this marriage. Twenty-five years filled with anguish. She'd be crazy to stay.

Tears roll and turn into sobs. She fumbles for a tissue, blows her nose, and hears a gentle knock on the door.

"Come in." She looks up and Mick is standing in the doorway. He looks concerned and helpless as he makes his way toward her, sits on the bed, and puts an arm around her.

"Mom...don't leave us."

Chapter 11

It is unseasonably warm. A full March moon hangs over the Kelly house as Griff, Little B, Brittany, and Cait row up to the dock and tie the small boat to a pier.

"Quiet," whispers Griff. They steal across the grass toward Mick's bedroom window. Little B trips on a sprinkler head, falls, and the girls cover their mouths, laughing. Cait taps the window and Mick opens it and crawls out, carrying a sleeping bag, a bag of energy bars, and a sports drink. He kisses Cait as moonlight glances from her hair.

"Let's go, son," Griff says. They run down to the water, untie the boat, hop in, and push away from the dock. Little B rows as Griff uncaps an 800 malt liquor, takes a sloppy drink, and passes it around.

"Griff, is this your old man's boat?" Mick asks.

"Nah. It's the neighbor's. He's in Aspen; he won't miss it."

Mick smiles and high fives Griff while Cait shakes her head and says, "Damn it, Griff. You told me you borrowed it."

"I did. I just didn't have time to ask anybody. We're going rogue."

Griff lights a joint, takes a hit, holds the smoke deep, cheeks puffed, and then lets out a power exhale, passing it to Little B.

"Dude that sold me this got a prescription for medical marijuana. He and his buds are doing like ten grand a month." No one disbelieves.

"I don't know why you guys smoke that crap," Mick says. "It just makes you both stupid."

"Sometimes you need to be stupid," Griff replies. "You got to mellow out, son."

"Try living with my old man," Mick replies. "There's no being mellow. He'd say that's for sissies."

Cait is wrapped in Mick's arms and holds the sleeping bag as Griff rows.

"This is cool, guys," Little B says, "but I can't be out too long. My old man's sleeping on the couch again. He might hear me coming in."

"B, you're always talking smack. Don't be such a puss," Mick says, reaching over the side of the boat and splashing water on him.

"Puss?" Griff adds. "He's not really a puss, in the literal sense. He's just afraid his dad's gonna go psycho when he finds out he's not in his room, whacking off."

"Just row, retard-o," snaps B.

"And lighten up, B. We're just screwing with you," says Griff.

They row across the lake past the big homes with docks and boats or Jet Skis tied up. The lake is empty, and they navigate by the town lights. About twenty-five yards from Millennium Park, Griff drops the oars and starts to slip out of his tennis shoes and jeans.

"What are you doing, nutcase?" Mick asks as the boat slides and rocks slowly.

"I'll race you to the park," Griff replies, pulling off his shirt.

Mick won't shy from a challenge and starts undressing fast.

"Don't be stupid," says Brittany. "It's cold."

Cait laughs. "You're idiots."

"B, you got the boat," Mick says. Griff stands in the moonlight and dives in. Mick follows, and as he dives, the boat nearly flips.

By the time B grabs the oars and starts rowing and Cait finds the flashlight to follow them, the boys are at the edge of the park, walking out of the water.

"Phew. That was colder than shit," Griff says, standing on the park's manicured lawn.

Mick is out of the water a step behind. "I froze my balls off." Mick shivers.

A few moments later, B guides the boat into the dock next to Millennium Park. He ties it up. The boys dry off and dress, and Griff grabs a small cooler as B carries a couple of blankets. They all dash along well-tended walkways through the quiet, tree-lined park, passing a fountain and a sculpture of three beavers that faces the lake. They slow their pace, rub the beavers for good luck, and jog until they reach the monument of a marine from the Vietnam War. The bronzed warrior is helping another wounded marine off the battlefield. The floodlight at the base of the statue lights the two marines' faces. The marine carries his wounded comrade with an arm around him and a rifle in his other hand. His head is up, his face taut, while the wounded marine's eyes dart to the side, showing the slightest hint of fear. Mick stops for a moment to look at the statue. He can imagine carrying the wounded marine. Five years ago, his father led a campaign to have the city donate the property and raise funds to have the statue built. Pacifists and former antiwar folks threw up objections and lawsuits before Mike finally pushed it through city hall. Mike wrote an anonymous check for the final twelve thousand dollars to complete the construction. Mick remembers that summer when he helped clear the ground with his dad. He liked working a pick and shoveling dirt. He figured it was patriotic, and anyway, it helped strengthen his baseball swing. He worked in the dead of summer with the cool lake beckoning and pubescent girls in tiny swimming suits walking by. That was a good summer. He liked the statue, was proud of his dad, and felt ownership of the project.

"Come on, Mickster," Griff calls, looking back over his shoulder. Mick pulls Cait by the hand as they sweep out of the park and across the street. They glide through the shadows of closed sandwich shops, Paradise Tans, and the hardware store with outdoor furniture stacked, chained, and padlocked. Reaching the side of Lake Parrish Gourmet Grocery, they sneak to the cyclone fence hiding the garbage and recycling bins. Mick gives Griff a boost up the fence, and Griff clamors up to the roof. They have done this before. Once, when Griff's parents got divorced, he and Mick sat up there drinking peppermint schnapps in the dark.

Little B climbs on top of the fence but falls into the open garbage bin, full of rotten fruit, old pizzas, eggs, and spoiled milk. Griff reaches down, helps Little B out, and tells him, "You're a joke, dude."

With Griff on the roof and Little B on the top of the fence, Mick tosses their supplies up, gives a boost to Cait and Brittany, and follows them to the roof. Quietly, they spread out their sleeping bags and drop a few cans of beer and some cookies that Mick swiped from the grocery.

The rain earlier in the day cleaned the air. The stars are out in force, and the moon has turned to silver. They can see lights from nearby shops and buildings. Occasionally, a car drives by. A slight breeze brings the smells of the donut shop, where the night shift bakes till morning.

Brittany turns on her iPod, the boys crack a beer, and they all settle in a circle. Soon Griff fires up another joint and passes it around. Only Mick and Cait decline.

"You need something to cut the edge, bro," Griff says, taking another deep hit. Little B agrees, and Mick tells them to kill their own brain cells. They share beers, and Mick listens to Brittany talk about who's hooking up with whom and why one girl's a ho and another one's not. Mick is barely taking it in though, thinking more about what an asshole his dad is and wanting to smash him in the face. Living with an ex-marine who gets so intense isn't as scary to him as it used to be, like when Mike grabbed a guy by the throat one time in the grocery store. His dad's just embarrassing now. Mick never knows what Mike will say or do. The little jokes he sometimes makes bug him. One day Mick brought a black friend home, and after an hour or so, Mike wandered into Mick's room and, trying to be funny, said to the kid, "I didn't know you were black." Shit like that. But mostly his mind is on Cait's ass. He's hard and wants her.

Little B gets up and announces he's taking a leak. He wanders to the side of the roof and lets go.

"Watch this," Griff says, picking up the flashlight. He catches Little B in midstream and everyone cracks up.

"Come on, dick brain," B says, leaning over the edge of the building, trying to stay focused. Griff tells him he's a wuss, and they banter back and forth before Mick stands up, grabs a sleeping bag and Cait's hand, and they go off to another dark place on the roof. They spread the bag and lie down, looking up at the Big Dipper and what's left of the moon.

"B and Griff are so immature," Cait says, turning toward Mick, resting her head against his shoulder. "They're like twelve-year-olds."

"I know," Mick says, cracking a smile. "But I grew up with them. They're my buds. And Griff, he's got my back, and if there's something bad going down, he's money." Mick turns into Cait, touches her face, and tells her how beautiful she is. He can smell the slightest hint of perfume and feels the warmth and softness of her body. He kisses her neck and lips again and again and then rubs his hand over the outside of her sweat shirt. He reaches inside, and she has no bra. But Cait touches Mick's hand gently and pulls it away.

"Not now."

"What's wrong, babe?"

"Maybe we should go. If we get caught up here, we'll be in so much trouble."

Mick rolls from Cait and lies back, filled with desire and frustration.

"Don't be mad at me."

Mick doesn't respond. He is so hot for her that he can't listen to reason. They hold hands, and neither speaks for a long time. They can hear the boys and Brittany giggle, and they can see the tiniest glow of a joint being passed.

"What are you thinking about?" Cait asks, turning onto her side again. "And not sex."

"Getting out of here. I just want to get out of here, out of my house, this town. Do something different," Mick says, the urge for her simmering. "My dad has been such an asshole. He broke a wine glass against the wall the other night and cut Mom's face. I wanted to cream him. We had to take her to the hospital for stitches."

Cait shudders and says, "How awful."

"And he's always bossing me around. Making me get up and hit baseballs at six in the morning. That's all he cares about. It's like he wants to live my life."

Cait kisses Mick on the lips and then brushes the side of his face with the back of her fingers. "I know what you mean. Parents always want to run their kids' lives. My mom gets freaked out over school. Like it means more to her that I'm valedictorian than it does to me."

"This is different. Vietnam is stuck in his head, and Iraq makes him act like a psycho. I just want to get away from him, have an adventure, do something exciting. You don't know what it's like living with a combat veteran who wants to protect and watch over you like you're a four-year-old. I'm a man. I'm eighteen. That's how old my dad was when he went to Vietnam. He acts like I couldn't hack it. I'd be a great marine…Let's talk about something else. OK?"

"I don't want you talking about the marines. You know I hate that. What about baseball? You said it was the most important thing in your life." Cait touches Mick's face, his hair, and kisses his cheek.

"I'm sick of baseball. I want to do something important." For a moment, Mick imagines joining the marines and how sharp he'd look in combat gear. And he can see himself rescuing a child from a building's rubble. The moon turns translucent and lights Mick's face as Cait kisses him again.

"You could do anything you want, Mick. Your SAT was huge. You could get into almost any college you wanted with those scores. You could go to Brown with me."

"I don't know, Cait. That's too preppy." Then Mick is quiet, thinking about telling Cait his plans. He can smell the bread from the bakery and hear a garbage truck pulling up to the trash bins, lights flashing, making noise as the Dumpster is lifted, emptied, and dropped.

He takes a deep breath, exhales, and says, "Griff and I were thinking about joining the marines." Cait is silent. Mick can feel her tense up.

"That would totally fry the old man. Me and Griff kicking some butt in Iraq. He couldn't talk anymore about his shit. And when I come home, I won't be messed up, freaking everybody out for the rest of my life like he does."

Cait sits up and turns toward Mick. "Oh, God, no! Don't say that. The war is wrong. It's so stupid. You'd get killed." She is nearly in tears and starts to stand but Mick pulls her back.

"Babe. You're so mental. Sit down. Give me a second," Mick says. "Listen. The war isn't wrong. Look at Afghanistan. Women can vote for the first time and get an education. When the Taliban were in control, women were like trash, and all the men had to wear beards or they'd get beaten. They couldn't even dance there or play music. It was sick. Kids couldn't even fly a kite. Did you know that?"

"Of course I knew that! But war doesn't help anything. Killing is wrong. There are humanitarian organizations doing good work there. And what about that mountain climber who has already set up dozens of schools in the mountains of Afghanistan? Mortenson, that's his name."

"I know. I know. We both heard about him in Mr. Runion's class. That's way cool. I thought about the Peace Corps, but if you join that, you never know where you're gonna go. You could end up in South LA, with gangbangers, or some hole in Mexico. And besides, peace workers are always getting offed somewhere. At least in the marines, they've got your back, and we can kill some terrorists, like the assholes that blew up the World Trade Center. My dad took me to the trade center when we went back for the Yankees game. That was in late August, and a couple weeks later the place was dust. How do you think that made me feel?" Mick drifts in thought and is quiet for a moment, reflecting. He can see the waitress and the windows.

"That was terrible, Mick. But going into Iraq is a lie. The 9/11 killers were Saudis."

"Damn, Cait, think of the people that served us. They're probably all dead. I remember looking out the restaurant windows. What a horrible way to die."

Cait huffs in annoyance. "Did you even hear what I just said?"

"I know, babe," he says, though he's not really listening. Mick feels it's no use trying to convince her the marines is a good thing. She's too caught up in soldiers dying.

"Come on, babe, I'm just thinking about things. I'm not sure what I'm going to do. I might end up hopping freights with the Griffter. And you know I love you." Mick lays her down and covers her with half of the sleeping bag and feels underneath her sweatshirt.

"Tell me you won't go in the marines," Cait says. "Promise."

"All right. OK. I promise." He'd say anything right now to be inside of her. His pulse has quickened, and he needs her. He can feel sweat on his back as he touches her carefully. "I love you, Cait," he says, as he pulls down her jeans. He slides a condom on, and they make love quietly, under the sleeping bag, as Griff cracks jokes on the other side of the roof.

Chapter 12

Mike is in his study, asleep in his recliner. The lights are off, and the TV is on. The History Channel is reliving the fall of Saigon. Choppers are on top of the US embassy as desperate Vietnamese civilians fight each other to get aboard. The sound of the chopper awakens Mike. He opens his eyes, and Jesse is in uniform, his arm broken, standing in front of the TV.

"Mike, they're all dead."

He stares at Jesse and is frozen in the moment the chopper went down. He can see Jesse's face clearly, his white teeth and handlebar mustache. He's covered with camouflage paint, and his utilities are bloodstained and filthy. He's carrying an M-16 in his left hand, and his right arm is broken between the wrist and elbow, a piece of bone protruding. Mike feels so peaceful. He wants to be with his friend again. Jesse dissolves, and the noise of the TV is startling. Mike stands, disoriented, and moves slowly through the darkness down the stairs. He feels fear—not for himself, but for his son. He sees Padre and Stoner lying on the floor, shot up, not moving as he walks down the hall to Mick's room. He shakes his head, and they disappear. Mike stands at the door, quietly opens it, and watches Mick sleep. He's checking in like he has so many nights before, as he does whenever he feels danger or loneliness. Just a glance at his children will remind him that he really is a decent man, troubled but not crazy. Moments go by and Mick rolls over, opens his eyes, perhaps sensing something. "Dad?"

"It's nothing, Son. Go back to sleep."

Mike closes the door, heads upstairs, and looks in on Claire. He can see her sleeping face in the dim light from the hallway. She makes a smooth sound with each breath, and the rhythm of her breathing touches him. He feels close to her. Protective of her. Thankful that she has stayed. This time he'll honor every promise he makes. He'll be a better husband and father. He *can* do that. He goes into his study, sits at his desk, turns on his computer, and thinks about Claire. About how she has loved him all these years. He sits at his blank screen in the darkness and taps a few keys.

I think I might be crazy. I hurt my wife the other night and wanted to die...

Chapter 13

It's high noon on a warm, cloudless day. Mick and Griff are driving in Griff's calling card: a beat-up 85 Ford pickup with 210,000 miles on it. It's Griff's way of setting himself apart from all the other kids who drive their daddies' cars. His parents own a paint company and live on the lake, and if he asked, they'd probably buy him just about any car he wanted. But he rejects that. He'd rather drive a bum-rushed truck than a new ride he didn't buy. They're tooling down the highway, headed toward Portland, windows down, listening to country on the radio. It's a warm Friday in May, and they're skipping class even though graduation is not far away.

Griff takes a pull from a big bottle of malt liquor and passes it to Mick. "I'm so fired up," Griff says. "Everyone's going to shit their pants after we pull this off."

Mick laughs and empties the bottle. He's not quite fit to drive. But neither is Griff. They barrel along, Griff pushing his beater, reactions wired on youth. The alcohol is not in control.

They reach downtown after fighting the throng of slow-moving traffic and find a space in front of the courthouse, next to the Park Blocks.

"I'm feeling good, my man." Mick smiles. "We're goin' zero to hero." He laughs and bumps fists with Griff and says, "Lock it," fists turning.

Griff says, "You 'bout ready, son?"

Mick nods, all confident and ready to go. "Yeah. Let's bounce."

They jump out of the car, plug the meter, and scat across the street, dodging cars. They jog into the city park, grinning; Mick's thinking they will always be friends and live forever. People are sitting on the grass or on benches, eating under the shade of the maple trees. The grass is freshly cut, and Mick notices the smell—like a baseball field. They jog over sidewalks and pass a couple winos unraveled on benches. Another sleeps under a tree. Three long-haired young men, whom Mick thinks are obviously stoned, play hacky sack. Two girls Rollerblade by. When they reach the other side of the park, they stop and look at each other.

"You sure, wuss?" Mick asks.

"Of course," Griff responds, and they bump knuckles again.

The boys walk out of the park with purpose in their stride, cross another busy street, and quickstep into the marine corps recruiting office. A US flag and a marine corps banner are mounted on pole stands, and the walls are covered with posters of marines and slogans about A Few Good Men. Both boys are stiff and somber, fighting smiles as they stand in the middle of the small office. Two marine recruiters secure two desks. They are spit and shine, heads shaved, uniforms sharp. You could open a Coke bottle on their jaw lines. One of the recruiters stands up. He is squared away, friendly, but all business.

"What's up, gentlemen?"

<hr/>

Mike pulls up to his house. The garage door is open, but the garage is cluttered with a ping-pong table, so he parks in the driveway under the basketball hoop. It's a beautiful, clear night. Laughter is coming from the neighbors' backyard, and the smell of barbecuing steaks drifts over the fence. *That's what I should be doing,* Mike considers. *Some rib eyes and fat baked potatoes. A glass of wine.*

Mike enters the garage, kicks aside Mick's baseball gear, steps over a bag of fertilizer, and opens the door to the kitchen. He smells pot roast and looks at Claire standing at the stove, stirring a pan of mashed potatoes. He sees snap peas on the counter and smells garlic bread in the air. Red wine rests in a decanter on the counter. *This is good,* he thinks. Mick is at the counter, looking big, reading the sports page and inhaling a bag of chips. Great picture. But it's quiet, and Mike can see the tension in Mick's neck and sense his wife vibrating with angst. Neither Claire nor Mick speaks or acknowledges Mike. He walks over to Claire, sticks his finger in the mashed potatoes, licks it, and then kisses Claire. No response.

"What's going on? It's like a morgue in here."

Claire looks at Mick hard. "Tell your father what you've done."

Mick hangs his head a bit and keeps reading, eating.

"Go on, Mick. Tell your dad. Tell him what you've done!"

"What is this?" Mike asks. "Oh no! Is Cait pregnant?"

Mick looks up defiantly and says, "Griff and I joined the marines."

The room freezes. Mike is speechless. It's a blow to the gut that triggers every damn fear and anxiety he's ever had. He imagines Mick on a gurney. Blood and broken bones. A look of disbelief in the boy's eyes. He feels how it must feel to see his son die.

"Mick...Son." Mike shakes his head slowly. He pushes the intrusive thoughts from his mind: Mick bleeding, Mick without legs. He feels like he's about to fall down. "Are you crazy?" He shudders. "Are you out of your god-damned mind?!"

"It's my decision. I thought you'd be proud of me."

"You're not joining shit! You're going to college and playing baseball."

"I'm eighteen; you can't tell me what to do!"

"Bullshit. I'm not going to let you go out and get yourself killed. I'll break your goddamned leg if I have to, but you're not going!"

Mick stands up, angrily throws his chips, and pushes his dad against the cupboards. Mike roars back, grabs Mick's shirt, and slams him against a cabinet door, dishes crashing.

Claire rushes toward them screaming, "Stop it, Mike! Stop it!" Then she forces herself between them, clutching the spoon.

"Go ahead and hit me, Dad. You're the reason I'm leaving. I've never been good enough for you. Tough enough. Remember when you use to tell me to quit being a pussy?"

Mike lets go. In that instant, he knows his son will die or come home horribly wounded and fucked up inside just like he is. He takes a deep breath, exhales, and speaks softly, "Son, you can't go."

Mick straightens out his shirt and looks Mike squarely in the eyes, lifts his chin, and says, "Can't go?...I'm already gone." He flies out the kitchen door. Claire backs to the sink. Mike sits down at the table, lowers his face into his hands, and closes his eyes. Claire's eyes are red, and she looks as if she has aged a dozen years. She looks at Mike with disdain, shaking her head. Her words come out filled with despair. "You promised me this wouldn't happen."

Chapter 14

Mike sits at his computer in his office downtown and watches a live feed of CNN, with news about a gun battle near the Baghdad airport. Suicide bombers ran up to the main gate and detonated. Six Iraqi guards and two marines were killed, as well as eleven schoolchildren playing soccer in the dirt just outside the entrance. The story reports a couple of trucks jammed with masked insurgents followed the explosions, firing rocket-propelled grenades and Iranian assault rifles. They broke through the entrance as a Black Hawk fired rockets and blew up both trucks. A quick reaction force spilled out of the chopper and quickly killed or captured those who were left. It was all over in a few minutes, which was about as long as it took for TV cameras and the reporters to swarm the area. *Actionable news* is what some call it. Mike thinks it's sickening. It triggers memories of firefights and enrages him. He wishes he were there, blowing the hell out of those murderous cocksuckers. They're not ideological defenders of Islam—they're brainwashed. They're mutations.

He brings up CNN International to see if there is a different feed as Glen walks in. By the scowl on his face, Mike can see he isn't happy.

"You missed another deadline, Mike. I had to fill the space with another shitty *New York Times* op-ed. What the hell? You need to get your shit together. You're putting me in a bad spot."

He looks at Glen as if he could give a rip. He's been here for decades, busting ass, and this dick treats him like a rookie. Screw him.

"What I don't need is you on my case giving me heat about it. I told production I was empty today."

"Dammit, Mike. I've got a paper to run."

"You can run it without me." Mike grabs his briefcase and blows out of the room. Glen stands there red-faced, muttering, "I've got to fire that son of a bitch."

Chapter 15

It's late afternoon. Claire sits alone at the kitchen table, having a glass of wine. She's been chasing late rents all day and getting bids for a new roof on the apartments in Beaverton. She doesn't want to prepare dinner or deal with anything else. Maybe she'll have something delivered. Chinese? Pizza? All she has to do is make a phone call, but even that feels like a monumental task. She thinks about Madie and her verbally abusive boyfriend, Cris. If Mike knew what Cris has been saying, he'd go down to her college and try to rearrange Cris's face. It's too hard to think. She doesn't know what to do. If Madie doesn't take charge and dump Cris, it will only get worse. She's got a broken chooser. That's what Claire's mother said to her about Mike: "You've got a broken chooser, dear."

Her mind is like a drunken monkey, leaping from one topic to the next. Mick slides in, and she's fear-thinking about him dying in a useless war, one nobody understands. Her baby carrying a gun. He's never hunted anything in his entire life, let alone other men. It all seems so tragic and hopeless. A car pulls into the driveway.

Christ, who's that? She looks out the kitchen window and sees that it's her friend Nancy.

By the time she answers the door, there's a smile on her face and a sense of relief.

"Hey, girl," Nancy says. "Was in the neighborhood and thought I'd drop by, and we could have a little bump." She holds up a bottle of red wine and hands it to Claire.

"Come in. Come in. I've already got a start. Grab a seat." Nancy wanders over to the table and sits down while Claire hides the ashtray, screws off the cap of the wine bottle, and brings it over with two glasses.

"Randy is working late or bowling or something. I don't know. I just needed to drop off some paperwork at our insurance guy, so here I am."

"I'm so glad to see you. I've just been drinking and worrying. Now I'm on overtime." They chuckle again.

"Tell me about it, girl. If I'm not worried about something, Randy will wonder what's wrong. Is it Mick? Mike? Madie?"

Claire fills the glasses and laughs. "It's Mike, Mick, Madie, the whole catastrophe!" And she smiles. "Like in Zorba the Greek."

Nancy laughs too, and they toast and click glasses.

"Let me get some cheese and crackers," Claire says, leaving the table.

"Tell me what's bugging you," Nancy says.

"It's everything. Madie's headed toward depression because her asshole boyfriend, excuse my French, is being verbally abusive. I can't really tell everything to Mike, or he'd be down there trying to put Cris in the hospital."

She brings over the cheese and crackers.

"Maybe that would do the jerk some good," cracks Nancy.

"Well, there's that, and Mike's PTSD is in full bloom. If he could get over being so self-absorbed, so caught up in his painful history, maybe he'd have room to think about others. I want it to be less stressful around here, more loving and fun. I want to laugh again, go dancing. See some friends. In the beginning of our marriage, the only friends Mike had were the guys he got drunk with or played softball with. Most of them were veterans. You would think that with Mike's fame, we would have more of a social life, but over the last years we've become more isolated. We hardly see you and Randy, and I can't tell you when we last saw Terry and Leslie."

"The four of us had dinner the other night and your names came up, of course," Nancy mentions. "We should all go to the beach again. Or up to our cabin. Randy is dying to show off the new wood chipper he bought. Gag me."

"I love it." Claire laughs. "Wasn't that in the movie *Fargo*? Sometimes I feel like putting Mike in a wood chipper. Anyway, we do need to get together. Dinner and a movie. I'm sure we can do something. The only times we really go out are to Mike's author events, where nobody wants to talk to me, or newspaper parties, which are so boring. All Mike does is go to work and come home and write some more and then watch the news or baseball. I'm going to shut off that damn TV. Cancel it."

"You're worried about Mick," says Nancy. "Not Mike."

"Yes, Mick, and yes, Mike. I mean, soon there will be no kids in this house. Just us. Do you know that scares me?"

Nancy lifts her glass. "I believe it." They chat awhile about Mick, Claire's mom, and Nancy's sister, who's getting a divorce and has breast cancer too. They promise each other to set up a double date with the boys, and before long, Nancy is gone, and Claire is alone again.

She drinks a bit, chews her cuticles, and considers Mike. She loves him in a deeper, sadder way than she did when they were young. He's brilliant, she reminds herself. He can be very gentle. He says I'm beautiful and often comes up behind me and kisses my neck and sometimes rubs my feet when we're on the couch watching TV. Let's see. He's a generous man too, but this isn't worth all the sadness he brings. Even his great gift of writing and the money and the fame all came because he's troubled and writes about it. Feeding the pain. She isn't sure that's what he's doing, but she doesn't believe the writing has helped. Maybe it would be worse without it...maybe.

No. The writing is valuable, but it's not enough. Look at all the writers who end up drinking themselves to death or killing themselves. Dylan Thomas. Hemingway. David Foster Wallace.

She knows every single story about the war. Buddies dying, the chopper going down, Jesse, the door gunner, and Padre—she knows all of them. At first the horror she heard was terrifying. When he writes, he describes everything in such detail, like he experienced it yesterday, not decades ago. Then he takes the experiences and gives them thoughts and feelings. When she read his first manuscript over twenty-five years ago, she was stunned. She admired him and felt sorry for him and thankful for what he revealed. She felt bad for not doing more for the boys who came home. After reading Mike's work, she wanted to reach out to veterans, understand them, and hear their stories.

She wanted to save him and let the world know what he could write and do. Through his writing, she could feel blood run through her fingers, as if Padre lay wounded on the kitchen floor. But most of all, Claire fell in love with Mike because in everything he wrote there was tenderness. The agony of battle was experienced by an exquisitely sensitive mind. He offered a unique juxtaposition of the worst and best of mankind. To Claire, Mike seemed bigger than life. On the outside, he was commanding and dangerous, a huge presence that could strike fear in people—in her. Mike could walk into a party full of strangers and stop their conversations. They too could feel what was inside of him. They could feel his physical power and were unsure of what he might do. And for years, Mike wanted it that way. He wanted people to fear him. She remembers when she thought he had changed. When he said, "I want people to respect me. Not fear me." She believed it. She still believes it, but she's afraid he's given up on finding respect. Not that he isn't respected by plenty of folks, but he can't allow himself to feel it; the anger and pain are too important to him. She knows he loves his family. He's always home at night after work. And Claire has never worried about where he has been. There was a time she felt lucky that she wasn't one of those women looking through their husbands' pants pockets or checking cell phones.

Claire calls for pizza, picks up her glass, and walks into the front room. She grabs a book off the mantle and sits down in the overstuffed brown leather chair. The light is good, and she is too tired to think about anything. She sets her glass on the tabletop next to the lamp and opens *Living with PTSD*. She reads about flashbacks and the "monster within," all things she has witnessed and lived with. She puts the book down, looks up at the mantle, and sees the pictures of Mike and the kids. She remembers how he loved to take Madie to volleyball tournaments. He'd get up while it was still dark, pack her a lunch, and wake her up for the long drive to the other side of Portland or across the big steel bridge into Washington and some distant city. Just like Mick's baseball, Mike lived for those moments. Watching Madie compete was exciting and made him feel proud. That was what was so frustrating to Claire. Mike was a good man. He would always compliment her, tell her she was pretty, and one night in bed, he touched her hair and held her close and said, "I want to touch you like this every night for the rest of your life." It made her feel so safe. She knew he loved her. From the very beginning, he could be gentle and thoughtful, but twenty years later, there was still that monster in him that could explode without warning. Or he wouldn't talk for days, and what she saw in his eyes was remote and terrifying. He'd want to die, he'd say, or kill someone.

His craziness makes me crazy.

She closes her eyes and rests back into the chair, thinking about their first date. They went to the Rose Festival that ran along the banks of the Willamette River in Portland in June. There were carnival rides and booths and throngs of people eating and enjoying themselves. Two stages, each with its own band playing, at opposite ends of the park. It was a beautiful night, and as they walked along the river, there was a fireworks display. Big rockets cut through the air and exploded in a brilliant display of pulsating greens, reds, whites, and blues. She had on a white cowboy hat. Mike wore a red shirt and looked so strong and handsome. But as the fireworks soared and burst above the river, Mike's face changed. He looked sad and began to shake as if he was fighting something terrible inside.

"I'm sorry," Mike said. "I just need to go inside." And so they left the park. He wouldn't talk about it back then, and Claire had no way of knowing what it meant. They were soon married. He was selling real estate and working on his first book, and as time passed, he became a journalist. She discovered the Fourth of July wasn't good for him. For years, he would stay in the basement on the Fourth. Not even come out to light fireworks for the kids. On certain days or weeks, there were times he would be very agitated. These were anniversary dates of ambushes and incoming and the chopper being shot down.

One Fourth of July, when the fireworks were over and the neighbors went back into their houses, Mike still wouldn't come out of his den. She figured he was writing or reading, so she went to bed. Later that night, she heard something outside. She got up and went to the window. He was in the garden, digging and digging. What was he doing? She went back to bed, frightened. She couldn't sleep. Finally, she went outside with a flashlight and found him in a shallow hole, sleeping.

The next morning he said, "For over a year, I lived in a hole I dug in the jungle. I know this sounds crazy, but I loved the holes I dug. I felt safe. I guess I was just trying to get back some of that same feeling."

The doorbell rings, and Claire opens the door, pays for the pizza, and gives the delivery girl a tip. She carries the pizzas back to the kitchen. Mike, Mick, and Cait are in a heated discussion about the school's gay students' club and something about graduation. Mick's in a tank top, as usual, and Cait is wearing a "Stop the War" button. Her nose has been pierced with a small diamond stud.

Claire sets the two pizza boxes on the table and says, "OK, no more politics. Let's change the subject. How were finals?"

"Good," Meg replies as she bites into a piece of pepperoni.

"Come on, Cait," Mick says. "Tell 'em. Tell 'em. She's going to be the valedictorian."

Cait beams and smiles.

"Way to go, Cait," Claire says. "You've worked so hard. I'm proud of you."

"Yeah, Cait," Mike says. "That's excellent. There's nothing more powerful than the made-up mind."

"Heard that a million times," Mick says, inhaling a piece of sausage and tomato.

"So, Mr. Kelly, do you notice anything different?" Cait asks.

Mike glances at Cait. "You've got something stuck in your nose."

Cait touches her nose, smiles, and everyone around the table laughs.

"I told you Pops wouldn't like it. He's too old school."

"Well, it looks better on you, Cait, than it would on me."

This cracks the group up, and they settle into a discussion concerning what Cait will say at graduation and what she wants to study. Has she been accepted to USC or is she still thinking East Coast? Mick is shrinking in his seat, Mike's nodding, and Claire is eating pizza and trying to listen.

A SOLDIER'S SON

"Cait, I like your button," Claire says. "You're not afraid to speak your mind."

Mick nods at his dad and Mike asserts, "All the buttons in the world won't stop the war. We're in a global war. We need to destroy al-Qaeda and send bin Laden home in a box."

The wine has loosened Claire's tongue and she snaps, "Global war—Christ. Mike, think what you're saying. I thought we went into Iraq because of weapons of mass destruction? And what did we find? Nothing!" The table is quiet.

"Mick, you don't have to go. Maybe your dad could still get you out?" says Cait.

"I've already talked to Glen," Mike says, with an edge in his voice. "And I called a couple congressmen, but the truth is, this is Mick's decision. I'm as sick about this as anyone. And what we're facing over there is a legion of fanatics who want nothing more than to kill as many Americans as they can...or anyone else who doesn't believe in their perverted ideology."

"Bush is such a liar," Cait says. "He should be impeached."

Mike is wound up. "Cait, you're being nonsensical." He stands, walks over to the refrigerator, and grabs a beer. "Al-Qaeda is a worldwide terror organization that wants to kill all of us. They want to impose radical Sharia law and blow Iraq and the rest of the world back to the Stone Age. They want women like you to be slaves. That should gyroscope your thinking. It should piss you off and every damn woman in the world who wants freedom and respect. And if you don't go along with their distorted theocracy, they'll just cut your head off."

Mick and Cait exchange an uncomfortable look.

"Mike." Claire has a look of anger on her face. Mike sits down, done with his minilecture.

"All right. I'll change the subject. So, how was practice?"

"I hit a couple bombs out," Mick says.

"And no baseball at the table! Please."

"Christ, Claire." Mike is agitated but backs off. "OK. How's your mom?"

"Thank you, Mike. She had a rough day. Tomorrow I want us all to go over and see her—"

Mike cuts her off. "Mick has a game."

"We can go after the game."

"I love Grandma, but it's a doubleheader, Mom."

"Shit! Then we'll go before the game," Mike demands.

Cait looks uncomfortable and has stopped eating.

Mick looks at Mike with disdain. "I've got to study for a final."

"Damn it, Mick!" Mike slaps the table. "We're going to your grandmother's before the game, and that's it!"

Mick gets up to leave the table.

"Sit down!"

"Screw you. I can't wait to get out of here. Come on, Cait." Mick grabs Cait's hand, and they leave.

Claire shakes her head, drops her fork on her dish, and looks at Mike. "And you don't think you're sick?"

Chapter 16

L ater that night, Mike sits at his computer in his study, under the lone light on his desk, trying to finish his Memorial Day column. The house is dark and quiet except for the soft sounds of his typing. He glances at a picture on his desk of Mick and Madie as small children and then jumps to a memory of Mick walking into his office one day when he was in preschool.

"Daddy, why don't you cry?'

"I don't know, Son."

For some reason, that moment popped up in his mind, and he realizes how little he has cried over the years. A couple times with Claire. Maybe if he started, he wouldn't be able to stop. His mind is in full-blown attention deficit disorder mode, skipping and whirling, one memory to the next. Forgot to take his pills. He's fighting to stay steady, trying to write and trying to block out Mick and Claire and think clearly. *My father and mother rest high on a green grass hill at the Veterans Cemetery,* he writes.

His mind is flashing a multitude of messages: the blowup at dinner, yell-ing at his son, Madie, Glen, and will Claire leave him? He can't write away the inconsolable truth that his boy is going to war. And nothing can change the fact that he has caused his family so much pain. He rests his head in his hands, thinking that for over twenty-five years, he has tried to have empathy and understanding for others but has mostly felt nothing. This flatness shakes the family and drives them away from him. Once he tried going to a twelve-step program when Claire thought it would help him find solace. But after a few sessions of listening to others, he couldn't understand their pain. It was silly or pathetic compared to seeing a leg blown off or half a face burned away. Each day, he'd get out of bed and try to control these miserable memories. *I'm going to kick misery in the ass,* he would think. Then he'd laugh and punch a hole in the wall.

He loves his wife and children, goddammit. He cares about people. Doesn't he give speeches and donate to charities? Doesn't he get physically sick if he hears or reads a story about a child being hurt? And doesn't he write the shit out of stories about the courage and tragedy of American soldiers? But now that Mick is leaving for boot camp and Iraq, everything in his life feels out of control.

Mike shuts down his computer, puts on a light sweater, and goes out for a walk. The neighborhood is quiet, and the night is clear. The moon looks like a bright-orange hole in the sky, and the scattering of stars is like fireflies snapping in the dark. He stops for a moment and hears the sound of cats hissing and then ripping through a neighbor's side yard and out into the street, past garbage cans stationed neatly at the curb.

Easing down the street, he slides in and out of lingering shadows cast by streetlights, writing his column in his mind. How war and alcohol ruined his father and how his mother was mentally ill. They are entangled in his thoughts of Mick going to war, which feels like the ruin of his life.

He makes his way to Little League Park, where Mick used to play, and sits in the bleachers behind the screen at home plate, thinking what a fool he has been. Suffocating his son. Preaching. Driving him away. From the light of the moon, he can see the dirt of the infield, the edge of the outfield, and the outline of a fence. For a moment, it is peaceful.

Sometimes, on the nights before Mick's games, he would come sit in the bleachers and visualize Mick hitting home runs or playing catcher and tossing runners out at third. Was that mentally ill? *My son brought me so much joy. I always felt Mick represented the innocence I left behind in the jungles of Vietnam. I just wanted*

Mick to be better than me in everything. Is that crazy? Is he building a newer version of his incomplete self? Claire used to say, "You have got to let Mick individuate. He needs to separate from you and be his own self." But Mike would dismiss it and ply Mick with his advice, especially before each game. "You're a leader, Son. People look up to you. They want you to be successful. Listen, you've got to visualize, Son. See that curve ball breaking in your mind. Feel your hips open and arms extend as the barrel of your bat makes contact. Believe in yourself, Mick; believe you can be the hero of your life." He told Mick things like that all of his life. It was as though he thought the power of his made-up mind could make up Mick's.

Now he feels agitated and afraid. Soon his son will lose his innocence and learn how to kill. He is trapped in a free-falling vision of his son's life. *He will end up just like me and all the others in every goddamned war. He'll feel terror and grief and great remorse. He'll learn how to remove himself from all feelings. How to be flat inside when a Humvee rolls over a land mine and soldiers are blown in half. Soon my son will shut down at the sight and smell of bloated bodies in the cooking sand. Bodies he helped kill days before. He'll numb himself and feel nothing when a gaggle of kids appears, some missing arms and legs, dragging themselves through streets of rubble, begging for scraps of food. Maybe one of them will smile and toss a grenade in the back of his passing truck. Maybe he'll see a woman holding a child and wonder if she is a bomber trying to kill him. And as the days and weeks grind on, he'll be tough and feel invincible. Or shake uncontrollably after months of IEDs and mortars, machine gun fire and suicide bombers blowing themselves up in a spray of flesh and bone.*

Mike starts walking back up the block, thinking, talking to himself. *Then one day, my boy will come home with his mind messed up. No medication or therapy can stop that. He'll have the same kind of nightmares and intrusive thoughts I do. And for years he will crave the same kind of unbelievable adrenaline surges I've always had—those heart-pounding moments of hyperalertness that come when you're surrounded by enemy or stalking them at night.* Mike's eyes water as he realizes the truth: *My boy will be just like me.*

Back at his computer, Mike finishes his column as dawn surfaces across the lake.

Memorial Day
by Mike Kelly
When I was a boy, we lived on a small farm not far from the city. I slopped pigs, rode horses, and climbed on bales of hay stacked inside our big, old barn. An owl slept in the rafters of the barn, and at night he'd swoop down and eat field mice. In the morning, I'd marvel at the litter of tiny, perfect bones left along the hay. I remember my mother in the front yard picking rhubarb while my father sat on the porch drinking beer. Every time I see rhubarb in a store, I think of her turning earth, planting, picking, and making pies.

The smallest things bring back the deepest memories, especially as I grow older. My senses and memory are more alive as I think of my parents' final resting or my fellow marines' last battles. I also grieve for our young soldiers who are dying in Iraq and Afghanistan. When I came home from Vietnam, every day was like Memorial Day. The wind in the trees might make me think of how Padre died or Jesse as I lifted him from the chopper. If I walked past a hole dug in the ground, I might imagine firing my rifle just before the rockets came.

The pastures of my childhood soon turned into housing, and we moved and moved again. We settled in a suburb, and my father worked long, hard days but began drinking his life away. Soon, my mother became harsh, disturbed, and unkind. When I was in high school, their marriage ended. He was always drunk and that seemed to drive her crazy. I joined the marines and when I came home, my mother moved away and my father was still drinking. I used to try to reason or threaten him sober but finally stopped trying.

Today, I want to be a more forgiving soul. Occasionally, I'm able to abstract the war away. I can review it without feeling like I'm living it. That's also true of how I feel about my mother. I can look back and see her in a gentler way. Perhaps it is remembering her as fragile that softens me. How I rubbed my mother's feet when she was dying. The night she died, I lifted her in my arms and laid her quietly on the gurney.

My father left slowly from cancer and alcoholism. In those last weeks, I'd carry him and bathe him and lay him on his bed. At night,

I'd listen to his moans, amazed that he never complained. He died at the Veterans Hospital, high on the hill that overlooks the city. He was fifty-four and had nothing. His belongings were a garbage bag full of clothes and faded handkerchiefs. I was more ashamed of him than saddened. I remembered him drunk, falling down at my baseball games or begging me to drive him to the store for a bottle.

Time and faith, however, have changed my life, opening new ways to look at things. A few months ago, a woman called about a book I'd written. She found it at a library sale in Enid, Oklahoma. My father and I share the same name, and she asked if my father was from Enid. I said he was, and she told me she used to live down the street from him. "He worked at the soda fountain in the corner drugstore," she said, "before he went away to war. He was a good boy, but when he came home, his eyes had changed, and he wasn't the same anymore."

A few days later, she sent me a package. Inside was a picture of my father standing proudly beside an army tank and a yellowed newspaper article about him coming home. He was awarded the Silver Star, the article revealed, and two Bronze Stars and a Purple Heart. I never knew. My mind shifted that day, and now I think of him as not just tragic but heroic.

Today is Memorial Day. The sky will be blue, and the sun will feel more than hot. Flags will wave in the wind as the neighbor pulls his boat from his garage. My wife will bake lemon chicken, but our kids have not yet arrived. When they do, we'll spend an hour or two outside on the patio by the lake. We'll eat and argue a bit about politics, and then I'll go inside, sit in my favorite chair, and wonder about Padre or Jesse, fresh rhubarb, and a photo taken a lifetime ago.

Chapter 17

Mike's grinding his teeth as he speeds up to the Veterans Hospital, gripping the wheel tightly. He can't stop thinking about his appointment. He feels shameful and cowardly. He's supposed to be a leader that veterans can look up to, not a weakling ruined by the war. Feeling bad because he survived. At a stoplight, a shaggy-looking guy with a mutt stands by the road, holding a sign that reads "Homeless Vet. Need food and work." He's in his fifties, and his dog looks sick. Its thin coat is pale, and there is mange on its hindquarters.

Mike motions for the guy to come over. He looks the right age to be a Vietnam vet. He's wearing an old fatigue jacket with an 82nd Airborne patch. When the guy approaches, his face looks worked over. His eyebrows are thick and scarred like he's been hammered in street fights, rolled for his wine. His eyes are bloodshot, and his breath smells like booze.

"Listen, man," Mike says. "Here's twenty bucks, but you better get your ass up to the hospital and get some help. Begging dishonors the memory of soldiers. If I come back here in an hour and you're still here, I'll kick your ass." A half a block up the street, Mike looks in his rearview mirror just in time to see the guy flip him off. He shrugs. How do you help these poor sons of bitches? What do you do? His mind flashes to Mick going to Iraq and how Claire must hate him.

I don't want to go the hospital. I've got enough problems. It's a beautiful day. Why should I waste time sitting in a circle, listening to that bitch empty another guy's vein?

As he pulls into the parking garage, he's pissed because the spaces are small and the ceiling is leaking again. *What were they thinking when they built this shit hole?*

Increasingly provoked, he walks into the lobby. It's less crowded than usual. No music or ice cream. An old guy is on the floor, having slipped out of a chair, attendants around him.

Late, Mike walks into the meeting room and sits in the circle next to the poor bastard in the wheelchair with tubes in his nose. Across from him is the same crazo who screamed about his meds last meeting. He's next to the smart bitch running the meeting. The guy fidgets in his seat, snorts, and takes off, rambling like a man possessed.

"It's those suicide bombers that mess me up. That and cutting off heads. Gooks used to do that shit too. You be in a firefight, and you got motherfuckers blown up, shot up, and dying everywhere. Afterwards, you see the head of someone you once knew, stuck on a fuckin' stick."

The other veterans look uneasy, eyes darting, aroused and distraught. Mike's thinking this counselor must relish these kinds of moments. Like Barbara Walters waiting for someone to cry on camera. A healing moment. Bullshit. Let it hang in the air like the smell of burning flesh and napalm. She allows the image its full impact so it can be absorbed into the other veterans' psyches! And the VA thinks this type of talk therapy is helpful?

The guy in the wheelchair starts choking and spittle runs from his mouth until he's coughed it all out. "Heavy, brother," one guy sighs. "Yeah, man," says another. Mike feels a pain in his knee and thinks maybe he should get out of here, take a couple of pills, and a get a drink.

"This work is very difficult," Ms. Counselor says. "But we must go through the door and into the pain before we can move to the other side."

Sounds like my wife, Mike thinks. She's on a roll. Mike sees her eyeing him... trying to read him like she does all the other poor saps. Mike looks for the door.

"That was a terrible and sad story," she says, looking up as she takes notes on a yellow pad. "And I know it must have touched a nerve or two on many levels."

No shit, Mike thinks. She has that perfectly practiced look of concern, honed from hours of listening to veterans relive their horror. Mike watches her eyes narrow and her mouth pinch, and he can see sweat circles under her armpits. She still seems startled at what men do to each other in war. Her eyes narrow again as they sweep the room, but Mike already knows who she wants to split open.

"Mike, you have been awfully quiet. Do you have anything you want to say?"

Damn it, he thinks. *I should have hit the door. All I need is to be souffléed in front of a crowd.*

"Mike? Can't you tell us something?" she asks, scratching her head with her pen.

He sits on her question for a minute, feeling like he wants to smash her in the face, punish her. Rip her open with one of his stories that even he can't stand thinking about. His brain starts fast, running through facts and realities like a race car running through a wall of fire.

"The wars in Iraq and Afghanistan bother the shit out of me. The butchery of it all. Every night on TV, Iraqis are killing our boys. One night, I imagined the TV was running blood. What people don't understand is when veterans see a boy blown up in a Humvee on TV or in the newspapers, we are also remembering. It's like we're in the event, drawing feelings, flashing back to it. We see it, smell it, and feel it. We can hear sounds from a photograph and can recall what we were thinking when something similar happened to us decades ago. Then my beautiful son joins the marines." The room is quiet. The veterans and the counselor have leaned into the circle, listening to each word. The tobacco-stained and gnarled fingers of one veteran clench and unclench. Another seems panicked as he rubs his hands together. The guy in the wheelchair nods methodically as if keeping rhythm to Mike's words, and a young woman veteran bites at her lip.

"I didn't want Mick to go. I wanted to keep blood out of his memory… You think I want my son to be like me, up here puking out the horror he went through?" Silence. "Forty years later, I still feel there's something dead inside me…" Mike's voice is resigned. "I'm in a different world half the time, where my dead buddies are alive. You think I want that for my boy? I served with seventeen different marines from February 23 to March 23, 1969. A thirty-day stretch. During that time, four were killed and thirteen of us were wounded, and I never saw them again." The room can't move, and Mike clears his throat. "Two weeks before I left, our company walked into an ambush, and when the fighting was over, eighteen marines were lying in a rice paddy dead. Or dying. They moaned with their heads back, biting at the sky. The NVA had dug in alongside a garden. Finally, the choppers came and cut them to pieces. Those of us who were able went back into the garden and killed them again."

In the circle, the guy in the wheelchair is crying. Several other men hang their heads in sorrow. The crazed one is smiling, muttering, "Right on, brother. Right on, motherfucker." The counselor bends over her yellow pad, eyes averted, taking notes, her hand shaking.

Mike straightens his back and settles in his chair. His face is numb, and he can see himself walking over dead bodies, shooting them again and again. Thinking, *I don't want my son to live like that.*

His eyes water, and he gets up and briskly leaves the room.

That evening Mike walks into the bedroom. Claire is in bed reading. She puts her book down and looks up.

"Something has changed," she says. "You look cleaned out."

He sits on the bed. His eyes are red.

"Do you want to talk?"

"No."

"I can listen."

"Maybe tomorrow."

"OK then. Come to bed."

He drops his clothes over a chair and crawls into bed in his underwear. But he cannot sleep. He's thinking of his son and imagines Mick is in his chopper, going down. He could never leave Mick behind. At 2:00 a.m., he walks into the bathroom and stands in front of the mirror, talking to himself, whispering over and over, "They're all dead. You can save him. You have to." He walks with purpose from the bathroom down the hall, moving in and out of intrusive thoughts, and takes a baseball bat from a closet. Downstairs he opens Mick's door and stands with the bat, looking at his son sleeping. A leg sticks out of the covers. He is tortured. *With one swing, I can save my boy. One fucking swing...*he stares at the foot for a long time, drops the bat in the hall, and walks away in the dark.

Chapter 18

Mike's Suburban is parked at the side of the curb at the airport. It's late June, and the sun is hot and hard. He sits in the front seat, gripping the steering wheel, feeling responsible for Mick joining the marines. He hates himself and wishes he could do something to himself. He'd sacrifice himself in any way necessary if it would make things change. Claire sits next to him, dabbing at her eyes with a tissue. Madie is in the back, eyes red, chewing her fingernails. They watch through the windshield as Mick says good-bye to Cait. Cait is crying. Griff is inside the terminal waiting.

Mike, Claire, and Madie exit the Suburban at the same time. Mike opens the trunk and lifts out Mick's one small bag. Claire slips a bit as she and Madie make their way around the Suburban to the walkway in front of the terminal. Skycaps move luggage as people stream by, going in and out of sliding glass doors. When Claire and Madie reach Mick, Cait steps back and wipes her eyes with the back of her hand. Claire's face is slack, her eyes are hollow, and she has aged another decade. The corners of her mouth have dropped, and she can't find words to speak. Madie hugs Mick and tells him she loves him. Then Claire holds Mick tightly, kisses his cheek, and clumsily hands him a bag with a few cookies she made and a sandwich.

"I...I just thought maybe you might be hungry." She looks longingly in his eyes and says, "Oh mercy. My dear, sweet boy." She has no advice to protect him, no means to keep him safe. She feels helpless and afraid.

"I will pray for you every day," she says, trying to hold back her tears. For a moment, fear streaks across Mick's face and settles in his moist eyes. He looks like a lost boy, frightened of where he is. It is the kind of fear that anyone could see. The fear of never coming home again. Then he collects himself, stands tall, and holds both of his mom's shoulders as he looks at her.

"I love you, Mom. I don't want you to worry now. I'm going to be fine."

Mike watches and wishes he could save his son, go in his place. My damn life is almost over, and Mick's has only just begun. But Mick would hate me for trying to interfere with his opportunity to do something, to prove something. To be brave and come home important. My boy wants to be a marine, and he imagines there's glory in war. Those are all the same kinds of things I felt when I was eighteen.

The night before, Mike wanted to give Mick some advice. Insight that might help keep him alive. But the only thing he could think of was, "Stay alert, keep your weapon clean. And if you have to shoot, Son, aim for the torso, not the head. There's more to hit."

Mick gave him a strange look, and Mike was reminded of all the years of advice he'd given Mick about baseball—as if all that was just a lead-up to this. Like someone—some alien writer—has been writing his life story, making every fucking detail mean something he never intended.

Watching the girls trying to be strong and hugging and kissing Mick makes Mike feel more distant. He longs to hold his boy, to cry, and to tell him how much he loves him.

Mike approaches Mick, takes his arm, and eases him from Claire for a private word. They stand next to a pile of bags. It is an awkward moment.

"I know you're upset with me. I know I haven't been the best father," Mike says, holding on to Mick's strong arm. He can feel his son tighten.

"You're intense, Dad."

"Son, I...I just wanted to...I'm..."

"I gotta go." And Mick picks up his bag and walks into the airport.

Chapter 19

It has been four months since Mick and Griff left for boot camp at the Marine Corps Recruiting Depot in San Diego. Mike and Claire's marriage is still strained, but to Mike it seems a little better. She made love to him twice, which was a relief for Mike, but she cried. Occasionally, they have gone to dinner, and she has told him she loves him. He often rubs her feet as they sit in front of the fire or watch TV, and that pleases Claire. Madie comes home more often and writes letters to Mick frequently. In his few e-mails and phone calls, Mick seems to be thriving. He said boot camp wasn't hard for him, and he didn't want anyone to come down for his graduation. He spent a quick week at home and hooked up with Cait, who flew in from Brown University. When Mick left to go back for his final staging, Mike felt even more estranged from him than he had before. Mick barely talked to him and never shared his experiences. When Mike asked him anything, he just said, "I'm doing this on my own. Gotta go." And, of course, Mike felt more fear. With Mick gone again, Mike is back watching news reports on TV for hours, every day. He stops going into the office at the *Portland Reporter* for days at a time. This gives him more time to visit websites about Iraq. *What are the best weapons and body armor and safest vehicles? What is the food like?* he wonders. So he buys a case of MRE field rations and learns how to cook them. Back in his day, all they ever ate in Vietnam were cans of C rations. He sends Mick e-mails reliving baseball games or giving advice on the best boots and gloves and protective eyewear. Things he can buy and ship to him, once he is in a war zone. Soon Mike orders those as well. Despite his attempts at connecting and understanding Mick's experience, he moves deeper into despair.

Mike stands at the kitchen window holding a paper plate, eating a turkey sandwich, watching the October rain pound the lake as boats toss in the waves. He was never a social climber, but when he was in high school, during the summers, he used to come up to the lake with his buddies to chase rich girls. Every time he met a girl, he wondered what it would be like to be rich and live in one of those big houses. He grew up on the east side of the Willamette River where his father owned a small farm and a small auto-body shop. His dad pounded dents out of cars, overhauled engines, and drank whiskey out of the bottle with foulmouthed customers. This is where Mike learned the dumb end of a broom, sweeping concrete floors amid the smell of paint fumes, oil, and gas. He was eight when he saw his first picture of a naked girl on a calendar hanging on the bathroom wall and found used rubbers in the backseats of cars he was cleaning out.

In those young years, he discovered that men were tough, kicked ass, ate pussy, and went deer hunting in the fall. His mother kept the books and would come in after hours to do her work and fight with his dad over his drinking with Kenny from the lumberyard or Captain Marty from the fire station. Marty drank so hard one night that he put a shotgun in his mouth. The next day, Mike saw his father cry for the only time he could remember. That's what the churning lake reminds him of: his life before his life. And any image is better than imagining Mick wounded, lying in the sand.

Standing alone, Mike is so nervous that he shakes like he has low blood sugar. The shakes come and go and are always preceded by thoughts of his son. He knows he is disturbed, just as he realizes he has no control of Mick's life anymore. There's no stopping him or keeping him safe. All that's left is worry. There are a million ways for Mick to die, he thinks, moving from the kitchen window to his office and sitting down on his cracked and faded leather chair. Mick could do everything right every minute of every day and still hit a roadside bomb or an errant mortar blast or have some stupid son of a bitch misread a GPS device and drop artillery on his position. Mick doesn't know shit about fighting in a war. Boot camp is bullshit. If Mike could just talk to him again, if he could get him to listen—but no, he has about as much control over Mick's life as he does over this goddamned shaking.

He pulls up a story he has been working on as Claire walks into his office. She has been shopping and has an armload of clothes from the cleaners. She sets the cleaning on the couch across from the desk and puts the bags on the floor. She has a look of concern on her face.

"You're home early again. I thought you were going to the office to try to work?"

"I can't write. I can't think. All I want to do is eat."

Claire walks over and stands by Mike. She runs a hand through his hair. He puts an arm around her and buries his head in her waist.

"I'm so scared," she says, touching his face.

Chapter 20

It is a cold October. Fall has worked its way into Lake Parrish, and Mick has landed in Kuwait. The US death toll in Iraq has reached over fifteen hundred. With the war raging, there was no homecoming before he and Griff and members of the Third Marines shipped out with their battalion. Claire and Cait make their way through Millennium Park, bundled in heavy coats and hats as they pass the frozen grass and sleeping rosebushes. They stop to look at the statue of soldiers that Mike helped fund, but it reminds them too painfully of Mick, so they move on quickly.

As they walk along the red brick pathway, wind blows off the deserted lake and lifts the dead leaves. They pass by white maples, brown flower beds, a fountain, and the row of stone beavers heading toward the lake. They leave the park and make their way along Main Street and into a coffee shop. Claire opens the door, and a little bell rings and makes her think of Christmas. The brisk air has made them both red-faced and glad to be inside.

Claire takes off her hat and says she will get the coffee; she asks Cait to grab a table as far away from the door as possible. Claire loves this little shop, where she often comes to read a book and get away from the world. It's a quiet shop with overstuffed chairs and couches, round tables, and folks working on their laptop computers or reading today's newspaper. Claire carries the coffee carefully, thankful for the heat of the cups in her hands and grateful for the smell of French roast. She sets the coffee on the table in front of the window that looks out on the park and hands Cait a napkin from her pocket. She sits down, loosens her coat, and gives Cait a look of compassion and concern.

"Finish with your story, sweetheart."

"It's awful," Cait says, with a tremor in her voice and a look of despair lining her eyes. "I told my parents I was almost four months pregnant, and my mom broke down and kept shaking her head and crying. And my dad? My dad is furious. Like I'm no good. Like I've just wasted my life. Thrown it away." Cait lowers her voice. "Of course I left Brown and am finishing the term online. I'll enroll winter term at Portland State."

"It's a lot to take in, sweetheart."

"I know I'm too young and all that, but I want this baby...and I just don't know what to do."

Claire listens to each word and measures her response. She can feel her face tighten and eyes focus as though trying to read something complicated and incomprehensible. What a tough predicament to be in. Nineteen, pregnant, and the father stuck in a war ten thousand miles from home. She reaches across the table and holds Cait's hand. All of a sudden, Claire's body relaxes, and she can feel the right words coming.

"We can't ever know what God has in store for us. All we can do is pray for guidance and turn to those that love us and ask for their support." The words sounded good in Claire's mind, but when they came out of her mouth, she feels they are inadequate. How can she help? She's been worrying about Mick every moment of every day, sometimes nonstop, and now this? And what will Mick do when he learns about the baby? It's foolish to get pregnant. This isn't the sixties. What were they thinking? It was stupid. What will Mick feel when it pops up on a computer on the other side of the world?

Cait considers her comments. They seemed to have composed her. She blows on her coffee, sips, and to Claire's surprise, the panic and dismay seem to have diminished.

"Well, I'm going to keep this baby," she says, her back stiffening with youthful pride.

"I never really questioned that." Claire takes a napkin from the red plastic stand. She's both glad and sorry for Cait's decision. Mostly she's glad she never had to make such a decision herself. She isn't sure how she feels about being a grandmother. Rushed, certainly.

"Do you have a plan for how to tell Mick?" Claire asks, touching the corners of her mouth.

" I'll e-mail him tonight. I want him to know. He doesn't have to marry me, but when he comes home, I'll be here waiting for him with our baby."

Cait sounds resolute, Claire thinks. Voicing her resolve is good, and she seems comforted.

"I'll just let my mom cry buckets if she wants, and Dad can chill and stop being such a dope. It's my life and my baby, and I'm not going to let my parents or anyone else change my mind."

"You know you can stay with us until things cool down if you want. It would be fun. There are a lot of people who love you, Cait." But that doesn't ease Claire's angst. How will Mick react? He's already on overload. And Mike? God. Claire shakes her head, reviewing that consideration. "OK, let's just do this. Let's set our minds that this will be a wonderful and joyful event." Claire raises her cup of coffee as a toast and touches Cait's cup. "We'll make this a huge celebration. A big birthday party for this new and miraculous child that will soon set upon the earth."

"Thank you for being so positive and supportive. I love you, Claire."

"OK, sweetheart. Rest with it for a day or two. It'll all work out. This child will be well loved and the greatest thing to ever happen to you. And I'm going to be a grandmother!" As Claire toasts her cup of coffee again, she thinks how terrible this could all be if Mick gets hurt or...

Cait walks into her lavish home, wet and cold and excited about her life again. She slips off her boots and damp socks under the bright chandelier, and her feet feel the warmth of the heated Italian marble. The winding white staircase is in front of her. To her right is her father's library and office, full of dark-cherry bookcases, leather furniture, and his handcrafted mahogany desk.

Cait is relieved after her coffee with Claire. She rushes upstairs, throws her coat across the chair, grabs her laptop, and plunks on the bed.

She sees the e-mail from Mick pop on the screen. She anxiously opens it and reads.

Dear Cait,

Griff n me r still in Kuwait and finished r training today with a 5mile run with rifles and forty-pound full packs. It was so fricking hot some of the guys were puking at the end, even as they poured water from their canteens on their head. I'll bet my old man never had to do that. Anyway, Griff wanted to show he was tough and bet a guy fifty bucks he could do the run carrying an extra twenty pounds of ammunition in his pack. Before the run, Gunny T gave a great speech about how someday when all the politicians stop lying, history will look on what we're doing as good and important. He's a squared away dude. And he said it in a way that made me feel good inside, glad that I'm a marine. Then he got Toby Keith's song "Red White and Blue" going on through loudspeakers as we set out on the run. U know the 9/11 song, where we're kicking ass over there, and the statue of liberty will be shaking her fist. We started out pumped up, Griff was guide arm, running out front, carrying our platoon's flag, and Gunny called cadence running next to us. Griff puked about three miles out n had to stop for a minute but caught up and stayed in front. He's so crazy. When he was done, he dropped his pack and helmet and rifle and did a back flip. He's nuts. A few guys were dropping at the end, but most everybody finished strong except this guy we nicknamed Boner cause he's got a hard-on a yard long…Anyway, he looks sort of like Little B. So training is done and we're pumped 'cause we take off at 3 in the morning for Iraq. I don't want u or mom to worry. I can take care of things. I'm ready. But I feel sorry for the guys whispering prayers at night and asking God to protect them. You know I believe in God even if I don't pray all the time. At night u can hear them praying or crying softly, their heads buried in a pillow. I heard Boner talking to himself one night. He was freaked, and I went over to his rack and told him it was OK. The next day Boner asked me if I wanted a piece of gum. Sort of like he was saying thanks. It's interesting what you think about and what you see. Sometimes I'll look in some guy's eyes and I can tell he thinks he's going to die. It's just a second, and then he remembers he's a badass. Anyway got 2 run, send me some E bars if you can. I love u Cait. I think about what you wear and how you love mini pizzas and what you look like dancing across the gym floor. I think u r beautiful...I dream about you lying down with me, by the lake on the edge of the grass, like last summer. I love you and want you. Don't forget me. Be good. Tell Little B 2 write. And I won ten bucks on a scorpion fight.

Love Mick

Cait reads Mick's e-mail again and again, trying to remember and visualize every detail. She feels confused and frightened as she closes her laptop, turns off her light, and curls up on her bed in the dark. She can hear her mom and dad yelling at each other. He's drunk again, and the last word she hears is *bitch*.

Chapter 21

After three fitful hours of sleep, Mick wakes up sweating in his bunk. It's pitch black. He looks at his illuminists watch; it's 1:00 a.m. His T-shirt is soaked despite the two churning fans at each end of the tent. He's in Kuwait in a box-frame tent with thirty other replacements from the Third Battalion Ninth Marines, who are about to convoy out of Kuwait to Camp Bravo in Iraq. Camp Bravo is a sprawling base, home to the Third Marines, and Mick and Griff have been assigned to Kilo Company, Third Platoon, nicknamed the "Ultimate Fighters." Their company motto is, "We may not be bad, but the bad don't fuck with us."

He is anxious as he sits up, rubs his buzz cut, and wipes sleep from his eyes. His mouth is dry, and his tongue is thick and pasty. His whole body is sore from the run a couple of days ago. He grabs his rucksack from under his rack and pulls out a plastic bottle of gummy bear vitamins his mom sent, shakes a few into his mouth, and takes a pull from a plastic bottle of warm water. The gummies have softened and fermented in the heat of the night, and the aftertaste is foul. He slips on his desert camouflaged utilities, pulls on his boots, blouses the bottoms of his trousers, and gathers his bearings in the dark.

A few marines are stirring; some haven't slept, while others are snoring, scratching, and farting as they break from their sleep. The sweat-sagging tent smells like rancid jocks and rotten eggs, typical for the humidity and humanity stuffed into an oven roaster.

Mick is alert and starting to charge up as he stands, tucks in his shirt, unbuttons the crotch of his pants, and pulls his shirttail tight, as he learned in boot camp. He feels the same kind of fear and excitement he used to feel when batting in the bottom of the ninth with the bases juiced. He pops over to Griff's bottom bunk and playfully slaps him awake, which inspires Griff to respond with a long loud gaseous blow.

"You better check your skivvies after that one," Mick deadpans.

Someone in the dark shouts, "Light a match, bitch."

Griff sits up and yells back, "Eat me, wiener."

Mick leans over and punches Griff in the shoulder. "Come on. Rise and shine; it's time to be a hero."

"All right, donkey dick. I'm up." Griff shoots out of bed, spreading a wake of foulness. He's already dressed, his boots on, as his feet hit the floor. He slept dressed, as he did every night from boot camp to Kuwait, in order to get a jump on the day when dawn squawked. He shakes his head and rubs his face awake.

"I'm wired," Griff says. "Ready to rumble. I'm a red-white-and-blue all-American boy. I love Mom, home, apple pie, and fried chicken on Sunday. I'm a high hooker, a good looker, a lover, a fighter, a wild bull rider. I got a hard-on a yard long, and I'm looking for something to start on."

"Shut the fuck up," a guy named Blueberry says from his bunk on top of Griff's.

Mick shakes his head and doesn't bother laughing because he has heard this same mantra in shorter and longer versions since they were in high school. Mick knew that when Griff woke up, he wasn't thinking about going to war, getting shot, or dying. Griff's mind didn't work that way. He ignored the future and never thought further ahead than "What's for dinner?" He was more into "Let's just kick it."

Griff is off to take a dump, and Blueberry rolls out of the top bunk and lands with a thunk. "Say, Mick. What the fuck's up with Griff? He's a nutcase."

"Nah," Mick replies, not offended that Blueberry is dissing his bud. "He's always been into thrills and chills. He didn't have to go to war to get adrenaline surges. He found that hang gliding or rock climbing or jumping off bridges. He used to have a Harley and was always redlining. That's Griff. Besides, we're all a little wacko, don't you think?"

Blueberry nods yeah. "It's cool."

About the same time Griff returns to his bunk, the platoon gunny, Gunny T, turns on the lights and shouts like the MC at a UFC cage match. "Gentlemen, get your shit together! We are going to Iraq, and rock and roll!" This is the Gunny's third tour, and at thirty-three, he is weathered and built like a bag of rocks. He's Semper Fi all the way, and for a short man, he commands big attention. He's got three purples and two silvers and is working on becoming a full-blown legend in the corps. On his second tour, a .50-caliber enemy round tore high above his ankle, shattering the tibia and fibula and leaving what was left hanging by a thread. He lost the foot, and his high-tech prosthesis starts four inches below the knee. Gunny T was the first marine ever approved for combat with an artificial leg. Just seeing him walk in a room motivates his marines, and within minutes he's got the tent stomping and shouting out *Oo Rah Oo Rah, Oo Rah!*

A smile crawls out of Gunny T's mouth, filled with white teeth and topped with a trimmed 'stache. "Listen up," he shouts, holding up his hands, smile dropping, eyes narrowed to a glare. "Listen gentlemen. Fill your canteens and hydration bags and make sure you ain't carrying any civilian contraband, and that means fuck books, dildos, cell phones, and pictures of your naked-ass girlfriend, who's probably banging some pencil-neck geek as we speak. No envelopes from momma with her address on it, so some terrorist son of a bitch can take it off your dead body and send some diaper head to blow up her house. There is a burning barrel out there; use it. Are we clear, gentlemen?"

Everyone shouts, "Sir. Yes, Sir."

"Any o' you shit birds hasn't turned in yer will, ya got about twenty minutes to pull that out of yer ass. Are we clear, gentlemen?"

"Sir," they shout just as heartily as when they were at boot camp, only louder. "Yes, Sir!" The adrenaline is pounding. The tears and prayers are buried with the charge of youth and the hunger for combat. The room is electric, fired up.

"And, by God, I want every swinging dick ready and on the road at oh three hundred."

"Sir. Yes, Sir!"

"All right then. And when we get on the trucks from here on out, you badass, hardheaded, ass-kicking sons of bitches call me Gunny T. You can drop that 'sir' bullshit."

With a slight limp, Gunny T walks out under the tent flap and into the darkness, leaving a room full of artificial light and stoked-up marines flying from cot to cot, bumping chests, slapping high fives, and talking trash.

"We're gonna kick some al-Qaeda ass."

"Semper Fi, brother. We'll be laying some hurt on those motherfuckers!"

There is purpose in their movements, quick and practiced, as they hit the head to shit, shower, and shave and come back to stuff their backpacks. Mick and Griff start with two pairs of socks and green boxers sent from home. They have a towel, a razor, and MREs. They fill hydration bags and two extra canteens at faucets in the head. They pack up first-aid kits with battle dressings. Then they toss in their night-vision goggles. They pack knee and elbow pads and gloves and slip protective goggles over their heads, leaving them hanging from their necks. Then they throw on thirty pounds of body armor with SAPI plates—small arms protection inserts—and their helmets and put their cased-up sunglasses in a pocket of their armored vests.

Mick and Griff stare each other up and down for a long moment, bump fists, and twist them at the knuckles. Each says, "Lock it."

They sling their packs over their shoulders and pick up their weapons. They've already stuffed four grenades in their nut sacks on the front of their jackets and seven thirty-round magazines. Griff has a modified M4 with a scope and a front-barrel pistol grip. Mick carries the seventeen pound SAW, the squad automatic weapon machine gun that will tear ass and punch holes in concrete. This opportunity came because Mick is six-foot-two and 210 pounds of "twisted steel and righteous attitude," said Gunny T...and because three other marines carrying SAWs were blown up by improvised explosive devices (IEDs) in Fallujah. Saddled up and ready to go, Mick and Griff walk under the flap and into the night.

The company stands in formation under the camp's lights on the pavement in front of the tents. Mick notices the weight of the pack and feels a little top heavy and tired. But it's nothing compared to the long run a few days ago. His weapon feels natural though, an extension of his body. Sort of like how the bat used to feel when he hit doubles deep to center field. His rifle gives him strength and power and courage few men will ever experience or understand. He feels himself. He's like a big, young bull, chained up, trying to pull free. He has trained for months and is strong and motivated, just as he was in boot camp when Drill Instructor Carll spoke. Carll was big, black, and formidable. When he stood on stage and looked down from under his flat, stiff, round, brown cover, he spoke quietly, and Mick froze. And when Carll said, "The most deadly weapon in the *entire* world is a motivated marine," Mick believed it. He believed everything Carll said and worked harder in boot camp than anyone else. A few times he even thought of his old man telling him, "Mick, no one controls how hard you work but you." Or Mike's favorite saying that Mick must have heard about a hundred thousand times: "Someone has to be the best; why can't it be you?" Mike's tired clichés emerged from somewhere deep in Mick's soul and helped inspire him. Not on a conscious level like a baseball coach's advice to keep your hands high to correct a hitch in your swing. This was something deeper—the words that stay in your life and help make you the kind of man you become. So Mick busted ass through boot camp. He was perfect on the rifle range and soared over the obstacle course. He was always first out on three-mile runs and marched better, learned quicker, and worked harder than any other marine in his platoon. And at graduation he was the Honor Man of his platoon, the best marine, a strong and quiet leader.

Soon the rumbling of seven-ton trucks, mounted with .50-caliber machine guns, can be heard. Several roll up. The trucks are older, with split side rails and no up armor like the army. Instead of having the finest bomb-blast resistant trucks and Humvees, the motor pool welded quarter-inch sheets of steel onto the side of some vehicles. Because of the weight, they could not reinforce the more vulnerable undercarriage. It was ugly, obtuse, and heavy protection, good against small arms fire but not effective against the powerful explosives smuggled by al-Qaeda from Iran into Iraq, bombs that could detonate in the middle of a road and toss a truck in the air like a toy, shredding it to pieces.

Gunny T called some of the Humvees "cardboard coffins" because the armor was just plywood boxes screwed onto the back and side panels and doors, filled with sandbags. "When an IED finds one of those lousy sons of bitches, it's all over but the cryin'." A favorite cliché.

Mick and Griff wait in formation with the rest of Kilo Company. Dim over-head camp lights shine down on the three platoons of thirty-six marines. The men stand at ease, quietly waiting, some whispering about a smoke or asking, "Permission to take a shit, Gunny T." He'd nod, and the marine would be fly-ing, pack and all.

Mick stands behind Griff, stolid, showing no emotion. He imagines Cait and the color of her hair and the one eye that has shades of blue and green. He sees her face and her body and remembers being inside of her on the roof across from the lake and the backyard and that first time when they hooked up on an air mattress down by the lake. Then he worries about the things all soldiers do when they first go to battle. Will I be brave? What if I get shot in the face or gut shot or my legs get blown off? I'd rather die than come home a cripple. Maybe I'll be a hero and win some medals. Me and Griff popping caps and rescuing people. Wish I had been there when they caught Saddam. I would have worked him over, pulled that puke from his rat hole, and let everyone take a piece.

I don't know. I don't want to die or end up in a wheelchair and have to shit in a bag for the rest of my life. How bad would a sucking chest wound hurt? Like my old man's. Did he scream and cry? Who took care of him, and what happened, really? And then he thinks of the hole in his father's chest and playing catch with him, summers in the backyard with his shirt off. And how all his life, he barely noticed the scar tissue, the sunken dent in his chest. But now, as he is about to go risk his life, he can see Mike's wound clearly. The layered smooth flaps of skin that were once stitched, sutured, and pulled into a mass of melded tissue. He can also see the joy on his father's face as he releases the ball, and he can see it spinning, red stitches on white. Maybe he'll never see that again. Maybe he'll never throw another ball or feel a bat. Then he recalls Sergeant Carll saying, "You'll be on line someday, crossing an empty chunk of desert, assaulting a bombed-out vil-lage, and your best buddy will get shot in the throat. You won't have time to stop and cry. You'll be firing back, thanking God it isn't your ass laying there, groveling in the sand, trying to suck your last breath. There it is. One day you'll understand it's better him than me."

It is still dark as the convoy pulls away and leaves the safety of camp. The troops are quiet. The moon has disappeared, and the headlights lead the way. Mick bounces in the darkness, holds onto his weapon, and whispers to himself, "What the hell have I done?"

━━━━━○∞○━━━━━

It is early morning as a flash of pink rises over the horizon. The marine convoy has been on the road for two hours, barreling along a rugged stretch of desert in southern Iraq. Mick, Griff, Blueberry, and twenty other replacements for Third marines, ninth battalion are in the second troop truck back. Following them are Humvees; another troop truck; a Stryker armed with machine guns, TOW missiles, and six troops inside; and then more Humvees with M240 machine guns up top and a gunner in the turret. They are headed north toward Basra, where British and American troops have established a base with truck refueling, a supply depot, an ammo dump, and a twelve-hundred-meter-long airstrip. After they pick up more supply trucks and combat vehicles, they will travel four hundred miles north to Camp Bravo, their battalion headquarters, which is one hundred miles south of Baghdad.

The early morning air feels cooler in the back of the truck. The metal bed is slightly cold to the touch, and the sounds of the wood railing creaking and the truck shaking are muffled by the sandbags underneath their feet. Packs are spread out across the bags, and some marines are stretched out or have fallen asleep sitting up, despite the roar of truck engines and gears shifting. The truck bangs as it rolls over potholes and bad roads. The convoy stretches for over a mile, with Strykers, armored personnel carriers, trucks, and Humvees. One giant trailer truck carries two Abrams tanks. Humvees carry riflemen and officers or special agents. Other Humvees are mounted with .50-caliber machine guns or belt-fed Mark 19 grenade launchers, with gunners who stand in the backseat area, exposed through a roof turret. The troop carriers have drum-fed .50 calibers or lighter M240 machine guns mounted on top of the cabs, while marines stand behind their weapons wearing sunglasses or goggles. They present an imposing sight, with their guns that can cut through steel and destroy humans with a single round. Interspersed with combat vehicles are huge, white Mercedes trucks. These monster eight-wheelers are driven by Kenyans hired by contractors from KBR. They carry food, water, trailers, flat-screens, air conditioners, and every other kind of supply or tool needed to run a war. Each truck also has an armed marine shooter riding shotgun.

As the sun rises, the road turns to packed dirt, and dust thickens and forms a layer on the marines' faces, helmets, body armor, packs, and weapons. Now every marine wears goggles. Some wrap small green towels, green T-shirts, or white hankies over their mouths to filter out the brown-and-red clay dirt that engulfs them.

Mick and Griff sit opposite each other on flat bench seats, mouths covered with green cloth masks Mike sent them. They're hypnotized by the monotony of the barren landscape. Desert and rock and occasional flat-roofed brick and adobe homes and buildings and shacks are scattered across the countryside. Three or four hovels have donkeys and carts out front where stray dogs, noses to the ground, scour the dirt for scraps of food. Kids play soccer in the dirt or stand and stare as the convoy passes, perhaps numbed by the terror it might bring. Women dressed in black burkas or head scarves feed chickens or beat ragged rugs draped over sagging clotheslines. Some of the scant villages look abandoned, discarded, left with nothing but despair. Occasionally, a cluster of palm trees pops up around the desolate villages, and a beaten car or worn-out truck sits idly by. Then the road is empty, and there is nothing but desert or bombed-out trucks and tanks pushed to the side of the road.

"Eastern Oregon," Griff shouts to Mick across the sandbags.

"What?" Mick asks over the low roar of tires turning and the truck shaking.

"I said this looks like eastern Oregon, high desert but scrubbier."

"It's Mad Max," Mick replies, thinking of the *Road Warrior* movies he and his dad used to watch, full of machine gun–mounted old Chevys and torn-up Harleys loaded with guns…rockets shooting from their handlebars.

"Yeah, boot," another marine replies. "Just wait till the costume freaks arrive."

Mick nods off under a blistering sun and dreams about Cait. In the dream, he starts flying toward the water near the railroad trestle where they used to go diving. But he's jarred awake by the sounds of horns blaring.

Now the road is paved and runs through a populated area, picking up traffic as more vehicles line the road going in the opposite direction. Some are military vehicles or empty KBR supply trucks with Turkish drivers. Beat-up Russian cars and new black Chevy Suburbans with dark-tinted windows escorting luxury Mercedes Benzes speed by.

The convoy slows. Canals run along both sides of the road, four feet wide and six feet deep, feeding the village and irrigating the fields with the same filthy water pulled from the Euphrates. Iraqis drink from it, bathe in it, and their backyard slit trenches drain into it.

People of all ages walk along the side of the road, carrying bunches of firewood wrapped in twine, baskets of chickens, or plastic jugs of water on their heads. Some walk alongside donkey-pulled carts. Mick notices dozens of burned-out vehicles with no wheels, doors missing. In the opposite direction, a pickup drives by, crammed with twenty Iraqis wearing black or red-checkered headscarves, waving AK-47s. The hair on his neck rises and a wave of chills dances down his spine. "Insurgents. They're assholes," the gunner shouts over his shoulder.

Mick wonders why they don't engage the enemy. Are they the enemy?

More ancient buses pass them, going in the opposite direction with baggage tied on top and people hanging from the windows.

It's six in the morning and already hot as piss as the convoy rumbles on the outskirts of Basra. Concrete blast walls are placed in several sections of the road, and more bombed-out Iraqi military and civilian vehicles are shoved onto the shoulders. A KBR sewage tanker truck was blown up by an IED the day before, and the ensuing stench of shit and body splatter is left cooking in the sun.

"Whew," Griff says as they pass the stinking hull, trying to block the smell with his arm, "I never should have listened to you."

"What are you talking about, douche?"

"Bite me. I never should have listened to you. It was your idea to join, not mine. You thought we'd be heroes. What the hell were you thinking? Now we're riding in the middle of this shit storm."

"Quit complaining, bitch. You thought we'd look cool in dress blues."

"You're the bitch," Griff shouts over the sandbags, his mask down and marines still sleeping. "I'll put a foot up your ass, bitch!" Both of them laugh.

"Fuck both of you," the gunner shouts. "You're both too new to be saying shit!"

The convoy passes Muslim temples with spirals, arches, and columns and a line of bearded men in robes and turbans waiting to get in. Around noon, the trailer truck in back of them has a flat, and the convoy pulls to the side of the road. Troops drop off the back and sides of the trucks, and Humvee doors swing out as marines unload. All of them carry their weapons and take a piss or a shit in the canal next to the road. They watch each side of the road, and Mick's senses jump up a notch. For fifteen minutes or so, they mess around with the flat tire with Gunny T bitching and Mick grinding his teeth, up on one knee, his eyes on the side of the road.

Gunny shouts, "Load 'em up." And the marines are up and on their vehicles, pushing down the road.

Marines suck on tubes from their CamelBaks, water bottles, or canteens. Riflemen watch each side of the road.

The convoy stalls around a curve, nearly slowing to a stop. The road has narrowed, and Mick feels uncomfortable. On the right are a canal and a collection of villagers, including children milling around in front of some flat-roofed concrete homes. Off to the same side of the road, behind a small wall on a stretch of green grass, is a well. Next to the well are four men dressed in flowing robes, kneeling on small prayer rugs, kissing the ground, arms outstretched, palms up, praying to Allah. A stack of AK-47s is piled next to them.

The marines in the back of the truck are alert. "Check it out. Look at those rag-heads," someone says as the column slows to a crawl. "What? Hey. Look! We're driving by? Let's light 'em up," says another.

Mick feels his gut tighten and heart quicken as the truck moves slowly by.

"A couple diaper heads aren't stopping this roll," the gunner says. "They'll drop some shit on those punks from the air."

A gang of kids runs up to the back of the truck, begging, and a man in Nike sweats jogs up to the side of the truck. His eyes are bright and his teeth are rotten as he smiles and shows long knives and pornography for sale. He holds out a booklet of ugly women with their legs spread.

"Got any hoes bangin' a dog?" The gunner laughs, cutting the edge Mick feels.

Mick and Griff look in their packs and throw hard candy from home to the kids, and horns blast as the gaggle of kids fights for it in the dirt. For a moment, Mick feels good, and then the convoy speeds up, and the village with the gun-praying Iraqis slides out of sight. Soon, a couple guys piss in plastic bottles and toss them away. The day drags on.

Mick and Griff eat dust in the back of the truck, bouncing around with the rest of the marines. The convoy slows again as they cross over a sturdy bridge spanning a rushing canal and approach another village. The village is clean, with green brush and palm trees lining an oasis of single- and double-level well-kept buildings. A mosaic-tiled mosque is set back off the road. Its ornate, blue domed roof and spirals tower over the village and can be seen from several miles away. Goats and cows wander by the side of the road, heads down, chewing scrub grass. A few kids stare but do not shout or wave. As the long procession slows, no one rushes the trucks. Mick notices that the people seem quiet when the gunner turns and announces, "Don't feel right." Blueberry, who has been silent for hours, says, "Fucking A."

Just outside the village, on the right side of the road, the desert goes from sand to rocks, changing the base of modest hills. The convoy slows to a crawl and stops. Mick has his mask down as he stands up near the gunner and looks over the cab at the Stryker, trucks, and Humvees.

"What's up?" Griff asks.

"Looks like a car hit a donkey and turned over on its side, and they're blocking the road."

"Fuckin' ragheads," the gunner says. "They don't know how to drive worth a shit."

The lead Humvee is moving slowly as it tries to go around the donkey when a huge explosion erupts, blowing the donkey apart and blasting the Humvee off the road. Marines jump from the trucks and the Stryker. The car sitting in the middle of the narrow road blows up in a thundering explosion, spraying lethal pieces of engine, fenders, bumpers, and glass into the marines and the front vehicles. The marines in the front are decimated. Bones break, eardrums burst, and shock waves rock the convoy. A plume of black smoke billows up into the sky.

"Incoming," someone yells. More marines jump from their trucks and fan out on both sides of the road. Mick and Griff dive from the truck into a culvert, their weapons pointing frantically toward the horizon. A couple of marines fire wildly. The convoy becomes a fury of officers screaming into headsets. "Get those fucking choppers."

Back toward the village, maybe three hundred meters away, Mick can hear Iraqis cheering. He feels small and helpless and unsure of what to do.

First Lieutenant Bittner, strapped with a .45 and wearing a headset, and Gunny T are standing behind the truck's open door. Gunny T's rifle rests at his side.

"Hold your fire!" Bittner shouts. "Hold your goddamned fire!" Bittner calls back down the line. "Gunny T, get first squad and a corpsman up there." Gunny barks for his men, grabs his rifle and a first-aid kit, and runs toward the explosion. Bittner jogs down the convoy away from the explosion, shouting at marines. Some of the troops are frozen in trucks or lie prone by the side of the road. He stops at a marine who sits, his weapon pointed at the sky, slaps the back of his helmet, and points to the horizon.

"Shit bird! Point your weapon out there."

The marine scrambles.

Captain O'Callahan, the company commander, walks up to Bittner, chewing on the stub of a cigar. He's been through this many times before. His face is pockmarked, and he's not much more than five foot six. "What is this cluster fuck?"

"IED," Lieutenant Bittner says, "stuck up a donkey's ass. Then they blow a car, and we got some KIAs and WIAs. Got Gunny T and a squad checking it out."

"Goddammit! Who trains these sonofabitches? We've seen this kind of shit before," the captain says. "Who the hell's on point?"

"Butter bar just in. Some young guns. We warned them last night."

"Yeah, yeah, and we talked to all you officers about how shit happens, Lieutenant. Grab a couple more squads and move them up about three hundred meters in front of this mess and make sure there're no others looking for us. And put another squad just off the road and secure an LZ. I'll take care of the rear. I'll headset you when it's good to drop a smoke and mark the LZ."

There's no firing. Captain O'Callahan strides away, and Lieutenant Bittner jogs back toward his truck, a corpsman following. Mick and Griff lie flat, their weapons trained on opposite sides of the culvert. Bittner kicks Mick's boot.

"You two go help the gunny," he orders. They jump up and hustle toward the front of the column.

Mick's heart is racing as sweat drips under his sunglasses and into his eyes. His helmet and body armor shake as he runs and nearly stumbles. He feels great fear as he and Griff beat along. Smoke rises up front in a funnel, and the smell of creosote fills the air. They press on to the wreckage of the Stryker, where marines are staggering out, faces black, stunned, blood running out their ears. The Stryker is damaged in the front, the windshield blown out, and a marine sags, lifeless, in the turret.

The Humvee was blown to the opposite side of the road. The entire right side of the vehicle is totaled. All the glass is broken out, and the passenger door is caved in. The wood boxes filled with sand were useless. Blood and sand are everywhere. In the front seat, the passenger's head is blown open in a mass of broken skull and brain matter. His shoulder and arm are mangled. Mick and Griff stare at the gunny, trying to pull out the driver. Mick has never seen or imagined this kind of carnage. He gags and pukes as Griff stands and stares blankly.

"Shitheads. Get over here," the gunny shouts, calm in a moment of madness. "Help me get this boy out."

Mick and Griff snap to and rush to the driver's side of the Humvee. The gunny works fervently on the driver, whose right arm is mostly missing and whose face is covered with blood.

"Help me lift him. He's still alive."

There is the sound of choppers in the air as Mick and Griff pull the wounded marine from the Humvee and place him on the ground. Griff turns his head away and pukes on his foot.

"Give me your canteen," the gunny barks.

Mick hands him the canteen, and the gunny pours water on the young man's bloody face. "It's Boner!" Mick says, horrified.

As Gunny T clears the blood away, an artery in the soldier's neck is spurting blood. An eye is missing, and the orbital rim is cracked like it was hit with a hatchet.

"Here! Here! Put your hand here!" Gunny demands, pushing Mick's hand into the beating wound. Jaw tight and eyes focused, Mick kneels by the marine. With each heartbeat, blood oozes through Mick's fingers. He is focused only on the moment, only on the task. He's dead, really. He can see that, but it is a secret now.

Another marine runs up to help, and he and Griff pry open a twisted door and pull another body from the backseat. The dead man is not a marine. He is dressed in a white short-sleeve shirt, soaked with blood, and shredded khaki pants where the bottom of both legs used to be. A large shard of glass is driven into the side of his head.

"This is Robinson. He's CIA," the marine says to Griff. "His buddy is riding with me."

Griff is silent, staring at what is left of what once was a human being.

Mick continues to hold the bleeding wound with one hand and Boner's hand with the other. Then Boner, the boy from a small town in Kansas, gurgles, opens his eyes, and looks up at Mick, searching and afraid.

"Hang in there, pal," Mick says, trying to be brave. "You're gonna be OK."

Boner's eyes begin to close as the gunny searches through streams and pools of blood for an artery, and then he pinches it with a clip and works an IV into the dying marine.

"You!" Gunny T yells at Griff. "Get the fuck over here." He hands Griff the plasma bag and moves on to help two corpsmen treat other wounded marines. One is in shock, sitting up next to the front of a Hummer, smoking a cigarette, his legs crushed. Two others are bleeding from the face, thrashing at their eyes, and shouting, "I can't see. Help me. Help me."

"Hang on, pal. We got a chopper coming," Mick says again to the dying young man. But no chopper will save this marine. No modern medical miracle will keep his heart beating and lungs breathing, Mick thinks. Only God could save him, and where was God five minutes ago?

Bittner sprints back to the wreckage. "Where is that damn medevac?" he screams into the headset. "We need it on the ground now!"

A man dressed in blue jeans and body armor jogs up, an assault rifle slung over his shoulder. He looks at Robinson in khakis, his legs gone, and freezes. Suddenly his cell phone rings. It is long and loud, and Mick is still trying to comfort Boner, who is already dead, and Griff is holding the empty bag and Bittner screams, "Fuck this!" And the cell phone rings again.

Bittner takes the cell phone from the civilian's hand and yells at him to answer the damn thing, and he does. And he says yes into the phone, listens, and then explodes.

"We just got hit, asshole! No! No! I'm not all right. Robinson is fucking dead. No! No! I don't want to talk to Adams." Then he snaps his phone shut and pulls a black flask from a front pocket on his vest. He unscrews the cap, never taking his eyes off his friend. Then he takes a long pull, throws the flask away and walks back down the line of the convoy.

A medevac chopper lands, as gunships hover above. The dead and wounded are loaded and lifted away. Mick wipes the blood from his hands on his pants and body-armor jacket and takes a drink from his canteen. He feels stunned, speechless, but the water is good as he swallows and, for a moment, he notices the water rush down his throat, cooling the heat in his stomach.

Griff picks up his rifle, and Mick bends to puke. They both jog back to the truck as a squad of marines pushes the dead wreckage to the side of the road.

"Load 'em up," Bittner yells, walking down the convoy line. Gunny T tosses his cigarette in the sand and pulls himself up into the cab while Mick and Griff jump on board, the vehicles fill, and the convoy moves on.

Chapter 22

Claire is in her home office, filling out a deposit slip for the tenants' rent and then entering it in the rent roll. When she's finished, she checks her e-mail, hoping for word from Mick. There has been no news from him for two weeks. Some days, when Mike is at work, she will look at the few downloaded pictures she has of her son from his time in the marines or a scrapbook she started when both of the children were small.

Madie is home from college for a long weekend, and her life is going well. She ended the relationship with "butt face" as she calls her ex-boyfriend and is playing volleyball.

Madie walks into Claire's office. Her hair is wet and wrapped in a towel. She is sending a text message on her cell phone with one hand and eating an apple with the other. Her fingers jump a few times, and then she snaps the phone shut.

"What's going on, Mom?" she asks, taking a bite. "Whatcha doin'?"

Claire turns in her chair, motions Madie over, puts an arm around her, and leans her head back for a kiss. Their lips meet for a peck.

"Nothing really. Bank stuff and checking my e-mail, hoping Mick will send something soon."

"Oh yeah, Mom. I forgot I got an e-mail from Mick a couple days ago."

"Madie! Why didn't you tell me? I'm about ready to jump out of my skin. I haven't heard from him for over two weeks." Claire's voice cracks, her lips are tight, and she has on her condemning face, the one that makes Madie dive for cover.

She catches her growing angst and takes a deep breath. "OK, honey, what did he say? Where is he? How is he? Is he all right?"

Madie sits across the room in a big-backed overstuffed chair. She is in no hurry. She crosses her legs in a yoga pose and bites into her apple without responding. "I'm mad at you, Mom."

"Mad. Now listen here—"

"OK, Mom, catch a breath. You know you really bug me sometimes. So Mick just said that he's at a new base or something and that it's hot and boring. And they sometimes go on patrols but nothing happens. Oh, and he knows all about Cait. He knows she's knocked up. What do you think of that?"

Claire is relieved to the point of wanting to immediately call Mike or Cait and Griff's mom, Shandel.

"Oh, mercy. Thank you, Madie. But please, next time you get an e-mail or letter or whatever, let me know right away." Madie nods and Claire makes her promise.

"I promise. But you know, Mom, all my life I've felt like you loved Mick more and, well...I just wish you'd show some interest in me." Before Claire can respond, Madie removes herself from the chair and walks back over to Claire and says, "I love you, Mom." She kisses her again and asks, "Did you want me to order the pizza yet?"

"No thanks, honey. Wait till six. And I love you very much. The same as Mick." Madie leaves the room, chomping on her apple, her cell phone vibrating.

Claire turns back to her screen and starts surfing. For the past several weeks, she has been on the Internet searching for support to deal with the trauma of having a son in Iraq. She found an organization called Marine Moms that gave her some guidelines on what to expect when your marine is deployed overseas. There were numerous projects that she was either too late or too early for, but she discovered she could create a local chapter and send out shoebox care packages to Mick and Griff as well as other young men and women. For the past couple days, she has been working with Griff's mom and her friend Nancy to raise donations to purchase razors, toothpaste, baby wipes, sun lotion, sunglasses, and socks. Tonight the mothers are meeting at Claire's to begin assembling the shoeboxes.

Relieved by the good news, she stops her search and composes an e-mail to Mick.

My dear, sweet boy,

I must force myself to stop referring to you as a boy. You are a man. A good young man—but you will always be my boy. I know learning about the baby is a shock, but it gives you one more thing to look forward to when you come home. Mike has settled with it, and we have agreed to help you and Cait financially. So please don't worry; all of that will come together as God intended. I talk to Cait almost daily, and she knows she is always welcome to come live with us. You two can stay with us for a while until you decide what to do.

I do worry about you every day, but God is watching over you, and I know you have the strength to make your way through it all. The country is getting more and more discouraged about our involvement in the war, and many of us want everyone home now. Don't get me wrong, sweetheart, we all support you; it's just—oh well, I shouldn't get into it. You are my son, and I just want you home. Is there anything you need? Tonight I have the Marine Moms coming over to pack boxes. If you get right back to me, I'll send you something special.

Little B came by and dropped off a package for you. He wrapped the package in the sports page and even agreed to help on our projects if we need it. He's so sweet. He says he loves the University of Oregon and tried to walk onto the basketball team but was cut the third day. Something about the coach not understanding his game.

So, sweetheart, please set aside any worries about home. We support you and love you and pray for you every day. Last night, when your dad thought I was asleep, I heard him praying for you, Son. He was whispering and thanking God. He's so proud of you, Mick, and misses you terribly.

Kisses,

Mom

Claire pushes send, and in an instant, her message is sent halfway around the world to a server in Kuwait where it is scanned, reviewed, and pushed out to Camp Bravo.

⎯⎯ ∞∞ ⎯⎯

It's just past 7:00 p.m., and the pizza truck arrives. Madie and Cait meet the driver at the door. They pay him and give him a tip and set four hot boxes of pizza on the granite countertops in the kitchen. Bottles of beer and white wine are on ice in a large blue ceramic bowl, and a bottle of wine stands open on the counter.

In the front room, Claire, Nancy, Shandel, and a handful of other moms are busily filling shoeboxes to be shipped to marines in Iraq. In each corner of the room are cardboard boxes full of assorted gift items, while two hundred empty shoeboxes are stacked against a wall in neat rows. There are boxes full of hard candy, toiletries, comics, and paperback books donated by the VFW and Mormon Church. In Mick and Griff's boxes, Claire and Shandel have placed a few clippings of local news and sports articles. Claire sent a new *Sports Illustrated* and a weatherproof Bible she had blessed.

All of the moms wear red marine T-shirts with Marine Mom in gold lettering. Some have worn their shirts at antiwar rallies or to the store in other hometowns. No one in Lake Parrish has the courage to wear them in public, as if somehow they will seem polarizing. They sit on the floor, packing and talking about their boys or what they do to ease the pain. They stop only if someone starts to cry.

"Sometimes I feel like I'm losing my mind," Shandel says. "I go to sleep worrying and wake up every morning thinking about Griff. How is he? Where is he?

What's he doing? Is he hurt? I'm always checking the Third Marines website to see if there are action reports or information about casualties. Throughout the day, I'm hoping for e-mails from Griff. The waiting is so hard. Hard on me and the family. It can be so depressing. I hate the war." Her eyes start to water and then she says, "But I'm thankful to be here."

"We're with you, hon," says a black woman from across town. "Terrance is my second child to go. My first child, Florance, finished her tour as a nurse last Christmas. She was with the marines as well. Now she's working at Providence in urgent care. So you see, things work out for most families. You keep the faith, hon."

There are a few other comments moving around the room when Claire stands and announces to the group, "If everything works perfectly, we can ship the first hundred boxes out by the end of the week, and they should be in our boys' hands before Christmas." The words fill her with a sense of purpose and urgency. She is lifted from the darkness of her thoughts and imagines the look on Mick's face when he opens his box. It will connect him to home.

"I wish we never had to do this," Cait says, slipping some tootsie rolls, baseball cards and a couple of pictures of her into Mick's box. "I think the war is a crime," she adds, which draws a few stares, a frown from Claire, and an eye roll from Madie.

"Remember the rules, Cait, no politics."

Nancy interrupts, "We all want our boys home, but this is good. Claire, you always come up with the best ideas. The last good idea I had was taking a long trip to Mexico without Randy!" There were smiles around the circles and a "Right on, girl!" from Silvia, a heavyset mom who drove in from the coast. She doesn't know her son was wounded by a sniper only hours ago.

As the women work, share, and support one another, Mike is in the bedroom, grinding his teeth, fixated on TV, watching more brutal news about the terror in Iraq.

Mike has barely slept for the last three days, watching hour upon hour of late-breaking news and trying to think what he could do. He paces the room, chewing a nail, thinking: *This war has been going on for two fucking years! Saddam's rotten sons are burning in hell, and these maniacs still want to fight.*

Then there is a news alert. "Sadly, we report eight marines were killed today in a suicide attack outside Fallujah," the newscaster says. The picture flashes to a war correspondent in front of a crumbling wall, wearing a helmet and flak jacket. His hand shakes as he holds a microphone. His eyes sag and dart as he speaks, and he ducks whenever he is startled.

"Moments ago, what appeared to be a mentally retarded boy," the reporter says, "or perhaps a Down syndrome child about twelve, walked up to a coalition troop check point carrying a basket of fruit. Witnesses reported a remote control device blew him up, killing assembled marines and a young mother holding her child. Moments later, a frenzied crowd could be seen dancing in the street chanting, 'Allah Akbar,' as the marines' bodies were set on fire."

Mike looks at the screen, hands still in his pocket, shaking his head. He turns to leave and then explodes and punches a hole in the wall. "Those rotten fuckers," Mike says under his breath. "I'll kill all of you sons of bitches; I swear to God I will!" He is breathing hard, his face is red, and his fists are clenched at his side. But he stays in the moment. He forces himself to calm down. *Keep your head,* he thinks. *Take a breath. Don't panic.* He slows down, and there is a knock at the bedroom door.

"Mike. Mike, what is it?" Claire asks, walking into the room. "What happened?" Mike knows she can see the hole in the wall, and he can see her face fill with shock...and then resolve. "What's happened?"

"Those rotten bastards just killed eight more marines. And they're doing it with kids. Suicide bombers. Putting them in suicide vests and convincing them that if they blow themselves up they will go to paradise. Just blowing them up. Claire, I can't stand it anymore. I've got to go over there, and maybe I can—"

Claire interrupts. "Mike! Stop it! That's crazy talk. Please. We have people here."

"I'm not going to sit at home and watch my son die."

She approaches him and touches his arm gently. "I'm as terrified and angry as you are," Claire says. "We are all terrified, worried, and angry. Maybe you can send Mick something to touch, something from home that is comforting. Find some pictures. Something."

Mike breathes easier. His face relaxes. "I love you, Claire, but this war is far beyond the realm of normal combat. The enemy is evil. These Islamic fundamentalists are inhuman. I used to think God saved me in Vietnam to come home and write about war. You know I've always believed that, but now, I think maybe the reason I'm still alive is for Mick. I'm going to Iraq to somehow save our son." She looks at Mike for a moment, touches his face gently. There is a sad look of disbelief in her eyes. She turns and walks out the door, closing it behind her.

Later that night, before light has lifted, she rolls from a dream and sees Mike in the dark. He is standing at the edge of the bed pulling on his knee brace, dressed in sweat pants and a hooded sweat shirt. Claire glances at the clock; it is five in the morning.

"What are you doing?" Claire asks incredulously.

"I'm going to get in shape. I have to be in shape."

"Mike, get back in bed."

Mike doesn't answer. He ties his tennis shoes and moves quietly through the shadows of the house. His legs feel heavy, and his back is sore. In the kitchen, he opens the refrigerator, and the light makes a wide splash in the dark. He throws some pain pills in his mouth and drinks milk from the carton. Out on the street, there's frost on the grass; its forty-three degrees, and the feel of dew is in the air. The neighborhood is dark except for the long, cold metal light poles shining. Mike walks, stretches, jogs a block, and then stops as puffs of steam roll from his mouth. He bends over and can feel the tightness in his back as he rubs the soreness in his knee. "God help me," he whispers, and then he straightens and slowly jogs down the street.

Chapter 23

A few weeks have passed, and Mike is up at predawn, stretching, working for twenty minutes with his dumbbells on the flat bench in Mick's room. Being in Mick's room inspires him as he goes through his routine and watches the early morning news. When his upper-body work is done, he puts on his knee brace and back brace and walks and jogs around the neighborhood. This happens every morning. He's trying to get in shape, as if he is going to carry a machine gun to Iraq instead of a notepad. He stops drinking and changes his diet, cutting the carbohydrates—no bread or potatoes. After his morning run, he showers, weighs himself, ices his knee, and then makes a fruit-and-protein drink in his blender. He pops an anti-inflammatory, vitamin B, and creatine, to enhance muscle growth. Mike is in his home office early, writing and preparing to leave. At noon, he downs another protein drink and an energy bar, and he's off to the gym. He hires a personal trainer at his club to push him. Over the coming days, his weight drops, and he can feel himself getting stronger. Not like a young man but, as Claire says, like an old war horse, trying to pull one more load. Twice he has his doc drain his knee. The doctor inserts a long needle in the joint and sucks out the fluid with a syringe. Over the years, he's torn his knee up in Vietnam, in college football, and in accidents at home. The last time was three years ago when he stepped awkwardly off a ladder and landed on the kitchen floor.

"Well, Doc, what do you think?" Mike had asked after the fall, sitting on the edge of the table in the exam room. The doctor had looked at the X-rays and newly minted MRI and had explained, "You tore it up good this time, Mike. Complete tear of the ACL, partial tear of the PCL, and the meniscus is pretty much shredded."

"Well, OK, what should I do?" Mike didn't acknowledge bad news from doctors. Problem? OK, fix the problem—like it was nothing. He felt that if you weren't dead, you could overcome anything. Pain was just a reminder that you were still alive.

"You need a new knee. Plain and simple."

"I don't have time for that. What else can I do?"

So the doctor scoped his knee again, cleaned out the floating cartilage, shaved the meniscus, and put him in rehab. He worked hard for a few weeks so he could walk and put the knee replacement on hold until he couldn't stand the pain anymore.

"Wait till the level of pain is a ten for a month," the doctor said back then. "One day you'll beg us for a new knee." What the hell did that mean? That was one thing Mike always had a hard time measuring, the degree of his physical pain. He'd always considered the question in terms of being tortured or enduring gunshot wounds. Ten would be the worst, and that might mean a marine strung upside down in the jungle, being slit open by a Viet Cong, and having his entrails hanging down into his face. His pain was never that bad. Or he'd think of the Bataan Death March or other morbid stories before he could reach a real number. And every time he named a number to identify his pain level, he felt bad about himself because he had not experienced level nine or ten as other marines had. He refused to believe he had survival guilt, even though he often wrote about other soldiers who did. They had lost arms or legs; that was real pain. Not being able to get out of bed or walk without feeling like someone had driven an ice pick in his knee was an inconvenience and nothing in comparison.

His body is feeling good as he pulls into the garage at the *Portland Reporter*. He waves to the new guard on duty and almost has a smile on his face as he steps out of the elevator.

"Morning, Sandy. You look nice today," he says to the startled receptionist. As he moves across the bullpen toward his office, he slaps a couple of high fives, tells the sports columnist he likes his morning story, and nods toward Cody, who is chatting up the new girl in research. By the time he walks into Glen's office unannounced, he is confident and strong.

"Well, damn," Glen says, looking up from his meticulous desk. "You look like the cat that swallowed the canary. Either you got laid last night or you're working out again."

Mike sits down in one of the two black leather chairs in front of Glen's cherry desk. He wishes he had gotten laid. It feels good, though, to have someone notice he is looking better.

"Been hitting the gym, jogging a bit, trying to turn back the clock."

"Well, you look better. It makes me want to get off my fat ass. How's the boy doing? Any word from him?"

"Mick's doing great. He's out of Kuwait, convoyed into Iraq, and is running patrols out of Camp Bravo." As he thinks about Mick, he can feel anxiety building and can't remember if he took his antidepressant this morning.

Glen reaches in his desk drawer and takes out a couple of nicotine-laced pieces of gum. "Well, if your boy's half as tough as you are, he'll be all right. So what brings you in this morning? You want some more time off? 'Cause if you do, we can work on that. No pay, though."

"No. No, not that," Mike says. He pauses to catch his balance. *Maybe my blood sugar's low.* "I've been thinking about going to Iraq. My old unit 3/9 is deployed again, and I'm sure I can get embedded. I've already contacted the battalion, and they would be thrilled. All I need is you to support this. That shouldn't be too difficult."

"You're joking."

"I'm serious as shit. I've been thinking about this since before the invasion, and it's something I want to do. So I made up my mind. I'm going, either with your support or without. I'll freelance if I have to."

Glen looks like he is about to jump out of his chair. "Why don't you stick your goddamn head in a blast furnace? You're too beat-up to be climbing on tanks and getting shot at. What about your boy? What's he going to think?" Glen reaches in his desk drawer, nervously pulls out two more pieces of nicotine gum, and shoves them in his mouth, chewing hard. "Jesus, Mike. You'll have a fucking heart attack, sure as shit. I don't give a damn what kind of shape you're in."

Mike's jaw tightens, his eyes narrow, and his face changes from resolute to fired up and defiant. "I don't much care about arguing the point. I'm going. I just thought I'd get your support and continue my column and use the paper's credentials."

"Fuck that shit! All I need is you going to Iraq and getting yourself waxed and then having everybody in town all over my ass."

"Listen, Glen," Mike says, leaning forward in his chair, "I've got to do this. You're right—I'm old, but I'm in shape."

"And we don't have the money for it anyway," Glen says, starting to calm down.

"I'll pay for it."

Glen rubs his face with one hand, thinking, and then shakes his head slowly. "Well, shit. I don't suppose it will do any goddamn good arguing with you, you hardheaded son of a bitch. OK. OK. I do like the father/son angle, and I know you'll write the hell out of it, but you better think hard about this. Iraq is a hell of a lot more dangerous now than when we first went in."

Mike stands up. "I don't give a damn how dangerous it is," he says and leaves the room.

A couple days later, Mike walks into Glen's office, sits down in front of his desk, and immediately smells a foul and familiar smell, similar to how his feet smelled when he had jungle rot.

"What is that?" Mike asks and looks at Glen and around the room. "The smell? Don't you smell it?"

"Well, of course I do, and you're the third goddamn nose hound that's brought that to my attention. I've got a damn abscessed tooth that's about ready to explode and tear my head off. My mouth smells and tastes like I've got a big turd in it. So let's make this short. I found the money. You're going to Iraq. I cleared all the channels, but it cost me an ass-chewing from the boss. Anyhow, you'll be with your old unit, 3/9."

Mike is pleased, and it shows on his face. "Thanks, Glen. I owe you."

"Life is full of crazy shit, Mike. I'm amazed at what you're doing, but if you keep from getting killed, your work might help make sense out of this god-damned shitty mess."

"I appreciate that, Glen. Your support, I mean."

"Good, but I never told the big shots your son was in 3/9. I didn't want them to throw a shit fit and find something wrong with that. So I don't know, understood?"

"Trust me. Besides, Mick will be glad to see his old man. Between you and me, I'd like to see if I can get him transferred to something a little safer." Mike leans back in his chair and feels his back getting stiff.

"Sure. Who wouldn't? Anyway, you need to do some background on your unit, some up-to-date info, get shots, and figure out your will. Our insurance policy won't cover much if you get wounded or get your ass killed. Shit, Mike, you're too old for this kind of thing." Mike nods and says he's already covered.

"And one more thing, Mike. I'm sending Cody with you."

Mike rises from his chair, not believing what he's heard. His face is stuck between an expression of disbelief and *I'm going to kick your ass.* "What? Cody? You have got to be kidding. We never discussed, never mentioned, anything about me dragging along some kid. I've got a point-and-shoot that will give you all the shots you'll ever need."

Glen isn't listening. He gets on his phone and tells the receptionist, "Find Cody now!" And before Mike can move into another objection, Cody swings open the door, camera around his neck, his hair greased up into a rooster point. He's smiling like he just got laid.

"What's up, boss? I was about to bounce to North P when you rang. Some gangbangers from Brother Speed blew out the front window of a titty bar, thought I'd scope it out, riding with Jolene. Hey, what's that smell?" Mike is pissed and stands up, about to interrupt.

"Forget the damn smell," Glen bellows, and both Mike and Cody catch a hint of what's living in Glen's mouth and grimace. "You and Mike are going to Iraq in about ten days, and I don't have time to listen to either of you piss and moan about it. Someone stuck a shit grenade in my mouth, and I'm about to blow, and if you don't mind, I'm going to the dentist!"

Glen grabs his coat that's lying across the chair next to Mike and flies out of the room, leaving a slight tailwind and taking the odor with him.

Mike stares at Cody, trying to sum him up. He looks like he just stepped out of a teenage reality TV show. *What is he? Twenty-four, twenty-five tops?* He's Vietnamese, and he has a splash of red in his hair.

Cody's arms are at his side, hanging loose, wrists jangling with a gold bracelet on one arm and a gold chain on the other. On the inside of the wrist with the chain is a tattoo of the Chinese symbol for the I Ching. He is still grinning and says with great admiration, "I'm so juiced. I read all your stuff, man. You're money!" Then, raising the camera to his eye, he asks, "Can I get a quick head-shot for the paper?"

"Put that shit away," Mike orders and walks out of the room.

Chapter 24

The sky is blue on an unusually warm day as Mike pulls into his garage in Lake Parrish. He passes through the laundry room, carrying two plastic bags of groceries, a bouquet of white lilies, and a box of dark chocolates, the kind Claire loves so much. He is in a much better mood, glad to be going and resigned that Cody is coming with him. He enters the kitchen and places everything on the kitchen counter next to the sink. He slips off his shoes and stores them in the shoe stand by the kitchen door. From one bag, he takes out a nice bottle of Napa Valley cabernet for him and a French chardonnay for Claire. In the other bag are a thick, well-marbled rib eye for him and a piece of pink Alaskan salmon for her. They will each have fat baked potatoes and fresh asparagus. Everything they both enjoy. He takes off his jacket and folds it over the back of one of the three bar stools, washes his hands in the sink, and tucks a tea towel in the front of his pants, hanging down the way his father once did. He wipes his hands, turns the oven on to four hundred degrees, and is scrubbing the potatoes as Claire walks in. She is wearing her black Marine Mom sweatshirt and tight white jeans. Mike thinks she looks sexy. She is already sipping a glass of white wine.

"Well, partner, what a nice surprise." She smiles. "That's my old Daddy Dog," she says, coming over to place a kiss on his cheek.

He can tell she is feeling no pain, but it is nice to hear her words...to hear her talk gently and kiss him without him asking. He loves to be called Daddy

Dog or Major Bud and even Rebobble Sr. and any of the half-dozen other nick-names she's made up for him over the years. They are terms of endearment that she calls him when she is pleased.

He puts his arm around her and holds her, saying, "I love you, Claire." She plants one on his lips and opens her mouth just enough to slip her tongue in; then she pushes away, moves to the counter, and sits on one of the stools.

Mike forks the potatoes, rubs them with salt and Irish butter, and places them on a cookie sheet in the oven. Claire is sipping wine, content to be watching.

"That looks so good," she says as he unwraps the steak and salmon and uncorks the white wine and asks her how her day went.

"Saw Mom again. She's a little better than last week. Hospice has assigned her a new caregiver named Gina who brings her guitar when she visits and sings to her in Spanish. So, yes, she's doing better. I had the new appliances I ordered installed at the duplex. It's becoming a little money pit over there. How'd your day go, Diego?" Claire asks, tossing her head back and laughing a little at her small joke and making Mike's normally rigid face crack a smile.

He didn't want Claire to ask about his day. He didn't want to ruin the rare moment they were having and avoided the question by pouring a glass of red wine and clicking glasses.

"To your health," he says, tipping his glass toward her.

Claire smiles and nods. Her face is soft, showing Mike the gentle side of her he so loves. "Did you hear from Mick or Madie today?" she inquires.

"No. Not today."

"Well, I just got a nice surprise. Madie sent me an e-mail and said she loved us and thought we were good parents." Claire's eyes go moist. She touches her breastbone like she always does when she is near tears. "That just makes me want to cry. To think our daughter appreciates me. It's been such a struggle." Mike hands her a paper towel, and she dabs her eyes.

"I also heard from Mick," Claire says, finishing her glass.

"What did he say? Where is he?"

"Well, he couldn't really say what base he was on or what they were doing, but he did mention that he and Griff are fine and mostly just bored. Thank God."

Mike sighs a breath of relief and places the steak on the grill on low. He cuts a lemon, squeezes it over the salmon, and spreads on some butter.

"Do you want me to grill some green peppers?" Mike asks, shaking salt over his rib eye.

"No. No thank you. So tell me, what did you do? Did you work on your book at the office or are you writing an essay?"

Mike pours wine in Claire's glass. "Well, I'm putting the book idea on hold, and I have an essay crawling through my mind. I just need to sit down. But I talked to Glen and worked out at the club. Started swimming too."

"That's good. Swimming's good," Claire says, her eyes widening. "So what did Glen have to say?"

Mike drinks some wine, bastes the asparagus, and wants to walk away from her question. He knows the evening will be shot and any chance of romance or good will is about to vanish.

"So what did you guys talk about?" Claire asks again.

He can feel the joy leave the room and sees that Claire already sensed what was about to happen. It's all over but the crying.

"I'm going," he says, bracing himself. He watches her face shift and change and take on the look she might have if Mick or Madie were hurt or someone she cared for suddenly died. She holds her glass with two hands on the granite counter, lowers her eyes, and shakes her head slowly.

"Oh my God."

"In ten days."

The words are crushing. Her chin drops. An instant wave of grief consumes her. Claire feels like the night her father died when she nearly fell. Or the time her childhood friend got hit by a car. It is unbelievable. It's hard to breathe. She feels like collapsing.

"Why are you doing this? Her head is bowed and slowly shaking. "You can barely walk." As she lifts her eyes to Mike, her mouth quivers slightly. "I never really thought you'd go through with this," she says, as her eyes meet his. "I thought you would know better, realize we need you here at home and stable. Madie needs you, and I need you, and Mick needs you most of all."

Mike comes from behind the counter, wipes his hands on the tea towel, and embraces her.

"I can help Mick. I know I can. And I'm a writer. That's what I do."

Claire pushes away and raises her voice in anger. "You could stay home and write all you want to. You don't have to go halfway around the world to write. You can do it here in our house."

She finishes her wine in a long gulp and sets the glass down on the granite so hard the stem breaks.

"You're not going to Iraq to write, and you sure as hell can't save Mick. You're going because you're sick. Because you think, somewhere in that selfish, egocentric mind of yours, that you can control Mick's world. That's why you're going." She stands up and goes to the sink, bends, and then she opens the cupboard where the trash is and drops in the broken glass. She turns around, arms crossed, anger building. "Or maybe you're going because you want to be a hero again. Relive what you failed. God, I don't know." The anger doesn't come. Instead, Claire gives up. "Well, I'm through with it. Do you understand? I'm done! Go get yourself killed." And she walks quietly out of the room.

Mike is staggered by her words. Exhausted. Maybe she's right. He turns off the grill and oven and puts the food in the refrigerator. He pours himself a heavy glass of wine and walks into his office and sits down at his desk. He knew this would happen.

She blames it on me, as if I'm so screwed up. Maybe there is truth to what she says. Maybe I am a self-absorbed asshole. Or maybe it's a death wish. Or maybe…oh, I don't know. He looks at the screen, takes a sip of his wine, buries her words somewhere in his compartmentalized mind, and says, "Screw it. I'm going."

Mike starts his column but gets nowhere. He's thinking he should write about how sorry he is. He finishes his glass and shuts down the computer. She will never, ever understand. He walks into the bedroom, feeling there's no use in trying to reason with her. Instead, he decides to let her cool down. Maybe tomorrow they can discuss it without the drama. He'll try to explain to her again what motivates him to go. This is his gift for compartmentalized thinking, honed on the battlefield.

There is still a hole in the wall from where he punched it, and Claire's half-packed suitcase stands in the corner next to the wall. Claire is reading in bed. He changes into pajamas and rolls two dumbbells out from under the bed. He stands and starts doing curls. Claire puts down her book and looks at Mike standing in front of the mirror.

Mike glances at Claire and then looks back in the mirror. There is a long silence before Claire says, "I hate you."

Chapter 25

Claire sits on the floor in the great room off the kitchen, looking out on the lake. A rough storm is blowing wet and cold on another typical, gray November day. She is surrounded by food and photos. She packs a shoebox full of essentials for her boy: socks and sunglasses, lotion and small plastic containers of jam, hard candy, and snacks. She looks at the storm and then a picture of Mike and Mick flexing their biceps together, and she realizes that, for the first time in his life, Mick won't be home for Thanksgiving or Christmas. For the first holiday season, the family will not gather, Mike won't carve the turkey, and Mick won't make the gravy. There won't be TV and football or a big mess to clean up. She sighs and places their picture in the box as well. She packs a few other photographs of Mick and Cait and a picture of herself holding him as a child. They sit together in a rocking chair reading *Goodnight Moon*. He always loved *Goodnight Moon*. For a moment, she fills with joy, thinking about Mick as a baby. But it has been a terrible, exhausting week in the Kelly home. Claire has been drinking too much and sleeping less. Conversations with Mike are nonexistent. Mike sleeps in the spare bedroom or stays up all night in his office writing and watching news, while she reads in bed or tries to sleep. Sometimes she'll see him leaving for a jog or with his workout bag and laptop, and then she won't see him again until the next day. And she doesn't want to see him, really. What she wants is a partner to consult with and plan with, not someone who has spent most of his life wrestling to be in control—of her and of the monster inside of him. Now all she wants is to move on. To leave before he does—to just get in the car and drive. Screw you, Mike. Go to Iraq not knowing where I am. The childishness of that strikes her; then she's angry again, realizing he's doing something very similar, letting his emotions control him.

She finishes the package as the rain beats on the roof and falls on the lake. Soon the wind picks up, and the window is awash with sheets of rain. She moves to a chair, leaving everything on the floor. What she wants is impossible now. She can't leave. It would upset Mick and make his mind wander. He can't be thinking about anything but staying alert. She knows that; Mike's told her so many times. He needs to look forward to coming home. Then there's Cait with a baby on the way. Oh, what a mess. Her father is so upset, she'll probably need a place to stay after the baby is born. I'll be here to care for her and our grandchild. For now, I'll try to stay clear of Mike's madness and support Mick the best I can.

It's hard not to think about Mike leaving. About being here alone, not having anyone to talk to. *My son and my husband both might be...*Can't worry. Can't worry. He probably won't get hurt. The young marines will watch over him. Maybe he'll stay in the Green Zone, with its movie theater and beautiful buildings. It's like its own city, other moms have told her. Those young officers will see he is old and can't really run or be placed in a position of real danger.

Yet just last night, there was a woman reporter broadcasting from Baghdad; she must have been fifty. And that CBS anchor, who looks older than Mike, is there, the one riding on a tank as convoys roll toward Baghdad. What is his name? He's always broadcasting from bunkers or inside bases with sandbags and blast walls. But Mike isn't careless, she reasons; he knows what can happen. Even though some American journalists get hurt, Mike will be all right. Then she recalls the reporter Daniel Pearl. He was kidnapped and killed in Pakistan a few years ago. February 2002. They cut his head off. The murder was video-taped and shown on the Internet. A wave of darkness assaults her, imagining Mike in a video like that, his exhausted face on the Internet—no. She won't think about it. She can't.

As Claire packs Mick's box in the great room, Mike is in their bedroom, filling an old North Vietnamese Army pack he took off a Viet Cong he killed with the blade of an entrenching tool. He restored and reinforced the pack several years ago. He is used to seeing it and filling it from time to time, but the memories come flooding back. He still has the E-tool; both pieces of equipment were featured in a story he wrote twenty years ago. He flashes to the jungle and the E-tool coming down.

He packs his meds and socks and the outdoor wear that matches the camouflage uniforms of soldiers. There is a first-aid kit and hygiene products; a handheld recorder; a dictionary with Arabic translations; a book called *The Enemy Within* by Michael Savage, which is about protecting America from liberal attacks on its schools, faith, and military; and a copy of War and Peace. There's room for his laptop and a plate-sized satellite dish. He places an empty holster and shoulder harness on top of an envelope with pictures of Claire and his children. This is the holster he carried many years ago. But he always kept it empty. Never once in twenty-five years did he buy guns or rifles or keep them in the house. He was always afraid he'd use them.

He goes to the bathroom and grabs a package of disposable razors, powder for his rash, and a hairbrush. When he walks back into the room, Claire is standing just inside the bedroom doorway. Her arms are crossed, and she looks at him in a way he has never quite seen before. It isn't hate or anger or pity on her face; it's a look of terrible loss.

Claire stands staring at Mike, a sad realization buried in her eyes. Her marriage is over. The father of her children is leaving, and she may never see him again.

"Mike. Please. You don't have to go."

He stands there next to the bed, looking at her with razors in his hands, and feels a deep moan inside. But it is too late now and hopeless.

"I have to go. It's my job."

Her eyes tighten. "It's not your *job*. The paper didn't just decide to send you, their veteran war correspondent." Her tone is harsh, and he closes his eyes. "It's your choice, Mike."

He doesn't answer.

"You'll get hurt. I know it."

Mike crosses the room, places the razors in with his other gear, and then turns to Claire.

"I'm sorry for all the trouble I caused you all these years, and I hope you can forgive me, but this is something I need to do. I can't explain it. This is something I have to do." He walks toward her and puts his hands tenderly on her shoulders.

"I have always loved you, Claire, and wish I had been a better man. But this is so clear to me. I'm happy to go, and I'll see our son. And I'll help him come home to you."

Claire's arms are at her sides, and tentatively, she reaches to hug him. Her anger has turned in an instant to a deep longing, as if she hasn't touched him in years. As if he is already thousands of miles away.

He holds her and holds her face next to his and whispers in her ear, "I love you." He has on a black silk Hawaiian shirt with birds of paradise and a black zip-up sweatshirt as he picks up his bag and walks out the front door to the waiting taxi.

Claire stands on the front porch, watching Mike get in. She watches it pull away. It is a moment of agony. Not the same kind of helpless grief she felt over Mick leaving, but a twisting torment like having the life sucked out of her. She walks inside and collapses on the couch. She stares at the walls and feels as if her body could break into molecules. He's gone, and the house feels empty. She closes her eyes. He's gone, and beneath the sadness, so is the tension.

Chapter 26

Mike and Cody are in their seats in the exit row on the plane. Cody is hooked up to his iPod, head back, eyes closed. The window shade is pulled down, and most of the cabin is sleeping. Mike's overhead light is on; he's wearing earphones, watching Oprah interview the author of the sensational bestseller *How a Woman Thinks*. The author, Kelly Kelly, is an attractive redhead with high cheekbones, big breasts, and a shiny white smile. *Nice name*, Mike thinks, amused at the thought. What intrigues Mike further is that she is in a wheelchair. She's beautiful. *Wonder what happened?* Mike listens as the author explains the top three things a woman wants in a lover.

"First off, a woman wants a man who is confident," Kelly Kelly says. "Not overbearing or narcissistic but sure about where they are and what's about to happen." The audience claps, and Mike says under his breath, "I'm confident."

"Next, a woman wants a man to take his time. Don't check the roast before it's really cooking." The crowd explodes with Oprah, and Mike's not quite following it.

"OK. OK. And this is the third thing, what a woman wants more than anything. More than an orgasm, and believe me, sisters, we all want that," Kelly says, showing all of her teeth in this smile. "So the main thing a woman wants in her lover is for him to be playful."

Mike takes the headset off and chews on that for a moment. Playful? Hmm? By the time Mike puts on his headset, the station is into commercials. He thinks about Claire and when they were young and remembers when he was playful. What happened?

Cody opens his eyes and takes off his headphones. "What's up, boss?"

"Never mind. Go back to sleep." He watches the next guest on the show— who happens to be a chef in a tall, white hat—demonstrate how to make a blackberry pie. Mike thinks about his mother and then turns off the TV screen built into the back of the seat in front of him.

For the next couple hours, Mike's nose is buried in *War and Peace*. It is the second time he's attempted the book, and he thinks now he'll finally finish it. Cody wakes, and Mike puts down the book.

Cody shuts down his player, takes off his earphones, and turns from the shadow of his seat. "So, Captain, how's the book?"

"Complicated. But Russian writers are. I read a biography about Tolstoy, and we have two things in common. We write about war and our wives are unhappy."

A few flat moments later, Cody tries to engage again.

"So, Captain, that backpack of yours—it's from back in the day."

"Vietnam," Mike replies. "It's a gook pack."

"Right. And, of course, we don't worry about being politically correct."

"Not much. That's one of the things wrong with the world; everyone's always on edge about what they say and afraid they might use the wrong word and offend someone's sensibilities. Cody, if I use the word *gook* and you get pissed off, then this is going to be a hell of a long trip for both of us."

"Sure, Captain. But I'd like to know how you got it."

Mike shifts in his seat as a flight attendant comes by, offering breakfast. Cody takes a beer even though it is early in the morning. Mike asks for a Diet Coke.

"You were gonna to tell me about the pack?"

"We made contact with a squad of NVA and killed a few. One dropped his pack and ran."

"Intense. Find anything cool?"

"Typical gook—" Mike catches himself. "Typical stuff. Shorts, shirts, let-ters, a photo, and some pot. About the most unusual thing we found was a red Frisbee."

"A Frisbee!" Cody says, his interest piqued. "Holy shit."

"It blew my mind…thought about it for years."

"And do you still have the photos and the Frisbee?"

Mike tells him to read a magazine; he's going to sleep. Then he turns off the overhead light, pushes his seat back, and closes his eyes.

It is midday. Mike and Jesse are sitting in a heavy jungle off the side of a trail some-where in the mountains of Vietnam. It is quiet. There are no sounds of men moving or birds chirping and no wind under the thick cover of jungle growth. They are alone and have on camouflage paint and utilities and carry M-16s and grenades. Mike is eating peaches with a white spoon from a green can of C rations. The taste of the peaches lingers in his mouth, the best sensation he has ever had. He chews and swallows the heavy sugar and juice and can feel a slice of peach sliding down his throat. He stops eating, looks at Jesse, and hears the sound of sandals padding down the trail. Vietnamese voices. Mike and Jesse push slowly from the trail, back into the jungle. He sees an enemy team of four in brown uniforms with backpacks, walking single file up the trail, carrying weapons casually on their shoulders. They are talking louder than a whisper. A patch of sunlight has pierced the thick canopy of broadleaf, ferns, and trees and warms Mike's face. His heart beats in his neck. His thumb finds the switch that clicks his M-16 to automatic. The lead soldier is wearing a bush cover and a green T-shirt with a black peace sign. How curious, Mike thinks. This boy carries an AK-47 and seems happy. He moves closer to Mike and stops at Mike's feet. He can smell me, Mike thinks, his forefinger riding the trigger. The soldier turns and looks down with great curiosity at the white spoon lying by the side of the trail. A white spoon? He bends over and picks it up, and as he does, he turns his head slightly and gazes into the brush and into Mike's eyes. He smiles for a moment and then must realize he's dead. Mike squeezes the trigger, and three rounds break open the boy's forehead. At once, Mike and Jesse open fire, jump to their feet, and in a moment of violent exchange, the enemy soldiers are shot and shot again. Six or seven seconds, and they're history.

Four dead and rifles scattered along the trail. Mike kneels on one knee, searches a pack, and pulls out clothes and letters, pictures, and a small leather pouch of marijuana. Jesse is standing, eyes searching the jungle. Mike is surprised as he digs further in the pack and discovers a Frisbee. He holds it over his head and whispers, "Jesse." Then he throws the Frisbee. It spins and floats slowly over the trail and the bodies lying flat until it rests at the feet of his son, standing where Jesse used to be. Mick is dressed in his baseball uniform. He looks strong and happy. He's smiling and has black stick under each eye. He's wearing catcher's gear and carrying a machine gun.

"Dad, how'd I do?"

Mike's eyes open as Cody steps carefully over Mike's feet, moving to the aisle.

"Sorry, boss. I gotta pee."

They land in the middle of the night in Kuwait. The flight has taken a toll on Mike's back, and his knee is throbbing. As they deplane and walk through the terminal, Mike is limping hard.

"You know, Captain, all you need is a new knee," Cody says as they head to collect their baggage. "High-tech coil. You'll be gliding."

"I know. I've been putting it off for twenty years. Maybe when I get back," Mike replies. "I've had it scoped three times. I'm due for a new one."

They bus over to the Third Marine Staging Area and are assigned a tent and a rack. The heat is searing, and it takes them both three days to acclimate. During this time, they get shots and desert cammies and are briefed with other reporters on what is acceptable once embedded. As he and Cody enter one briefing being held in a tent with wooden floors, and folding chairs, Mike sees Howard Avery, a Harvard-educated reporter with the *LA Times*. He has met Howard a couple of times at literary conventions. Howard admired Mike's Vietnam writings, partly because he was too young to experience the war himself. Howard's series on international child slavery was something Mike read with great interest.

"Howard," Mike says as he approaches him. Howard wears glasses with thick lenses. He's a dozen years younger than Mike, but when he looks up, he seems a little older and confused. Mike slaps him on the back. "Why, you son of a bitch, you look good. You must be off the sauce and in the gym."

Howard ducks the hard comment, stands, and gives Mike a great smile. He reaches to shake Mike's hand. "Thanks. I lost sixty pounds and only have about twenty to go. You look good for an incorrigible old fart," Howard says, patting

Mike's stomach. "But what the hell are you doing here? I thought you were a novelist now."

"Well, yes, I am," Mike says. "But I still have a local column. And I needed an adventure. Thought I'd check out the war and punish my body one last time. I'm not as young as you are. I can't wait around for another one to happen." Howard nods his head in understanding, and then Mike introduces Cody, whose hair is combed into a point. His bracelets and tattoos are dancing on his bare arms. He has a camera ready in one hand and a maple bar in the other.

"What's shaking?" Cody asks. "When did you set down?"

"Yesterday. Just getting my feet under me."

"Who you assigned to?" Cody asks.

"National Guard unit out of LA County."

"Very cool," says Cody as Mike smiles and winks toward Howard.

They all finally sit down for a cultural briefing, in front of a white screen and a petite female marine, Major Dunnly. She stands next to an American flag on a stand that's placed near a podium.

"Welcome," the major says. "Let's get to it. You men and women are stepping into a very dangerous situation. Much of the Iraqi population wishes you harm. Once you are embedded, we are the only ones you can trust. You will be treated like one of us. And if you are wounded or captured or killed, we will afford you the same standard of care we would our other fallen warriors. But bear in mind, we want you safe, so do what we say. We do not want you to create news by getting blown away. Are we clear?"

The group mutters as Cody shifts in his seat and gives Mike a startled look. Mike thinks about the major's words and how it felt to get shot in the back so many years ago. The lecture ends, and Mike, Cody, and Howard drink a couple beers back at Howard's tent.

———— ❧ ————

Days move quickly. Mike's knee is better, his back feels good, and he works out a couple times in the marine's gym. But he's restless and worrying about Mick. It's been Mike's intention all along to hook up with 3/9 at Camp Chesty and find out where Mick actually is and how he can reach him. He has his papers and clearance; all he needs now is a way to get there.

In a cube in the communications center, Mike is pounding out a column for the *Portland Reporter* on a community desktop. He mentions all the things good reporters do, such as the environment and conditions and the general attitude of the marines. But his writing is flat. He finds it hard to concentrate. He cannot bear the irony that he's so close to his boy, typing on his keyboard, while his son could be shot by a sniper or blown up by an IED.

After a couple more days of waiting and filing updates on his blog, word comes that things have changed.

"Damn," Mike says to Cody, as they walk to the showers in shorts and T-shirts. Towels are tossed over their shoulders. It's a nice night—full moon, hint of a breeze—and they're walking downwind of the shitters. "I forgot that's what I always hated about the green machine."

"What's that, boss?"

"They're always changing things at the last minute. Where you're going, what you're doing, and how long it's going to take."

"That's what Glen's always doing to me."

"Yes, but you can always tell Glen to buzz off and quit. You can't do that in the corps. They'll throw your ass in the brig."

Cody acknowledges with a shrug and keeps walking down the path. "So where are we headed? What base?"

"To Ali Sid Airbase in Iraq. It's massive is what I hear. It's where Saddam and his two asshole sons, Uday and Qusay, used to hang out and rape women and young girls. And if they resisted, their goons would kill the girls' families." Mike bends over and scratches a sore on his shin until a tiny stream of blood drips down his leg.

"I know they were bad dudes," Cody says as they stop at a long line, waiting to get in. The line is twenty deep with guys moaning.

"Shit, Jackson," a brother at the front of the line yells. "Hurry up."

"Quit pounding it in there, dick wad," shouts another marine with big arms and a tattoo of a heart and the word *Mom* on one of them. A bucket flies out the door of the low-rise concrete building. Guys jump.

"Shit ass!," someone shouts.

"What was it you said about Saddam's kids?" Cody inquires.

"One of my best days was in July of '03," Mike says. "That's when those two psychopaths were killed in Mosul."

"Saw it on the tube," Cody says. "And I remember your column. Something about victory."

"I got a lot of heat for that one. Too graphic, people said. Too real. Can you believe that? It was a great day. We killed a couple of rats that relinquished their right to live long ago. But I almost wish we didn't kill the cocksuckers. We could throw the bastards in a cell. Then let families of girls they tortured and killed pay them a visit and beat the shit out of them."

The shower line putts along and is about ten deep; there is a stream of swearing and banging around in the shower room. Marines scramble out, mad as hell, shaking their heads and shouting.

"Damn shower's dry."

"Piss on it. Third time this week."

"Well, goddammit!"

Mike looks at Cody, and they turn around and head back down the path.

The next day, Mike, Cody, Howard, and some other reporters are flown to Ali Sid Airbase on a Black Hawk helicopter. There they will catch a hop to Baghdad International Airport and convoy to Camp Bravo or another remote base. Ali Sid Airbase is a sprawling fortress, once home to Saddam's Red Guard and a number of palaces. It is rumored that Saddam and his sons flew in Russian prostitutes for wild sessions of sadistic sex, cocaine, and the finest Russian caviar and vodka. There were also rumors that some of the women were sold into slavery and were never seen again.

At Ali Sid Airbase, a tangle of razor wire is strung across the top of the cyclone-fenced gate. In front of the gate is a succession of blast walls and concrete barriers vehicles must negotiate before they enter. A green-and-red, six-by-six wooden sign reads Ali Sid Airbase. Inside the gate, on both sides, stand reinforced concrete bunkers, with .50-caliber machine guns manned by marines. The bunkers are lined with sandbags and strands of concertina wire.

The gates swing open to a sandbagged tent city the size of a small university, encircled by bunkers and gun towers with machine guns. There's a landing pad for choppers and heavy artillery emplacements. Row after row of brown military tents sag in the unrelenting sun. Some tents have signs in front of them designating Kilo, Lima, Indian, and Mike Companies. There are two mess tents, a mail call tent, dozens of Porta-Potties, and an AT&T phone tent filled with banks of phones and rows of computers, each one in use.

Each tent is protected by rows of sandbags or freestanding bunkers with corrugated steel, sandbagged roofs. Trucks and Humvees move along the dusty, flat dirt roads. Marines in combat gear carry rifles or shoulder holsters and far outnumber those dressed in shorts and sunglasses. A detail of marines fills sandbags. Another is stirring flaming half barrels full of shit, with long, blackened two-by-fours. The smoke and rotten smell drifts across the camp.

A small group of marines cruises toward the showers in shorts and flip-flops, towels draped over their shaven heads, with M4s or 16s or .45s in holsters slung over their shoulders. A black marine has on headphones and carries an MP3 player as CIA operatives wander through the camp dressed in desert vests, using cell phones, packing M4s with short barrels. There is a three-on-three basketball game on a concrete court with five shirtless marines in shorts and a woman marine dressed in a green T-shirt, desert shorts, and boots. They're running, shooting, and rebounding. Another group of marines wearing bush covers, some of them women, sits in lawn chairs next to the court, rifles at their side. They hoot and catcall as they would at a college game, letting loose, cheering madly.

"Jerk-off!" a guy yells from the chairs at his buddy being guarded by the girl. "It's hard to shoot with a hand in your pants." The girls erupt in laughter, and the girl steals the ball and runs downcourt for an easy basket.

The media tent is huge and crowded with sixty bunks or cots on raised plywood floors. A string of four-foot-long light fixtures with fluorescent tubes runs across the tent's ceiling. A flat-screen TV blares on a table in the corner, with no one watching, while two large fans blow air from each end of the tent. A dozen reporters are lying down, two others talk on satellite phones, and another reads a book. Five guys tap away on laptops on their bunks, and two guys play chess on top of a green footlocker. The tent smells of sweat and farts. Mike has his boots and socks off and is sitting on a lower bunk, rubbing shaving cream on his feet. Cody slides up, wearing shorts, cameras hanging from his neck, hair still spiked, and snaps a couple pictures.

"What's up, boss? What are you doing, shaving your feet?"

Mike looks up, a little annoyed at being interrupted. "If you rub shaving cream on your feet, it keeps them from cracking. You should try it." He tosses the can of shaving cream to Cody, who catches it awkwardly with one hand as his cameras swing.

"Sweet."

"And if your feet start to smell," Mike continues, "piss on 'em. Kills the bacteria."

Cody seems to struggle with that suggestion and sits in a brown metal folding chair. He messes with a lens and then bends and scratches the dozen angry, red flea bites on both his legs. After a few moments of silence and itching, he says, "I fired up the satellite and talked to Glen, told him what's up. I asked him if he wanted to talk to you, but he said no, he was in bed, and it was three o'clock in the morning." Mike smiles and says that's funny as he digs through his pack and pulls out the old shoulder holster, wrapped in a white towel. First he examines it and then starts rubbing it with shaving cream thoughtfully, just like he used to rub Mick's gloves when he was a boy.

"Are you packing?"

Mike shoots Cody a look like he's stupid. "It's for my boy. Used to be mine. Almost forty years old, and it still looks great." Mike's mind drifts for a moment. He sees the chopper going down, looks at his hand, and misses his .45. Then he drifts back to the room and Cody.

"I used to have this need," he says, rubbing the holster while speaking in a voice so low Cody can barely hear. "I used to pull it out of the closet on anniversary dates. Then I'd rub it with shaving cream or mink oil and remember."

"What are you talking about, Captain? What anniversary? You mean like the war? When you got hit? Is that what you mean?" Cody slips a camera strap over his head and places the camera on the floor.

"Cody," Mike says, acting a little bit testy. "I want you to stop calling me Captain. I'm not a captain and I never was. You can call me Mike or anything else, but quit calling me Captain. Come on, let's go eat." Mike wipes the last of the cream from the holster, wraps it in the towel, puts it back in the pack, and stands up to leave. Cody grabs the camera and pops up as Mike turns and half limps through the tent flap.

Chapter 27

A couple days later, at high noon, the sun hangs in an empty, blue sky. Occasionally, choppers buzz through, dropping off troops or supplies. Sometimes an unmanned drone returns from a mission. The ground is so hot that snakes of heat dance in the air. Mike and Cody and two marines walk to the mess hall. Mike is in a yellow Hawaiian shirt with green leaves and red flowers. A large sweat stain clings to his back. Cody has on a Bob Marley T-shirt, shorts, and flip-flops. They're in conversation with Privates Tyler Andre and Billy Bratcher from Drain, Oregon. Drain is about 150 miles southwest of Portland on the way to the Oregon coast, with a population of roughly one thousand. It's an old timber town, with lots of trees, high unemployment, and a median income that falls far below the national average. Cody met the boys in the PX, and Mike is interviewing them.

"So, Billy, were you and Tyler stud athletes at Douglas County High School?"

"No, sir," Billy says. "I just played all the sports."

"Mr. Kelly, don't let him BS you," Tyler says. "He was all-state in everything."

The chow hall is a good two hundred yards ahead, and Mike moves slowly, in no hurry. "How about baseball, Billy?"

Mike guesses Billy is about five foot ten, a buck sixty in his shorts. He has cobalt-blue eyes and a teenager's bad complexion. He never makes eye contact with Mike and speaks softly. "Sir, I love baseball. I pitched and played first."

Mike fires up. "My son caught for Lake Parrish. Graduated in June. You ever hear of Mick Kelly? He was second team all-state."

"No. But he must have been good. Is he playing in college?" Billy asks.

This stops Mike just in front of the mess hall, by an outside table. He thinks through the whole disappointment of Mick. Man, if he had only walked on at Oregon State. But, no, he pulls this crap. He snaps back to Billy's question. "Mick's not in college. He joined the marines just like you. In fact he's in Iraq right now."

"That's awesome," Tyler says. "Maybe you'll run into him." A group of ten black marines walk by. Some carry rifles or iPods, and one has a basketball.

"That would be nice," Mike says, noticing Tyler's chipped front tooth, wondering why the corps hasn't fixed it.

"Cody," Mike says. "I got a story for you."

Cody jumps in front of Mike and the boys and snaps off a few pictures.

"When I was in the head this morning, shaving, I ran into another reporter, back for a second assignment," Mike says. "The guy tells me this mess hall used to be a warehouse piled high with marble toilets. It was crammed with heavy slabs of granite and the kind of marble you'd find in Italy." Billy, Tyler, and Cody are dialed in as they stand around Mike, listening. "Anyway," Mike continues as he sits on the corner of the table, "when the war was first rolled out, US troops were moving through this area with almost no resistance. There were Iraqi soldiers running away, not even firing a shot. But when US troops bore down on this place, they were met by hard-core Iraqis with heavy weapons, shoulder-fired rockets, and Saddam's elite Red Guard soldiers in trenches, willing to die."

They are hanging on each word. Cody looks at the clean white concrete mess hall and the banner on the outside announcing that Pizza Hut and Burger King are coming soon. "I wonder what the hell they were protecting." He bangs out a few shots with his camera, and they keep walking.

"This is way cool," Tyler says. "I haven't heard this story. What happened?"

"So they dropped air strikes, and Black Hawks worked it over, and when they were done, the First Marines busted inside and found granite and marble and thousands of toilets." Mike shakes his head and says, "Can you believe that?"

"Shit," says Tyler. "Toilets?" And they all laugh at his comment.

They move on and stop at the entrance to the mess hall to have their IDs checked by the British trooper on duty. Once inside, Cody scans the place, turns to Mike, and says, "You jerking me, boss? What's the rest of the story? Come on, that makes no frickin' sense."

Billy and Tyler let out a little laugh. Inside they grab Styrofoam serving trays and utensils and stand in line with marines and Iraqi soldiers, news reporters and TV camera crews. All of them are waiting impatiently for the KBR employees, some of whom are Iraqis, Romanians, or Africans, to serve them hot food.

Mike nods at a reporter he saw earlier that day and stands behind the three boys, waiting to be fed.

Lunch is a tray of chicken and gravy or meat loaf, steamed vegetables, baked potatoes, and a salad bar with fresh fruit. They fill their trays and stop at the silver milk machines. Mike draws a glass of cold chocolate milk and at the same time feels a sharp pain in his kneecap. He shifts his leg, and the cartilage floats back into place.

"The best meal I ever had in Vietnam was a cold piece of dry turkey," Mike says as Cody, Billy, and Tyler stand just in front of him. "We were in the middle of a monsoon, dug in on the side of a mountain. We hadn't eaten for about a week. People were pissed and fighting over a can of crackers or telling long stories about fresh strawberries and the dinners their moms used to make. I remembered how good a chocolate milkshake tastes, especially when it's summer and the humidity is almost too much to bear. Then one day, with the monsoon rains still pounding, a CH-46 chopper, with those two massive blades churning, came hovering overhead with cargo nets full and swaying. They were able to drop us green vats of yesterday's turkey. It was so good."

Mike grabs a picnic style table with benches, and he and the boys from Drain sit down. Billy and Tyler bump knuckles with a couple marines in their platoon and plop down opposite Mike and Cody.

"Dude, finish the other story. You got me hangin'."

Mike doesn't like to be called dude, and it shows on his face. "OK, dude. So now this place is full of toilets, hundreds of them. I mean, up to the ceiling. So the marines start hauling the toilets out, and when the warehouse is empty, they start looking for trap doors. They brought in ground sensors, X-ray machines, and smart guys from Washington. Finally, they locate some kind of vault under the floor. They jackhammer it up and find an old bank vault and…" Mike stops in midsentence and stands up.

"Wait, where you going?" Cody asks. "Finish the story."

"Be right back."

Cody and the two marines are quite anxious by the time Mike returns with a diet cola extracted from a tub full of ice and assorted soft drinks. He sits down, and by now, the other guys at the table are also leaning in, wanting to hear.

"Let's see, where was I? Oh, yeah. So engineers carefully blow the vault and…Cody, could you pass me the salt?" Cody hurriedly does. "And the pepper."

"Come on, boss. So what's in the vault?"

"What?" Mike asked.

"I said, what was in the frickin' vault?"

Mike waits for a moment for effect, then deadpans, "It was full of shit just like I'm giving you."

The others at the table laugh out loud, and Cody is as red-faced as an Asian can get. "I can't believe it. Captain…uh, I mean, Mike, actually told a joke."

They eat awhile, and Mike smiles to himself as he scopes out the room, how it's laid out, and where the exits are. He watches the wide screen for a moment, marveling at how the military has changed and thinking what a dinosaur he is. When he was in Nam, back in the rear, they didn't have anything like this. No Cokes or chocolate milk, and they didn't even have a mess hall at LZ Stud. They barbecued steaks, though, on fifty-gallon drums turned on their sides and cut in half. Here, a guy goes out on a mission for a day or a week or so and comes back to soap and hot showers. Back then, Kilo Company might be out for a couple months, with no shower and no change of clothes, slopping in monsoon rains so cold you might piss yourself at night just to stay warm. And when they did come back to LZ Stud, they'd go down to the river, their uniforms smelling like sweat and pus, torn and rancid with jungle rot. They'd strip down and toss the uniforms in a bonfire and step into the muddy water where open, portable showers were set up. Twenty guys standing naked next to each other getting showered off like they were in a two-bit car wash in the heat of summer—but the guys were happy as hell. Best showers he ever had. Dried blood and ground-in dirt and smell would wash off into the moving river. When Mike stepped out of the water, the stench of the clothes burning and the other marines' stink was striking. It made him think: could I really have generated that kind of gagging smell?

Mike pulls a prescription bottle from his pants and takes a couple of pills to slow the pain and swelling in his knee. He chases them with the milk and watches a group of marine brass and an Iraqi businessman file in. The Iraqi has a short-cropped beard and is wearing a black turban and a freshly pressed, pinstriped suit and is carrying a silver briefcase. Interesting, Mike thinks, as he watches them pass through the food line in front of the wide screen, holding their trays of food, and then quickly disappear out the exit.

"Mike. That story you told was so not funny," Cody says, smiling. "You're a player, boss." Mike takes it as a compliment. Then Cody says, "I think I'll skip around the camp and work it out."

On the other side of the room, not far from the wide screen, next to a couple tables full of men and women marines and KBR German contractors, an Iraqi soldier finishes a glass of milk. He stands up and yells "Allah Akbar" at the top of his lungs, and then he reaches inside his jacket and explodes in a fireball of flesh and bone, nails and ball bearings.

The soldiers closest to him are blown into pieces of human flesh, piles of shattered arms, broken femurs, and torn-open torsos, spilling organs. Faces are ripped apart and heads splayed open, separating into sections of skull and brain matter. The explosion destroys a good-sized section of the room, blowing holes in the ceiling and breaking the wall, tearing the screen apart, and killing a cook and four food servers. The marines who did not die immediately lie wounded, nails sunk in their faces, ball bearings tearing at their skin, their limbs at odd angles, broken in unusual places. Chunks and spears of tables and benches are embedded in bloody bodies that lie alone in fetal positions or tossed on top of one another.

Cody is knocked down, and Mike is blown back off his bench while the rest of their table and the other tables are shoved over in different directions. It's as if a bulldozer has cut a swath through the crowded room. The dirt and spray of blood and flesh splash the room and rain down from the ceiling. The room is engulfed in smoke. Coughing and groaning and gurgles of breath lead a cacophony of guttural sounds. A loud siren blares and marines stagger to their feet from under collapsed walls and rubble. Then the shouting and hysteria begins. One marine stands crying, her face a mass of blood and her left arm missing at the shoulder. An eyeless marine keeps standing and falling, screaming, "I can't see! I can't see!" as others flounder with eardrums broken, blood running from their ears.

Mike and Cody are pinned under their table with marines and reporters slammed on top of the table trying to stand up. Mike pushes on the table and struggles to his feet. He's splattered with blood and food and pieces of shredded flesh and other human debris. Billy, who was sitting opposite him at the table before the explosion, has nails driven into the back of his neck and head and is quite dead. Tyler, too, has a mortal head wound. Already, there is the familiar smell of creosote floating in the air, with tiny particles of the bomber and those sitting closest to him. It is common for suicide bombers to have their bodies mutilated while their heads often are popped up and, like this one, left intact, sitting in a pile of wounded soldiers. The dead eyes stare blankly, hatred and faith wiped away.

Mike makes it to his feet, helps Cody, and grabs his camera too. Cody's face is smeared with blood, and Mike tears off the shoulder of Cody's shirt, takes Cody's hand, and forces him to press the gash in his forehead. A fire is raging in the cooking area and a propane tank explodes, sending another fireball full of metal into the room, wounding more in the kitchen. The siren is sounding its call to action, as if the base is under attack by a ground force of insurgents with mortars and rockets. There is shouting and destruction everywhere. Marines with fire extinguishers work on controlling the grease fire. Others help each other as they stagger and limp or are carried from the blast, through the doors, and lain outside.

Iraqi soldiers and workers and other KBR kitchen help are carried out as marines treat them and corpsmen try to save them. Marines run from all directions and trucks and Humvees and Strykers and stretchers appear to pick up the injured.

Mike limps badly as he and Cody make it outside. Mike rubs the blood from Cody's face with his hand and locates the small gashes in his forehead and the top of his head.

"What the hell happened?" Cody asks, hands at his side as Mike works on his wound.

"Asshole blew himself up," Mike replies, tearing off a piece of his Hawaiian shirt sleeve. He wipes Cody's face.

"Where's my camera?"

"Shut up!"

Mike reaches up and pulls a piece of nail and splintered bone from Cody's head.

"Jesus!" Cody cries out. "What was that?"

Mike takes Cody's camera and wraps the strap around his neck and tells him to go sit down until someone can help him. Cody won't listen and grabs his camera and follows Mike back toward the building, holding the bloody shirt to his head with one hand, trying to take pictures with the other.

There is devastation everywhere. The worst of the wounded are being tended to by other marines or are moaning by themselves, trying to tie off their arms or legs with belts or torn shirts. A marine lies on a row of sandbags next to a trench, both legs bleeding profusely. A young medic with bloodstained white gauze wrapped around his head is on one knee by her side, working frantically. He wraps a compress on her left thigh and one on her calf as she rocks side to side, crying "Oh, Lord! Oh, Jesus! Please." Her voice is high-pitched and pleading as the corpsman applies battle dressings to her other wounded leg, his young face flushed with panic and his hands shaking. Mike approaches them, takes off his belt and bends down slowly, his knee catching. "I can help," he says in a voice that is calm and reassuring. Blood from her femoral artery has sprayed the face of the young medic as he works to save her. Mike uses his belt as a tourniquet, wrapping it above her knee, slowing the flow of blood from the artery. Below the knee, her leg is cracked, bone protruding. It looks like a splintered baseball bat. The corpsman and Mike work carefully, applying pressure and more bandages as she rocks and pulls at her hair. "Oh. Jesus. Jesus." The corpsman sticks her with a morphine syrette and pins the tube to her utility shirt. Soon the rocking and the crying slow. Mike takes a pack of cigarettes from her rolled-up shirtsleeve, lights one, and gives her the smoke. Finally, she is quiet.

The siren has silenced as Mike swabs the blood from her legs. Cody is still staggering and trying to shoot pictures of Mike and then of a young navy chaplain blessing a middle-aged contractor from Oklahoma who lies dead, his mouth open, head flopped to the side.

She handles pain better than most marines he's seen, Mike thinks, but now she wants to sit up and see what the damage is. She forces herself up on her elbows, looks down at her broken and shredded legs, and says, "At least I still have my pussy."

Mike and the corpsman glance at each other; their eyes meet for a moment, and then Mike forces himself to his feet.

Inside the mess hall, the smoke clears. The fires are put out by marines from the motor pool. Most of the thirty-five wounded are gone or being rushed away in Humvees and trucks. The twenty-eight dead are already picked up or shoveled gently into black body bags and lifted into the back of a seven-ton truck.

Mike spends another hour tending to the wounded, moving slowly and limping. His body is covered with the thick, sticky, and obscene effluvia of war. He is beyond exhaustion as he and Cody walk back to their tent. He leans on Cody for a moment and says, "You're a good kid." In that moment, he feels more alive than he has in decades.

Chapter 28

Dearest Mick,

My sweet boy. I pray that this reaches you at a time when you are safe and things are less stressful. I worry about you every minute of every day. I am so proud of you, Son, and I know God will protect you. I hope you're happy with Cait staying with me. She is such a dear. She is so beautiful with her mama's belly. She can stay here for as long as she wants. Her being here makes it easier to wait for you to come home. Grandma is holding on, and I took her a picture of you from your boot camp graduation. I hope you're not too upset that your dad is going to be working in Iraq for a few weeks. I didn't want him to go, but he insisted. He's on the edge now, and when he makes up his mind, nothing will change it. I know it's a shock, but Glen called and said he won't be anywhere too dangerous.

I saw Gay McCormick, and she sends her love and is worried about you. The whole Mormon congregation is praying for you, she says. David is on his mission and heard about you joining and told his mom he should have enlisted. He hates knocking on doors every day. Cait and I are actually going on a walk together in a little bit. We walk when her class schedule permits, and it is so good to have her around. She gave up the big car her dad gave her, and so we bought a used Toyota for her at an auction. The first day, we had a chance to preview the cars, and later that night we investigated their history on CarFacts.com. It's sweet looking, and Toyotas have an excellent safety record, and it is a V6, so it should be good on gas. This weekend, I've got rents to collect and bills to pay. Tomorrow night, we're going to a lecture titled "Raising Your Child with Music." So take care, my lovely boy. The Lord blesses you, and we are counting every day until you come home. I pray you're safe and hope you and Cait and the baby will stay here for a while. Cait wants to say hi so I'm turning the computer over to her. I love you so much, Son, and pray for you every night and day.

Blessings,

Mom

Mick

I miss you Babe 2 much and wish you were home. I want to hold you and kiss you and tickle you all over. (And some other things.) Saw Dr. Palmer the other day and he said the baby has a strong heartbeat and the ultrasound was perfect! But I am nervous but I'm going to be positive. I just pretend you are out of town for a while and stay busy. My back hurts a little and I'm fat. I hope you like fatty girls because I am one. I really like staying with your mom. She's so cool and thoughtful and is really like a BF. My parents will come around. Mom already has. My dad took back the big ride, so she gave me $6000 from my trust fund. Then your mom and I went to a car auction and bought a car! It was so fun. Claire chipped in $1200 and said it was a wedding gift. "No pressure." I bought a 2001 Toyota Camry with only 40,000 miles. Little B went with us and pretended to know something. He's nice but so lame. He got three MIP's (drinking) and dropped out of school and got a job selling advertising for a sports radio station. I told you he was a tool. Anyway, he almost wet his pants, you know how excited he gets. Your mom really did the bidding, and it was awesome. I love ya Babe and will email later. Love and singles...Cait.

Mick sits in a crowded phone room full of marines, on a stool in front of a desktop computer screen. He's in his clean uniform and body armor, M4 at his side. He reads the e-mail again and again. He listens for the textures and decibels of their voices that sound so clear in his memory. He imagines Cait's belly and Little B going crazy and his mother on her knees praying for him. He remembers how she used to tuck him in bed at night when he was a boy and read to him. Then they'd say prayers. "Now I lay me down to sleep. I pray the Lord my soul to keep. If I should die before I wake, I pray the Lord my soul to take." And he'd bless all the animals in the world and all the relatives, name by name, and all his friends, and maybe Claire would bless a person for him that she read about in the newspaper that morning over breakfast. And most nights, when prayers were done, Mike would come into the dark bedroom, bend over, and say, "I love you, pal. I love you, big buddy," and kiss his cheek. For a moment, he marvels at the purity and power of those memories and forgets how unbelievably stupid it would be if his dad came over here. Christ! Just like that. Boom. His old man in Iraq. What was the old man thinking? It makes Mick angry; his mind spins like a cyclone, ready to touch down and destroy. "What the hell?" But he catches himself, just like his father could. He's able to slow his mind down and compartmentalize it all. He'll just stash this thought somewhere in the deepest recesses of his mind. Forget it!

He prints a copy of the e-mail and folds it carefully so that the edges are crisp and even, and then he places it in a plastic baggie, tucks it into his breast pocket, and buttons it down safe. That's the way he saves all his important e-mails and letters. He has a stack of them, all wrapped in individual bags he swiped from the mess hall.

"Griff," Mick shouts across the crowded tent, over the shaved heads of marines on the Internet, looking intensely for some sort of connection to home. "Let's roll."

Griff is on the net, searching for girls to chat with and buddies to share some of the drama he's seen. It helps him to let go on his keyboard and gain a little instant sympathy. He's into a styling thing today, as much as you can style wearing cammies. He has a black handkerchief tied like an ascot around his neck. Mick has already ribbed him about it. He spins on his stool toward Mick's voice and says with a dopey grin, loud enough for everyone to hear, "Just check-ing out some skin, Mickster. Found some naked pictures of your squeeze, and she's looking double tight. Right, guys?" Mick knows that's impossible, but the other marines let loose with a big "Hoorah" and burst out laughing.

"Come on, dog," Mick says. "That's so not funny. Let's go to the PX."

Griff shuts his computer down and meets Mick at the exit. They start their hump across the dirt and paved pathways, past the gym and weight room housed in a barn-like two-story building with a roof made of shiny corrugated steel, and on to a huge steel hangar converted into a PX. It's good to be in the rear at Al Asad Airbase, one of the biggest in Iraq, where you can grab KBR hot food, warm showers, and clean sheets.

Al Asad is located in Northern Iraq, about 150 miles west of Baghdad, not far from the Euphrates River. White trailers have been brought in and set along-side the cream-colored tents. The trailers are for NCOs and officers. Some elements of the First and Third Marines and the army and navy also stay there. Coalition forces from Uganda and KBR employees from all over the world are housed in tents or steel huts, called tin cans, each with air conditioning.

There are long runways and chopper pads, a permanent air tower, and a hospital.

Areas are being fortified with dirt and gravel berms by KBR employees, and they build Hesco barriers made of metal-mesh frames, lined with cloth and filled with truckloads of dirt. Al Asad has an eight-mile perimeter and was originally built by Saddam. It was captured early in the war by Australian troops, who found Soviet Migs buried in the sand. It's loaded with comfort and often referred to as Cupcake City.

Mick and Griff playfully push on each other just like they used to in high school and head toward the PX, where they can buy anything from soap to wide screens, Bibles to mail order cars or fast motorcycles, shipped home, with pay-ments taken directly out of their military pay.

Griff is a PFC, and because Mick made Honor Man out of boot, he was a PFC before Griff and now is a lance corporal. They both make about a grand a month, which is ten or twelve times less than Halliburton security guards make for driving trucks or protecting VIPs.

They cruise into the PX, and immediately, Mick slides over to jewelry, which irritates Griff. "Don't tell me you're thinking about getting Cait a ring," Griff says as they bend over a jewelry case. "Why don't you just start planning the wedding, or better yet, see if they have bridal gowns, and you can have the wedding over here. Son, I can see it now. You and Cait married in Iraq and taking off after the wedding, riding on a camel, dragging cans." Griff laughs harder than he should.

"Dude, why don't you go watch TV?"

"Lighten up, bro. I'm gonna to look at DVDs while you drool over the rings. Maybe after chow, we can go swimming or hit the gym." Griff walks away. He gets lost in the cameras, stereos, TVs, and DVD players. There are hundreds of videos to choose from. Mick is helped by a pretty Filipino woman behind the glass case whose KBR nametag reads Mary.

He scans the case looking for something for Cait that won't cost him six months' pay. Something simple, he thinks, as Mary smiles, nodding like the bobblehead doll he got at a Yankees game. He starts thinking about that summer again. He was fourteen when Mike took him to New York. They rode bikes through Central Park, and Mick played pickup hoops while Mike fed pigeons and watched Mick play. The next day, they visited the World Trade Center, waiting in line with other tourist families, riding the elevator up, and having lunch, looking out over the city. Mick peered through the telescope mounted by the railing and walked all the way around, seeing the views from every angle. It was his favorite part of the trip, after the game. Two weeks later, three thousand were dead. The blonde. The waiter. People jumping from the towers. That moment still stuck in his brain.

He leans over the glass and looks at jade rings and silver rings and bands made of twenty-four-karat gold. As he does, he thinks about Cait and her being pregnant and how scared he is. He is too young to be married and a dad. His life changed so fast. He just wants to go home and be safe. Maybe go to school and take Cait camping or to Las Vegas. But now he'll have to get married and be a grown up. Have a child. That seems more frightening than the war. Where will they live, and how can he support them? He searches through the glass some more, feeling inspired, leaving handprints as he goes.

"Mary," Mick says, pointing. "Can I see that silver ring with the blue stone?" Mary stops her bobble but keeps smiling as she reaches in the back of the case and pulls out the ring Mick is pointing to.

"It sapphire. Berry beau-ti-full," Mary beams. "Only twelfth hun-red dol-lar." Mick likes blue, but that's too much, and he shakes his head and says no.

"OK. Special price tomorrow, I give for you today. Nine hun-red dollar."

Mick says that's still too much and starts to walk away. He's sure he can get it for less now.

"OK. OK. What you pay? What you pay?"

Mick's thinking seven hundred and wondering why he even needs to get married, and then he lets the words stumble from his mouth. "Seven hundred and no more."

Mary frowns a frown she must have practiced and applied a thousand times before and says, "OK. For you, very special price, seven hun-red, fifty American," and she starts wrapping it in a little box and placing it in a sack before Mick has time to respond.

Mick reluctantly agrees, hands her a debit card, and exchanges smiles with the happy, nodding Mary. He hopes it will fit as he calls to Griff, and they leave for the mess hall. They show their IDs to the Ugandan soldier in the khaki uniform holding an M-16 and standing guard at the entrance to the PX.

"Why do you think they have all those damn pockets?" Griff snorts, looking at the half-dozen large pockets on the Ugandan's shirt. "It's weird. Looks like a frickin' nerd."

"Maybe he needs all those pockets to keep track of the contraband he's selling," Mick jokes. "You know, pot, roofies, porno from home." Mick laughs. Griff shoulders him and then Mick puts Griff in a headlock and rubs his knuckles on his head. Griff reaches between Mick's legs and tries to lift him, and Mick releases his headlock.

"OK, OK," Mick says, "Let's race to the mess hall." They both take off running and laughing and breathing hard as they pull up.

"Son," Griff gasps, a little out of breath. "You'll never have my wheels."

The mess hall is crammed with over a hundred tables, and once inside, they grab Styrofoam food trays that KBR charges the government twenty-six dollars for, empty or not. The food is good and served by a Filipino crew in matching white uniforms and caps, one hand placed rigidly behind their backs. Griff places three slices of pizza on his tray and Mick chooses a burger and fries and a slice of meat loaf. They search for a table to sit down.

"I think I'll put on weight," Griff says, finishing another glass of chocolate milk. "This is awesome. As good as Pizza Hut."

"It is Pizza Hut, brainiac. See the sign above the servers?" Mick points. Griff reads Proudly Serving Pizza Hut Pizza and shrugs.

Mick is about halfway through his meal, dipping fries into ketchup, when the speaker system blares, "Kilo and Lima, report to your company headquarters immediately."

"Oh, shit," Griff says, working through his last piece, sauce sliding out of his mouth. "I thought we were chilling. I just wanna kick back. Slap the monkey for a while."

Mick picks up his tray. "Come on, beat-off, we're outta here." Then he dumps everything left on his tray into the garbage, and Griff follows, grabbing a wrapped cheeseburger on the way out.

"Fuck this," says Griff as they hurry out the door.

"Just keep your feet moving, Private. You can complain next week."

"That's PFC, dog."

At night, the desert air is cool and clean, and the sky is stashed with stars. The smell of shit-filled cities has disappeared. The sliver of moon hangs sideways, casting a sweep of light across the flat sand. It's three in the morning, and the desert is empty except for the nocturnal crawling creatures, four armed Humvees, an open-bed truck mounted with a .50, and ten more combat-ready marines. The night is quiet; the only sounds are grinding gears and the hum of fat tires rolling.

Mick and Griff are in the first Hummer with Corporal Thomas, a calm and experienced marine from Kentucky. Thomas is riding shotgun with Beans, the wired-tight driver. Thomas is composed; Beans is chewing on his lip. He's survived two IEDs that blew up, just missing his ride. Willy, who is thin and stork-like, with a hook of a nose, is on the .50 caliber and is standing up in the back, his head protruding through the open roof. Corey, from New Orleans, Mick, and Griff are in back. They will be the tip of the spear going in.

Thomas looks at the green GPS screen on the dashboard and studies the shifting images of the landscape before staring out the Humvee's dark front window. With the headlights running, he can clearly see the road off to the left that winds toward the target village.

"Beans," Thomas says, "hang a louie. Kill the lights; we're going black." The other vehicles following do the same.

Mick's platoon has day-patrolled this village before and caught sniper rounds from rooftops. They bounced off the armored Humvee doors and the gunner's steel glacier plates up top. And every time they patrol in this sucking rat hole, they've been cursed by locals shaking their fists and bombarded by rock-throwing kids, screaming, "Screw America!" This is a hostile Sunni town full of former Ba'ath and Saddam loyalists who would rather cut your throat than have you toss candy to their kids.

The area is also crawling with foreign al-Qaeda fighters coming in through Syria, Iran, and all along the sieve-like border. These are the bearded fanatics who drive nails in the heads of disobedient women, skin victims alive, and record decapitations in the name of Allah. These wild-eyed jihadists walk into schools, hospitals, and marketplaces, packed with families, and blow themselves up. They are the targets in tonight's mission.

Last-minute, confirmed intelligence from reliable Iraqi informants say the house they are hitting is filled with a team of al-Qaeda suicide bombers, bomb-makers, and shooters. It will be hell fighting these fanatics, who have no fear and would rather blow themselves up than have life on Earth.

The Humvees and trucks roll into the village. Both sides of the narrow street are lined with beat-up cars and one- or two-story stucco and concrete homes, surrounded by tall concrete walls. The target is easy to spot. It's on the second corner in and has a satellite dish on the roof and a bullet-riddled painting of Saddam on the second-story wall. He's dressed in fatigues, wearing a beret, cradling a child in one arm, and holding a rifle in the other.

For a moment, Mick is touched by the image and symbolism. Then he recalls a column his dad wrote about Saddam killing a village with nerve gas. There was a photo with the essay of dead women and children lying in the dirt. Next to them was a small dead boy, clenching a dog. The dog and the boy were unforgettable, and Mick's mind moves to hate. *I wish I could kill that prick.*

The convoy slows. Thomas tells Beans to stop fifty meters short of the target and shut down. A drone hovers silently, five thousand feet in the air, armed with missiles and cameras that are sending images through space. Back at camp, in a reinforced bunker, officers and technicians gather around a flat-screen and catch the dark-green images and watch the night unfold.

First Mick and Thomas and then Corey, Beans, and Griff dismount. Griff will stay with the vehicle along with Willy, his .50 locked and loaded. This is Willie's last month in his third tour, and he has developed a tic, a quick snort and a shake of his head. Drinking Robo—Robitussin cough syrup—at night calms him, but the tic keeps him stuck on the gun, too corked to carry a rifle and assault.

The second Humvee drops four snipers and then squeezes past Willy and parks up the street to block and support. The third drops off four men and, with the fourth Humvee, turns the corner to block the rear. The truck drops off another four-man team for the assault and then turns around and takes six marines to guard the opposite end of the block.

The Humvees form four corners of a box. Their two-story target is surrounded. Sniper teams set up on the rooftops of adjacent buildings. Thomas, Mick, Beans, and Corey are on one knee beside the Humvee. Eight more marines and a navy corpsman hustle up behind them. Each marine's face is painted with black camouflage. They spread out in line along the shadows of cars and busted-up sidewalks and bullet-pocked walls. From the drone, the target building looks like a small compound, with goats and trees and a courtyard bisected by a line of laundry stretched between two poles. A thick, wide wooden gate, big enough for two cars to pass through, is tightly closed. The walls that surround the target are at least eight feet tall. The only thing visible from the street is the second story, the roof, the dish, Saddam, and the tops of several palm trees. A strong odor of sewage and rot ruins the air.

Each marine wears body armor, night-vision goggles strapped to his helmet, and black kneepads and gloves, and each carries a weapon. There is caution in their movement and tension on their faces as they sweat through their utilities, despite the cool air. The sliver of moonlight rests on the walls and gate and polishes the leaves of the palm trees standing in the courtyard.

Corporal Thomas walks point. Like Willy, he's on his third tour. He carries a Remington sawed-off shotgun and wears a .45 strapped around his waist. Under the stars, his blue eyes are focused. He is ready to move quickly and with purpose.

Thomas crouches in the shadows across the street from the target and runs his hand over the barrel of his shotgun thoughtfully. He turns to check if everyone is on one knee. Beans is next going in, and Mick follows, carrying the squad's automatic weapon, referred to as a SAW, with Corey on his backside. Corey is six months down and carrying an M4 with an attached grenade launcher loaded with a beehive round.

Thomas moves down the line, tapping each shoulder and whispering, "Do you know where to go?" He stops when he reaches Mick, who is sick to his stomach and wants to pee. "This is just like we practiced. You can do this, Mick," Thomas whispers, looking into Mick's eyes. The words are firm and comforting and help diminish the fear that tightens Mick's throat and causes his body to shudder. He can hear his breath and Willy down the street ticking.

"Follow me, Beans," says Thomas. "Watch the left side of the road; I've got the right."

They rise and scramble quickly past cars and darkened buildings, moonlight slapping at their backs. Thomas lifts a fist and drops again to one knee next to the gate, and the men respond one by one. He looks down the deserted street at the other Humvee. He can see the gunner. Thomas is trying to feel what is about to happen. Trying to anticipate and work that sixth sense that good soldiers can tune into. That voice inside that tells them when something doesn't look right or feel right. That internal radar that has developed from twenty-one months of combat, two purples, and countless patrols and ambushes.

Mick, meanwhile, has no history to draw from. He has yet to develop the keen, adrenaline-induced senses that come with hyperalertness. The kind of senses that can see in total darkness, hear drops of sweat fall, and feel enemy movement in the dark.

Thomas is bent over as he steps back toward Mick.

"Open the gate, let the other guys through, and then follow me and Beans," Thomas whispers. "You're the third one inside the building. I need you. Do you know where to go?"

Mick nods, and he can feel his spittle dry as he asks God to please take care of Cait and their child. He wipes sweat from his eyes and tries to imagine what it will be like, breaking into the house and killing someone. He thinks about how his father told him that the first time is hard, that it eats at your soul. He hears those words again, "If you have to kill someone, move quickly and shoot for their torso. Better him than you."

Better him than me, Mick thinks, balanced on one knee, gripping his SAW. The torso.

Corporal Thomas moves quickly down the line to Griff. "Stay outside the wall, and do not move from the corner. When the shit hits, shoot anything you see that's not a marine."

He makes his way back to Mick and taps him. It's time to go.

Mick pukes a little spittle as he slides along the wall, bent over, moving in and out of the moonlight. Every ounce of adrenaline he has collects and then explodes through his body.

He reaches the gate but can't find the handle. He panics and runs his hand over the door until he hits a metal latch that clicks loudly, but the gate won't move. He almost drops his weapon as Thomas runs up and breathes, "What the fuck?"

"It's locked," Mick whispers in desperation.

"Oh shit. Blow the bastard."

Mick backs up from the gate, nearly trips, and squeezes the trigger, but it won't fire. His mind is reeling.

"Chamber a round in the son of a bitch!"

Mick chambers a round, and the sound can be heard up and down the line of young marines. He's hearing Mike's words, "Shoot for the torso. Shoot for the torso." Goats start *baaing* behind the gate as the marines rise from their one-knee stances, tension pounding, hearts racing, and their backs flat against the concrete wall.

Mick squeezes the trigger and blows the gate to pieces. He and Corporal Thomas race through the shattered gate, swim through sheets on a clothesline, kick aside goats, and make it to the front door. Mick's mind is on fire as first one, and then two grenades fly out of the top window and explode away from them, killing goats and wounding two marines coming in. Six more marines fan out around the building and into the palm trees. Thomas shoots the front door, kicks it open, and tosses in a flash grenade, and then rushes inside. Beans and Mick and Corey drop down their night-vision goggles and follow quickly. More rifle fire outside and another grenade is tossed from an upper window and explodes. The window is sprayed with rifle bursts from the marines below and Willy on the .50 from across the street. The heavy thunk of the shells busts up Saddam and the windows as the concussion vibrates down the walls. Then the firing stops. The house is quiet.

Mick's vision through his goggles is green like a reversed negative as he follows Thomas and Beans, his weapon ready. The room is long, with two doorways hung with beaded curtains in front of them. Mick sees a table in the corner and chairs, pillows, rugs, and prayer mats. A glass buffet and a TV are on the other side of the room.

Windows are dressed with flowing curtains, and the long strands of beads covering the doorways are shaking. Mick hears the click of beads touching and the slide of his boots stepping softly over Persian rugs.

"Get me a fucking corpsman!" someone screams from the courtyard. In perfect harmony, an old Iraqi woman runs screaming through the beaded doorway into Mick's green vision, followed by two Iraqis firing wildly. Mick, Beans, and Thomas open up, killing the people, spraying the wall and the floors. Fear races up Mick's arms and blood rushes to his face, jaw muscles clenching and neck bulging till the firing stops. Only twenty rounds are gone, but he drops the magazine and pulls another from his nut sack, snaps the fresh one in place, and loads up. But in this brief period, Corey catches a round in the eye and falls into the buffet, tumbling heavily to the floor. Mick sees him dead on the other side of the room and freezes. Stuck in the moment.

"Light the hallway," Thomas screams, and Mick pulls his trigger, banging away. Whoever fired at Corey is shredded. Thomas fires another shell into the bodies lying on the floor, reloads, and heads for the beads.

"Right," shouts Beans, moving through the beads on the right doorway.

Mick snaps to, swallows, and feels his Adam's apple stick.

"Left," barks Thomas, going left through the other doorway.

"Left," Mick yells, following Thomas.

The torn-apart hallway is narrow, with a staircase in the middle and two more doors, one on each wall.

"Clear," shouts Beans, "All clear." And he raises his goggles and flips on a light from the kitchen.

Thomas turns on the flashlight attached to the gun barrel. He raises his goggles; Mick does the same. Thomas tosses flash grenades into each room, clears them, and finds a light switch on the wall. He exits the room, backs into the hall, flips on a light, and signals for Mick to take the stairs. Mick nods, trying not to shake. He grabs a grenade pulls the pin. It is round and cool, and he thinks it feels good, like a baseball. He flips it underhand far up the stairwell, onto the landing, and backs away fast from the coming explosion. When the boom settles, he moves cautiously back to the stairs, thanking Jesus God.

"Mick! Hit the stairs," Thomas shouts from down the hall. "Go! Go! Go!"

Mick's shoulders touch each side of the narrow staircase, making him feel trapped. One step, two, quickly three, four, five, six, and suddenly a figure appears at the top of the stairs. Mick fires toward the middle as a grenade hits his helmet and bounces down the stairs, blasting a hole in a wall and pushing Mick forward and taking out part of the staircase. He can feel a sting in his ass.

At the top of the stairs, Mick pushes up and gathers his feet under him. The spotlight guides him as he steps over the small, shirtless body of a young girl, her torso torn apart, soaking in a pool of blood.

There isn't time to think, to stand above her staring down, mouth gaping, feeling something. There isn't time to memorize what's left of her face and the color of her pajamas. He has to move and clear and shouts, "Left," as Thomas bounds up the stairs, shouting, "Right. Right."

Thomas stands to the side of the door on the right, tosses a grenade, and blows up the room. When the explosion begins to clear, he dashes inside and kills two bomb-makers by firing through a closed closet door.

Mick can hear crying inside the other room, and before he throws down a grenade, he listens to the whimpers again and imagines children. His jaw tightens, and a tooth cracks as he clears one room with its empty mats, pillows, and a teapot. He's steady. Heart pounding but steady. The cries have stopped. He approaches a closet, and his rifle's spotlight hits movement. His brain sends a flash down his arm to his finger, but his nerves twitch at a half-pulled trigger. A woman, two children. He can see them trembling in the faint light, feet covered by suicide vests and surrounded by weapons and explosives.

The woman starts screaming, "No. No. No. Nooo!" pleading and begging and screaming a sound so shrill and ungodly that he can barely think.

"What the hell is going on?" Thomas yells, stepping inside the doorway, his light finding Mick.

"A woman and some kids," Mick says.

"Let's get 'em the fuck out of here."

Thomas motions them into the center of the room. Two small boys cling to the woman's nightgown. He picks up a blanket from the floor and tosses it to the gagging and sobbing woman. Mick picks up the children's sandals.

"Get out!" Thomas shouts. "Get out of here," as if screaming will make them understand a language they almost never hear.

They head down the staircase as Thomas shouts all clear, and more marines storm inside. There is no more firing.

"All secure!" comes a shout from outside.

Mick steps into the moonlit courtyard, feet tangling in the pulled-down laundry, and sees the bloody corpses of dead goats and chickens. Under a tree, a swing is swaying, and next to it, two wounded marines are on the ground being patched up by the corpsman. The sound of the Hummers as they roll in interrupts the crying of the woman and her two children being led from the house. A woman marine and an interpreter gather the mother and kids as the interpreter speaks. More marines go in and out of the house, bringing out AK-47s, ammunition, rocket-propelled rifles, and grenades, leaving behind nine suicide vests, lined with explosives to be blown in place. Corporal Thomas talks on the radio in the Humvee Griff and Willy brought up. He's telling the Command Post what happened as neighbors peer over walls and through iron gates.

"We got one KIA. Two WIAs," Thomas explains, confidence in his voice. "Nine dead hajis. Six in the basket and three running away. And we got a woman, sir. And it looks like her two kids and a ton o' weapons and explosives. That's it, sir… I'm looking forward to it. Out."

Mick stands in the middle of the courtyard, drinking from a plastic bottle of water, feeling numb and disoriented, and holding the kids' shoes. His body and brain are exhausted, and his feelings have drained away.

Now he can feel his butt and reaches behind. It's wet. He can feel a small cut, a piece of metal. The corpsman notices him and finds the wound and pulls out a warm nail and bandages him. "You're a real hero, dude," the corpsman says, laughing. Mick doesn't react; he feels nothing. Flat like he is void of emotion. He's alive, but fuck it.

Soon, Corey is brought out and laid flat on a patch of grass, away from the goats and chickens. His head lists to one side, and his eye and orbital rim are gone. His legs are limp, and his feet are lying sideways in the dirt. But Mick feels nothing. No anger or regret or thanking God he is alive. Just nothing.

Griff walks into the courtyard and sees Mick.

"You OK, pal?"

The woman has stopped screaming but is still sobbing. The kids are silent, clinging to her gown.

"What?" Mick says, his face ashen in the dim light.

"I said, you OK, Mickr?"

Corporal Thomas walks up to Mick and puts an arm on his shoulder and turns him away from Corey. "Get this marine covered," he shouts toward a corpsman just walking through the gate. He takes a step or two with Mick and stops and faces him and looks him in the eyes. "You'll get used to it. You did good. Made good decisions. And don't sweat the fuck stick that threw the grenade. She's just another haji. I wonder what paradise she's going to?"

"Thanks," Mick replies. But he thinks, *He's so full of shit. I'll never get used to it. She was younger than Cait.* Then he turns away, walks over to the kids, and crouches down and gives them their sandals. The woman screams and spits in his face. He takes it.

Chapter 29

Mike and Cody and twenty marines from the Second Expedition Company sit on webbed seats in the belly of a turboprop C-130, bouncing their way to the Baghdad airport. The plane is the workhorse of the war, just as it was in Vietnam, and is carrying supplies stacked on pallets wrapped in netting and containers filled with weapons, packs, and sea bags. The pallets run down the middle of the plane, separating the rows of passengers, and are secured on a bed of recessed steel rollers. When the plane lands, the supplies will be rolled out the plane's ramp and off-loaded by crews waiting with forklifts.

Mike is wearing a camouflage marines baseball cover he picked up at the PX in Kuwait, camouflage pants, a USMC green military-issue T-shirt and body armor, just as Cody does. The shirt is a little tight, and he notices the roll in his belly as he leans forward, working on his laptop. He thinks, *I've got to get my fat ass moving.* He is writing a letter to Madie while Cody taps away on his laptop, searching through the photos he has taken so far on this journey. The trip is a short hop from Ali Sid to the Baghdad airport, and almost as soon as the laptops open, they are closed as the plane readies for its descent.

Flying at thirty thousand feet to avoid incoming fire, the plane begins a sharp nosedive, corkscrewing its way toward the airport. Mike, who never cared too much for flying after his war, fights the loaded gravity sucking his face and body down, like the drop on an extreme roller coaster.

"Having fun yet, boss?" Cody says, smile washed out by the earth's pull.

Mike isn't enjoying the ride, and it shows in the tension of his sagging face. His neck bulges with veins as he grips both sides of his seat.

The plane makes its final sharp bank, levels off, and slaps the ground in a hurry. It coasts to a stop, and the engine roar subsides as they back the engine off and the props stop turning. A ground crew quickly surrounds the plane, bringing tractor-pulled flatbed trailers to load up the cargo.

Lieutenant Jarvis, a "buzz-cut muscle head," as Cody said when he first saw him, is on his feet, making his way around the pallets of supplies toward Mike. He's twenty-seven, with green eyes, a ton of freckles, and a Texas twang in his voice. His sleeves are rolled up to his biceps, and his forearms are cut and vascular. Mike imagines that he could be on steroids. Either that or he lives in the weight room "back in the world," as marines used to say in Mike's day.

"Sir," Jarvis says as he reaches Mike and Cody and extends his hand. "Captain asked me to make sure y'all are doing OK. Correction. To make sure you're not puking on anybody." He smiles and winks and nods his head to let them know he's just joshin'. Mike shakes his hand and notices the strength and calluses and cracks. This is how a working man's hand feels. For a moment, his hand disappears into Second Lieutenant Jarvis's big paw. Mike is embarrassed that his hands are soft and smooth from typing all these years.

"We're doing good, Lieutenant, although I feel a little naked without a weapon," Mike says, looking at Jarvis's silver lieutenant bar on both shoulders.

"I can understand that, sir. I can't sleep without my babies," Jarvis says, tapping his .44 Magnum in the holster tied to his leg and lifting his short-barrel M4.

Mike likes Jarvis. Cody looks impressed, taking it all in.

"You play football?" Cody asks.

"At navy, for a couple of seasons. I was a skinny linebacker."

"Quick shot?" Cody asks as he stands and raises his camera. Jarvis is straight and erect, white-chalk smile, shoulders back, muscular chest stretching his shirt and lifting his body armor, making him look huge. Mike's thinking that with that all-American grin, he's a poster. What the public wants its heroes to look like. Not wounded in wheelchairs with brain damage and spittle dribbling down their chins.

Cody moves around excitedly. He looks small standing next to Jarvis. "And one more?" he asks. The lieutenant responds to a round of catcalls and clapping from his troops, who are moving to get off the plane.

"You're working it, LT," someone shouts as others laugh. "You're working it, babe." A little embarrassed, Jarvis's face turns the color of the bright red on a marine corps emblem. He orders everyone at ease.

"Uh. By the way, sir, I want to compliment you on your fine bulldog," Lieutenant Jarvis says as the ramp in the back of the plane opens and the men stand. "Oceanside?"

Mike glances at his faded bulldog tattoo and his arm that has atrophied over the years and looks back up at Jarvis. "No. I actually had this done on Okinawa. I was incorrigibly drunk on Singapore slings, getting ready to go to Vietnam. That was 1968."

"Before I was born, sir. I'm a child of the eighties. My mom calls it the disco generation."

"Don't tell me."

"I'm a lifer. Whole family is. My dad did two tours with the Third Marines."

Mike perks up as Jarvis squats down beside him, and the back of the plane begins to unload. "You're not Colonel Jarvis's son?"

Jarvis nods, smiles, and throws another wink to clarify the truth. "He retired major general, but I do believe he was a colonel on his second tour. Did you know him?"

"I remember the colonel back in the day, out in the bush. He was my company commander. He was bald as a boulder and had big forearms, like yours, Lieutenant, big as a bison's front legs. He was shorter though and looked like a bulldog, no offense intended."

"None taken, sir, but we need to deplane."

Mike, Lieutenant Jarvis, and Cody stand by the side of the last container as it rolls down the ramp and is picked up by a yellow forklift.

Lieutenant Jarvis shouts to his men to gather inside the concrete hangar. "The smoking lamp is lit, and you can hit the head." This surprises Mike. He feels at home. The jargon hasn't changed. At least with this young buck.

Cody is open-eyed and intense as the three walk away from the plane, across the asphalt tarmac, and into the shade of the hangar.

"Is it safe here, Lieutenant? I mean, from suicide bombers," Cody says.

"Yes, sir. That was bad trouble back at the mess hall, but we've got fewer shitheads working on base. And I'm sure security will be kicked up now."

Cody's face relaxes a bit, and he steps back to check out the area and take more photos.

"Sir, tell me more," Lieutenant Jarvis asks Mike, as the men in the back of the hangar smoke and bust out of formation for head calls.

"Well, your old man was a tough bastard, but he never cursed or raised his voice. I can remember, one time, he's pushing us through jungle on this steep slope. He'd been wounded, and his arm was broken. A corpsman must have tied some sticks together to hold the bone in place and wrapped it. The jungle was a bitch, slashing and cutting everyone's arms and hands. I was fairly new. That day it was hot, and the jungle was thick, pulling at my legs and boots. A guy would disappear in a tangle if he was more than ten feet in front of you."

Mike spots a Coke machine, a metal table, and a few chairs on one wall, wonders about it for a moment, and then walks toward them. "Got to sit down." Before he drops some money in, Jarvis stops him.

"It's free."

They sit down. Mike drinks a Diet Coke, Cody sucks a 7 Up, and Jarvis just grins, shaking his head like he's amused. "I bet you're addicted to them diets, right, sir?" Jarvis asks.

"I am. It's my caffeine high. But back to the story. We had walking wounded with battle dressings soaked with blood, and we're carrying several dead, looking for a place to blow an LZ. We were carrying them uphill, hands and legs tied together, swinging on poles, like animals. They were so heavy. Colonel Jarvis came up and touched me on the shoulder and said, 'Come on, men, you'd want to go home if this was you.'

"At the time, I thought, screw that. If I was dead, leave me. The climb was only three hundred meters, but the strong were falling and tripping, bent over exhausted from carrying their brethren. We would help each other up, hand by hand, grabbing onto vines and branches and clumps of soil."

Jarvis is transfixed, and Cody is hanging on each word. A couple other marines walk up and listen.

"We used ropes that tore at our hands, and some were dropping from heat exhaustion. Stray mortars were falling, AK-47s snapping, and our forward artillery was hitting the valley and dancing a circle around us for protection. It was a son of a bitch. But the Colonel kept moving up and down that line, blood all over him, directing fire with the radio man, and when it eased, he'd encourage us, shouting, 'We're almost there, troops, we're almost there.'

"Spent three days on the side of that hill," Mike says. "Before we were able to get the dead and wounded out."

Cody is shaking his head in disbelief. Jarvis is listening hard, his back straight and his eyes focused.

Mike's thoughts jumped back from the jungle, carrying a different memory. "Last story. That was in the A Shau Valley, where we were up to our asses in NVA. We'd been humping and fighting for weeks in the thickest jungle and steepest terrain, our uniforms torn and rotten. Morale was low, and there was no scuttlebutt on when we would get out of that mess. We were running patrols off a ragged firebase full of trees blown down with C-4, concertina wire strung out, and holes and sandbags everywhere. It was often too hot with enemy fire for resupply choppers to land, so supplies were brought by choppers on slings and dropped. One time, they dropped some rolls of concertina wire that ripped out of the netting and rolled downhill, killing a guy in Indian Company. So the colonel finally gets us resupplied and has a pallet of beer dropped too. Actually landed on an NVA bunker and killed a couple of those poor bastards. The beer was warm, but it was the best damn two beers I ever had."

Jarvis chuckles along with the other marines who are standing around, hands in their trouser pockets. Cody laughs out loud.

"Sir, you're kidding me," Jarvis says.

"That was no bullshit," Mike replies.

Lieutenant Jarvis stands and says to Mike, "Excellent. Thank you, sir. And if y'all need anything, let me know."

Mike thanks Jarvis and tugs on his Coke as Jarvis moves to the back of the hangar with his men. Off in the distance, Mike can hear and see Black

Hawks working the outside perimeter of the Baghdad Airport, firing rockets and machine guns.

A sharp wind pushes sand through the air-hangar entrance and to the table. The sand is swirling and nips at Mike's eyes as he pulls on his sunglasses and stands up. At the same moment, he feels a bit of cartilage shift in his knee. He bends over and presses his thumb on a soft spot at the front top of his kneecap until the debris floating inside shifts, and he can walk again.

"Is it messed up, boss?" Cody inquires, reaching in his armor-jacket pocket and putting on his shades.

"It's nothing."

"It's karma," Cody says. "Happens to me all the time."

Mike thinks about it for a moment. "Karma? I sure as hell hope not."

As he walks outside the hangar through the swirl of sand, Mike is disturbed by Cody's comment. He wonders if he has bad karma and if it will somehow interfere with his plan to see Mick.

It's a hot one, he thinks, and he notices again the sound of a battle—small arms fire and the distinct snaps of AK-47s. Cody looks worried, and Mike wonders if that disaster at the mess hall will have a long-term, negative impact on him. He's too young to see that shit. It would make anyone crazy. And Mick. God, it makes him sick thinking about it.

A gunship makes a pass over the terminal and unleashes a fury of rockets about five hundred meters outside the perimeter. In moments, another chopper soars by and fires another salvo. It is impossible to see the battle from Mike's position, so it seems like a long way away. *That's what a change in topography does for soldiers,* Mike thinks. *It gives a false sense of security.* On one side of a town, carnage is served, and on the other, Diet Cokes.

"They keep hitting the perimeter with mortars and small arms and a few RPGs," Jarvis says, walking up behind Mike. "Don't know why the brain power don't jus' level the village and let God sort it out." His helmet is on; his shades are in place. "Instead, the bad guys drive up in a pickup they stole, jump out, set up a tube, drop a few rounds on the perimeter, throw the tube in the back, and drive off. If they're shooting RPGs or small arms, they do the same thing...or else they fire from the vehicle. A lotta times those dicks get up on the rooftop of a school or home and fire away. Usually in some residential area that's packed with kids."

"I know. And if you fire back into a neighborhood, you're the assholes, and the media has a field day."

"Yes, sir." Jarvis closes a fist and bumps knuckles with Mike and Cody as a rain of mortars hits about five hundred meters down the runway. The rounds fall harmlessly but get everyone's attention. Mike's worrying about Mick: where he is, if he has seen this kind of shit. Jarvis jogs over to his platoon that is standing in formation, at ease, loaded with gear, ready to move out. The crew moves more quickly around the plane, unloading.

"Hope those morons aren't trying to walk rounds in," Mike says to Cody. "You get used to the sounds of incoming. And four or five football fields away seems like quite a distance. Especially if you've lived with rounds falling on your buddy in the hole next to you."

Mike and Cody walk over to the marines. Lieutenant Jarvis is barking into his headset mouthpiece, the thin, black receiver cord running down his cheek. "We got to get rolling, six! It's raining tailfins," he says. "No, sir. No wheels have shown up, sir. No trucks." Just then a line of trucks, Humvees, a couple of all-terrain Cougars, and an Abrams tank appear on the tarmac.

"First squad, first truck. Second squad, split the Humvees," Jarvis shouts out. "Rest of ya on the big cat. And y'all best hustle ass," he says as the marines load the vehicles with supplies.

"Since we're convoying to Bravo, you guys can hook up with me," Jarvis says to Mike and Cody, who, as always, has a camera stuck in his face. "We got a good crew, but some of these young'uns are new to the blues, if you know what I mean."

Mike listens. *This kid is the corps,* Mike thinks. Like Mick. Was he ever that young or strong? Maybe if he had stayed in the crotch a few years instead of going in at eighteen and being discharged before he was twenty-one. If he'd stayed, he could have been an officer.

Cody bumps Mike from his reverie and asks him if he needs help carrying anything. "I mean, your knee and all."

"I'm good," he says. "The knee's fine."

Jarvis has his pack on, rifle in hand, and tells Mike it's time to go. "The bastards are just agitating, but we need to move out, sir." He turns to two black marines who are about to slide into a more comfortable Humvee and shouts through the whirling wind, "Nunez, Hop. Get out of the taxi and help these guys with their shit. They're riding with you on the truck."

The two marines are wearing shades and reluctantly back away, packs slung over their shoulders, holding their weapons.

"Suck this," Nunez says under his breath. "Got no time for this bullshit. Yes, sir. No, sir. I'll kiss your ass, sir. I'm short as shit. I need me some more back in the rear, taking it easy, checking e-mail, instead of riding in the back of no goddamn truck. If I wanted to be riding in a truck, I'd joined motor pool and sit on my ass all day driving one of these noisy, big ass boats."

"You got that right," Hop replies, his head draped with a towel as he finishes a bottle of water. "I just wanna get my young butt out of the situation. You know what I mean? Like, I'm so short my dicks dragging, bro." They both snort and grin, tap tapping their fists, and acting like that was funny as shit.

As the wind picks up, Nunez and Hop start tossing gear up on the truck to other marines. A couple of choppers are still circling above as another C-130 lands, and two more workhorses take off.

Mike notices that Cody's cameras are put away in his bags for what seems like the first time. He thinks that Cody has turned out to be good company. He's quiet, and that's all right with him. But, damn, the back feels sore. Mike's got a sharp pain that flashes if he turns wrong or steps on uneven ground. The knee, too, is a little sore, and he can feel it expanding with blood, making it feel stiff like a sprain. That means any cartilage floating will shift out of place, and a wrong move feels like an ice pick in the knee. Before he gets on the truck, he'd better take something. He reaches for the bottle of anti-inflammatories he keeps in one of the pouches of his armor and pops a few to calm everything down. "Stay ahead of your pain," is what Claire always said. For a moment, he misses her and wants to go home.

Cody is up on the seven-ton truck with the help of an extended hand, and Mike follows with a push on his butt by Hop. It's hot and nasty with the stinking wind blowing dirt and sand and the smell of shit through the air. But Mike feels pretty good as he sits on the flat wooden bench and leans back against the wood and hard steel. His boots rest on sandbags next to his pack and his bag full of gear. The truck engine is running as he slaps at a sand flea. The wind picks up some more, causing the bed full of young bloods to pull on goggles and wrap their mouths with towels, handkerchiefs, or T-shirts. They grab a little at each other, shouldering for space on the benches, holding their weapons between their knees, by their barrels, butts down, resting on the sandbags. All of them are irritated. Nobody really likes riding convoy, getting shot at and knocked around.

"All I needs is another ball slapping, bouncin' round in this piece o' shit," says Quiz, a private from Mississippi. This gets the troops stirring, and a round of bitching begins.

"Them kiss-ass, douchebag lifers always got the Humbags," Rossi from Florida says, blowing snot out one nostril. "Why don't we ride in style? Whose dick you gotta suck?"

"Hell if I know," Quiz replies. "But I heard you already sucked everybody off in battalion and what that get ya?" That gets a howl or two and a quick reply.

"Your mother. That's who. Fool," snorts Rossi and his buds hee-haw and bump fists.

"Y'all can stop the bullshit," Jarvis demands, raising his voice. Then he turns to address the whole of the truck. "We need to be tight, shit together. Your mind right. We'll be catching AKs, RPGs, and IEDs. You can count on it. So you better not be thinking of far-off bullshit. I want you focused. Locked and loaded. Check your frags again; make sure the pins are bent and taped, and be careful with your water. We got a hard day in the sun coming, so don't waste it." The boys settle down, on benches and sandbags, waiting to roll.

Mike's attention is back in the truck, dumping daydreams of Claire. He's watching the way the lieutenant tilts his head, the way he speaks, and the inflection in his voice. He hears Jarvis's every word and watches his jaw muscles work. Mike can see that he's got command of his troops and respect from them. A good leader, Mike assures himself, pulls his men back to focus. At the same time, Mike feels a rattle inside. A kind of shaking from something buried so deep not even a mess hall full of dead could retrieve it. A feeling that shreds the numbness he lives and never acknowledges. And that is fear. Not for Mick or his girls back home but for himself. He shifts on the bench and thinks that Cody is onto him or that Jarvis can sense it. Out of nowhere, he's struck with the kind of fear that rushes through your body when your chopper's shot down, spinning in the night. Or when you're lying in a hole with a wounded buddy on top of you as he gets shot again and again. A fear so powerful that it takes away control and leaves you trembling, pissing yourself at the bottom of your hole. He feels exposed and ancient as he looks at the strong, youthful soldiers. And for the first time, he is afraid for himself. He feels like a young blood and doesn't want to die. And he feels guilty. Like the time they were all shot to hell, lying in a rice paddy, and he was on the radio, so confused he couldn't talk coherently to the chopper flying above them. He couldn't tell them the coordinates or where they were lying, and he screamed in the handset, "We're below you, in this fucking field, getting shot to shit!"

Thirty-five years later, he feels that pang of helplessness again. Jarvis said they'd get hit. If they do, what will he do? He has no weapon. If they are ambushed, how can he defend? How can he provide any kind of help if it's needed? He has spent so much time worrying about his son, fearing for his son's life and well-being, that fearing for himself was never there. Now, in this most mundane of moments, where no real threats are visible, he's scared hopeless. He looks at Cody, who is swatting at fleas and flies and picking mites off his neck, and at the boys sharing the back of the truck. He wonders if they can see that this old man is afraid. How pathetic. Broken-down old man. That's what he is. A joke. He wants to smash himself in the face as he used to do when he made a mistake or felt he was wrong. And now he realizes that he's feeling sorry for himself. That's great. His brain is being critical again, telling him a plethora of negative things. Old. Scared. Damaged. Useless. Things he can't reveal to anyone. Nothing new. He once told his shrink that he had this fear that if he told someone how his mind worked, how crazy he is, that person wouldn't be able to stand it. Wife, friend, shrink, whomever. None of them would be able to comprehend how sick his thoughts could be. They were a kind of wrongness that has no name.

"Nunez. Hop. Get your asses up here," Jarvis shouts above the sandstorm, which is picking up more speed.

Nunez, shades on, is oblivious to the whirlwinds and clearly still on a run of *woe is me*. He turns to Hop as they stand by the back of the truck, sharing a cigarette, spitting sand.

"Don't know why I signed up for this bullshit," Nunez says, taking the smoke from Hop and drawing deep.

"You wanted to be a hero, asswipe." Hop pulls himself up onto the truck and reaches back to give Nunez a hand. Nunez exhales with a loud *phew*, tossing the butt, watching it blow away toward the empty plane. He reaches up and grabs Hop's hand.

"Hero?" Nunez says. "You lost your mind, nigger?"

The convoy of four troop trucks, four Humvees, a tank, and two Cougars powers up and stutters, gears growling as it shakes like a big snake, turns, and moves out. Another C-130 passes over the convoy as the convoy leaves the front gates and turns onto a flat, smooth road with concrete dividers. They move out, away from the Baghdad Airport, heading to Camp Bravo.

Mike's truck is in the middle of the convoy, with two armed Humvees in front and the Cougars and two more Humvees in back. The truck is reinforced with sheets of steel plates welded on the side and moves slower than the rest of the vehicles.

Once they start moving, Mike's mind has turned the corner and built its own barrier to what he feels. He has kicked fear in the ass again, forcing it to release its grip on him. He used to tell Mick, "Son, you have to just kick fear in the ass. You have to compartmentalize. Stash that sense of fear or failure in some box, and leave it there. Think only about what you need to do and what the best outcome will be." He didn't say that his own fear didn't feel like what he thought manly fear must be, that his own fear always seemed more low-down, more toxic. He gave his son smart advice and felt stronger for it.

The wind is blowing sand up Mike's nose as he leans across the hard bags and gear and shouts to Jarvis, "We get hit, I can still fire a weapon."

Jarvis gives Mike a thumbs-up and grins under his goggles, nodding his approval. Mike takes that as, "Don't be a fool, old man," and shifts his attention to the mounted .50 caliber with a gunner standing up, holding both handles. The thought *forgot how to fire that son of a bitch* races down his brain stem. There is a stack of AT4 antitank weapons resting at the gunner's feet. They remind Mike of the piece of crap marines used to carry, called Laws. They, too, fired a single shot that could blow up bunkers or thatch-roofed huts with one round. Problem was, half the time they didn't work and were tossed out on battlefields and blown up later by the good guys' own men. "Hope these work," he whispers in the wind.

Mike pulls on clear goggles issued by the marines and stretches a small, white shred of bed sheet that he ripped off back in the rear. He runs it across his mouth and nose and ties it behind his neck. He feels a bit like the Lone Ranger or Superman, fighting for truth, justice, and the American way. He should have brought some of the masks he sent Mick.

Cody has on a blue doctor's mask and the same kind of goggles and military-issue gloves that Mike and everyone else wears for protection. Even so, the wind and sand bite at uncovered skin, leaving tiny welts on their faces and neck that will be scratched into open sores.

Mike looks up through his goggles as the sky turns a mustard color, filled with strong winds and grains of sand the size of tiny pebbles. The smell of diesel, shit, and garbage from the passing villages still lingers, but at least the sandstorm washes the taste. Soon the storm slows, and the sun brings patches of gold as a backdrop, and the convoy moves on. They roar past scores of low-slung, flat-roofed buildings, some shut down, some boarded or blown up, and quickly the road runs rough as they leave the neighborhoods.

The convoy drives around standstill traffic, honking horns, drivers shouting out their windows in English to "get the fuck out of the way," and when the truck bounces, Mike rubs his back and grimaces. The storm ends as suddenly as it began. The air is clear, and Mike can see the unending broken-down huts and houses that line each side of the road. They are heading east; on one side of the road are fields, and on the other side are flat desert and occasionally rocky hillsides. Everything is brown, dried up, and useless. The only things moving are the convoy and the traffic running toward them.

Mike closes his eyes and imagines the convoy getting hit. He's younger, bolting up, firing the .50, cutting down waves of black masks standing up in the back of their beat-up pickups, firing wildly. He swings the .50, and rounds punch through their windshields, fenders, panels, and engine blocks, ripping them with the same kind of brutal impact the suicide bomber had in his mess hall explosion. Assholes. They're all assholes. And when he thinks of the explosion and the wounded and the piles of dimorphic arms and legs and flesh torn away, he remembers the black marine and the critical injuries she suffered. Would she ever be the same? Could anyone, after experiencing so much horror and pain?

He feels guilty again, as he has for all these years. Guilty for surviving. Guilty for just being knocked off the mess hall bench and not being wounded. When he was a kid, just back from the war, he'd walk through the ghetto part of town, the dangerous part. Where the Black Panthers blew up the McDonald's because they didn't cop enough free food for the Panther school's breakfast program. Down on Knott Street, there was a boxing club where Mike used to train and where he won a Golden Glove trophy when he was seventeen. Back then, he was the only boxer who wasn't black or Mexican. That was the part of town where being white was a liability during the day and a death wish at night. Where cheap hookers with their tight, short skirts; big hairdos; and high heels walked the streets looking for tricks, while their black pimps sat in shiny cars, keeping guard from the corner. One day, two pimps were arguing in front of the boxing club. The fat one called Jelly was going off on Sugarman, a skinny freak, coke dealer, and rip-off artist. Sugar, who'd been down for a dime and had just been released a couple months before, was hoping to bullshit his way out of the predicament. He'd been trying to sleep with one of Jelly's girls on a pro bono basis, which didn't sit with Jelly at all. Jelly was up in Sugarman's face, half drunk, sweating like a fat man. His white shirt and turquoise pants had traces of various foods he ate, and his garlic breath was backing Sugarman away.

"You 'bout a sorry nigger motherfucker, tryin' to steal my bitches. You cocksucker. You be stealing my money now," Jelly snorted. Sugarman kept backing up but trying to save face.

"Gimme a break, you fat ass. I just tryin' to sweet talk me some pussy. You can't blame a nigger for—"

"Fuck I can't," Jelly said, his belly quivering. He pulled out a .38 snub nose from the back of his waistband and started waving it at Sugarman. "OK, cock bite. How 'bout I shoot you in your boney, black ass?"

Manny, an ex-pug who ran the center, came running out in his sweaty sweatshirt wearing a thick pair of leather mitts, used to catch boxers' jabs and hooks. He yelled, "Knock this shit off! Jelly, I told you not to bring no trouble down here. Now get the hell outta here before you in some real trouble." Jelly was suddenly amused and swung his .38 toward Manny.

"Screw you and yer sister. Turn around, you beat-off dumb ass, and get out' my face."

Manny put his big mitts up in the air, saying, "Be cool, be cool," and he turned around, walking slowly toward the building. Mike saw it all going down from the glass doors at the front of the boxing center. He thought about sneaking out around a car or two and jumping the scumbag and beating the hell out of him, but just as that thought entered his brain, two pops rang out and two slugs hit Manny in the back of the head. Manny stopped, grabbed the back of his neck like he was stung by a bee, turned around, and started falling down slowly, in sections, onto the broken sidewalk.

"Get that fuck," someone said, looking out the same windows Mike was. Both pimps split, and when the ambulance came, Manny was dead, face down in a puddle of red, a plum-colored bubble of spittle on his lips. Just as the ambulance men loaded Manny, a bus pulled up and dropped off two more young black boxers carrying white shoes and sack lunches. When the police arrived, no one had seen anything, except Mike. He carefully reconstructed what he observed, which was a righteous deed, he thought, but maybe unhealthy. Soon after, he stopped boxing and joined the marine corps.

For a number of years after the war, he'd go back and walk through the same streets and hope he'd run into the dude that shot Manny. He'd beat Jelly's ass down and stick a .38 in his mouth and show him face-to-face how it's really done, marine style. That was one reason he'd wandered the streets, mixed up in his mind, feeling angry. Another reason was that he felt bad he had survived Vietnam, so he hoped a car would drive by and shoot him. Maybe if he was shot again or lost a leg, maybe then he would be worthy of the emotional pain he felt.

The wind rushes through the back of the truck, bringing a fine powder of red dirt and clay. The marines' white masks are dark and their faces caked. Their goggles need constant wiping. A series of potholes jolts Mike awake. He stretches his sore back and straightens out his swelling knee. The extension of his leg jars the back of Hop's head. Hop is lying back, listening to some scat on his headphones. This catches Cody's attention.

"Enjoy your siesta, boss?"

"I'm not your boss."

"You keep telling me that, but Glen said you were. He said, and I quote, 'Cody, you better look after that snarly old son of a bitch. He's got worse knees than a ten-dollar whore dropping for blowjobs.'"

"Amazing. That's the most you've said since back in the world."

"Well, he did instruct me to do what you ask and help you carry the gear."

"OK. All right. I'm going to rest my eyes for a minute or two. Dream up a way out of the back of this truck."

"Yo, boss. I'm working on it too."

Mike shakes his head and closes his eyes, listening to the seven-ton truck run through its gears when it comes to a curve in the road, stalled traffic, or a herd of goats crossing the road. After a while, the terrain is a wash of flat desert as far as the eye can see on both sides of the road.

"Gentlemen," Lieutenant Jarvis shouts, jerking Mike back into the truck. "We're coming up on Ambush Alley."

Mike is alert, adrenaline kicking in as he sees the desert changing into berms of sand and rock on either side of the road. On the right side of the road, as they head north, there is a narrow ditch, an offshoot of an irrigation system that runs through the fields on the opposite side of the road. Just ahead is the beginning of another desperate town, ground down from centuries past and air strikes and ongoing poverty.

Mike analyzes both sides of the road and the hillside, and he notices the way the road dips toward what looks like a shallow canyon dotted with battered tin and cardboard huts and a few peasants walking around. Cody stands briefly and rips off a couple of shots before Jarvis's stare drives him back down to the sandbags. Up ahead on the left, a burned and bombed Iraqi tank is buried on its side, followed by a pile of destroyed jeeps and small pickups. The vehicles have been picked clean from years of desert winds and destitute villagers. On the right side of the road, the town climbs into the hills on switchbacks of rugged dirt and rocky road. It looks something like the red hills of Sonora, California, Mike thinks, only scattered with mud huts and falling buildings. On the flat rooftop of one of the sturdier buildings sits an old satellite dish the size of a hot tub, catching CNN from outer space.

"Sir, you might stay down lower now," Jarvis tells Mike. "We always get a round or two from this Sunni village. Rumor is some of Saddam's relatives still live here."

Mike obeys and backs down below the steel plates welded to each side of the guardrails. Cody lies almost prone, clicking off shots of Jarvis and the gunner. The lieutenant and the other marines seem almost bored, as though this is hardly anything to get juiced up for.

"Fuck this shit," Nunez says, lighting a cigarette. He passes it to Hop, who's sprawled on the sandbags, scratching his nuts and taking off his headphones.

A couple of barely audible cracks from AKs snap through the air, rounds bouncing off the convoy, like peas from a peashooter. One of the few armored Humvees breezes through the light fire into the beginning of an ambush.

Half of the convoy has passed the berms and the huts staggered on the hill when a Cougar at the center of the convoy hits an IED made of five buried artillery shells wired together. The sonic-sounding explosion lifts the vehicle and flips it over. It comes down wrong, like a bucking bull with its back broken, and flops on its side. The column grinds to a halt. A heavy machine gun, firing from the village, punches the Cougar and marches down the convoy, blowing holes in more vehicles or swooshing overhead and impacting with a thud on the other side of the road. A daisy chain of explosions starts down the line in two-three-four earth-rending explosions, blowing huge holes in the road, damaging vehicles, and spraying sand, rock, and discus-sized pieces of asphalt.

The front of the convoy turns in place and barrels back toward the ambush to where the convoy has been severed. Already, help is in the air. With vehicles smashed, overturned, and blocking the road, marines are unable to push through the killing zone and are forced to fire madly toward the village and berms. Marines are diving from the trucks, some of which are on fire or catching round after round from enemy hiding in rat holes or firing from the sides of buildings.

Mike jumps awkwardly from the truck, hits the ground, and rolls slowly, like an old man falling. He grabs his knee and crawls to safety behind the big truck. Cody leaps from the truck, rounds zinging overhead, and lands gracefully, like a cat, his camera strap tangled and clinging. The trucks are empty, and marines scatter on the road to seek cover in the culvert or alongside the trucks and Humvees. They pound out rounds toward the hills and huts in a disciplined manner now. Four small pickups full of insurgents roll over the berm at the front of the village, The men are wearing black masks or red-and-white-checkered headdresses. They're firing RPGs and rifles at the wounded convoy. Hop and Nunez and Jarvis are on the ground with the rest of the marines, firing. Quiz takes a round through his hand, and Rossi is shot through the neck, dead instantly. Behind the big truck, Mike pushes on his knee, forcing the cartilage to shift, and Cody snaps away from behind the front tire.

The gunners in the backs of the convoy trucks and Humvees pour .50-caliber rounds in sheets of thumping steel, blowing off the shoulders and heads of the black-masked enemy and spinning their pickups with their withering fire. An enemy pickup passes the berm and heads straight for the Abrams, its wild-eyed driver looking through the shattered windshield. A moment later, a round from the tank tears through the front windshield and driver. Truck and insurgents disappear in a booming explosion, raining chunks of metal, flesh, and broken bones.

The Abrams tank cranks on, fire burning on its turret. The hatch opens, and a marine douses the fire with an extinguisher as more enemy shots crack at the tank and kick up dirt, missing the marine, who lowers the hatch.

Mike watches another kid, face down in the road, lying between the back of the truck and the Humvee that was following. The kid looks like Mick. Oh, crap. The marine is shaking with fright. The kid's rifle is lying a few feet away. The firing has slowed. That can't be Mick. Then Mike hears what he thinks is a mortar tube popping and the sound of several rounds impacting close to the convoy. Suddenly the kid jumps up and starts tearing off his body armor and screaming, "Fuck you. Fuck this. Fuck you!" His face is distorted, like a madman's, as AK rounds dance toward him.

Mike is closest to the marine and gets to his feet. He crouches behind the seven-ton truck and takes one step with his good leg and tackles the kid, driving the still-screaming marine to the ground. One mortar and then another explode, along with a spray of small arms fire coming from two directions.

It's not my boy!

A drone and two gunships circle overhead. One gunship dives toward the village, unleashing rockets, followed by the other gunship with miniguns, sweeping the area.

A corpsman runs up to Mike, who's dazed and exhausted from holding this kid down. The corpsman drives a syringe into the thigh of the howling boy, and in a minute, the howling and fighting turn into sobbing. This time Cody misses it all, caught up staring at the remains of an enemy soldier lying by the side of the road, his corpse dissected by a .50 caliber.

The choppers make another pass, sweeping the village with miniguns and rockets, turning the earth, destroying buildings, and finding the backs and necks of young zealots in Nike shoes, fleeing.

Suddenly, the firing stops, and the frenzy is over. The firefight has boiled down. What's left now for the marines is to tend to their dead and wounded, call in medevacs, and sweep the village. Four marines from the Cougar are dead, and four are pulled out, severely wounded. Six other marines are walking wounded, who will also be choppered out, along with a dead kid from Kentucky, who ran hard, face first, into the sharp edge of a truck's steel plating.

The convoy is left staggered and smoldering as marines regroup and the medevac chopper sets down. The casualties are bagged up, and the wounded stagger aboard, including the freaked-out marine who is still sobbing. Jarvis calls to his trucks of men, now gathered along the side of their trucks.

"Spread out. First and second squads, watch the road. The others come with me. We're going to do a quick recon. Then git outta here. A company from battalion headquarters will follow up most shortly." Jarvis puts a grumbling Nunez on point, and the group of twenty or so moves out on foot along the road, over the culverts, past the berms, and into the village.

Mike limps along toward the tail end of the patrol and swallows a couple of pain pills. He opens a water bottle, wets his cracked lips, and feels the water run over his tongue and slip down his throat in a rush of satisfaction. Cody follows him, snapping.

It is not easy for Mike to climb or keep his balance. The training he did back home on flat surfaces or in the park where the terrain was gentle and giving was no preparation for walking over hard rock and slogging through sand. He's doubting himself. He's thinking about Mick and what he could ever do to help him. Every step seems like a challenge, and his knee is bad. But he stumbles along, blocking the pain, watching the terrain and Iraqi's as they emerge cautiously from bunkers or come flooding back into the village.

Mike turns to Cody. His mind is clear. "I'd guess it's mostly al-Qaeda, shot up and on their way to paradise. Probably some Sunni and Syrian fighters. I'll bet there's a fist full of papers on one of those dead fucks. Or ID. That will let us figure out who the hell they were." Cody is in shock as he follows Mike and methodically snaps pictures of dead attackers. Marines in back of the patrol tell him to hurry up.

Some of the insurgents are with Allah, and others are on their way. Two insurgents were shot in the head by marines before they could trigger their suicide vests, while several more are taken away on stretchers as compliant prisoners. Four village women were killed by choppers, and two are left groveling in the dirt next to dead children the insurgents used to hide behind.

The patrol searches a few huts and gathers weapons and explosives into a pile off to the side of the road. Marines drench the weapons with gasoline and set them on fire. The pile is still exploding and burning as Mike looks over his shoulder from the back of the truck. And the convoy moves on.

"You're the man." Hop leans forward across the width of the truck full of sandbags and tired marines and bumps knuckles with Mike.

"Yeah, well, I'm too old for this shit."

Nunez leans in too. "Nice work, Grandpa. You're bad for damn sure!"

"Grandpa Rambo." Hop chuckles. "Knocked that shit head down. Beat 'em down." But not all is well as Jarvis scoots his way across the bags and looks Mike in the face.

"Sir. Mike. You guys all right? I noticed you limping there."

"Just the same thing I contend with every day in this old body. Happens all the time. No problem."

Lieutenant Jarvis tells everyone to clear their weapons and checks in with his boys again; everyone says they're fine. Then he is back to tracking Mike and Cody.

"Sir. I don't know what the hell y'all were considering back there," Jarvis says. "You put yourself in jeopardy and my men in jeopardy. You could have made the situation worse. And how is this going to look on tape, back in the rear, you grappling with one of my men? Shit. Damn, sir. If you're ever in that kind of situation where you think you can do something to improve what we're doing, forget about it!" Jarvis's face is red, and his eyes are fired up as he hammers Mike. "Are we on the same page?" he growls. Mike nods, but his rage factor flips on, and he wants to show the lieutenant what he could fucking do, but just as quickly, the flash runs through his body. He breathes deep and stays calm.

Jarvis shifts his attention away and tells his guys how good they did and what they could do better.

"Now, don't be thinkin' the rest of this trip is gravy. We still could hit some shit."

Cody is freaked out. His eyes are wide open, and he's drinking water furiously. "Those pricks back there are so fucking crazy. What motivates them to just blow themselves up? They're young men! What's up with that?"

Mike drinks from his water bottle and listens to the question but is too tired to think about it. Too tired to really answer more than, "I wish I knew." He looks out the truck's side rails and sees nothing.

After a few minutes, Mike's brain shifts back to Cody's question. "All their lives, they have been studying the Koran, being told that paradise is just a battle away. Most of these suicide fighters are uneducated and force-fed extreme views. They have been taught that we're devils. They have been indoctrinated that their belief is the supreme belief, and if anyone disagrees, they should be killed. We are offensive to Allah, to the word of Mohammed. In our culture, we live to live, and they live to die. The families of martyrs get big bucks when their sons and daughters die. They're like rock stars. Blowing themselves up just starts the party."

Jarvis has been half listening and has lost his intensity. He thinks he should have waited and told Mike off at the next stop, away from his boys. He moves over by Mike again. Tries out Cody first.

"So, y'all good? I think we'll be fine now. They shot their wad, least for now I do believe."

"They're nuts," Cody says. "Crazy as bat shit. Blowing themselves up. How do you fight that way of thinking?"

"Well, we don't. We let God judge the terrorists. We just try to set up the meeting." Cody laughs out loud, and Mike is smiling. Nunez and Hop and half of the rest of the crew are rolling.

"That's for damn sure, LT. We gonna set up a lot of meetings for those motherfuckers," says Hop.

"Seriously," Jarvis says. "We lost some good marines today, and most of them ragheads back there can't shoot for shit. Now we're headed for some hard-core Islamic terrorists. They're cutting off heads in Fallujah, and they sure as hell can shoot straight."

Chapter 30

Claire sits in the waiting room at the hospital not far from home, waiting for Cait to finish her prenatal appointment. She wonders, not for the first time, how the heck Cait and Mick could have been so stupid. Cait could have been at Brown University by now, on her way to a great education, instead of pregnant and attending Portland State, for Christ's sake. Then she recalls that this is the same hospital she came to that night Mike broke the glass. She touches the place below her eye and is shaken with sadness, remembering his volcanic anger and the blood on her face. She picks up a magazine, thumbs through the pages randomly, and falls on an article about the failure in Iraq. Going it alone, the Bush administration is in a quagmire. There are no weapons of mass destruction. It's hard to read. She tries not to think about Mick risking his life in a failed war, built on lies.

Everything feels like a failure: her marriage, her family, and the war. The only thing that keeps her steady is caring for her mother and the coming of her grandchild. If something happens to Mick—oh God, please. She folds the magazine closed and sets it down neatly on the table. She glances around the room at the pregnant women, some with small children, and notices that there are no men present. Maybe they are at work or in the war; or else why wouldn't they be here? When she was carrying Madie and Mick, Mike was always there. Always. And then she thought about how he used to rub cream on her swollen belly and work a breast pump on her engorged breasts. Even though she felt fat, clumsy, and unattractive, he always complimented her, and at night, he would read to her from whatever she chose, she remembers, softly smiling. And then she thought of her labor. Mick was easy. He came out with a grin. All his life, he was a happy child. Oh, but the labor with Madie was so long and so difficult. Waking up in the middle of the night, so sure the baby was coming, and grabbing the packed bag. And Mike was so excited as he drove her to the hospital. Then the news that it was false labor, and she was only—what was it—two centimeters dilated and would have to go home. Twice that happened, and each time she was sure her baby was coming because it hurt so much.

She stares at a little boy crawling onto his mother's full lap. He must be around two, she thinks. He looks a little like Mick did at that age. Climbing on things and jumping off. Mick was a breeze compared to Madie. She watches the little boy sit on his mother's lap as they turn pages in a magazine. Maybe it was because Mike thought Mick could be a better person than he was. A better athlete and human being. He felt more in charge of Mick's upbringing. He loved them both so much, but differently. What did Mike write one time? That Mick was the innocence he left in Vietnam.

Her stomach growls, and she checks her watch. It is after one. *When Cait is finished, we'll catch a bite to eat somewhere and talk about this antiwar thing Cait is still insisting on doing.* This was a worry that wouldn't go away. What would Mick think? How would he feel if he knew Cait was helping organize the event and his mother was supporting it? Mercy. It's too much to contemplate, so Claire picks up another magazine with front-page photos of Hollywood stars and who they're sleeping with.

Soon the door from the exam room opens, and Cait steps out, smiling like she belongs on the cover of a parenting magazine. *She looks so fresh and pretty,* Claire thinks. But much too young to be pregnant. *She kind of looks like I used to look—rounded belly, a blush on my face. Perhaps less terrified about being a mother.*

"How did it go?" Claire asks, looking at Cait's big blue eyes.

"It was so awesome. I saw his tiny feet and watched his heartbeat. I got so excited that I forgot to ask you in. Next time. I promise."

"You said 'his.' You said 'his feet'!" Claire says excitedly. "Did you?" She smiles.

Cait's shoulders rise and fall, and she sighs with a cute grin curling up her lips. "Yep. It's a boy." They do a little hop, like teenage girls do, and hug each other and walk out of the office so pleased. They zip down the elevator, chattering and giggling all the way to the car, and still the look of joy is on their faces.

"Let's go to downtown Portland, to the top of the Hilton for lunch," Claire says. "I'm starved, and we need to celebrate. It's my treat."

"Claire. You've done so much. Thank you. I'm so excited. I'm going to love this baby so much. Maybe we can call him Mick. I don't know. I'm going to e-mail Mick right now." She pulls out her Blackberry and starts typing away. Her fingers are tapping more quickly than Claire can imagine, her face radiant and filled with the knowledge that soon she'll have a son.

The hotel is bold and austere, and they pull up to uniformed valets who open their doors as college boys run to park their car. The lobby has ornate glass chandeliers, marble floors, and cherrywood-lined walls with big, stuffed leather couches. Suits and ties and elegant ladies walk through the lobby looking important, carrying leather briefcases or folders as they hurry through.

The restaurant is packed with the late-lunch crowd, having chardonnay and salmon or plates of tiny, odd-looking food, admired more for its presentation than its taste. Executives and their secretaries talk quietly, and the newly rich clink wine glasses.

Their table is at a window that looks out across the city and over the bridges and the Willamette River that connects the east and west sides of Portland. It's still cold and cruel in February, but there is a split in the gray cover that lets a sliver of winter sun dance across their table.

"So how are things going?" Claire asks as they sit at their table.

Cait has a frown on her face. "Well, I'm excited, of course. Going to Dr. Palmer and all. But when I woke up this morning, I felt fat and ugly and didn't want to go to class."

"I'm sorry to hear that."

"I've got this English lit class, and it's being taught by a grad student from Pakistan. The guy barely speaks English," Cait says, shaking her head in frustration.

"How alarming. Does he know the material?"

"I don't think so. And he's always commenting on the war and how our soldiers are killing innocent women and children."

"That's got to be hard."

"It is. But I spoke out in class. I told him I'm against the war, but my boyfriend's in Iraq, and he should stop talking about our boys that way. Then this black guy stands up and says 'Yo. Get 'em, girl.' Then he tells the professor he's a vet and calls him an 'F-ing moron' and says something like, 'Don't be talking no BS about my brothers.' Some of the class applauded. That felt good."

"Good for you," Claire says, unwrapping a cracker from the basket in front of them. "I'm proud of you, Cait."

Cait blushes a bit. "How have you been?"

"Well, the truth is, things could be easier. I haven't been sleeping too well. I woke up with a terrible headache, and then I had to get some garbage bags from the garage, and I looked down, and the water heater was leaking."

"What a pain."

"Yes. I called the plumber and then got a couple of tenant calls, and all the time I'm thinking about Mick and Mike and my mom," Claire says. "Then I remembered today was your appointment with Dr. Palmer. And I got excited. I just love him."

"Dr. P.'s the best," Cait says, reaching across the table, touching Claire's hands. "I just am so lucky to have your son and your support. And I am so excited about our little boy."

"He'll be a sweet one, and you'll be a great mother."

The waiter arrives and stands with one arm behind his back and a clean white napkin on his forearm. He pours water from a glass pitcher filled with slices of lemons.

"Do you need a minute?" he asks.

"Yes, please," Claire says, scanning the menu and then looking toward Cait. "I am so hungry." Both of them pick up their menus and banter back and forth. The waiter comes back, and they order turkey sandwiches with cranberries.

"I'll have a chardonnay. Cait?"

"Can you make a chocolate shake? I'm eating for two."

They smile and laugh and talk about a baby shower, and they write notes on a pad from Claire's purse. They discuss dates and funny gifts to give to the women who will attend. Finally, they brush up against a couple of topics neither wants to address.

"You know how much I love you, Cait, but I feel like its time for your mother to step in now. She and I have always liked each other, and she's your mom. You need to talk more with her."

Cait's smile drops like a plate on the floor, and Claire can see her body tense up.

"I know. I know, but it's hard dealing with my parents. If I let her get involved, she'll want to take over everything."

"That's something you have to deal with. You're an adult, and you have made a decision with Mick to have this baby, and you're going to need all the help and support you can get."

The food comes. Their plates are garnished with parsley and a shaved, curled red radish that perturbs Claire. "I don't know why anyone would want a radish with a turkey sandwich," she says, her face twisted in a look of bewilderment. "But let's see." She takes her first bite and then nods her head, pleased. "This is good. Now, where were we? Yes. Well, whatever you decide...but your mother loves you and will love this baby, and maybe you should let her hold the shower. That's best, and tell her I'll help her if she wants."

As Claire takes another bite she can see Cait run this idea through her mind. *She's just headstrong. All this girl needs is a push in the right direction.*

She drinks from her wine glass and touches her napkin to her mouth. "Besides, Mick needs to know everything is good on the home front. OK, honey?"

Cait has a bite of turkey in her mouth that she chews methodically, and then she takes a long sip of her shake before responding. "I'll try. And if I can get Dad turned around, that would sure help. He's just pissed about everything." She sucks on her straw and then stops to catch her breath. "I'll really try."

They talk about the baby—how big he'll be and the color of his eyes—and Claire tells some mildly funny stories about being pregnant, and then they talk about Mick and e-mails. Neither mentions their fear. With the last bites, Claire turns to a topic that they have both avoided for weeks—the mid-March antiwar demonstration Cait has been so much a part of.

Claire is nervous, and there is a hesitation in her voice, but she feels she must broach the subject. "Are you sure this is what you want to do? Don't you think this could make Mick unhappy—having you protest the war in such a vocal way?"

Cait touches her napkin to her mouth and then drinks some water. "I don't know. I'm not against Mick or the soldiers. I'm just against war. I feel it's so wrong, and it seems like our government is always fighting. And does it ever do anything good? Does it ever solve anything?"

Claire doesn't want to offend Cait, especially on this special day. It is all so complicated, she thinks. She believes the major reason Mick joined was to defy his father and prove he could do anything Mike could. As she speaks, she chooses her words carefully.

"Sweetheart, I really don't think you should participate in this protest. It's just the antithesis of what Mick feels. He's hardheaded. He believes in this war and doesn't want anyone saying anything different."

"I know that, but I made a commitment, and maybe this is my way of helping. If we can just put enough pressure on Bush and the right wingers, maybe we can get them to start bringing our marines home."

"Well, it worked in Vietnam. We were in the streets by the millions. But I wouldn't mention it to Mick. He doesn't need to think about anything but taking care of himself."

Cait nods her head and tells Claire she's right again. "But I'm still going through with it. And I want you to come. I want you to say something. Please. Promise me you will."

Claire shifts in her seat. Of course, she won't speak. But she is resigned that there is nothing she can do to stop Cait.

Chapter 31

A crowd of about two hundred is gathering at Millennium Park, on the lake in Lake Parrish. The rain comes down, mixed with gusts of wind that grab at hair and coats and catch umbrellas. A big white tent erected on the reddish-colored paver bricks billows in the wind, as does the American flag atop a fifty-foot pole. The statues of soldiers that Mike and Mick helped build stand unfazed by the weather. People park their cars on the street or arrive in buses, carrying signs, not pleased to have to fight the elements.

"I told you this should have been scheduled in June," grumbles Ralph Bunch, a retired professor from Portland State University. "I told Cait that," he says to his wife from underneath a big umbrella.

"Hush, Ralph," his wife intones. "Cait and all the rest of the students have been working on this night and day. This is the only time they could get the park. And tell me, how many more have to die before you consider it convenient to protest?"

"Yeah, well, I—"

"Come on. Pretend it's the sixties all over again. Let's go inside. They've saved us seats."

"Easy for you to talk about the sixties, but I'm in my seventies, freezing my butt off!" The professor carries a placard that reads No More Blood for Oil.

"Come on, you old fart," she says, leading him toward the tent.

Separate little booths back up to the lake with signs that say Veterans for Peace, Gays for Peace, and The Peace Coalition. Opposite them are food booths with fruits and vegetables and hand-ground multigrain breads. Next door to the fruit are corn dogs, burgers, and snow-cones.

Despite the weather, there is a sense of gaiety as several young men play hacky sack in a light drizzle and kids and dogs run by. But it's cold and gray, and the sky looks like it's ready to burst open with buckets of rain. As if the weather is on a timer, the clouds crack a bit. The gusts of wind fade, and the rain stops. There is a slice of sun and blue sky. A man on stilts, dressed in a red, white, and blue Uncle Sam outfit, carrying a Stop the War sign, walks through the crowd. Soon more people collect around the tent as a guitarist inside stands on the stage playing. Next to him at the microphone, a pregnant woman with her belly exposed and a peace sign drawn on it sings "Blowin' in the Wind." The smell of pot lingers in the air.

The sides of the tent are rolled up as steam rises from the ground and dissipates into a growing crowd. Claire and Nancy walk through the park past folks they don't recognize. Claire's wondering if this is where she should be. They are both bundled in rain gear and ball caps, hands stuffed in their pockets.

"I smell pot," Nancy remarks, a pleased look on her face.

"I know. I kind of assumed it would be here."

"Well, if someone offers me some, I'm going to take it," Nancy insists.

"Believe me, Nance, no one offers pot to sixty-year-old grandmas."

They walk along, and Claire notices several police standing in corners of the park with their white helmets, dark sunglasses, black leathers, and black nightsticks. It seems like most of Lake Parrish's rich have left the protesting to people from out of town. Maybe they're students from PSU or high school. The kids are about the same age as Mick, some with beards and long hair, but none of them look familiar. Hmm. Maybe that's a checker from Palisades Market sitting on one of the concrete benches. But she's smoking. How odd it seems. It all feels a little overwhelming as Claire winds her way to the Peace Coalition booth. Inside the booth, Cait stands next to an overweight woman a little younger than Claire. Both the woman and Cait are wearing white T-shirts with the words Peace Now in blue letters. The T-shirts cover long-sleeved blue turtlenecks, and they are handing out information on "How to Adopt a Platoon." They are also asking for signatures on a petition calling for the immediate withdrawal of all troops from Iraq and Afghanistan.

Out of the corner of her eye, Claire catches a group pushing through the throng of protesters, holding signs that read Support Our Troops and Marines Don't Run.

Claire watches the prowar advocates, and it feels like 1968 all over again. She remembers Mike talking about how hurt he was by the antiwar movement. Maybe she is wrong to be here. But there was a lot more ferocity directed at soldiers in those days—"baby killers"—she remembers, wincing. She glances at Cait and sees herself, when she was young, working as a candy striper at the Veterans Hospital. The war was raging, and soldiers were being killed by the thousands each month. More than twenty-eight thousand died in 1968 and '69. She remembers Mike telling her that more marines died in Vietnam than in Korea. The streets held tens of thousands of sign-carrying protesters, not just a few hundred. There were battles with police, and she watched from the windows of the hospital as the ambulances brought in more wounded. It was her first day volunteering. She was only seventeen and scared when the orderlies brought that first boy in from the military hospital in Japan. Like all of the worst-wounded soldiers, this kid had been on a naval ship after he was first hit and then was transferred to Japan and finally sent to her hospital. He had a sucking chest wound that had nipped his aorta, and he almost died on the medevac chopper on the way out to the ship. His transfer to Japan was a disaster as well, with no one quite sure about his internal bleeding. They gave him six units of blood on the plane. All they had. In Japan, they found the problem and grafted an artery from his ankle to repair the damage. When he could be moved, he ended up in Bremerton, Washington, to recover.

They brought him in on a gurney with IVs stuck in both arms and a tube up his nose running to his stomach. In Japan, he had been on a ventilator and, though he had a strong heart and a strong will to live, he had lost a lot of blood and was near death. Now he was fighting an infection as well. When she saw him, he looked so vulnerable. His eyes were closed and his lips were cracked as she helped lift him onto the bed. The window was up, it was summer, and she could hear the sounds of protesters gathered at the gates. *That seems so long ago,* Claire thinks. As she looks at Cait, she remembers how gentle the boy was and how he thanked her whenever she came to his bedside for the first couple days. He was from Missouri, she remembers. He pronounced it *Missoura.*

He was still nineteen when he died suddenly in the middle of the night. The next day, when she went up to see him, his bed was empty, and he was gone. *Ben,* she thinks. *Ben was his name.*

"Claire," Cait shouts from the booth across the paving stones, above the noise of children yelling and running through groups of people. Claire's daydream fades, and she smiles, and soon Cait grabs her in a big hug.

"Claire, I'm so psyched you came. Both of you. Isn't this amazing? And we got so many people out in the rain. You're the best."

"Well, Claire told me we could score some dope, so I'm here," Nancy jokes, and Claire shakes her head.

"You're too funny," Claire says to Nancy and then turns to Cait. "You've got a good crowd, and the weather is finally cooperating for you, and the girl singing in the tent has a wonderful voice."

"She's the bomb. So nice. I met her at school, and she told me about a Lamaze class and everything. You'll go with me, won't you, Claire? Please."

"Yes. Of course." But for a moment, she can't believe that this young, beautiful girl is carrying her son's child. That she and Cait will be connected for the rest of their lives.

"Griff's mom is here and Marilyn Devault and Mrs. Davis and some of the kids Mick went to school with."

"What about Little B?" Claire asks.

"I shouldn't tell you, but he got a DUI and has to spend the weekend in jail. His folks could have paid his fine, but his dad says he's got to grow up. Anyway, we've got more speakers and some TV coverage, so this is totally cool."

"You've done a good job, Cait."

"Oh thanks! But now listen, Claire. Could you speak to the crowd? Just for a minute or two, and tell them you're against the war, and tell them about Mick. Could you?"

This is what Claire was afraid of. She doesn't want to risk betraying Mick in some way. "I don't think so. I'm not a good speaker anyway."

"Oh, come on. I know you want this war to end, and I know you love Mick, and maybe this can help," Cait pleads. "If every little town like ours held protests, maybe Bush would wake up and see that we don't want this war, and we shouldn't be over there."

Claire feels queasiness in the pit of her stomach. It feels wrong to speak out when your son is in harm's way.

"I just can't, Cait. What would Mick think?"

"Oh, hush," Nancy slips in. "No one's going to advertise this or tell Mick. Besides, you heard Cait. Even Griff's mom is here. You know that sometimes moms know better."

Claire considers it again and thinks maybe it will do some good. "OK. I'll do it. But just a few words. That's all."

"Thanks so much," Cait says and grabs Claire's hand. "Come on. It'll be fun."

Cait leads Claire from in front of the booth, passing a juggler who keeps dropping his hacky sacks.

To Claire, nothing about speaking out reminds her of fun. She flashes on the boy in the hospital and the first time he opened his eyes to her and how he smiled when she wet his lips with the tiny blue sponge. And she thinks of Mick somewhere in that desolate country. He, too, could someday be in a hospital with tubes in his arms and legs.

They walk under the white flaps and into the packed tent. On stage, a young woman in her thirties is announcing a countrywide planned demonstration, scheduled in Washington, DC, to mark the two-year occupation of Iraq. They want a million people there. "And we've got MoveOn.org giving big money and most of our Democratic senators and representatives are behind this, and *we want you there!*" she shouts to applause and shouts of "Peace now! Peace now!"

Claire takes it all in and sees the stage and the lake outside the tent and the statue of the Vietnam soldiers in the park.

"I can't do this," Claire says to Nancy.

"Oh, don't be such a wuss. Get up there, girl." Nancy gives Claire a little elbow. "You'll tear 'em up."

Cait squeezes Claire's hand and says, "You're a mom. Just say that, and tell them you want the war to end. That's all."

Claire listens to Nancy and Cait's words and feels hypnotized by the energy and grief she's feeling. She can hear her stomach growl and feels faint and reluctant as Cait leads her by the hand through the mass of people, some joyful and others looking stunned. Some are her age, and maybe they, too, are reflecting on what they experienced forty years ago.

At the stairs leading to the stage, a young man has painted himself black and written *OIL* in big red letters across his chest, while another stoned-looking kid stands holding a pole from which a string of plastic naked baby dolls is suspended, splashed with blood paint. The crowd is chanting, "No more war! No more war!" as Cait and Claire ascend to the stage. Cait pulls Claire along and takes the microphone, trying to quiet the crowd that has reached a frenzy.

"All right. All right," she says into the microphone. She raises her hands and drops Claire's. "Quiet. Please. Please. Thank you all for coming and a special shout-out to Professor Ralph Bunch from Portland State University and his wife Cilia for their time and money to help this happen. And to Mayor Nancy Clark, who wouldn't back down even when most of the other city council members were ripping on her, trying to stop our protest." The crowd cheers and claps. As the applause wanes, the gathering quiets to a murmur.

Claire is fascinated by the confidence Cait displays and is so pleased that she is Mick's girl.

Cait speaks into the microphone again. "I need quiet now. Please. All right. I'm so excited. Some of you know me," which draws a screech from two of her girlfriends drinking Diet Pepsis and rum from paper cups. "But for those that don't, my name is Megan Chambers, and I am a freshman at PSU. I also want you to know that my boyfriend, Mick Kelly, is a marine, and he's in Iraq right now, with his best friend Griff Goings." A few boos emanate from the crowd, and the prowar group starts shouting, "Support our troops. Support our troops." Cait raises her hands again and the grumbling and shouting ebbs. Then she pats her swollen belly and says, "And this is my son." The crowd cheers wildly for a moment. "And this is Mick's mom, Claire Kelly," she says proudly, holding Claire's hand in the air. A round of cheers and a few whistles and modest applause fills the tent as Cait and Claire stand at the microphone at center stage.

Claire looks out over the faces and sees Griff's mother and another woman she knows standing next to her. They have on their Marine Mom shirts, and she suddenly realizes she should have her shirt on as well. She doesn't know what to say. After what seems like an eternity to her, she clears her throat and leans into the microphone, slightly tipping the stand. She says, "I just want to say I'm against the war." Immediately, the sagging tent is filled with the roar of "Peace now, peace now" in collective euphoria. Claire begins to feel something warm inside and can feel the corners of her mouth turn up and, at the same time, a sense of relief.

I can do this.

Somewhere in the middle of this glowing choir, a man's voice bellows like a bad note. "You want terrorists in your backyard? You want them blowing up our schools?"

Voices put the man down with shouts of "Peace now," until Claire raises her arms in the air and brings them to silence.

"It feels like Vietnam all over again," Claire says, raising her voice and scanning the crowd. Applause follows, and suddenly Claire is angry. It shows on her face and in her voice. She grips the microphone stand hard, and from somewhere deep inside of her it all comes out. "Why in the hell are you applauding?" she asks, both mystified and upset. "Don't you know Vietnam was the worst mistake of our generation? It tore our nation apart. We lost almost sixty thousand of our boys and over a million Vietnamese were killed." She pauses for a moment as if inspecting the crowd's responses. "It was the greatest tragedy of my generation, and it makes me sick to even to think about it."

There is silence. Feet shuffle. People look at each other. Then a different loud voice that is not moved by Claire's words says, "Your son is going to think you're an asshole being up here. Going against him." The argument strikes Claire like a blow. It reverberates in her soul. It's the question she has asked herself for weeks leading up to this rally. But she thinks for a moment and realizes how shallow the words are. Not worth the energy it takes to argue. It's a trap, in a way. Forcing her to confront her feelings and fears.

"My son knows I support him. He knows I would give my life for him. What he didn't know when he left—what he was too young to know—is that this and any other damned war is awful. And the sad thing is that this noise we're making might not change any of that." She shifts the weight in her feet from side to side, looking for the Marine Mom sweat shirts and some kindred spirits to draw strength from; she sees Nancy. Nancy gives her two thumbs-up, and then the words just spill out of her with no hesitation. "Our soldiers are dying now, every day. Or they come home with arms and legs missing and the war stuck in their minds." The tent is quiet.

"My husband Mike used to say our soldiers will come home with their minds damaged, their thinking affected, perhaps forever," Claire continues. She is confident and poised now, with the fervor of an evangelical pastor. "Mike was wounded, shot through the chest. That healed. The wounds inside him never did. Even now, he sometimes scares me with that cold, faraway look in his eyes. So cold that I have to go out of the house and take a breath and walk around the block and remind myself it's not me he hates, it's what happened to him. He's a tortured soul and has been for more than thirty years. Do you think this war will produce anything different than broken souls?"

"They're heroes!" someone shouts.

"They're all heroes," Claire responds, and now the crowd is listening to each word. Listening to how it sounds and hangs in the air with mental images and feelings so deep that they trigger some great sadness inside most of the people in the crowd.

"But what good are heroes when our kids come home so damaged inside?" Her voice is loud and then soft, and no one speaks as her message resonates through the tent. "And this damage isn't limited to our men or women soldiers. It spreads out and affects their families, their children, and their wives. Like dropping a pebble in a pond. The whole community suffers." The sun comes into the tent in a flood of light, and Claire can see the light sweep across the tent, filled with dust particles, as she searches for words. "I don't know or pretend to know the long-term damage war does, but I know it's profound. And we can put out all the damn yellow ribbons in the world and wave all the flags but…" She shakes her head and her voice drops. "I don't want to sound hopeless. But my God! We have to do something to stop this madness. My boy was playing baseball last summer." Her voice tails off, and her eyes squint as though she is seeing Mick again. It is so quiet in this tent in Lake Parrish. There are a few whimpers. Kleenex are pulled out. Cell phones are raised to photograph her. No one leaves. She inhales and exhales and looks at all the faces turned up toward hers and says, "I just want the war to end." It is quiet for a long moment as Claire shifts her gaze to the ground and then the tent erupts with applause.

A moment later, Claire takes Cait's hand. They descend the stairs. The guy painted like oil runs up on stage, grabs the microphone, and starts chanting, "No more war! No more war!" Soon the tent is lifted with the same slogan from the same young people while the older ones exit.

Outside, folks follow Claire and sing her praises and want to touch her and have her attention. A woman Claire's age pushes past the bodies clamoring at her side and confronts Claire. She looks Claire in the face, her eyes swollen and red from crying. "My…my son Steven was…was…" and Claire pulls the woman to her and holds her, whispering in her ear, "I know. I know." Nancy watches, her eyes wet, and touches Claire's shoulder.

The circle grows, while across the street, a man in his eighties, wearing a "Veterans of Foreign War" hat, stands beside a woman in a wheelchair who is holding a small flag. She has a hand-painted crooked-letter sign that reads We Love Our Country.

Chapter 32

From the air, Camp Bravo spreads out in almost a perfect circle with the command post and communications buildings at its center. Originally named Ali Dang, it's a small city dropped in the middle of a desert with over a twenty-mile perimeter, complete with paved streets, two twelve-thousand-foot runways capable of landing anything that flies, and thirty aircraft hangars made from concrete and reinforced steel. Numerous palatial office and recreation buildings line the streets, as well as housing for private contractors, officers, enlisted men, and various troops from a smattering of countries including Britain, Australia, Uganda, and the United States. Buses crisscross the base twenty-four hours a day. The base was built by Saddam and partially destroyed by American air power during the first Gulf War and then again in the original assaults in Iraq. One section of the base holds a two-square-mile graveyard of destroyed Iraqi military vehicles and planes.

Not everything was decimated by US air strikes, however. Saddam, anticipating the inevitable, moved dozens of older Russian Migs and four Mig-25 foxbats, considered to be the fastest aircraft ever built, out to the middle of the desert and buried them. Perhaps he thought it would be just like the Gulf War, where the United States withdrew before it was over. He must have planned to fight another day. Another unusual discovery was a tanker truck stopped by

American forces as it attempted to flee the 2003 onslaught. Turned over by an air strike, it was filled with gold bars worth hundreds of millions. Where the gold ended up is part of a senate investigation.

All branches of the service have some sort of contingency troops at Bravo, as well as choppers, fighter aircraft, heavily armored vehicles, and artillery. It is a complete modern base with training facilities for Iraqis, two hospitals, canteens, four mess halls, three gyms, and two movie theaters. Along with several thousand American troops, coalition forces from Britain, Australia, and Uganda do most of the patrols and operations and the building and technical work. Over two thousand KBR contractors are employed in support from the kitchen to the once-secret underground bunkers that lie beneath the Communications Center. Some troops are housed in rows of cream-colored tents that sleep forty, others in prefabricated white trailers that sleep up to six. All of the housing accommodations and buildings are sandbagged, and most are surrounded by concrete blast walls. There are numerous twenty-foot-high gun towers around the concertina-wired perimeter. Each is manned with heavy machine guns, grenade launchers, and inflatable slides for a quick exit. Bradleys, Strykers, and tanks point out from the perimeter, equipped with machine guns and TOW missiles. The Communications Center is a one-hundred-thousand-square-foot building that once housed Iraqi troops, communications equipment, an indoor pool, a soccer field, and a basketball court.

The camp is in full swing, as any major base would be, in midday in the middle of a war zone: choppers moving troops and supplies and planes landing, unloading or loading up. Work details and construction projects are building more housing and warehouses where mechanics work on everything from a general's Humvee to jet engines. An outdoor amphitheater also welcomes USO shows, where movie starlets and beauty queens, with long hair and long legs, walk across the stage in tight shorts and high heels, smiling with their perfect teeth and waving to the crowd of wildly cheering, lonely soldiers.

Cody is on a small dirt basketball court, near the front lines of the perimeter, playing one-on-one with July, a female marine chopper pilot. Both are sweating profusely under a blanket of heat and humidity. It's 120 degrees in the shade, and Cody dribbles the ball, trash-talking July even though he's down a bucket in a game he needs to win by two.

"I can see you're fading. You got nothin'. You're history, and I'm going to drop a trey in your eye." Cody laughs. "Fact is you might never touch the ball again."

"Go ahead and shoot, pretty boy."

Cody handles the ball well, bouncing it in front of him, switching hands; sweat and dirt help control his dribble. He bounces the ball back and forth between his legs, jab stepping, jab stepping, kicking up dust. "Watch me now, Ju-ly. I'm coming. Watch me." He drives for the basket and goes up for a shot. July jumps after him, and her fast muscle twitch is quicker. On the way up she swats the ball from Cody's hands, lands, and grabs the ball. Black hair flowing through a cloud of dust, she spins toward the basket and lays it in off the backboard, soft as butter, like she's done it all her life.

"That's sick," Cody says, bent over, hands on his knees, panting. "You're dope."

July has the ball on her hip, grinning like she just won Olympic gold. She says, "You owe me five bucks and a beer."

Meanwhile, Mike is sitting in a lawn chair at a card table, under a tarp strung between a Bradley and a sandbagged bunker. He's working on his laptop, a small satellite dish next to him, composing a *Portland Reporter* entry.

What bothers me most is not being young. Every morning, I wake up, and my back aches, and my knee throbs, and I shovel in a handful of pills just to make it through the day. I'm a wreck, falling apart in front of the eyes of these young, smart, and strong marines. Then, if I put my own selfishness aside, I see the sad reality that some of these young marines will be maimed and disfigured, and some will die.

Met a kid from Kansas the other day, kind of small and thin. He was carrying an old M60 machine gun, like we did back in the day.

I told him I used to carry one in Vietnam and wondered where he got it. "And do they let you use it in combat?"

"Oh no. It's too old. We carry stuff that really kicks ass. We took it off a haji we fried in a firefight. I'm takin' it to Weapons Recovery."

I asked the young marine to hand it to me. I was bracing for some heavy duty muscle memory. As I grabbed the stock and butt plate, the only thing I experienced was a shooting pain running through my backside.

Occasionally, Mike looks out through the rows of wire to the wide, empty expanse of monotonous desert and then back to the screen and the keyboard as he forges a story. He's not pleased and deletes it all and starts again.

Nunez and Hop sit next to Mike, eating some meals ready to eat (MREs) and looking at naked pictures Nunez bought off a kid about a month ago. The black-and-white photos look like European women from the forties with their frilly tops, big eyes, and Greta Garbo hairstyles.

"Sheeet, Hoppy. This one's got some fat tits there, and look at that bush. Damn! Wish I was eating that instead of this sack of shit. Pass me some o' that Tabasco."

"Quit cryin', donkey. We off this watch at five and then we can get us some real food."

"This gonna set my sweet ass on fire," Nunez says, shaking sauce over his packaged meal. "It sho is nasty." Nunez takes a couple bites and looks in his meal, seeing if there is something strange down there that's causing trouble in his mouth. But he's hungry, and they both are stuck on the lines until dinner. Tired of trying to gag it down, he looks up at Mike keyboarding away.

"Say, old-timer, you hungry?"

Mike welcomes the distraction. "No. I think I'll take my chances at the mess hall."

"Come on," Nunez says. "Try some; here, let me help you out." He laughs with Hop and dumps some more hot sauce in the pouch and stirs it with a spoon and hands it up to Mike. This is a challenge. Pussy out, or be one of the guys and take a bite. Mike looks for water and sees his bottle, lying on his pack under the card table.

"You know, I think I will." Mike takes the pouch and white plastic spoon and takes a big bite. Immediately his mouth is on fire, but he won't let it show. "This is good, a little sweet. Needs some salt." Then he ingests another spoonful, swallows, and can feel the heat burning down his throat into his stomach like a hot briquette.

"Go to hell! You see the old-timer? He's the bomb!" Hop laughs. "You could take on that Chinese guy, you know, the dude who eats like a hundred hot dogs? You could put him to shame."

While the boys are distracted, bumping fists, laughing, Mike quickly drains his bottle and feels the warm water rush run down his throat, drowning the fire, wishing he had a cold beer.

"That was good," Mike lies. "Better than C rations."

"What's C rations?" asks Nunez.

"Before your time."

Cody slides up, dripping sweat like he just stepped out of a sauna. His shirt is off and Mike looks at his slender frame and compares it to Mick's.

"Who's that?" Hop asks. "She be looking fine. Schooling your scrawny ass."

"I was laying back. Gotta let the girl win."

"Bullshit! I saw her make a move and damn near break your ankles."

Cody doesn't defend himself, and Mike enjoys the conversation, his face relaxed and the corners of his mouth lifting.

"Met her at the gym the other day," Cody continues. "She was shooting hoops, running with the boys. I was in my sandals just taking pictures, looking for something interesting, and so after the game I hit on her."

"Wooeee! Catch this shit. Mr. Cameraman trying to hook up!" Hop gleams and does a knuckle punch on Nunez's shoulder and slaps a high five.

"I wouldn't kick her outta bed," Nunez says. "I'll show her some of my everything." And he grabs his crotch. Cody is turning red. His head brushes the top of the tarp, and Mike is all smiles, a look Cody has never seen. Cody shakes his head and says, "She's not—"

"Don't tell me," Nunez interrupts. "Don't tell me. I gotcha. I gotcha. Let me guess. *She's not that kind of girl!*" This triggers everyone. They slap knees and rock with laughter, and even Mike lets a snort of laughter break through his grin.

"I'd like to know what kind of shit you two been smoking?" Cody asks. "Whatever it is, save some for me. I'm going to shower. I'll see you cartoons later." Cody turns and starts to jog away.

"Wait, Cody," Nunez calls. "What's her name?"

Cody, not breaking his stride, yells back over his shoulder, "July. Lieutenant Debby July to you."

"Damn! An L-T. For the cameraman," Hop says. "And she got some pretty titties."

When things slow down a bit, Hop takes apart his M4 and cleans it. Nunez rolls to his back on the poncho liner spread near Mike's feet and closes his eyes, and Mike snaps his laptop closed, thinking he can write tomorrow or tonight, when the sun isn't frying.

He's been thinking about Mick, discreetly asking some of the men if they know him. But it's a big battalion, and he might not be in the area. Even if someone is in the same company or platoon, they don't necessarily know everyone. And he isn't quite ready to take it up with any of the officers in charge yet, thinking they might get pissed, which could threaten his mission. And what is his mission? He pops out the thumb drive, places it in a plastic bag, and stuffs it in his pocket. What the fuck is he really doing here? Is he here to somehow save his son? Or is he hoping to kill some of the assholes that are killing marines? Somewhere in his confused mind he thought he could come over here and save Mick. Or at least help him. Or maybe talk to someone and get him moved somewhere safe like supply, or shipped to the Green Zone, which is R&R city from what he understands. Being here brought clarity. None of those ideas make sense anymore, and he wonders if he is here for something else. Maybe he's here just to write the hell out of the war. Write like he used to, to punish people. That was his main focus in the early days. Make readers feel ashamed for what they did by protesting in the streets, calling soldiers baby killers, and shaming veterans. He'd show society that sat back in judgment of veterans. He'd show them what war was, what it did to their boys. He'd ram it down readers' throats. Tell them how soldiers felt and suffered—for them. He wanted to remind all those shithead protestors that most Vietnam veterans were a good and proud lot. That they were capable and confident, not the losers that Hollywood imagined. That's what all the movies were about, Mike says to himself, and he drinks from his water bottle as a gust of wind lifts the tarp and makes it flutter.

Back in the sixties and seventies—and even eighties—to gain traction as a veteran, to get people to listen to you, you had to say being in Vietnam was stupid, and what you did was wrong. Then you had to blame it on the government for putting you there. There was no honor in serving your country back then. Only shame and guilt and drunken nights when you thought you couldn't stand to live anymore. You couldn't talk about the heroic nature of the men you served with or that the Vietnamese were glad you were there. If you said shit like that, you were considered a fool.

He takes another sip from his bottle, twists the cap back on, and considers how he used to be. It was a twisted view the country had about the war and the boys that fought in it. And it was his purpose back then, he supposed, to shame them all. Shame them for not loving their soldiers.

The blast of thought and memory makes him angry as he watches Nunez and Hop get up, stretch their legs, and walk along the perimeter and then back to the cover of the tarp. By the time they sit down again, the afternoon is waning, but Mike is still fired up. What war protestors said forty years ago continues today. And he hates it. He hates it when those against the war say, "We're not against the soldiers; we're just against the war." He doesn't accept or believe it. If that were true, then why protest when soldiers clearly don't want that? Why inspire the enemy? Why, if people are really for the soldiers, don't they push for victory in Iraq? This is a war on terrorism, isn't it? Why not show support and rally behind the troops, like in World War II? Where are the posters of our soldiers? And the slogans, like V for Victory, and campaigns and personal sacrifices? What will you give the soldiers who are willing to give their lives for you? There is the clarity, Mike is considering, but now he's tired.

"Hey, guys," Mike says, shooing away flies and brushing off some sand fleas. "Have either of you run into a kid named Mick Kelly?"

"Yo! Kelly? Is that your kid?" Hop asks. "Your nephew or some shit?"

Mike doesn't want to go into a big explanation or have the guys hammering him with questions.

"Mick's my son and is with the Third Marines, and he's in Kilo."

"Wow," Nunez says. "When I was growing up, my old man wouldn't even drive cross town ta go to my ball games. He was too busy hooking up with the neighbor bitch on the second floor. Damn, man. So ya jus' buzz over here to see yer boy. " Nunez couldn't have been more amazed.

Mike feels self-conscious, trying to figure out a way to get them to understand that coming here is just work. That's all. But a lie is a lie. Nothing he can dream up will change that. His being here is about his boy. Of course, the marines realize that. Everything else is secondary.

"Never heard of him," Hop interjects. "Might've met him, but we've only been in shit city here for 'bout a month." Hop takes another slug of water from a plastic bottle and shakes his head. "No. No way."

"Just asking. Keep this to yourselves, OK, guys?" They both nod their head in agreement. Mike's still looking for some justification for coming that doesn't involve Mick. He's a journalist for God's sake. A Pulitzer Prize–nominated journalist, so why should he be concerned about what anyone thinks? They can go to hell. He's here to record history; seeing his son would be a bonus. And if he can somehow get him out of this hellhole, would that be so bad?

He puts his gear together, takes down the dish, and is about to leave to go catch a shower before chow when Cody appears under the tarp, sweating through a white T-shirt that has Boston in blue letters on the front of it. He's got a camera hanging from his neck and is drinking a cherry sports drink he ripped off from mess. He sets his drink on the card table.

"Hey, dude. Get a picture of me and Burr head," Nunez says, putting his arm over the shoulder of Hop. "Something nice we can send the sisters back home waiting for the big one," Nunez laughs.

"Big?" Hop says, a joke written on his face. "You so small you needs a magnifying glass and tweezers just to find it." Cody checks them on his screen, adjusts for light and distance, and brings life to a still shot.

"I'll put it up on my Facebook."

"You way cool, dude," Hop says.

Mike and Cody emerge from under the tarp. It feels to Mike as if the temperature jumps twenty degrees. "Shit, it's hot," he says, putting on his shades.

They walk for a bit. Mike limps past bunkers and rows of trailers and canvas tents. "You're limping, old man," Cody says. "You going to make it OK?"

"Knee keeps locking up on me."

"That blows. You get compensation for that? How did you hurt it?"

"I stepped the wrong way." And that was that.

"Hey, I ran into Jarvis," Cody says as he slaps at some fleas and scratches his neck. "Frickin' fleas. Boss, he tells me they're doing a snatch tonight, and we could go if we promise to keep quiet and stay out of the way." This piques Mike's interest. "They're after this asshole that's funneling money to the insurgents. Jarvis says he's al-Qaeda, and it could be rough, but we can go if you can walk."

"Walk? No problem. I'll just tighten my brace and drop some meds. No hill for a climber."

"No what?" Cody asks, a silly look of confusion slapped on his face.

"It means if you're a…forget it. I'm all in. I'll catch up with you tonight. "

Chapter 33

Mike is back at his laptop in the tent he shares with Cody and thirty or so marines. He's finishing a column that he started a few days earlier, and he's reading the *Portland Reporter* sports page, checking out the baseball scores to see if Boston won and whether their center fielder Billy Fast Horse, from a small town in Oregon, did well. He loves the little left-hander who grew up on an Indian reservation.

Billy was three for four with an RBI, and he even stole home. That's a big deal. This tickles Mike, and he thinks about Mick and what he could be doing if he'd stayed and played in college. He reads the last page about the Portland Trail Blazers and how they have the first pick in the draft. From there, the section leads into the obituaries. He scans up and down, making sure he's not there, and comes across a small death notice about his friend, a veteran named Kenny Rose. It shocks him. He saw Kenny just a couple of months ago walking along the waterfront with his wife and child. It angers him that little is mentioned in the obit. Mike decides his next column will be about Kenny. He searches in the archives of the *Portland Reporter* for information about him and the event he was famous for. And he thinks of all the decent things Kenny did for veterans. It wasn't right for him to go unnoticed. Mike writes the last words about Kenny and e-mails it to Glen.

Glen, you bastard. I guess I should have stayed home. The knee's screwed, and I'm too old anymore. I haven't seen Mick yet and hope to soon, that is if the guys at the top don't cut off my nuts for being here. Call Claire for me, and tell her I love her, will you? Tell her I'm still trying to connect with Mick. Here's a column about a buddy of mine. The attached article isn't about being here, but it's about a veteran I knew. I pulled some info from the archives and e-mailed some other folks for info. Isn't it amazing? I'm here in Iraq writing like I'm home at my desk, sipping a soda.
Mike

The Siege at Fort Vancouver
by Mike Kelly

In the early morning of August 30, 1988, Kenny worked alone. It was still dark as he gathered ropes, a grappling hook, ammunition, fuses, and blasting powder. He stuffed his pack and bags as thoughts of SWAT teams and snipers lingered in the air. He might get headshot, he imagined, but he'd risk it if the country listens.

Earlier, he had placed an anonymous phone call to the *Portland Reporter*, telling them something big might happen. He filled the trunk of the beat-up car he slept in, headed north across the bridge, and parked near historic Fort Vancouver long before sunrise. His bags were heavy as he crept through the shadows to the wooden walls. He dropped his gear, tossed the grappling hook over the wall, and struggled to get his heavy frame to the other side. He unlocked the gate, brought the bags inside, and left a sign that read, "If anyone tries to enter, we'll blow up the fort." Then he padlocked the gate and moved toward the cannons.

Kenny was a marine in Vietnam during the bloody years, 1968 and 1969, when over twenty-eight thousand American sons died. He didn't tote a rifle or fire a machine gun or drop violence from the sky, but he served as a cook in a tent during the bloody Tet Offensive. He was nineteen when enemy rockets tore through the sagging canvas, erupting in a wide swath of dead and wounded soldiers. He survived, and the guilt left him psychologically damaged—forever.

When he came home, he was one of thousands of homeless and unemployed veterans across the country. He often got drunk, and he lived under the Burnside Bridge alongside his countless comrades. One day, he decided to change and get sober and serious about his homeless brethren. He set up coffee and hot dog nights under the bridge's dark and dangerous corners. He fed the homeless, surrounded by the roar of traffic overhead and the stenches of alcohol and urine floating through the air.

As the sun rose over Fort Vancouver that August morning in 1988, Kenny worked furiously, fixing fuses, setting cannons with gunpowder, and filling their barrels with his ammunition of crumpled newspaper. He didn't want to harm anyone. He only wanted to call attention to his anguish and the plight of a generation of homeless veterans.

A guard came to open the fort and saw Kenny's sign. He called the police. Soon the building was surrounded by cop cars and nervous officers shouting out orders and demands. Kenny started setting off cannons with loud explosions blasting paper in the air, and the cameras and the reporters came, along with SWAT teams and trucks full of snipers. I-5 was shut down near the bridge. Nobody knew what this "crazed veteran," as one reporter called him, might do. The siege lasted for hours and moved into the midday sun. By now, with radio and TV reports, the one-man siege had blown across the state and nation. The *New York Times* and CNN picked it up, and soon millions would know.

The FBI arrived with a hostage negotiator, and a two-way radio was lowered into the fort. Eventually, Kenny surrendered and held a news conference in which he spoke about the plight of homeless veterans and the trouble with the VA. "It's a national disgrace," he said, "to see veterans sleeping under bridges and eating from garbage cans."

He went to court and was given thirty days of jail time and two hundred hours of community service. He was penniless; ironically, a group of former South Vietnamese soldiers thought he was a hero and paid his fines and damages to the fort.

After his release, Kenny began a decade of volunteer work. He wasn't firing cannons anymore, and the *Portland Reporter* reported in 1989 that "his ammunition is words and his battlefields are boardrooms and the halls of government." He worked with former commissioner Bob Koch to try to find city money to buy and build a homeless shelter for veterans. There was a vacant congregate care center on SE Division he tried to pitch, as well as the long-vacant and run-down Kenton Hotel in North Portland. But the money never came.

In 1991, he created Vets for Vets, and with the assistance of the Red Cross, the Oregon and Washington Employment Divisions, and the Veterans Administration, he launched Oregon's first Stand Down at Delta Park. He arranged for three days of food and tents and cots to sleep on. He brought in medical, legal, and housing services for hundreds of veterans. Everything was donated, and to this day there is still an abbreviated Stand Down held in Oregon every year.

Last year, Kenny developed a brain tumor, and the doctors said cancer and twelve months to live. He was treated at the Portland Veterans Medical Center that he once despised. His sister Linda Wilson said, "It was a glioblastoma, the most aggressive of brain cancers. Ken thought it was from Agent Orange."

"Rose, Kenneth Donald, was born in Portland. He is survived by his wife, Melodina, and daughter Alexa."

This small, nondescript obituary says nothing about his passing, those whose lives he touched, and the scores of homeless veterans he helped lead toward respectability. And that's one of the sad parts about being a veteran. Soldiers we know and love often leave this world in anonymity. And so it was with Kenny. Sometimes we honor them with small parades and lightly attended speeches. But the imprint of their lives and what they have done is often forgotten. The way they walked in war or peace vanishes. In the public's eyes, they disappear like Kenny under the small paper flags that wave across a veteran's cemetery.

Mike shuts down the laptop and gets ready to move out with Cody and Jarvis and a couple dozen or so marines bearing arms. He puts on a clean, camouflaged shirt and pulls his knee brace over his matching trousers. He can feel the swelling and tightens his brace with Velcro straps, slips on his brown desert boots, and pulls the laces tight against the eyelets. After a double dose of pills to cut the pain and reduce the inflammation, his knee will soon be numb. As he slips on his body armor, he feels the same kind of sensation he had when he was a young man. He feels his heart quicken and his adrenaline surge. For a moment, he is excited, but when he takes a couple steps, he feels old again.

They load up four Humvees and a Cougar. Each Humvee is mounted with a .50 caliber or M240 machine gun. The same for the Cougar. Lieutenant Jarvis is in the front seat of a Humvee, with PFC Adam Bloomfield driving. Corporal Marlantes is standing in the backseat, his body sticking out the roof opening, holding on to the .50 and chewing tobacco nervously. He spits to the side. Cody is in the backseat, holding a hand-sized digital camera, and Mike is talking notes into his tiny voice recorder.

Jarvis has a headset on, obscured by his helmet, and is talking to Command. "Roger that, Sky One. We'll be hitting the bars, looking for some ladies at 0100," he says in a stupid code that Mike thinks wouldn't fool anyone. The lieutenant leans over the seat. "Mike, y'all sit tight, and don't leave the vehicle until I say so." His voice is firm and direct. "And, Cody, you keep yer ass down when yer shooting that camera. We cool?"

"Yes, sir. I'm just glad to have the opportunity—"

"Knock off the bull. Just do what I say." Cody sinks back into his seat. Their team will be responsible for communications and coordination and will call in support if needed. They roll out in convoy.

Through the side window and up through the open roof past Marlantes, Mike can see the moon, almost full, and a sky filled with the brightest stars. It reminds him of nights with his dad in eastern Oregon, near the Wallowa Mountains and the tiny town of Joseph. They'd hunt during the days and camp at night under stars that always looked bigger than they did in the city. He never actually carried a rifle as a boy or shot anything. Come to think of it, as a man, the only thing he ever hunted was other men. The four Humvees roll through the desert. A drone is hovering over the target, sending images of the suspected house. Choppers are on call for fire support or emergency medevacs if needed.

Mike feels his adrenaline draining. What if they get hit? He can't move for shit. He feels heavy, weighted down, with his camouflage uniform, helmet, and the night-vision goggles strapped to it. Lieutenant Jarvis is in the front, looking at the green screen on the dash and talking on his headset. Marlantes is holding his weapon easily, swinging his gun as if he were swinging a baseball bat in the on deck circle.

Cody looks around Marlantes's legs at Mike. In the light coming through the roof, he notices that Mike's wearing the holster under his flak, and he's packing a gun. "Boss," Cody says, not too loud. "What the hell are you doing?"

"What does it look like I'm doing?" The sound of his voice is buried by the hum of tires turning, and Mike's in no mood to talk bullshit. Broken down or not, he's ready. He feels like he's nineteen again, scared but jacked up, hoping he sees some action.

"I saw your gun," Cody whispers. "You've got a weapon. What's up with that?"

"It's a semiautomatic Sig Sauer P232. Bought it off a guy just in case."

"In case of what? You can't carry a gun. You shoot someone, you're up shit creek."

"What are you, a goddamned girl scout? We're in a country full of jihadists that want us dead. And I don't give a shit what any other reporters are doing. I'd rather be judged by twelve than carried by six."

"Keep it down! We're going dark and silent!" Jarvis says, pissed. The convoy's lights turn off in unison, the vehicles slow, and hearts quicken.

Mike turns his face to the window and doesn't talk any more. He won't get caught up trying to justify why he's carrying. If something does happen and marines go down and need support, he can sure as hell help. He may be an old man, but he's not going to roll over and die. Besides, when he finds Mick, he'll give the pistol to him. That should help.

The convoy travels a few more minutes, with the stars and the moon as the only illumination. Mike touches the holster and feels his handgun and checks his body-armor pocket for the four other magazines. With four seven-shot magazines and the one in his gun, he has thirty-five chances to kill someone if he has to. If some of the psychos get close enough for him to shoot, the patrol is in trouble anyway. But imagining some dickhead in a turban and tennis shoes running toward him is exciting, just like the last convoy. In his mind, Mike's back in the game, emptying a few rounds in some fuck's head.

Lieutenant Jarvis leans over the back of the seat again and says, "Y'all listen up. Just got a call from the Big Boy and the mission's dead."

"What the hell is going on?" Mike asks.

"Heck if I know, but we're turning back."

"Goddammit," Mike says under his breath.

Cody lets out a sigh, and it's obvious he's relieved.

The convoy turns around near a cluster of palm trees outside a small village. The moon is at their backs as they cut through the sand on their way to Camp Bravo. Mike rests his head against the glass, closes his eyes, and drifts off. He's back at Grand Slam. Mick is hitting, Jose pitching, and everything he swings at is hit hard. Mick stops and wipes sweat off his brow and turns to Mike with a big smile. "How's that, Pops?"

Chapter 34

"I t's hot as a motherfucker," Nunez says, playing cards at a table in a tent with Hop. The big fans that keep the tent cool are broken, so the flaps are up. Hoping for a breeze.

"Look, man," Nunez reaches out his arm to show Hop. "It's so damn hot I ain't even sweatin'. I drank me some Gatorades, but I haven't taken a piss all day."

"Fool, you dehydrated." Hop grimaces, looking up from his cards. "You need to take on some more water, or you be on your ass, and I'll be standing over you pissin' in your face, coolin' ya off." Hop's wearing a big grin and seems quite pleased with the idea.

"Bite me."

"Bite you and your mama, dog shit. That's what you do when somebody goes into heat exhaustion."

"Well, I don't have no heat exhaustion."

"Shut up. Play your cards, and drink this." Hop reaches down on the floor, picks up a plastic bottle of water, and tosses it to him.

Across the tent, a marine with a big white shaved head and a dozen stitches in it is racked out in his skivvies on a lower bunk with his iPod cranking. He's got speakers hooked up, with music booming.

Mike and Cody are sitting at another small metal-and-plastic folding table, working on their respective laptops.

Mike leans into Cody. "What the hell is that noise?"

Cody looks up from his screen, looks around, and finally realizes what Mike is referring to. "He's playing T Man, a coke-freak rapper," Cody says. "Kids like him 'cause he's been shot like seven times, doing drugs and crimes. It enhances his gangster authority."

"Refreshing," Mike says. "Any punk can get shot."

"People also think he's cool because he's built like Superman."

Mike shakes his head in bewilderment. "Where's he from?"

"LA. Most of his music is inspired by living in a Mexican borough outside of LA. He's the real deal. Got a bunch o' top hits like 'Nutin' Like a Good Bitch Slapping' and 'Stick a Gun in His Face,'" Cody explains. "Now that he's rich, he writes songs about his new life."

"Garbage. So tell me about his new crap."

"He just writes about living high, banging movie stars and first-class whores, getting wasted, and burning through life and money."

Mike's face has taken on an exasperated look. "And the white kids like him too. Right?"

"Pretty much true. Even the white marines don't care about his skin color. They just like the way he commands and demands and gets all the girls."

"Life has changed so much. I grew up in the sixties, and when I was in the marines, there was a lot of racial tension," Mike says. "They had all this Angela Davis, Huey Newton black-power stuff. You had to be careful; that's all I'm saying."

Cody nods as if he understands, and they both dive back into their screens.

The rest of the tent is cleaning rifles, gear, and their feet, reading magazines sent from home, or getting some shut eye, as they snore away. The nostril snorts rumble through the air. They sound like a far-off motorboat, sputtering upriver.

Mike is composing a message to Claire when a couple of young marines breeze in carrying small, handheld video recorders, one-third the size of a football. They look like country boys, big and square, loud and unassuming.

"Tater Heads," one of them shouts, rousing the tent. "Hey. I'm Mickey, and this here's Cris, and we're shooting a documentary. We just want to cruise through, shoot some vids, and ask a few questions. We cool?"

The tent is not juiced because this kind of thing happens all the time; being filmed is old news. Mickey and Cris try to tape Mike and ask a few questions, but he runs them off with his best annoyed look. Cris starts talking some bullshit to a guy from Enid, Oklahoma, and convinces him to play the guitar next to his rack. Mickey persuades the iPod man to bust off a couple break dancing moves. The boys will edit the footage on their laptops, download some tunes, and blow it out to YouTube or Facebook, hoping for a million hits. They're dreaming red carpet, Academy Awards, and Hollywood, baby.

"This will be the best documentary on what it's like to be a marine in Iraq," Mickey shouts. Of course every other dog and cat already has that idea. They've posted so much on YouTube about the war that it's hard to believe they have time to fight it.

It's instant war, Mike thinks, looking up from his screen. A way to unwind and have fun maybe, but also a way to anesthetize people into thinking war is something good. He returns to the screen, sweat forming on the inside of his forearms and dripping onto the keyboard. His back itches from heat rash and reminds him of the little needles he used to get when he was sweating in the jungle. A strange rash still bothers him to this day, no matter how clean he is or what medication he spreads on it or ingests. It goes away for a few days and then comes back. None of the dermatologists have been able to cure it. So it's a double type of fungus working away, rash on rash that causes the itching.

Cody snaps his laptop shut, bags it, stands up, and says, "Boss, I'm in the shower for an hour."

"OK, kid." Mike punches the keyboard.

Claire,

It's so ungodly hot and humid. The dry desert heat is different from the jungles of Vietnam. My lungs feel like I'm breathing hot cotton. I forgot what it feels like to sweat all the time. My rash is driving me up the wall, but at least I brought my medication, and that helps. Too bad it doesn't stop the fleas or ticks. Stepped on a scorpion this morning when I was coming out of the shower, but I had on the flip-flops you gave me, and that saved the day. No word on Mick. He's not even e-mailing. I'm sure he's on a forward firebase not far from here. I have had a couple discussions recently with Lieutenant Jarvis and some officers, and somehow they got the word that I'm looking for my son. No one's happy about it, and I guess I understand. It's interesting how being in a combat zone affects me. It brings up all of the same feelings I had when I was a marine. Even the kind of muscle memories you used to talk about. When I first encountered this wave of heat, it reminded me of Vietnam. It felt like Vietnam, and I began feeling like I was young again. But then I'd step wrong or turn too quickly, and my knee would bark, and my arthritis would flare, and I was back to the reality that I'm old and nothing like I used to be. I used to be able to climb through the jungle with an eighty-pound pack on my back and go days without food and with only limited water. I could lift a wounded soldier by myself and carry him, running all the way to a chopper. My body has failed me now, and that is the bad part of being over here. I am reminded that if there were real trouble, I might be a liability. I thought I could somehow help Mick, but now I'm worried that if things got rough, he'd have to help me. And I don't want to be a burden. Oh, Claire, what have I done?

I still feel this huge need to see Mick. To hug him and feel his strength. I remember when he was a baby, and I used to take him in the shower and rock him in my arms and say, "How you doing, big buddy. How's my buddy wuddy?" The shower and the soap. I can almost smell the soap and feel his tiny body in my hands. That was so important for me. It made me feel like I was decent and good and that I could take care of this child that God entrusted me with. Maybe that's why I came over here, to feel decent again. I don't know, but I've got to see Mick and let him know how much I love him.

And I miss you and can see that I've caused you enormous pain over the years. I'll be a better man, a better husband, Claire. I promise you I will.

Please give Madie all my love and tell her I miss her. And tell Cait I'm thinking about her and looking forward to a grandson.
Mike

He sends the message flying through cyberspace, and it lands halfway around the world in Claire's inbox. She's in her office paying bills, Mike guesses. Or maybe she's in Mick's room, sitting on his bed, looking at his bench press and weights. No, that's probably what he'd do. She might be at her mother's, sitting by her side, rubbing her mother's feet and talking about what she read in the newspaper that day. He loved it when Claire would tell him stories or read articles that he missed. It seemed like she knew all the characters involved and the situations they were in. He is recalling the story she told him about a Zen Buddhist Monk who was a Vietnam veteran when Cody walks up, a soda in his hand, shirt off, and hair sticking up like a rooster's comb.

"Where's your weapon, Rammm-bo?"

Mike looks up. "Look at your hair. You look like a goof. And why are you giving me heat?"

Cody self-consciously runs a hand through his hair and flattens the top.

"I'm not trying to mess with you. Anyhow, I got some good news. A scoop, you might say."

"Don't tell me. You're in love with little Miss Long Brown Hair with the uh—"

"I'm not in love, but we are going to hook up tonight and watch a movie on my laptop. But that's not my news. The LT checked the roster and confirmed that Mick's with Kilo Company, and they're on a small fire base not far from here called Jessica."

"Jessica?"

"Like Jessica Simpson. You know, she's hot; it's hot. Lot of action. Forget it." Cody cracks up, snorting. "Sorry, boss. But he's there, and it's way cool."

Mike grins, clenches his fist, smacks his leg enthusiastically, and then pauses as if to reconsider his excitement. "He's OK?"

Cody pulls up a green plastic chair, like the kind used at barbecues, and sits down. He takes a hit off his soda and offers it to Mike, who shakes his head no.

"So what did Jarvis say? Can we see him?"

"The LT said the camp is like a listening post for Fallujah. They're catching a lot of shit, mortars, a few rockets, but they run patrols off the base every day, and they've got a ton of air support. I guess they are also doing some humanitarian project. Something about a school. I don't know—you'll need to talk to him." Cody finishes his drink and tosses it like a basketball toward a cardboard box by the tent entrance. When it lands in the box, he shouts, "Bam! In your eye."

"Christ. Fallujah. That's about the last place I want him to be."

"Yeah, well, LT thinks Mick's company might be rotating a platoon in for a few days to get some downtime. He said some of these guys are doing two tours now, and they need a break."

Mike's not slapping high fives or showing any emotion.

"You should be stoked, boss; he could be headed this way, or maybe we can go check it out and build a story."

"Screw the story. I just want to see my son." Mike stops for a moment and considers what Mick might feel. "I'm worried."

"About Mick getting hurt?"

"No. Well, yes. Hell, I'm worried about how he's going to take it. You know, me being here."

"Are you kidding? He's your son. He'll be glad. What's not to like?" Cody sits back, pulls a package of cigarettes out, lights one, and coughs.

Mike looks at him, puzzled. "When did you start smoking?"

"Yesterday."

Mike stands at the door of Lieutenant Jarvis's small trailer, calculating what to say and how to say it. If he had been thinking clearly, he would have broached the situation with Jarvis earlier. He'd have persuaded him that he was a journalist first, and it was chance, not design, that he happened to be with the same battalion as Mick, at the same time in the same location. Shit. The lieutenant would never buy that. No one would. OK, so he fucked up and should have done it differently, but it is what it was. He's here now and wants to see his son. What the hell had he been thinking? Maybe thinking he could save his son was a fucked up excuse just to come over here and be tested again. Write about the war from my perspective, not from my history or an interview with real warriors. From living it again. Blow up my ego. Act like I'm young and strong and not afraid. Maybe I'm just full of guilt.

He knocks on the door, over the sound of the air conditioner turning. Each trailer had one, another perk for being an E-4 or above. Mike could have gotten one if he'd kissed ass or claimed he was a big shot back at the paper. Or he could make some colonel out to be a hero, get it picked up by the AP, and he'd get anything he wanted.

"I'm coming," Jarvis says from inside the trailer.

When the door opens, Mike gets slapped with a large charge of cool air, like he had just opened the door of a walk-in cooler. It feels good all over.

"Lieutenant, can I come in for, uh, a moment?" Mike stutters. "There's something I want to say."

"Yep. I bet there is. Well, come on," Jarvis says, holding the door. "Yer losing my cool air."

Mike brushes off the dirt he picked up on the walk over and steps inside. His sweat cools almost instantly. Inside, there are two bunks, a fridge and a one-burner stove, a few storage places, and a sign that says *Shitter*. Mike sits on the empty bunk across from Jarvis, who's eating an MRE of beef stroganoff out of a plastic bag, cold, like he was in the field.

"Love these sons of bitches," he says, raising a white plastic spoon to his mouth. He's in his green underwear and tank top and just lifting the spoon to his mouth makes his muscles hop. Mike notes the gold cross and how it looks so small on his massive chest. Used to be me, he thinks.

"I haven't been honest with you, Lieutenant."

"Go on," Jarvis says, stirring his mix, listening, and shoveling in a couple more spoonfuls.

"Lieutenant, my son's here in Kilo and—"

"Mike, I know that," Jarvis says, pointing his plastic spoon at Mike. "Y'all must think I'm an idiot? I know who you are, how many books you wrote, and everything else important. This is 2005, sir, not Vietnam in the Stone Age."

Mike is irritated, and his rash itches, and he wants to scratch his balls and is trying not to lose his temper.

"I can Google and use search engines and damn near know everything about you, sir. No disrespect, but we have information technology that you never even dreamed of happening here."

"So you must have known for a while that my son was here. Am I right?" Mike asks, scratching his neck.

"Yes, sir. We've been trying to figure out how to get you out of here as diplomatically as possible. Without the press havin' a shit fit."

Mike is not dumbfounded; he's embarrassed, as if what he thinks and feels really isn't important. He's just a nuisance, an old man in the way. He feels his face begin to redden, and it makes him angry. Screw it. "OK. So how am I going to get to see my son before they kick my ass out of here?"

"You probably aren't," Jarvis says, finishing his meal. He tosses the sack and spoon in a small green garbage can on the floor. Then he gets up, takes a step across the room to the counter, opens the tiny fridge, and pulls out a couple cans of German beer. "Here." He hands one to Mike, who is distracted but takes the cold beer in his hand, knowing it's contraband.

"Thanks. But you know they can't boot me. I'm here to write for the *Portland Reporter*, and I got approved, and I'm here for a couple more months. That's my assignment."

"Nobody gives a rats ass about your assignment. You're here by the grace of whatever high-brass pogue shuffled and stamped your papers. I expect in a few days, y'all will be going home, sir."

"Bullshit. I've got to see my son, and that's that. After I do, I'll finish my assignment, and get the fuck out of here." Mike springs to his feet, and his knee lets loose with an audible crack that sends a stabbing pain deep into the tissue, so deep he clenches his teeth and turns for the door to hide the look of pain on his face. He pushes the door open and still has the cold beer in his hand. He grimaces, turns, and looks at Jarvis sitting calmly on the edge of his bunk, amused, beer half empty.

Mike takes a long pull and chugs it, his old bulldog tattoo twitching. "I need to see my boy, Lieutenant." Then he sets the can on the bunk, turns, and is out the door.

Chapter 35

It's night at Camp Bravo. There's a moon and bright clusters of stars. The temperature has dropped to ninety degrees. With no wind and high humidity, it is sweltering. Air conditioners are churning hard. Some are breaking down in trailers, command offices, and bunkers. The perimeter is on alert; towers are manned. Humvees and tanks, Bradleys and all-terrain vehicles are ready to respond from anywhere in the perimeter. The camp is so big that hundreds of marines and soldiers are on watch behind the layers of concertina wire, tangle foot, and moveable blast walls. The concrete airplane hangars are busy with marines or army and air force personnel working on choppers and planes and every kind of vehicle the war deploys. In the mess halls, contractors from around the world finish cleaning after the last meal service and get ready for 5:00 a.m. breakfast. Burger King stays open all night, as do three other full-service mess halls to handle the twenty-four-hour needs of work crews and soldiers. Weight rooms are a major place to pass the time and are blistering with activity all hours of the day. A nineteen-year-old marine working in supply, let's say, comes in weighing a buck sixty. If he hits the weight room hard, eats right, he's going home ripped at one eighty. And if he juices, who knows how much he balloons.

Camp Bravo is a city, with all the good, bad, and ugly. It's got everything but women who'll lie down for money. There are plenty of romances started but rarely finished, blowing up the same way they do anywhere else. The difference in romance between here and the world is that here you're living on the edge. If you survived a rocket attack together and fuck in a trailer, not wanting to get caught, intense is too timid to describe it. That's the way it is—intense, day and night. Then you go home to your wife or husband, a nine-to-five job, and everything is flat, and there is no edge unless you create it. By drinking, drugs, fighting, or whatever.

Mike and Cody move slowly through the camp. Mike limps and Cody turns down his stride to half speed so Mike can keep up. Mike is wearing another Hawaiian shirt, khaki shorts, and a black knee brace. His knee is about the same, even though a corpsman drained it again. The swelling and tightness have dissipated. Cody wears a tight, white T-shirt, tattoos jumping off his small arms, blue jeans, and a Yankees baseball hat on backward, and he carries a small digital camera in a pouch with a strap, which he has wrapped around his waist. They walk through an area near the front lines, past bunkers built from sandbags and tarps, past the towers and heavy Bradleys and Strykers with their TOW missiles and machine guns.

In front of the airplane hangars, sparks fly and arc welders crackle, as soldiers work on planes and choppers and military vehicles. The moon is high and full and casts light on Mike's aging and weathered face.

In front of one hangar, two marines are launching another drone. One launches the plane with four-foot wings, and the other follows it on a handheld screen like a video game. Mike and Cody watch the drone leave the marine's hand and disappear into the darkness.

"That's so amazing," Mike says. "We have weapons and technological support that people didn't even dream of when I was a young marine."

"Yep. And it's changing every day," Cody adds.

"The thing that really is unbelievable is the medical care and how traumatic injuries that would have killed soldiers decades ago are handled almost effortlessly. And now we have soldiers with artificial legs going back into battle." Mike stops to adjust his knee brace.

"Yeah. And did you see the story on TV about the guy who lost both legs and is running on these blades with Olympic-caliber athletes?"

"Speaking of legs, mine are tired. I'm going to sit for a minute." Mike slides onto a pile of sandbags on the side of the road as Cody stands by, both hands in his pockets, scratching at his jock rash. "I feel guilty sitting," Mike says. "Maybe I should just replace this son of a bitch," Mike declares, straightening his leg.

"You do need some new wheels, boss." Cody pulls his hands out of his pockets. "I gotta get some stuff for this jock rash; it's driving me nuts."

"Tell me about it. I've had it for decades. Anyway, here's a story for you, kid," Mike continues, his toe catching on the end of a bag, tugging his bad knee. Just a tug and a spark, like one from a welder, slashes through his knee. His face contorts, but he keeps the pain inside.

"You OK, boss?"

Mike ignores Cody and bites into his story. "So one night, a bunch of us are at this bar."

"Which bar?"

"I don't know. It's not important to the story."

"I'd just like to know is all."

"I don't remember. Maybe it was the Candlelight Room on Fifth Street, behind the *Portland Reporter*. OK?"

"There's no Candlelight bar there anymore," Cody says, annoying Mike further.

"I know. I know. This happened ten years ago or so. Shit! Listen," Mike says as a team of choppers buzzes overhead, their lights flashing.

"We were at the Candlelight Room, okay? It was at least ten or twelve years ago, when you were still in junior high, all right! I was with guys from the *Portland Reporter*, having a few bumps, shooting some pool. "

A couple other marines walk by, and one of them says "What it is, gentlemen?"

What it is? Mike's thinking. What the hell does that mean? "Yeah. Semper Fi."

"Semper Fi, sir," one of the guys replies.

"So we're in the bar, knocking a few back, and I just shot and scratched and wanted another beer. Back then, the Candlelight was a real wild hangout. A buddy of mine, Joe Shore, owned it. We went to grade school together and even played Little League All-Stars together. He was a big left-hander and hit a lot of home runs."

"Never played Little League. What is that?"

"It's baseball for kids. Didn't you play baseball?"

"Nope. Vietnamese kids didn't play baseball. Soccer."

"That's a shame. Anyway, Joe's family was poor. When Joe was a kid, he didn't even have a bed. He slept on the floor in a sleeping bag. I know you're getting bored."

"No. No. I'm not, but I'm starved. Let's hop over to Burger King." They ease off the bags and walk.

"So we're at Joe's, juiced. The place is packed, and I go up to the bar and slide onto the one empty stool and order a shot of Johnny's with a beer back. There's a gal on my right who's probably in your next wet dream. On my left is a rough-looking guy with a missing forefinger."

"Wish I had a beer," says Cody as they walk the dimly lit road, past closed warehouses and rows of trailers.

"So I started talking to the guy, and he tells me he was a marine. So I'm questioning him about where he was, to see if he is bullshitting or not. I pity those sons of bitches that say they were in the war and are just lying through their teeth." Mike stops for a moment, bends down and shifts the cartilage in his knee, and then stands up. "I hate this," he says, referring to his knee.

"I sure hope I don't end up with a bum wheel when I'm a geezer," says Cody.

Mike just lets the comment ride and says, "There's a whole lot worse to deal with. Or you could be dead."

Cody flashes him a smile. "Not me, boss."

Some flares drop in the distance, and there is the faint popping of artillery reaching through the night. Another chopper with its lights flashing *whaps* through the night.

"So where was I? And so I said to the guy, 'How'd you lose your finger?' Well, he gives me this look like his brain is drunk, and he suddenly sobers up and is serious as shit.

"'Well, it's kind of complicated,' the guy tells me. So I'm listening, and I drop a quarter on the floor, and when I bend down to pick it up, I can see that he's strapped with an ankle holster. I come back up feeling his energy, and he says, 'I did some bad things in the war. Things I'm not proud of.' He's been drinking boilermakers and drops a shot of Jack in his beer and drinks it all down, easy."

"Were you worried about the gun?"

"Not really. Then he says that one night he was feeling bad and was fucked up on dope and went up to Forest Park, took a hatchet, and chopped his finger off and nailed it to a tree."

"Don't bullshit me, boss."

"It's true. It's no bullshit, and so I asked the guy why did he do it? And he told me it was 'payback, brother.' Atonement for what he had done when he was a soldier. And you know, Cody, that is a big part of any war. Trying to live after what you have done. I think deep down, it's against human nature to kill another man. Especially if you grow up in a religious society where life and creation are so important. Where bringing children into the world is so important. I once read an article about an Iraqi woman whose son was a suicide bomber and had just blown himself up. She said she was happy and only wished she had more sons to give. That disturbed me for a long time. It seemed inhuman. For our soldiers, killing is against God and society. It takes training to learn to do it without hesitating. And then decades to get over it, if ever."

Cody's face was somber. Mike can't tell if he's really feeling that way or is putting on the expected expression. "Did you ever do anything you regret?"

"Yeah. Bringing you on this trip," Mike deadpans, and Cody hesitates in his tracks. "Just kidding." Mike snorts. Another chopper passes over, this one landing on the helipad next to the hospital.

They walk around the back side of some more sandbagged tents and past the showers and latrines and the last of the tented areas, where a group of hard chargers are gathered around a DVD player set up on sandbags. They're laughing, joking, and passing around Listerine bottles filled with whiskey, each taking a hit. Mike walks slowly past, thinking of his youth, remembering nights at LZ Stud getting stoned, smoking pot in the rear. He remembers the shotgun they sometimes used to blow dope in your face. Getting so loaded off high-grade

Vietnamese grass or Thai stick that he felt like he was hallucinating. He could buy a party pack of kick-ass weed. They called it a ten-for-twelve—ten bucks for twelve tightly rolled joints, delivered in plastic sandwich bags. Open the bag and the smell alone could get you high.

Off in the shadows between tents, Nunez and Hop are toking on a hash pipe. Mike and Cody don't see them, but the air is full of the unmistakable, sweet smell. Mike remembers that he used to toke up with Jesse. They'd never do it out in the field, but whenever they came in off an op, they'd find someone who could score a party pack. Then they'd wait until dark, crawl inside their two-man hooch made from shelter halves, sit on the dirt floor, heads brushing against the plastic ceiling, light up, and be gone. Delivered from despair. Delivered from the rotten, stinking jungle. Removed in a minute from arms and legs, twisted, broken, and bloody. Ripples and rivers of it. Gone. Just like these young marines. Mike's thinking that was over thirty-five years ago.

"You smell that?" Mike asks.

"Dope," Cody says, looking back over his shoulder.

"I know what the hell it is. How are they getting it here?"

"Babes send smoke in deodorant sticks, anything really. Booze is usually in mouthwash bottles, and sometimes dudes can cop stuff from the hajis."

"You sound like an expert. Come on, let's sit down." They walk to a wooden picnic table set under a dim light, opposite a horseshoe pit. The sand is softer here than the asphalt or packed-sand pathways that run all through the base. Mike eases to the bench. Cody sits across from him.

"Boss, they tell me stuff they won't tell you because you're, well, you know, like from the Stone Age to them. No offense."

"All right." Mike pauses, taking in the moment. "I remember what it is to be young and dumb and full of cum," Mike says and quickly wishes he hadn't. Cody's face shifts oddly in the light, and he looks uncomfortable. "All I'm saying is that I did all that back then, and that's what kids do when faced with death. Then they do it after the war to ease the pain. I used to smoke pot, but I'd end up eating everything." Mike squeezes out of the conversation and moves into a new topic. "Tell me about your family. When did they get out of Vietnam?"

"In '74—everything was nutso. I heard the stor y so many times from my mother and uncle that I feel like I was there." Cody takes out a cigarette, lights it clumsily.

"Those will kill you," Mike says. "Helped kill my father."

Cody ignores the comment and fires up, the lighter's flame dancing in the dark. "We lived near Nha Trang. Have you heard of it?"

"Yes. North of Saigon on the China Sea."

"Exactly. My mother, father, two sisters, an uncle, aunt, and another family from our village escaped in the middle of the night. They carried a few clothes, food, and possessions. They walked five miles, carrying my sisters, sneaking past guards and informers, through an old rubber plantation with land mines. My father had practiced the route many times but never in the dark."

Mike watches the glow from Cody's cigarette and listens to his words carefully, imagining the villages and the danger he once walked in.

"When they came to the cove, my family hid in the water for three hours, because the captain of the boat was afraid to come in to shore. It was the end of the monsoon season, but rain began to fall. My sisters would cry, and sometimes my mother would hold their mouths, with the water splashing above their waist. My father finally took a sampan that was tied next to a dock out to the Chinese junker, but the captain would not come in. The rain and wind were bad. He made several trips out to the boat."

"That was tough. Your father had courage. Your whole family did."

"Yeah. I know. He was a little man, my mother said, but he had the heart of a tiger. So the boat left a couple of hours before dawn. They glided by the early fishing boats that could have sounded an alarm to the Viet Cong or naval patrol boats, but they didn't." Cody scratches at a leg bitten by fleas and feels a scab break and a trickle of blood run down to his ankle. "Fuckin' fleas."

"I want you to finish, but we should be headed back to the tent. Here, use some of my bug spray." Mike pulls the bug spray, stuck in his sock, and hands the small squeeze bottle to Cody, who quickly sprays his arms and hands and wipes it on his face and then hands it back. They leave the soft sand of the horseshoe pit and hit the path, winding through the base.

Cody stops and lights another smoke and snaps the silver lighter shut. "The voyage was very bad. I won't freak you out."

"I don't think you need to worry about that," Mike says, and suddenly he has a deeper appreciation of Cody. Like all the wounded veterans he's ever met. They have a commonality; that's what Mike thinks. A relationship of pain.

"What I mean is, well...I won't go into all the gory details. But here's some of what I know. After they left the harbor, the rains got bad that night. Rain and wind and my mother and the girls cried out. They were almost howling. The rain stopped, and the engine worked, and they were happy for a day. Then the engine started smoking and blowing oil and finally stopped. All they had were the sails in this beat-up, piece-of-crap junker. Boss, it wasn't more than twenty-five foot max." Cody is working into a state of astonishment when suddenly there are one-two-three loud explosions somewhere in the camp, followed by sirens and a fury of activity as tents, billets, and trailers empty. Marines and cooks and civilian personnel pour out in the night, scrambling to bunkers, or stand looking in multiple directions, trying to get a sense of what is happening and where. People are running into each other and falling.

"Let's go, boss," Cody screeches, but Mike grabs Cody by the arm.

"Calm down. It sounds like rockets, and they're impacting no closer than five, six hundred meters away."

"Shit, boss, what should we do?"

"Just be calm. We'll wait here till things slow down and let the men do their jobs. Then we can hoof over there and see what's happened."

Mike is reassuring and his heart rate has barely risen. He lets go of Cody's arm and Cody says, "Thanks. You're right."

They walk through the tents and trailers while choppers roar overhead, and they approach the position where Nunez and Hop were getting loaded. The place is empty now. Huey gunships are working off in the distance, firing lines of red tracers and using spotlights to identify targets, followed by a stream of cannon fire. It's a great fireworks show, and when the choppers fire rockets, marines stand outside their tents or trailers, cheering.

Suddenly a huge explosion shakes the earth. The vibration carries to Mike and Cody, like an earthquake tremor. Mike slips. Cody wobbles.

"Bunker busters," Mike says, moving over to a large box air conditioner that cools the mess hall. He sits down again. "If the explosion doesn't kill you, the concussion will." The large charge brought more marines out onto the street.

Guys with towels wrapped around their waist or in briefs and flip-flops gawk at the light show and talk about the "heavy duty shit my boys are laying down."

"Those ragheads are hurtin' for certain," one marine tells another.

"How'd you like some of that ass kickin'?" says another.

"Boss, here comes Lieutenant Jarvis," says Cody.

Jarvis steps into the lights near the tents and sandbags. He's moving quickly down the road, wearing body armor but no helmet. Mike rises from the air conditioner and walks to the middle of the path. Cody hangs at his side.

"If y'all with First Platoon, get back to your tents or trailers and jock up," Jarvis tells the guys milling around. "This ain't no fireworks show. We got some heavy contact going, and we're going full alert." As he speaks, the siren sounds. "We may take some more incoming. You men in First Platoon, I want you to spread out along the perimeter at your day positions. Do it. Now." Assholes and elbows start flying.

"Sir," Jarvis says to Mike. "You two get back to your tent and put on your body armor and wait till you hear an all clear. They're a long way away, but shit happens."

"Who's taking fire?" Mike asks.

"We've got Third Platoon at firebase Tiger, west of Fallujah. They're patrolling off the base and ran into some heavy contact. Shitheads already shot a Black Hawk down. That's about all I know for sure."

The firing in the distance is intense. Streams of tracers fire back and forth on the ground, and choppers keep working hard from the air. Explosions and faint flashes of light bleed through the night.

"Did you say the third?" Mike asks.

"Yes, sir, I did."

Mike is shaken and hurries to stand up on a stable stretch of sandbags looking for a better view of the fight.

"Jesus! That's my son!" Mike says, stumbling off the bags.

"Yes, sir. I know it is."

Mike is unnerved, and Cody climbs to the top of the bags searching the horizon. Fear is inside of Mike in a way he has not experienced since he was a soldier. Worse even. It's his boy out there.

"Lieutenant, I need to get out there. I gotta get out there. It's my son."

"Get serious. That's not possible."

"It's my son, and I didn't come seven thousand miles to sit on my ass and watch my son get killed."

Jarvis grinds his teeth and glares at Mike, about ready to explode. Mike can see it on his face in the streetlight and shadows, and he can feel it just as clearly as he can feel danger. *Fuck Jarvis,* Mike thinks. *I'm going to get out there somehow. Go with a support team. Yes. That's what I'll do.*

Nunez and Hop walk up, wondering about the commotion.

"Sir, I don't have time for this shit. Don't be stupid. You put yourself in this box. You could jeopardize the entire platoon. You think we're going to send you out there so you can babysit? Is that what you think?"

"Fuck this. I'll talk to the top."

Jarvis growls and bangs a finger into Mike's chest. Mike doesn't move; his fists are clenched, and he's not impressed. "As far as you're concerned, if anyone knew you wanted to hang your son, you'd still be home."

"This is bullshit!" Cody jumps in and stands by Mike's side. "This is a story. Our job. Other crews get outside the lines."

"Y'all might think this is bullshit, but in a couple of days they're going to chopper your ass right outta here. Now get back to your tent! That's an order!"

Jarvis jogs off, disappearing around a sandbagged billet. Mike can hear him shouting orders and hears boots slapping against the asphalt road. Off somewhere in the dark, the sky is lit with chopper lights flashing and streams of red lights from miniguns banging. The sound is like a giant stuttering, but the noise does not do justice to the damage tens of thousands of rounds can do to buildings, vehicles, and humans.

Mike walks back toward his tent, dejected, feeling like a moron. Cody flashes by with a "Hey boss" and runs ahead of him. By the time Mike pushes through the flaps in his tent, it's empty. Cody and his other cameras are gone. Mike puts on his body armor, takes some pills, and then opens his laptop. The screen lights up with a montage of photos of Mick, standing in his catcher's gear, holding his face mask, streaks of black under each eye. He's smiling, and his face looks so perfect; his teeth are so white. He is like an angel to Mike.

There's a graduation shot with his boy in robes, smiling, standing next to Cait, Griff, and Little B. And more photos of Mick and Madie taken the weekend the family went camping near Crater Lake. And the trout Claire caught. Mike continues to punish himself by revisiting the past, reminding himself that there is another world out there. A place that is relatively safe and full of love, where his son doesn't have to worry about getting shot in the head or rolling over an IED and coming home disabled, captive to whatever new kind of leg or arm they've just created. Mike helped build that safe environment for Mick, and yet, for the first time, he feels responsible for Mick being here. Deep in his soul, he acknowledges bringing the war home and letting it become such a negative part of his family's life. How the things he used to do could only trouble his family. Everything from insisting he keep his back to the wall whenever he sat with them in a room to make sure no one could sneak up on him to patrolling the house at night, checking the doors. From no fireworks or BB guns to making sure that whenever he took the kids to school he took a different route to avoid ambush. He lived in fear for their lives. And he wrote books and columns about war and talked about it as if it was the single most important thing in the world. And when he did bring home friends, they were always wounded vets like Louie, with no teeth and three fingers blown off, or Ron, with one leg, or Chuck, who was blind and spoke through a hole in his throat. It was always war. The focus of his life.

A siren sounds all clear, and it is quiet. Mike is alone and feels like he's breaking apart. What has he done? What has he done to his family? The troops are moving through the area, back to their jobs and routines. A bell sounds for chow time, and Mike understands what pain he has created. He buries his face in his hands. He can't save Mick or himself. He has no power or control, and in that realization, he sobs quietly.

At daylight, a small convoy made up of Humvees and Cougars from Mick's platoon passes through a run of concrete blast walls and pulls up to the razor wire gates of Camp Bravo. They have returned for rest and a rotation from firebase

Tiger. Marines from the heavily fortified towers and sandbagged bunkers on each side of the gate change guards as the gates swing open. Men drag up and down the tower and clamor in and out of bunkers.

"'Bout time, brother man," a marine says, stepping out from a bunker to his buddy going in. "'Bout mothertruckin' time."

"Let's grab some chow and rack out," says another marine to his buddy, who is coming off guard duty.

The vehicles unload in a drop-off zone, which is used as a helipad most of the time. It is a simple slab of asphalt, poured in place and marked with a white circle. Some anonymous joker filled in the circle with a white peace sign. Then a couple weeks later, the base commander thought visuals from the air would be good for morale, so he had a gold marine corps emblem painted on another helipad.

Marines crawl out of their dusty, sand-soaked trucks and grab their weapons and packs and begin the short hump to the Kilo-area tents. There they will lick their wounds and kick back for a while. They are haggard—clothes torn, faces dirty—but walking tall. Other marines or civilian workers greet them with awe because they know what these warriors have been through. Wounded marines have battle dressings on their hands, arms, legs, and heads. They are exhausted. Up all night fighting, only just now have they let down their guard and given in to the weariness they feel. They are too tired to cry about what they have seen...or they are just numb to it all.

Lieutenant Bittner is in front, followed by Corporal Thomas, with a scatter of other marines in tow. Cody is busy snapping pictures, close-ups of dirty boots and filthy faces, hands wrapped with battle dressings made from crudely ripped cloth. Two of the wounded are carried on litters. Three are in body bags. Mike watches the patrol wind past him. He prays that Mick is OK. And he searches for his face.

Then Mike sees his son. Mick is carrying a litter with one arm and an M240 machine gun slung over his other shoulder. He looks so powerful and changed, Mike thinks. *My son! My boy! Mick!* He's a man now, his tired face brown with dirt and stubble. He's got a .45 strapped across his chest. His head is up, but he looks sad. The flash in Mick's eyes has faded. Mike knows his boy made it through hell last night. That what he experienced is beyond the realm of normal human experience. And he understands whatever he saw or felt or did will be inside of him for his lifetime. *And there's Griff! Behind him on the same side of the litter.* They're carrying a boy whose leg looks mangled, his arm hooked up to an IV.

One leg of Mick's fatigues is torn, and a dirty hunk of white gauze is wrapped around his thigh. The flat, dark color of blood has soaked and dried through, but he is not limping. Mike watches his every move as fresh marines come to carry the litters of dead and wounded. Ambulances and marines who have been standing by scoop up the damaged troops and carry the fatalities away as another group of vehicles loaded with clean marines passes out beyond the wire.

Mike can no longer control his emotions and shouts, "Mick! Mick!" He catches his son's attention. Mick is startled, stops, tilts his head to the side, and stares. He recognizes Mike, but doesn't. Then a big white smile blooms from his dirty face.

"Dad? Dad? Is that you?" And they both tumble toward each other. Mick sets his weapon down and looks at Mike as if he is in a dream, and then he hugs him, and for a moment, they are wrapped in each other's arms, and Mike is the happiest he has ever been in his life. He can feel the broadness of Mick's back and the strength in his body, and as he kisses his neck, he remembers the texture of his son's skin and how they used to hug when Mick was young. He is overwhelmed with relief, and Cody captures the moment from every possible angle.

"Damn!" Griff shouts excitedly. "Mr. K!"

Mike pushes away from Mick's embrace, still holding his arm, and looks at him. "You're as big as a damn horse!"

That mutual recognition and jubilation has reached its crescendo, and the light in Mick's eyes and the smile on his worn face fades. His look of joy turns to confusion. He looks hard at his dad.

"What are you doing here?" His body is stiff, his jaw tight.

"I'm on assignment."

"No, really. What the hell are you doing here?" Griff and Cody look at each other like witnesses at a head-on collision.

Mike is searching for the truth and skips it and grasps at another possible reason. "I'm with the paper. I'm covering the war. Glen sent me."

"You're full of shit, Dad! They wouldn't send you over here. You can barely walk."

"Son——" But before Mike can gather his excuses, Mick's temper flares.

"Don't give me that crap! You thought you could come over here and watch me like it was some freaking game? Dad, what were you thinking?"

Mick's body stiffens, his chin lifts, his jaw tightens, and veins in his neck start to expand. His energy is big and threatening, and Mike is drowning in guilt. He's lost his resolve. All he has are pitiful explanations that dissipate in the air.

"I wanted to come, Son. This is my last shot at covering a war, and I thought I could see you and maybe——"

"Get fucking real. I've killed people." Mick starts to turn away and then snaps back. "And people are trying to fucking kill me!" His face is tight and filled with the kind of rage a parent might have for a child who picked up a loaded gun. He shakes his head and then calms down; he looks embarrassed and then very, very sad. "You need to get out of here, Dad. Go home. Take care of Mom. Come on, Griff." Mick picks up his gun, turns his back on Mike, and walks away. He takes a half-dozen steps, hesitates, and hangs his head for a moment as though he is considering something, and then he once again turns to Mike.

"You can't even walk a hundred yards without your knee blowing up. Jesus, Dad." Mick and Griff trudge off, up past the tents, and turn toward the mess hall.

Mike and Cody are left standing by themselves in the morning light. The base is busting ass. Choppers lift supplies and troops and F-15s equipped with 20mm cannons, and five-hundred-pound bombs roar overhead. The Burger King is open, turning out breakfast burritos, and a new group of Canadian troops and their convoy, full of supplies, leaves Camp Bravo. Bunkers and other small construction projects are being built as tanks, trucks, and marines charge by in a fury of activity. Mike's huge moment is lost in a camp that never stops.

"I'm hungry," Cody says. "Gonna grab something to eat and see if July is around."

Mike looks at Cody's skinny, tattooed arms and messed-up haircut and says, "Say hello to her for me."

———— ⊗∞∞ ————

Mick and Griff chow down at the Burger King, crash for a couple hours, shower, and then come back to their tent and flop on their bunks. Griff's reading a little magazine contraband, licking the foldout, and feeling himself get hard. Mick lies in the bunk below, thinking about the firefight, reviewing it as if it's a DVD that he can pause, reverse, or fast-forward. His old man said something about remembering. "Remembering what happened will be important someday. Focus on what you see and what's surrounding you. Then step out of it and memorize it. All of it. The color of the day, the sounds, and the fury. Someday, when you need to remember that day, it will be there for you." How could he forget? Mick stares up at the bottom of Griff's bunk. He stares and watches the movie roll in his mind.

The RPGs sliced through the darkness and hit east of Mick's perimeter, fifty meters from his position. Small-arms fire came by and the thundering noise of twenty marines returning fire. Our tracers snapping, flares popping, and enemy rockets and mortars exploding. He would remember it, all right. Everything seemed to break apart. There's no logical progression in most battles, he's thinking, just reactions. Haji unleashes some heavy shit on us, and we beat their asses down, bringing hell on them. If that doesn't work, we bring on the choppers and machine guns and rockets to blow their shit away. What's left? Wounded moaning and the broken dead, lying quietly on the battlefield. Mick's thoughts jump to the donkey and Boner's blood and the CIA agent flipping out. That was madness. It was daylight, and he could see it and understand it even as he was being pulled into the horror of it all. Last night was something different. He was getting used to it. Other senses kicked in. His hearing was acute and the hypervigilance soared, like on the first night raid, his heart beating in his neck. Seems like years ago. The moments of not knowing. In the firefight last night, he wasn't squeezed by fear, puckered up worrying he'd get shot; he was enjoying it. Bringing it down on those raghead motherfuckers. He smiles. Yeah. This is for Boner. Mick could see it all so clearly—firing his gun, feeling the power and feeling the recoil.

Suddenly his thoughts do another spin, and he's lying naked on top of Cait. He's in her. Safe. He can feel the perfect roundness and the soft tissue of his girl. She was his first and only. The virgin boy and the breasts he touched and the look in her eyes when they first joined. She welcomed him with trust and fear and a little tear. When they were complete, he was frightened, tying his tennis shoes, his hands shaking.

"Hey, douchebag," Griff says, rolling his head down under the side of his bunk. "Let's get lit."

Mick rolls out of his bunk and his bare feet slap the wooden floor. It's late and dark outside, and he looks at his luminescent watch glowing. He slips on a new pair of green socks, compliments of Marine Moms, and sees his mother in the kitchen as he pulls on his boots.

"Come on, son," Griff complains. "I want to get fired up and get something to eat. I'm starved."

The boys hop out together, carrying rifles and bottles of water into a cool night, maybe eighty-five degrees. Half moon rising. There's activity up and down the lines and a couple of parties going on out at the trailers, where it's safe from everything but rockets and mortars. This is where the more seasoned marines hang out. There are a couple of tables set up outside, and someone's got a TV hooked up, working a Nintendo, taking turns bashing each other's heads in with animated boxing. Loud laughter and bottles of mouthwash are passed back and forth. Mick sees a guy through the open door of a trailer with his shirt off. The marine is passing a bottle of Johnny Walker Red to another dude who looks shitfaced. Griff exchanges a few words with a drunken dude about where he's from and finds out he's a short-timer from Detroit. "And I sure as hell ain't coming back to this rat hole," the guy says.

They move on around another corner of the road, pass a line of shitters where the smell throbs the nostrils, and they jog a bit down wind. They stop beside a half-finished, sandbagged bunker protected by a concrete blast wall. Nobody is in sight, so they hop on top of the three-foot-high roof and look out at a quiet sky. Griff pulls out a plastic sandwich bag holding a few rolling papers and a few pinches of buds and shake. He opens the bag and inhales the aroma.

"Smell this, Mickr. This'll punch your lights out."

Mick takes the bag and lifts it to his nose. The smell is strong and sweet. He likes the smell of pot now and likes to get high after a mission. But never in the field. It helps him sleep when he's still jacked up on adrenaline. Won't smoke when he gets home because he's going to be a dad. That thought spins around. He sees himself holding his baby boy. Then there's sports and camping. That's what they'll do when he gets home. Take Cait and his son camping. Like the old man almost never did.

Griff grabs the bag and starts rolling a fat one, thick and tight, and then pulls out his lighter and says, "Fire in the hole." He lights up, takes a huge hit, deep into his lungs, and holds it like he's sitting under water. Finally, his puffed up cheeks explode out the smoke in a loud *phew,* and his mind is dancing.

"Here, Mickster." He passes the joint to Mick. Mick blows on the tip until there is a bright-orange glow and touches it to his lips and inhales.

"Son," Griff says as Mick takes a hit and holds it. "That is some baaaad shit!" Both boys giggle for a minute.

"Got this shit from Gramps over in Second Platoon," Griff says. "You know that old fart that's like a hundred years old? Got busted from gunny to sonny. Fucking PFC. So he cops for Hop and a couple other brothers."

Mick's brain started out clear; he was thinking, feeling the slight breeze, and noticing the moon drifting. Now his head is full of sausage, and the stars look like they're exploding. He is losing his balance sitting cross-legged on the swaying bunker.

"What is this shit?" Mick asks, amazed and suspicious. "What the fuck is that, bro?" He starts laughing, which triggers Griff, and then Griff teeters back too far and tumbles off the bunker and lands on his back in a pile of sand.

"Whoa, dude." Mick looks over the edge of the bunker. He reaches down to give Griff a lift up. "You're a nut case. Better put that shit away."

Griff makes it back on the sandbags, messes clumsily with his pot, puts the rest of the dead joint in the bag, and then stuffs it away. They talk about home and baseball, and how maybe when they get back, they can play for the marine corps team. The one that travels.

"Yesssss," Griff says. "That would be way cool. Maybe we could end up in Hawaii or some shit."

"That would be so great. I miss baseball," Mick says. "I miss the feel of the bat and the sound it makes when you hit a big one. And I'm not talking about your cans of corn, pop-up to second." They both crack up.

"Bullshit. I hit three-twenty-three senior year."

"Remember, I punked you. I hit three-forty-one with four bombs." And he could see each ball flying out, dropping over the fence into the golf course. "Maybe I should have gone to school," Mick laments, thinking again about that last ball he jerked out of the park. He thinks about hitting with Jose and driving with the old man. He wants to be back at Grand Slam, rakin' 'em, Pops drinking Diet Cokes.

"I'll tell you this much, Mickster. You gotta admit, your old man has got some balls. I mean, what the hell, he came over here. My dad sure wouldn't."

"No one's dad would. That's the point. He's still trying to run my life. I wish he'd get a grip."

"Yeah, well, you still ought to see him. He's the only dad you got."

"Shut up. You sound like my mother. Let's kick it. I want some pizza."

A couple of days pass, with Mick dodging Mike and Mike trying to track him down. Cody hooks up with Lieutenant Debby July, shooting baskets and having lunch at Pizza Hut. The next night, he bangs her inside the back of an empty Bradley, both of them sweating up a storm. He's so into her, and she's not just lying down for anyone; he means something. This could take, he tells Mike over dinner. Griff, meanwhile, has got a bad case of jock rot and heat rash and is hungover two days in a row.

Chapter 36

It's another scorcher, sun high in the sky, choppers choppin', and F-15s barreling through the blue, doing half-rolls and trailing white streamers. Mike is sitting under a green-and-white beach umbrella that a reporter from the *New Yorker* magazine gave him. He's working on his laptop near the tents on the same card table he's used before, sitting on a folding chair. He just got off the phone with a pissed-off Glen, who says some guy with the Pentagon called and wants Mike to get the hell out of Iraq. *Screw it,* Mike thinks. *I'll leave when I'm done or after I see my son.* His table is set on the sand next to the road and gives him a good look at the perimeter with its armored vehicles, blast walls, and bunkers. If he were standing on a twenty-foot ladder, he could look out over the perimeter and see the outline of Fallujah twenty miles away.

Mike starts to work on a story about Cody for another column, but his mind is wandering. He thinks his arm is good, and he could still play catch if there were a couple gloves around. "If I had a baseball, I bet I could one hop that Bradley out there," he mumbles to himself, looking out across the sand and blacktop. It's 150 feet tops, he figures. Then he thinks about baseball back when Mick was a little guy and the first time Mick played T-Ball. Mick was seven, Mike was coaching, and Mick played shortstop. His boy loved the game so much back then. Mike digs around in his mind, trying to figure out a way to make up with his son. Let him know he made a mistake. What a fool.

Not ten minutes later, Mick and Griff appear, wearing shades and carrying rifles, with Corporal Thomas in tow. They look strong in their tight, green T-shirts. Their camouflaged trousers are clean and tucked neatly into their worn, tan boots. Their arms and faces are tan and taut. Mike notices that Mick's arms are huge, and his hands look thick. He's a man, and Mike is so proud. For a moment, the fear of losing his son is gone.

The boys duck under the umbrella around the table and Mike cracks a smile. "Sit down, men. Sit down." There's only one other folding chair, but they make do with a stack of empty ammo boxes that are next to a trailer. Mick slips his glasses over his head so they are hanging upside down on the back of his neck as he and the others sit down. When he does this, Mike notices a small silver cross hanging around his neck and is touched: *my son believes in God, even in this rat hole, where, every day, men do the unspeakable to each other.*

"Mick, we don't need to talk about this if you don't want to, but I was worried the other night when you guys were getting hit. I thank God you guys are OK."

"Forget it, Pops. We're good. And we kicked haji's ass bad. We had eleven confirms and blood trails all over the place. But that's not why I'm here. I'm just going to say this: buy me an iPod, go home, and I'll forget you trying to babysit me." Mick lets out an *Ooh Rah* and Griff and Thomas guffaw out loud and bump knuckles.

"Well, yeah, sure...I meant no harm, Mick."

"OK. It's a done deal, Pops." He spins Mike's laptop in front of him, saves the writing on the screen, brings up Walmart, and starts his order. This happens so quickly that Mike is way behind in reaching for his wallet, for his credit card, and offering it up.

"Done," Mick says. "You got that card?"

Mike fishes past business cards and snapshots of Claire, Madie, and Mick before he finds his Visa. He hands it to Mick, whose mouth has risen to a wonderful smile. He's not the hardened marine Mike imagines him to be—he's just another teenage boy spending his old man's dough.

"Thanks, Dad. I'm going to e-mail Cait, if that's cool, and Mom?" Mike nods his approval.

"Tell her to let my parents know I miss them and everything over here blows big time," Griff orders, his shades still dropped over his eyes.

"Look at that bastard," Corporal Thomas says, standing up and pointing at a five-inch tan-colored scorpion crawling through the sand a few feet away. The scorpion's pincers are open, and the tail is cocked over his backside, almost touching its head.

"Let me kill 'em," Griff says, standing up.

"Bite me," Thomas says. "I used to kill these little guys in Texas. This time I'm going to catch that little shit and fight him over at battalion. We got to be careful. You know, sometimes if you corner them, they commit suicide and sting themselves to death."

"Good and no collateral damage," Mike deadpans.

"*Ooh Rah!*" Mick shouts, and they clamor around, looking for something to put their prize in. They take an empty water bottle and cut off the top with Griff's scabbard, and Thomas scoops him up. Then they take another plastic bottle, cut off the bottom, and place it on top of the bottle, like a cap, so the scorpion can't get out.

"One of those stings you, it'll knock your dick stiff," Griff chips in, but no one hears him.

Mick pounds away on the computer while Cody gathers more shots of their group. Griff and Corporal Thomas are enraptured with their new specimen. Mike sits back, getting a large charge out of seeing his son happy, when suddenly Lieutenant Jarvis walks up, a scowl on his face. The boys tone down their enthusiasm, and Mick stops finger-punching the keyboard.

Mike looks up, "Hey, Lieutenant. Want to join us?"

Jarvis looks stiff and resolute, as though he might be getting ready to demote someone. There's no passion on his face, nor in his voice, as he says to Mike, "I hate to break up your party, but Captain O'Callahan says to pack your shit. There's a chopper on the way, and y'all are going home."

Mike's staggered. "What?" Cody's mouth is open.

"You heard me, sir. You and Cody are history."

Mike can't believe this is happening. He blew past being shocked, and now he's really fired up—face red, teeth clenched, adrenaline surging. He's up out of his chair, barking.

"Lieutenant, don't give me this bullshit. We didn't come halfway around the world to be intimidated by some short-shit captain with a hair up his ass. We've got all our clearances and approvals. If we're pissing someone off, let me know, and we'll straighten it out, man to man."

"You can buck as much as ya want, but this is it. Trying to cover your son's unit is not only a loss of perspective, sir, but dangerous to him and his fellow marines. You're gone. What about this don't you understand?"

"I want to talk to the battalion commander. We can move to another unit if safety is the issue. This is not right."

"Tough shit. I'm fed up with this. These orders are from the top of the chain. They want y'all out of here. At 1700, be down at the pad, or I'll be back, and it won't be pretty."

Jarvis walks off, and Mike is momentarily speechless. The lieutenant's words about being a danger to his son might be true, and the realization makes him sick inside. But no one has told him what to do in thirty years, and that hammers his ego.

"What a bunch of crap," Cody moans, kicking up a puff of sand. "Shit, fuck, son of a bitch!"

Mick raises from his ammo box, ducks under the umbrella, and puts an arm around Mike's shoulder. He has a smile on his face, like he's thinking, *I told you so,* and then he shakes his head. "Like LT says, you're history, Pops. We're going to eat and take care of some stuff and I'll see you in a couple hours or so and help you carry your gear."

Mike and Cody drag themselves to the tent, not speaking. They flop on their racks, complaining back and forth to each other. The time moves quickly. After a shower, Cody begins loading up his cameras, computers, and satellite dish. Mike's got on a black Hawaiian shirt as he angrily stuffs his pack. He could get tough, throw a fit, and try to reach Glen or the lousy state senator or two he knows, but that would only embarrass Mick further.

Cody packs each lens and camera carefully. "This is shit," Cody mumbles. "Pure horseshit. I gotta talk to July." He leaves one digital camera hanging from his neck in a carrying case. An hour later, Mick and Griff show up in body armor and helmets, with goggles on top and their weapons slung over their shoulders.

Mike looks up and sees that Mick's carrying an M14. His front pockets are bulging with magazines. "What's up with the fourteen? I used to tote one of those babies."

"I didn't know they had those in the Civil War, Pops."

Mike smiles.

"Seriously, I used to carry the SAW, but it's a piece of crap. Kept jamming, and I got rid of it. Now, I carry the fourteen when I'm at a base like Bravo and the M-two-forty when I'm out in the field."

"It's a great weapon, Son."

"The fourteen was back in the day, but it's making a comeback. You like my scope and light?" Mick holds it out with a straight arm, and Mike takes it in his hands. It feels good in his hands, heavier than he remembers. But he likes the smooth stock, and it looks and feels substantial.

"You can damn near use it as a shovel," Mick says. "And it'll still fire all night long."

"I know. I carried one before you were even a thought in my mind."

"And the seven-sixty-two rounds tear it up. Better than Griff's peashooter."

"I like the M-four. It's a good weapon, as far as I'm concerned." Griff snorts. "If you keep it clean, it won't jam. Besides, it's light, and with the rails, I can put laser lights on it and a grenade launcher. I'm not a big-ass ox like your son here, carrying this heavy load," Griff adds, touching the stock of Mick's 14.

The whole conversation feels awkward and out of place, as if they're trying to fill in the gaps between moments of sadness. The suddenness of the orders to leave is numbing. Mike feels comfortable in a war zone, now that he can keep track of Mick and doesn't want to go. He lets out a big sigh. As he looks at Mick with awe and concern, he knows he should leave. This is my boy. My beautiful son that I love so much. He is a man now. He doesn't need me hanging on like a broken-down old fool. What was I thinking?

Mike composes himself and, like everyone else, pulls a couple bottles of water out of an ice chest and stuffs it in a pocket of his body armor.

Mike moves slowly as he finishes packing his gear, as if he's trying to still figure out a way to stay. But it's no use. They've got him by the short hairs, and maybe it's better this way.

"We'll get most of this gear, Pops."

"Mick, I wrote a note for Lieutenant July, because I didn't get to see her. Can you give it to her for me?" Cody asks.

"I'll give it to her," Griff says, excitedly reaching for the note.

"I bet you would," smacks Cody, brushing Griff's hand away. "I'll just leave it with Mick."

The boys snicker, pick up some of Mike and Cody's gear, and carry it toward the landing pad marked with a peace sign. The sky is the color of concrete and coal. Clouds shift, and a light mist begins to fall.

It's a short hump past the shitters and showers and down the road to the LZ. A Huey is just leaving the pad, and in the aftermath, dust floats in the air. Pallets of bottled water and boxes of latte machines and containers of espresso beans sit next to the pad.

"Look at this stuff," Griff says, snapping a grin. "Must be going out or just got in. I'd like one of these coffee makers. We could put it in the tent."

"Forget about it. It's not worth getting busted," Mick says. "So, Pops, Griff and I are going to hop over to Baghdad Airport with you and check out the PX they got going."

Mike is pleased but concerned. "Did you clear it with Jarvis?"

"Nah. We'll be in and out. He'll never know."

"Who the hell is running this war?"

"No one, Pops." And the answer brings a perplexed look to Mike's face.

"Glad to see nothing's changed. Most of those lifers have their heads way up their asses."

"You're taking it easy on 'em," Cody says. "I'm still furious. This was my shot. Those cocksucker."

"You developed quite a vocabulary on this trip," Mike says. "But don't worry—this conflict will last for years. The Sunnis and Shias and Kurds have been fighting for centuries, ever since Mohammed died. Hell, you can always come back. And then there's Afghanistan. The Taliban will be back there, brutalizing and killing women, blowing themselves up big time. Remember I said that."

The boys all listen to the mini lecture and take sips from their bottles.

The chopper approaches, dark green against the beat-up sky. The mist has thickened and is mixed with fine sand. *Storm is coming,* Mike reasons. He and the others look up at the old Vietnam-era looking chopper, blades whapping and making a churning noise they can hear from far away.

What a wasted opportunity, Mike thinks. Maybe he could have written something about the hopelessness of it all. About how the cycle of tribal violence will never end. We can support whomever we want over here, but when we leave, nothing will really change. They'll still be killing each other. It's not worth the risk to my son. He watches the Huey come in and shakes his head in despair. If I could take his place, I would.

"Mick, I used to ride in those all the time. And not in the Civil War."

"They're still bad boys, Dad."

"Where's the other gunship? They're supposed to travel in pairs."

"Just like up-armored Humvees, they're working on it."

"That's not good. They should have brought one other gunship, for Christ's sake. Maybe there's another one coming."

"Nah. It's a quick trip, Pops. Fifteen minutes tops."

"All right," Mike says. Well, we better get out of here. We're burning light."

The chopper lands in a rush of noise, wind, and sand kicking. The power from the blades' downdraft blows dust and sand into everyone's eyes and mouths. Mick and Griff bring down their goggles, and Mike and Cody slap on theirs as well. As the chopper hovers and lands on its rails, everyone can see the name Debby in white letters painted on the side panel next to the pilot's door.

The crew chief and door gunner wear flight suits and helmets with dark visors. The door gunner is holding the butt plate of a mounted M240, its barrel pointed down outside the door, the nose of the barrel's flash suppressor covered with a sandwich bag, held on with a rubber band. The crew chief yells, "Get on board. There's a sandstorm on our ass."

As they toss their bags on board, Cody shouts at Mike over the turbine's loud churning, "I'll miss this shit, Captain."

"Debby? Cody's squeeze?" Mike asks anyone as they sit on webbed seats and strap in.

"Pilot," Mick says. "Second tour. She's the best. And she's hot. Ask Griff; he tried to hit on her too."

Griff smirks. Cody looks embarrassed but is quiet. Mike looks at him and realizes who she is.

As the chopper lifts, they all pull on something to cover their mouths. As Mike stares across the chopper at Mick's young face, he feels his gut tighten. His hands cramp and his fists clench. He can feel his mind shift, and there's nowhere to hide. In an instant, he's flashing back to the jungle. Chopper down. Flares drifting. Surrounded by enemy.

Mike's in the chopper with Padre. He hears the sound of a whistle, and as flares flash in the night, he looks into Padre's eyes. He can see he is almost gone. His arms are broken and his legs ruined. He knows he can't carry him. The NVA will surely torture him. He pulls his .45 out and hits the slide. *Oh God. What am I doing?* He reads the boy's haunting eyes. "Help me." Padre's words stop him. He looks at Padre's face, and it is filled with the deepest sorrow. He can't. He returns his gun to its holster. But he can't leave him alone to suffer. He reaches up and covers Padre's mouth and nose with his hand and then leans in with his body to quiet the shaking. Soon Padre rests, and Mike imagines his soul has passed into him. And the life time of guilt.

Mike grabs the radio, slings another rifle and strap over his shoulder, and slips out of the chopper. He finds Jesse in the tangle of plants and vegetation and pulls him up, puts an arm around his waist, and they hobble along, pushing deep into the jungle. After several minutes, they stop and sit. The flares are far behind them.

"I'll fix your arm," Mike whispers.

"With what, your dick?"

"Shut the fuck up."

Mike lays down his weapons and body armor and takes off his utility shirt and green tee. He tears the T-shirt into strips and feels Jesse's forearm. The broken bone has ripped through the skin. He pours water from his canteen on the wound and wipes away a handful of crusted blood, and then he wraps the arm tightly with the cloth. Jesse grimaces and bites through his lip but holds the pain.

"Pops, you with us?" Mick shouts from the seat opposite Mike.

"Yeah." He refocuses, feeling an intense sense of dread. Not from Padre but from the huge realization of what a fool he is. Of what a mistake he's made. What the fuck is he doing here? As with Padre or Claire and the glass, he feels great remorse and no way to fix it. He's helpless. He's on a chopper with his son, and it feels awful, and he can't do a goddamned thing about it.

"You're day-tripping, Pops," Mick shouts above the constant pounding of the rotors pushing through the wind and then nudges Cody with a shoulder. "He always does that." He leans into Cody, voice loud from beneath the hanky pulled across his mouth. "Since I was a kid, he'd fog out all the time. Dinner, TV, the middle of a conversation."

"I'm working it out," Mike yells over the noise, and the guys laugh.

Griff says, "That's funny as hell."

Dust and wind pick up and blow through the door. The door gunner has his helmet visor pulled down and a white handkerchief tied across his mouth and nose.

Visibility is dropping.

"Maaan," the gunner shouts, turning from the door to the cabin. "We're in a sandstorm."

Everyone tenses up, fearing a crash, while Mike is trying to stay out of a flashback. Stay in the moment with his son. The chopper shakes and shudders, drops and rises, and then the engines misfire as the chopper tries to race out of the storm. It loses altitude and passes over a small village and out toward the desert.

Three pickups full of sweat suited, black-clad insurgents are stopped in the middle of the desert, five miles from the village, riding out the blow. Several point their weapons at the chopper. Another jumps out of an open-bed pickup and runs with an RPG.

At the front of the Huey, Lieutenant Debby July fights the controls and speaks calmly into her headset as the copilot follows her directions.

"This is Bravo two. I'm reducing altitude. We just got hit by a shit storm. Correction. Sandstorm. That's confirmed. I'll try to make it."

The sandstorm increases in denseness and velocity as the crew chief shouts, "This is going to be a rough son of a bitch. Just passed over the village where you guys built that school. We may have to take it down."

"Maybe, but I kind of fuckin' doubt it," the gunner shouts. "Sand niggers all over the place."

Everyone in the back holds on hard to his seat, gripped with tension, sweating profusely, except for Mick. He's acting cool, trying to keep the men calm. "Cody, go on up front and talk to July," Mick jokes, shouting over the noise of blades whapping and sheets of sand slapping against the chopper's panels. "That should help her fly this piece of crap."

Sand is flying in the open door, but the door is stuck, and the gunner can't slide it closed. Cody turns and flips Mick off as Griff laughs out loud and shouts to Cody from across the chopper. "And get a blow job!" Suddenly, the Huey pitches, raked by AK-47 fire and is hit by an RPG. There's a huge explosion at the front of the chopper. The co-pilot is dead instantly. July catches a round through her hand and blood is everywhere. She turns the chopper with her knees and one hand, and shouts into her headset, "We're hit. Can't correct. Going down."

"God dammit, shit," the gunner shouts, and slips and falls as the chopper shakes.

The chopper banks hard, maintains altitude for a few minutes, shaking furiously. Engines shudder, and it falls slowly, spinning until it crashes on its sides. The rotors still turn, tearing and breaking in the sand. The force of the crash and breaking of the blades causes the Huey to bounce up a few feet in a broken mess and crash again, settling upright on its skids.

Mick is shaken. He feels like he has fallen down a couple of flights of stairs, but nothing's broken. He looks around. Mike, Griff, and Cody have survived, still strapped in their seats. The crew chief is a train wreck—neck fractured, both arms snapped, and a dislocated leg next to his head. His mouth is a mess of broken teeth and blood. His visor rests across his eyes, covered with a splash of blood. He is dead.

The sandstorm has erupted into a howling tidal wave with lightning strikes and rain. It roars two hundred feet in the air. It looks as if the end of the world has come as it engulfs the crash site. Damp sand roars through the open door.

Mick shouts, "Dad, are you all right?"

"My back," Mike says, sand slapping at his face and goggles.

"Griff? Cody?"

"I'm fucked up," Griff says, struggling to pull his goggles back on. "I tore up my shoulder."

"I think I broke some ribs," moans Cody, as blood pours from a gash sliced in his ear from an AK-47 round. He shifts his cockeyed goggles.

Mick stands and fights his way to the fallen crew chief, takes his hip holster and .45, straps it to his leg, and rips off his dog tags. "Where's the gunner?"

"Blown out," Mike yells, unstrapping himself from the seat. His back hurts like a son of a bitch, but the pain is masked some by all the medication he has ingested. He feels like he's been spun in a turbine. Four of his teeth are broken, and he's bitten off a chunk of his tongue. Blood is running out his mouth, and he has bitten a gash in his lower lip.

There is another small explosion in the front of the chopper and a flash of fire.

"Get out! Get out! Get out!" Mick shouts.

Mick and Griff turn toward the front of the chopper, toward the pilots, but are driven back by the flames.

Mike picks up his pack and pulls it on; a sharp pain shoots through his back.

Mick picks up his pack, slips a shoulder in a strap, and lifts the door gunner's M240 out of its sling.

"Cody," Mick orders. "Get the ammo box. Griff, grab my 14."

Cody picks up two boxes of ammo, and he and Mike pass through the side door and step down. Griff hesitates, his shoulder pounding with pain. "Motherfucker!" He grimaces. Then he steps out into the sand and is knocked back by a blast of sand, smashing against the chopper. Cody helps him up. Mick follows as flames rise in the chopper.

The fire lights up the area and is fanned by the wind. The sandstorm is suffocating. Visibility is near zero as the men push around to the nose of the chopper. The glass bubble is broken. Inside, the copilot has an AK-47 round to the head. He caught most of the RPG round and is nearly blown in half. July rises from her seat, clothes on fire and her back to the flames, frantically trying to work the door open. Mick and Griff rush the door but can't budge it. Mike struggles to them. He opens his pack and pulls out his gun and yells, "Step back," and fires three rounds into the door, breaking the lock. Mick rips the door open and pulls July out and rolls her to the ground to smother the fire. He quickly drags her away from the wreck. The others follow, fighting to stay erect in the wind.

Griff turns on the light mounted on the barrel of his M4. Cody helps Mick turn July onto her back and flips up her visor. Her eyes are closed as the Huey explodes in a ball of fire, sending jagged pieces of metal and doors in all directions. A piece of shrapnel lodges in the heel of Mick's boot. They dive to the ground, and Cody shields July from the blast, as a small piece of hot metal rips over his head, close enough to slice his skull.

The desert is lit, the fire intense, and the men are breathing hard. The storm makes it almost impossible to see or hear. Everything said is a shout. Mike pushes himself up from the sand, struggles toward July, and then drops to one knee and catches another shot of pain in his back. He reaches out and touches her neck and feels for a pulse. His fingers drag through charred flesh.

"She's alive," he says, matter-of-factly. When he pulls his hand from behind her neck, a piece of burned skin pulls off with it.

Mick takes off her helmet and visor, arches her chin up to clear the passageway, wipes sand from her mouth, and begins mouth-to-mouth resuscitation. He pinches her nose closed and breathes into her mouth, forcing air into her lungs, again and again. Cody looks panicked. Finally, she gasps and comes to.

Mike bends over and looks into her soft brown eyes. He flashes to Padre and back again.

"Debby," Cody cries, his face at once full of anguish and joy. A stream of blood runs down the back of his neck.

Griff sits in the sand along with the others. All of them have their goggles down as the wind and sand continue to beat them. Visibility is no more than forty feet, helped by the glow from the crash. Mick takes the .38 and extra magazines from July's shoulder holster, but he leaves the holster on her. He stuffs the weapon and magazines in his trouser side pockets.

For a long moment, nobody says anything. It's as though they all are looking for someone to take charge from here.

Mick shouts, "We're not going to leave her." He looks up at Mike, and in that moment, they are connected to their cores.

"We can't," Mike says.

"We got to get the fuck out of here," Mick commands. "The shitheads that shot us down will soon be hauling ass, trying to find us. This fire is their beacon. If we get back to the village, we can get shelter. If the shitheads come, we can make a stand until the Quick Reaction Force finds us." Mike is astonished at what a man his boy has become. "I can carry July," Mick shouts above the howl. "Wait." Mick looks toward the burning chopper and then runs over and unfastens a stretcher from above the side rail and brings it back.

"I've got medical supplies," Mike yells and slips off his pack.

"Perfect," Mick says. "Griff, how you hangin'?"

"About eight inches," Griff jokes, favoring his shoulder.

"That's so not funny," says Mick.

Mike tears through his pack, sand ripping at his face. Moans are now coming from July. That's good, he thinks. He grabs the oxycodone that he rarely uses because it hurts his gut, and afterward he can't shit for a week. He'll take one, but he'll give one to Griff and two to July.

Mike places the pills in July's mouth and gives her a touch of water as the wind wails and showers them. She chokes and coughs but keeps the pills down. Mick takes a battle dressing wrapped in plastic from her flight suit and bandages her hand. There is no way to treat the burns, which run up her right leg and arm to her shoulder and neck. He tightens her right boot around an ankle that looks busted.

Cody opens the stretcher. It is still warm to the touch but intact. "I got it!" Cody yells.

July is coming to and is in immense pain but alert enough to answer questions.

"Do you have your GPS?" Mick asks, kneeling on one knee next to her. She nods and lifts her arm and points to a side pocket, and Mick pulls out her Global Positioning System. It's far better than anything he's seen, but it's simple to use. It's the size of a sandwich. In about a minute, the screen pops up their location, a bird's eye view of where they are, the topography, and the storm they are swimming in. The village where Mick, Griff, and their company built a schoolhouse is identified and is the place they can rally to. The wind is still blowing hard and visibility is bad. With the light dying, soon they will be in darkness.

"Pops, can you walk awhile?" Mick shouts.

"I'm good."

"We can head back to the village and take shelter in the schoolhouse. They like us there."

"Yeah. Well, some of your friends want us dead," Mike says.

"Let's get the hell out of here. I'm on point with the 240. Pops, you carry the M-fourteen, but keep the chamber clear. And here's some magazines." Mick hands him four from his flak jacket. "You still know how to shoot this baby?"

"Don't ask."

They move out like a shot-up patrol with Mick on point, carrying the gun with a short belt. Mike is behind him with the 14, with Cody following, pulling July on the stretcher. Griff is a weak tail end Charlie, staggering with his rifle and a can of M240 ammo.

The wind and the sand and the rain continue to bear down on them as they plow through the storm. Everyone has goggles on and some type of cloth still covering their mouths, except Griff. He's now wearing a mask his mother sent him that's been folded in a trouser pocket. It's blue and cone-shaped, like the ones car painters wear when they're in a paint booth, spraying.

Mick stops, sand beating at his front, kneels, and sets the butt of his gun in the sand, balancing it against his body. The others stumble to a stop, and Cody lowers July to the sand. Mick pulls the GPS out of a front pocket in his body armor, punches it up, and thinks for a moment. He consults with Mike.

"Don't ask me," Mike shouts over the howling wind. "I can barely figure out my cell phone."

Mick places the GPS back in his flak jacket pocket, picks up his machine gun, stands, and points with an extended arm. "This way. We'll just get to the village and set in at the school. If we're lucky, the assholes won't find us before the reaction team does."

Mick pushes on, his crumbling squad following behind him. The faint glow of the chopper burns in the distance.

They march on, bent over, fighting the unrelenting sandstorm. The little light they have is nearly gone, and the village and schoolhouse are at least a thousand meters away. Mick looks over his shoulder at Mike and can barely see Griff. He's disoriented, he thinks, and then stumbles and falls to the sand. Mick has tripped on something he can't see. He stands up, cradling his gun, and kicks the sand and sees the door gunner's body. The others stop and then slowly gather near Mick.

"Oh, fuck," says Griff, the last one to reach them. "Goddamn. Well, what do we do now?"

Mick pulls out the GPS, notes the location, and then puts it back in his nut sack in his body armor, over the outline of a SAPI plate.

"I've got our position, and when we get out of this storm, someone will pick him up. Now we gotta move." Mick bends over, rips off the gunner's tags, takes two grenades from his vest, stuffs it all in a side pocket of his pack, and moves out, his squad following.

Mick seems to bore a hole through the storm as the winds have shifted. Mike struggles to catch up, and for an instant, Mick disappears in the storm, and Mike feels lost. A moment later, Mick is facing him and shouts, "Hold on to my shirt if you have to." He points his machine gun in the direction of Cody, who has disappeared, and flashes the light on his barrel twice. No one. He flashes it twice again. Nothing. One more time and finally Cody appears but without July and the stretcher. Griff, too, is missing.

"What the fuck? Where is she?" Mick demands vehemently.

"I can't carry her anymore. I fucking can't. I had to leave her."

"No, you don't!" shouts Mike, pulling down the covering from his mouth. "We're not leaving anyone."

"Listen up. The old man's right. Cody, hold my weapon and keep the barrel out of the fucking sand. Every minute, flash the light once. I'll find them and be back."

"Mick, hold on," Mike says. His broken teeth hurt, and his tongue is thick, and it's hard to talk. Mike hands Mick his rifle and pulls off his pack and sits down. He reaches inside and pulls out a set of night-vision goggles and gives them to Mick.

"Pops, you're the bomb. Take your rifle. Flash the light every couple minutes." Mick turns, and at fifty feet out, he disappears.

Sandstorm all around them, terrorists after them, and Mike isn't worried anymore. For the first time in his life, he isn't worried about his son, who has been swallowed up by the dark. They may be a messed up bunch now, and the bastards that shot them down will be coming, but sweet Jesus he feels good about his boy. Confident they'll get out of here, knowing their lives are in his son's hands. Mike smiles to himself as he flashes the light and Cody mutters, "I wasn't leaving her. I was getting help." He sits down next to Mike.

The storm is slowing, but Mick fails to reappear. Mike flashes the light. The wind has slowed. Another flash. The waiting and waiting. Another flash. And they are in total darkness. Flash.

The moments drag on, and Mike's fear begins to crawl inside his mind. Is his boy lost? Maybe he should try to find Mick? Have Cody flash. But soon, Mick reappears and can be seen pushing through the curtain of sand. Moments later, he is upon them, pulling the stretcher with July, Griff trudging behind, carrying both guns. The storm is slowing. The wind is easing. Mick gathers his squad close and looks at his GPS. "We can make it to the village, but we have to push hard. When it's easy for us to move, it's easy for the bad guys too. Cody, I need you to man up. You carry the two-forty, and I'll pull July. She's hanging in there. Pops, those meds helped. Griff's doing better."

"I'm a frickin' Fourth of Ju-ly firecracker, ready to blow," Griff blurts from under his mask.

"These storms end as fast as they begin, so let's bounce, but stay close—assholes to belly buttons until it clears," Mick orders. He is out front again, and the sand is fading fast, and Mick is cutting through the wind. Mike is drafting behind him as the brunt of the dying storm hits Mick first. The pain pill is still doing Mike good. The sharp, stabbing pain is replaced by an agonizing ache that he can endure. Behind Mike, Cody holds the M240 by the barrel, the stock resting on his shoulder. He, too, is hanging in there. Griff's shoulder is almost numb but moving better as the storm begins to lift.

Finally, the wind stops, the sky clears, and the moon rises. What remains of the storm is a thin cloud of dust.

As they close in on the village, Mick stops and motions them to drop to one knee. "We're five hundred meters out, and it's clearing, so we can spread it out some," he says. "With this moon, they can see us from miles away. They'll find the chopper and then be on us. So we need to make it to the village." He looks at July, whose face is battered but still holds the look of a pretty woman. "How ya doing?"

"I feel like a sack of shit and hurt like hell."

"That's good. Isn't that right, Pops?" Mick turns to Mike.

"That's right. Pain means you're still alive and being alive is the main event."

Cody bends down. July looks at him and says, "Thought you were going to leave me."

"No. I just couldn't carry you anymore and went for help."

"We have to really move this next few hundred meters," Mick commands. "July, I don't think you're busted up inside, so I'm going to pick you up on my shoulder and carry you. It's going to hurt. Are you cool with that?"

July agrees, her voice not more than a whisper.

"All right then. Pops, you got to stay up. Knee OK? Back?"

"I'm right behind you."

"Cody? Griff?"

"Kick it, dude," Griff says, and they bump fists.

Mick bends down and lifts Lieutenant July easily from the stretcher, arranges her in a fireman's carry over his shoulder. She moans as her burned flesh tears. Mick takes off, moving quickly, and soon there is distance between him and Mike and the others. At about one hundred meters out from the village, Mick drops to a knee, and lowers July gently to the sand. He is winded. The moon is full, with enough light to read a book. That's bad, he reasons. The village looks quiet. Mick turns and sees Mike limp toward him, gasping for breath. Mick is touched by Mike's struggle. He sees him as vulnerable for the first time in his life and feels a closeness to him he can't recall ever having felt before.

Cody and Griff ease up to Mike. Both look exhausted.

"Want me to carry your rifle, boss?" Cody asks.

"Nope," says Mike.

Griff rotates his bad shoulder and feels it grinding inside and clenches his jaw, fighting the pain. "You got another pill, Mr. K?" asks Griff. Mike digs through his pocket. He's out of oxy but finds some aspirin and hands Griff three, and then they all push on, reach Mick and July, and sit down on the moist sand.

Mike finds the aspirin again and offers July four, which she takes and chews, making a face as she swallows.

They rest under the moon at the edge of the desert, the outline of the village in front of them. Mick thinks about Cait and being a father and wonders for a moment what it will be like to hold his own son someday. And he thinks about Mike and courage, and how he must now take care of him. But there's no time to think. They have to move.

"Let's go," Mick whispers.

"I want to try and walk," July says. "I think I can."

"OK. Hard-core," Mick replies. Mick helps July to her feet, but she buckles.

"I can't. It feels like my ankle's broken."

Mick lifts her again, and the battered group moves cautiously toward the village. Mick has July and the M240. Only a strong man could carry both. Cody now follows Mick, carrying Mike's pack. Mike moves slowly with his M14, and Griff follows, occasionally turning back to see if they are alone.

Close to the village, a dog barks. Mick stops. They all drop to a knee. July is lowered to the ground. Mick motions Griff to come up.

"Let's check it out."

"I'll cover you," says Mike. Then he turns and offers Cody his pistol, but Cody pushes it away. Mike shakes his head, puts the pistol back in his armored vest, and then bends to the sand and lies prone. He lowers the bipod on the 14 and points his rifle toward the village, maybe fifty meters away. Through the scope, he can see the village clearly.

Mick and Griff edge toward the village. Mick's senses are acute, his body tingling. He can feel the shift of wind and smell the slit trenches full of shit coming from the village. He feels the heat increase and the sand shift beneath his feet and hears his footsteps as the sand packs firm, closer to the village. He glimpses a camel spider near his boot the size of his hand and thinks he can hear it scuttle along. His boots squeak as he shifts from his right foot to his left, and the sand lifts and slides. He can still sense July on his back and the heat of her breath on his neck and the smell of her burnt flesh. He stops and drops to a knee. Griff follows.

There is a small rock wall running alongside the village, facing them as they approach. Every hundred feet or so, there are gaps in the wall that lead to the dirt patios attached to each home. This is a small village with a few palm trees.

Each home has doors and glassless windows covered with shutters. The storm has taken its toll. Outside tables are turned over, chairs scattered, some flung by the wind and broken in pieces. Satellite dishes have been swept off rooftops and left hanging by crude wires or buried by the sand. Big drifts of sand line the walls.

Goats and dogs and baskets of chickens must have been brought inside, Mick thinks, as they close in on the stone wall. They can hear cackles and the shuffling of hooves and paws. But no voices.

Mike lies flat in the desert, his face covered with dirt and sand. A cool rush of wind brushes his cheek. He reaches up and scratches, fingers full of filth from an ear. Without a helmet, his hair is stiff and caked with remnants of the miserable storm. He strains to see through his scope where Mick and Griff are. Through the sight, he sees them steps away from the stone wall. He feels exhausted, run over, and old. His back hurts with sharp pain again, and his knee throbs. He tries to concentrate. His pain medication is wearing off, so he rolls to his side, pulls a bottle of aspirin from his trousers, chews four, and sips water from a bottle that was in the side pocket of his pack. Behind him, Cody is comforting July, her head in his lap. The only sound Mike hears is a breeze lifting puffs of sand. He notices Cody sitting up and is pissed.

"Lay flat, dumb shit."

He looks up at the stars and sees the beauty in the quiet of the desert. His mind drifts. His war was different, fighting in the jungle. The chopper is shot down. Jesse's arm is broken. It's midday now. They're sitting up in dense foliage off of what Mike figures is a section of the Ho Chi Minh trail. They are resting, hiding. The jungle is so thick. It's exploding with every damn kind of broadleaf vegetation, scores of different plants and trees, and the sweet smell of nature: trees, plant life, and soil—all rotting together on the jungle's floor.

Some of the trees had been bent over the trail to hide it from planes that patrol and drop crushing bombs or tumbling silver canisters of napalm. The canopy is so thick that the sky seems like some faint, incandescent sheet of wavering blue. The sunlight works its way between the layers of leaves and trees and dries the jungle floor. He remembers feeling his back and neck full of stinging heat rash and his mouth was so dry.

Mike knows approximately where they went down and radios his position at first light. They are miles from the crash site and have been sitting for about thirty minutes.

Jesse fishes a can of C rations out of his pocket and motions to Mike.

Mike looks at him incredulously and whispers, "What are you doing, numb nuts? Holding out on me? I'm starving."

Jesse leans into Mike's ear, his broken arm the color of plums, and whispers, "Fuck you, turd bucket. Let's eat."

Mike opens the can with his John Wayne snip of a can opener, and they share a can of peaches. He eats with a white spoon and chews slowly. Mike remembers the feeling of the juice resting in his mouth and sliding down his throat. Suddenly he hears Vietnamese voices and sandals down the path.

NVA. Two of those sons of bitches, wearing brown uniforms and backpacks, are making their way casually up the path. Rifles on their shoulders. Must not have gotten the word; either that, or they're fuckups. He turns his head to Jesse, makes a fist, and then raises two fingers. They inch back from the path. Then he looks back to the path and sees the white spoon.

The first one walks by Mike and Jesse, missing the spoon. A second one follows. Suddenly, there is a third young enemy, bending slightly, dressed in brown like the others, with a floppy bush cover and worn rucksack. Only this man's eyes are sweeping both sides of the trail, searching. Mike can see his furrowed brow and oval eyes and how one hand rests on the trigger and one on the stock.

This boy knows what's up, Mike thinks, his heart beating so loudly that he can hear it. The third NVA stops. Studies the path. He walks up to the spoon and Mike can see his sandaled feet. The soldier has his foot a few inches from the spoon, which is not on the path but wedged in a clump of green plants. He bends down and reaches for the spoon, and Mike can smell the faint odor of fish soup on his breath. He sees his brown eyes and the black birthmark over his lip. Mike squeezes the trigger on his rifle, and Jesse opens up with Mikes .45, and all three are half dead as they crumble to the ground. Mike is on his feet, putting one quick round in each NVA's head as they lie twisted, legs flopped, minds empty. He looks down the path and listens hard. Nothing. He hurriedly grabs one pack as Jesse searches the other.

"Let's get the hell out of here, Cinderella," Mike says.

"Mike." Jesse is on one knee, a gook pack open. He pulls out a red Frisbee and smiles. Then he tosses it toward Mike, who is twenty feet away, and it floats across the jungle. Suddenly, shots ring out, and Jesse is killed instantly. Mike fires at three NVA soldiers who are advancing. He rips a *Chi-Com* off one of the dead soldiers and tosses it down the trail. When the explosion is done, the jungle is quiet. He grabs the radio and a pack and takes off, running down the path and into the jungle. For three days he moves in and out of jungle and travels parallel to the path. On the fourth day, he reaches a chopper on the net, and soon it hovers above him and lands in a small clearing. As he runs toward the chopper, small arms fire rakes the chopper, and he's hit in the back as he is plucked from the jungle.

They landed at Third Marines. He recalls being carried on a gurney—the pain and lying on a table. And when they used a rib spreader on him, he bolted up and punched the corpsman, knocking him across the room, and then fell back.

His reverie is interrupted by a loud moan from July behind him.

"Oooh!"

He glances back at Cody and wipes his brow. "Give her water and try to keep her quiet."

He's looking back through the scope. Mick and Griff scale the short wall and approach the door of a house, open it, and disappear inside.

Bent over, Mick and Griff move cautiously. As they do, sand from the door spills onto a concrete floor. Mick flips the light on his weapon. Inside the room, his beam of light hits a TV, chairs, and prayer mats. In the middle of the room, a family of five lies dead on the floor. A man, a woman, and three children have their mouths gagged, hands tied. They have been shot in the head and stabbed repeatedly. The woman is naked from the waist down, as is a girl close to Mick's age. An older man's head has been cut off and placed on a small table. The dead have fouled themselves sometime between life and death, and the stench mixes with the smell of their sticky blood.

"Those bloodsuckers." Griff snarls.

Mick wants to scream and cry, rave and swear and take his gun and shoot through every wall and door. The indignity. The inhumanity. What are we fighting? His hands shake, and his light skips from woman to girl to ceiling and then to the floor. He catches Griff's eyes glaring in a moment of anger. He shudders and forces himself to step out of the horror. To get his mind right.

"Fucking al-Qaeda," Mick says, his feelings grinding to a halt. "They probably didn't like us building the school. They're sending a message. Looks like they've been dead for just a few hours." He stares at the bodies and looks past the head, and he feels flat inside. Not angry, not shocked, not appalled. Flat. Like he has no emotion. Humans do this to each other? These were innocents. Children.

Griff's face starts to sag. His mouth turns down. "I want to get these guys," he says. "And blow their shit to pieces."

"You got it." And they bump fists. "Let's get outside."

Mick turns off the light on his machine gun, and as he steps toward the door, his boots stick, and he can hear the blood stretch as he lifts his foot. He opens the door slowly and looks out on the courtyard and wall. The night is almost clear. A light breeze carries a film of fine dust and the smell of death. Mick fears it's too light.

They move from one courtyard to the next and inside each house they find the same thing: men, women, and children slaughtered. In some homes, al-Qaeda's work was swift and skillful—a slash here, a single bullet there, a throat cut quickly, like the butchering of a calf. In other homes, the families were tortured, mutilated, and treated by their captors as if they were victims of homicidal revenge. Inside one house there are dead goats and chickens and a man who was gagged, tied with rope, burned with scalding water, and bludgeoned to death with a can of milk. He'd been hit so many times in the head that the can broke and milk spilled across his face and into his cracked-open skull.

In the next hovel they enter, the parents were slaughtered on the floor, awash in blood. The baby, too. Dogs were at them.

Why they didn't kill the dogs? Mick thinks. "Christ. We'll get the others, come back, and set in at the schoolhouse."

—<del>⧉</del>—

At Camp Bravo, it's night. Corporal Thomas stands over Nunez's bunk, shaking his shoulder, shining a flashlight in his face. "Wake up, dude. Get your ass up. Mick and Griff are in a world of hurt." A single lightbulb is on in the tent, and a couple marines are still awake, banging their laptops. The rest are racked out, snoring in their bunks.

"What the fuck?" Nunez says, flailing one arm and covering his eyes with the other. "Get that light outta my face, cock bite. I'm sleeping."

"Get up, shithead," Thomas orders and then bangs on the upper bunk where Hop is crashed.

"Whatcha say, Corporal T," Hop asks. "Who's in what?" Both Nunez and Hop have been drinking Robo and smoking pot all night and finally went down for the count about an hour ago. They are slow moving and not quick to wake up.

"OK, here's the deal," Thomas says matter-of-factly. "The supply chopper with Mick's old man in it was shot down or crashed because of the fucking sandstorm. They're about ten miles from here. We'll take a couple Humvees and a Cougar. Why do I have to spell everything out to you dick wads? You're on the Quick Reaction Team. Get your shit together. We're going out and bringing 'em back. You got that?"

"Why can't they just send another chopper?" Nunez says, wiping sleep from his eyes. "I mean, dude, we're tired. I did the last QRT. It's my turn to slide."

"Fuck you. Cobras and Hueys are tied up with some big shit the other side of Fallujah. And you know what, I don't give a rat's ass how tired you are. I'm tired. We're all fucking tired. Get up. You and Hop better be on the road in fifteen minutes or you're in some serious shit." Thomas spins away and heads for the flap, stops, and turns. "You fuck sticks shouldn't stay up all night smoking dope." Thomas drops the flap.

—<del>⧉</del>—

Mick and Griff glide across the desert sand, moving quickly under the moonlight. The topography is so flat they can see Mike, Cody, and July lying prone at a hundred meters. When they reach the three, Mick hears the click from Mike's rifle as Mike flicks the switch with his thumb on the handle to off.

They drop to one knee, catching their breath and trying to stay low. "You weren't going to shoot me, were you, Pops?"

"No. I got you covered in the scope."

"We got to roll," Mick whispers. "Al-Qaeda or some Sunni insurgents slaughtered the Shiite village. Everyone's dead. The ragheads are gone."

He rests the M240 by his side, barrel up and butt in the sand. "They must have been the bitches that shot us down." His lips are cracked, and he touches blood as he runs his tongue across them. "We're going to set in at the school and hope they send a quick reaction team out here ASAP. I'll be on point again. Griff, you're next. Dad, you follow. Cody, you help Lieutenant July. When we get to the wall, follow my hand signals and no talking. Not a sound." He looks at Debby, who is lying flat. "You gotta eat the pain, Lieutenant."

Everyone stands, and Mike's nervous system shoots a sharp pain in his back far greater than his throbbing knee. He swallows hard, sucks in a breath to steady himself, and his broken teeth scream. His lips curl, and he wants to shout, but he relaxes into the anguish. *God help me,* he thinks, and a flash of fear shakes his body. *Push through it, you asshole. You wanted to be here. Take it. Deal with it. Show your son.*

Cody holds onto Debby's arm, keeping her steady, until Mick says to spread it out. Mike guts it out as the four move to the village, spread out. They stop to rest at the base of the wall and flatten. A dog barks. Mick stands and signals them up. Griff's left arm flops almost uselessly, but with his right arm, he can manage his rifle. Lieutenant July grinds her teeth, beating back the agony, limping, and hopping with Cody's help. Mike's knee is still holding together, but his back is a knife fight. Cody's ear throbs from the wound, but the blood has congealed.

Mick moves slowly, no time for fear. No time to worry about Cait and the baby or his old man dragging behind him. The moon has dropped, and the light has diminished. His pupils have dilated as big as buttons. His heart is racing. His mind has passed into the clarity only soldiers know. He is hyperalert. He can feel the shift of a breeze and smell the goats and chickens. He can hear

Lieutenant July's shallow breath, her struggle to move. He pulls down his night vision, and the village is green. He turns the corner at an opening in the rock wall and glances back and then continues toward the school, wiping sweat from his eyes. He notices his heart beating and his nose crusting. He passes by two more patios.

A bicycle rests on its side next to a hut, where a car fender lies and a metal table is overturned. In the next patio, there is a clothesline; underneath it are a dead woman and a hammer lying in the dirt. He trusts himself, his hands, and the movement of his hips. He steps toward another patio, looks back again, and everything is cool. They are keeping up. Good.

Another patio has a broken pop, spilled in the dirt, a soccer ball, a dead dog shot through the head, a generator, and the smell of chicken shit. Suddenly, a goat runs out of the shadows, and Mick spins his M240 and stops. His hand is firm; his finger still rests straight on the side of his weapon. *Where the fuck did that come from?*

At the last house, there is no sound or sense of man or beast. The dog still lets out an occasional bark somewhere in the night. From the side wall, he can see the courtyard and the schoolhouse twenty-five meters away. The walls are mended and freshly painted. The back of the school looks out onto a soccer field with goals and a swing set.

It's twenty-five meters from the edge of this dirt patio to the one-room building and around front to the door, a step up to the concrete floor. It seems like a long way. Mick thinks for a moment. Window openings. No shutters. This is where we set up the swing set and repaired and painted the walls. Where those poor kids got to go to school for the first time in years. Where girls, heads covered with scarves, actually laughed in front of him and where the teachers shook his hand. But he knew that death could be waiting.

He closes his fist and pulls it down to let Griff know everyone should stop. Griff turns and does the same. They all drop to their knees. With the moon gone, so are the shadows. Against a wall, Mick disappears in a pocket of darkness. Moments later, he is back and hand signals Griff that he will cross to the school. He raises a flat palm to let Griff know they should wait. Moving quickly, he slips out from behind the house and over to the side of the school. His finger slides down to the trigger. He is a shadow as he creeps around the side of the school to the front of the building, pausing beneath the glassless window. With one hand, he reaches out and pushes open the door. Everything inside is green in his vision: the room, tables, and bench. The two bearded teachers are dead on the floor, hands tied behind their backs, their throats slit, all of it green in his vision. Allah Akbar is scrawled in big white letters on the chalkboard. He ignores the scene and creeps back out the door and around the building. He taps on Griff's shoulder. Griff turns and taps Mike, and Mike touches Cody. They stay close and shuffle into the school.

Inside, Mick moves around the room freely. The storm has dumped sand across the room. Each footstep makes a scratching sound. For the others, the room is dark and confusing. Mick leads Mike by the hand around benches and tables, past the murdered teachers, to the back window, where Mike sits on a bench, holding his rifle, back to the wall. Griff stays at the front window, down on one knee, looking out, his M4 in hand. Mick sets Cody and July away from the windows, underneath the blackboard. He picks up Mike's pack, steps over to Mike, and drops it.

Mick sets his machine gun on the classroom table. Then he drags the teachers to a far corner. Cody helps July down to the floor, takes his shirt off, and slips it gently under her head.

"Thanks," she sighs, her voice weak but steady. "I think...I think I'll just close my eyes for a moment." Cody touches her cheek gently.

Mick considers how best to defend their position. With the M240, he can cover the courtyard and have a bead on the buildings across the street. There are three or four maybe. He remembers that one is a home with a Coke sign hanging on a shed next to the main house.

Mike sits on a bench in the darkness at the corner of the window and looks out onto the soccer field. It's flat and quiet except for that damn dog and the squeak of a swing being pushed by the wind. He squints and imagines what he'll do if they're hit. Stay calm; squeeze the trigger. Short bursts. Duck back behind the wall. He hasn't shot a gun in over thirty years. But it feels right; just like when they would run night ambushes near the village. Sometimes they would dig in along a tree line, waiting for Viet Cong to cross the middle of a rice paddy. *We always dug a hole back then,* he thinks. No one does it here. Dig a hole and wait. Gooks could see better than we could. If we only had night vision back then. Not that shitty Starlight scope but these high-tech goggles and GPS. Unmanned drones and TV screens. It's a joke. Used to be able to smell VC. Now they're watching these pricks on TV. That's the difference. These poor fuckers don't usually attack in the middle of the night because marines own it.

Mike bows his back and stretches and hears and feels something move along his spinal column. Pain. A crack and burning down his backside. He gasps and grits his teeth. Phew. He exhales, and the pain ebbs.

The room is quiet, and the early morning is quiet. Maybe al-Qaeda split. Those radical jihadists are so crazy. Maybe they came in and did a job and went on to terrorize some other hopeless shit hole. What kind of religion would tolerate this carnage? Maybe they're gone. Yeah, right. And maybe they fucking forgot they shot us down. Where the hell is that reaction team? *Christ I wish I had a beer,* Mike thinks, feeling his parched lips with his fingers and touching his damaged teeth and dry tongue. Can't use the bipod on the table; I'd be too open. His eyes catch something, and he holds his breath and tries to see a subtle shadow of night moving. It's nothing; he breathes, and his heart slows. Maybe they've got some sniper with a night scope, he thinks, and moves his head away from the window. He listens, swings the rifle, and ducks to the side of the window. The M14 is heavy in these old arms. Mike's thinking about getting shot in the face. Fuck that. He can't see out the window no matter how hard he tries. He sets the rifle butt down on the floor and leans it against the wall, and then he lifts his pack from the floor. He pulls out a couple pairs of underwear. He pops out his magazine and starts wiping it down with his shorts and wonders if these are the ones that say Mr. Happy. He snorts and chuckles just as Debby whimpers. He digs sand out of the magazine and wipes each round.

Mick moves back to Mike's window, drops to a knee, and tells him to lie down.

"I'll take the window for a while," he whispers. "Try to catch some Zs. And give me that rag."

Mike eases to the floor, exhausted. He puts his feet up on the bench and suddenly his back feels a lot less painful. He closes his eyes, and for a moment, he feels like he is resting.

Mick has a short belt in the M240 and a box of ammo, and with his night vision on, he can see the soccer field, the nets, a swing set, and the long, flat, green desert. But light is coming, and they'll find the chopper and come in trucks, he thinks. Those cheap, beat-up pickups, Russian or Toyotas. They'll have RPGs and AKs and probably a suicide fucker or two. That's what this place is full of, sand and suicide. If we can hold them for a while, the good guys will be here. Lieutenant Jarvis, Corporal Thomas, maybe Hop and Nunez. He takes a couple of M14 magazines from his nut sack and sets them on the bench for Mike, and then he switches knees and moves to the other side of the window. It's gotta be at least six feet wide and four feet high, which makes a nice opening for grenades. But we do have some firepower, he thinks, lifting from his knee and sitting on the bench. He quietly blows some sand out of his nose and runs a finger around the inside of his nostril, picks up his dad's underwear, and quickly brushes his weapon.

Cait is in his arms, and they are naked in his parents' shower, soaped up, water pouring on them. It's so warm, and the steam is rising, and he's sitting on the granite bench, back to the wall. She's in his lap, facing him. He's in so deep. So safe holding her. Warm and safe and it feels so good. And she rocked and arched her back, and he groaned, and she whimpered and let out a little cry, and it was all good. And that must have been when it happened. The condom slipped—how stupid. Now he's a dad. Wow. Gun cleaned, he loads a round in the chamber and sets the gun on the floor and then steps over Mike, bends down, and asks, "You OK, Pops?"

The hint of a smile plays on Mike's face. He takes another breath and coughs. "I'm good, Son."

Perhaps it's his father's cough, or perhaps it is simply that in that moment, Mick sees his father as vulnerable and in need of his protection. He couldn't love him more.

Chapter 37

The morning sun rises over the horizon. The air carries fine filaments of sand and lingers like LA smog or the vog from a Hawaiian volcano. The mud and brick and concrete huts, barely visible in the dark, form a half circle, facing the school across the wide courtyard. There are no sidewalks, only sand and dirt, a well in the middle of the courtyard, and the worn buildings, pockmarked by bullet holes. The dirt-packed patios are cluttered with stools and chairs that are tipped over, pots and planters, and empty clotheslines. A few tables and chairs are busted, and bicycles and rusted-out hunks of cars are covered with sand from yesterday's storm. Ravens peck the ground near a garden, chickens scratch in the patios, and a trio of dogs trots through, noses to the ground, sniffing for food. The village is deserted.

On the wall of the schoolhouse hangs a red sign with gold letters written in English that reads, Built by Third Marines May 2005.

Inside the school, the corpses are beginning to smell. Flies buzz, circle, and land where the knife was drawn and lap at the redness. Lieutenant Debby July sits up against a wall, asleep. From the right angle, she looks pretty, hair back, eyes closed, the second- and third-degree burns hidden just below her collar. Her lips are the color and texture of crushed, red rose petals.

Cody is also asleep, lying on his side, back to the wall, his head not far from Debby's lap. Her bandaged hand rests on his shoulder. Griff stands at the back wall, pissing out the window, one hand on his business, the other on his weapon. Mike sits on the bench, his head turned away, looking at table legs and dried pools of blood.

Griff is quick and settles his butt back on the bench at the corner of the back window. He can see the wide expanse of desert past the swing and the soccer field. Mick is at the opposite opening, looking out on the courtyard. Every hour they switch positions to stay alert. Thank God Debby had some beans to keep them wired.

"Mr. K," Griff says, turning his head sideways so he can see Mike. "I want to know how in the fuck did they shoot us down? They sure as hell couldn't see us."

"They probably heard us coming," Mike replies. "We were so low to the ground, they might have seen us and fired a Soviet heat seeker. That's how they want to knock our airliners out of the sky. Either that or they got a lucky shot with an RPG. I'd guess RPG because, with a heat seeker, the chopper would have blown up before we hit the ground. That's my guess."

Griff nods in acknowledgment and goes back to staring out at the empty soccer field.

One room, two windows, and a door. Mick covers the front window by the door. He's wired on beans and adrenaline and feels as if he drank a case of high-caffeine energy drinks. He's jittery and tired but still focused and filled with the driving desire to get out of this mess and bring everybody back alive. They can handle an assault or two, he figures, and they have enough ammo to last a few firefights. He's talked to Mike and Griff and made it clear that if they get hit, they need to use some discipline. Fire single shots, and don't hold down the trigger. In any case, his boys should be coming. Thomas, Nunez, Hop. Maybe Lieutenant Jarvis. They'll be here soon and as Nunez likes to say, "Fuck somebody up."

"You know, the problem with this war is we're too pussified," Griff says, turning from the window so that all can hear. "We need to muscle up. Get tougher on these ass wipes."

"What lit you up, donkey?" Mick asks, looking back over his shoulder and across the tabletops.

"Listen. I'm serious. Say a suicide bomber blows himself up. When we find out who the bastard is, we should go waste his family and all his relatives. You know what I mean?" He's on a roll now. "So that dipshit that's turning himself into dust has to know there is a consequence that lives on after he blows. He can be nailing all them virgins, but his family is going to suffer. Maybe for decades." Griff has a big smile on his face, and his chest is puffed up like he just took a huge hit off of a joint. "What do you think, Mr. K?"

"I used to think that," Mike says. "We used to say sweep the Nam. Kill 'em all, and let God sort it out, but it's more complicated than that. It is here, anyway. This is global. We're fighting an ideology, not an enemy we can bomb back to the Stone Age. I told you this already, didn't I?"

"Yeah, douchebag," Mick snaps at Griff. "Killing more Iraqis is pointless. It just breeds more hate, and then the world will start to hate us."

"Son, they already do," Mike says. "That's why this is so complicated. This is a very tough enemy. They're driven by religious, fanatical beliefs. And they won't be happy until we're all dead, or at least all of us are gone, and they can return to the same kind of torturous rule Saddam had. We can win this war, but we have to do it one village at a time. Problem is, al-Qaeda and other splinter groups are doing the same thing. Only they're trying to destroy the people's will by doing what they just did to this village. They want to strike fear in their hearts. And fear is powerful."

"If we kill enough of them, they'll understand," Griff says.

"Why don't you all shut up," Debby says, startling everyone, her eyes still closed. "You're giving me a headache."

The boys and Mike laugh and share a sense of collective amazement.

Mike picks up his pack and hobbles over to Debby and sits down. He fishes through his pack, pulls out some aspirin, and gives it to her. Then he hands her a bottle of water.

Mick looks over. He's at the back window now. "Pops, what the heck. You're holding out on us."

"I'm not holding out. I just wanted to wait, use some discipline."

July's eyes open to Mike's voice, and she says, "Yes. Thank you." And she takes a sip and passes the bottle.

Mike digs some more and finds a bottle of aloe lotion that Claire gave him.

"Let's try some of this," Mike says, reaching out with the green bottle.

Her face is twisted in pain as Cody and Mike help her slip out of her tattered and burned marine shirt and what's left of her burnt green tee. Then she turns from the wall so Mike is facing her back. The burns are mostly second degree, with flesh bubbled, and a few are black and deep-pink third degree, burning a strip down to her tailbone.

"This will hurt at first," he says, spreading the green lotion carefully on her shoulders. "But then it should cut the pain some." He gently applies it over the shoulder blades and down her backbone as Debby muffles her cries. Cody nearly retches.

When Mike is done, he takes a red silk Hawaiian shirt out of his pack and slips it over her damaged skin. She is sweating from the pain and exhausted and lies down on her belly, her head on Cody's leg.

"Don't you think some help should have come by now?" asks Cody.

"They better," Mike says.

Mick hears a pop and looks out from the corner of the back window. He sees a plume of smoke rising from the desert. He imagines trouble at the chopper, but help is on the way. Mike sits on the bench next to him, his back to the wall, checking the magazines in the M14. He's taking out one round so they will respond better.

"What the hell was that?" Mike asks. Cody gets up and walks over to the back window and stands inside the frame of the window.

"What'd you see? What happened?"

"Get down!" Mike orders. Before he can reach out to pull Cody down, a round from a sniper rifle tears through the window and hits Cody high on his cheekbone, knocking him back. He crashes into a table and then slumps to the floor. He is dead before Mick can turn from the window and recognize what happened.

Mike sees Cody on his back. His eyes are open as if he is astonished. Under one eye is a crushed red hole the diameter of a railroad spike. No time for loss. Mike turns back, head beneath the window, thinking, what a waste. What a fucking waste this is.

At the same time, a pickup truck full of black-masked insurgents roars through the courtyard in front of the schoolhouse and starts firing. Griff opens up. He squeezes off several well-placed rounds that turn the truck around, flee-ing out of the courtyard. At the back of the school, another truck careens onto the soccer field, packed with enemy in masks and street clothes, shouting, "Ali Akbar," and waving AK-47s as they open up on the school. Mike fires the 14 and misses everything, while Mick hammers the truck with his M240, knocking two off the truck's bed, before it turns them away.

"Stay out of the window, Pops!" Ducking low, Mick steps over Cody's body and pushes aside a table. Griff fires another short burst at the back of the truck by the time Mick reaches the front window, squats, and opens up too. One hand feeds the belt and the other holds the gun, its barrel resting on the windowsill. He blows the shit out of the truck and bodies spin and drop off the tailgate. A third small, beat-up pickup with a missing front fender idles up the street. A beard in a turban is standing in the back with a Russian light machine gun mounted on the roof of the cab. The truck continues to idle as the beard fires carefully, rounds ripping into the building, some flying through the window as a haji with an RPG drops on the other side of the courtyard. Griff watches him in his scope as he shoulders the RPG. Then, with perfect timing, Griff puts a bullet in his head.

At Camp Bravo, Corporal Thomas is in a briefing room full of maps and over-lays and a slew of computers. He's meeting with Lieutenant Jarvis, Captain O'Callahan, and Lieutenant Colonel Robert Spector. Behind the colonel's back, junior officers call him little Bobby Sphincter or just plain asshole. He's shorter than the captain and has been in the reserves forever, and he has never had a sniff of combat. How he became company commander of a grunt unit is beyond anyone's understanding. Eight weeks in the country and already he is hated. In Mike's day, he'd be fragged.

"I don't know. I don't know," Spector says, drinking a bottle of water with a straw. He takes a handkerchief out of his trousers, puts a little water on it, and wipes his brow. "This all seems a little risky, sending so many men out to rescue so few. Why, they might already be dead for all we know."

"Sir. Sir. With yours and the captain's permission," Lieutenant Jarvis chips in. "I do have a faint signal from the pilot's GPS, and we think we know where they are. We just need a chopper to get them. And I think—"

"Lieutenant," Spector says. "The answer is no. No fucking chopper. Most of the birds are in the air doing some serious work, and what we have on ground, we need for an emergency. Now I've got a meeting with the general, and if you gentleman will excuse me, we will reconvene at thirteen hundred hourse and revisit the situation." Spector throws a salute and the others follow. He turns and walks out the door.

"Captain? Lieutenant. This *is* serious shit," Thomas says. "Mick and Griff are two of my best men, and if even they're wounded or dead, we don't leave 'em behind."

"I know, Corporal." O'Callahan snorts, chewing on a stub of a fat cigar. "And all we need is a dead reporter and *his son*, goddammit. Next fucking thing you know, we get beat-up in the press and shit canned out of the corps."

"Captain," Lieutenant Jarvis interjects. "We could send our quick reaction guys on the ground and be in and out before 1300. I will personally make that happen, sir."

O'Callahan chews on his stub and paces across the room like the bulldog marine he is. "I built my career the old-fashioned way, from the ground up. Mustang style. I got twenty-five years in the corps. I sure as hell ain't going anywhere. Lieutenant Jarvis, get the crew together post haste, and do you think this corporal here can do the job?"

"Sir. Yes, sir."

"Then get 'er done."

In the early morning light, Lieutenant Jarvis is at the main gate of Bravo in a Humvee with a gunner standing in back, his head through the top, manning a .50 caliber. There's a driver and two experienced shooters inside. Behind him is a ten-passenger Cougar 4X4 with blast protection. Inside the Cougar, Hop is in the top hatch with a mounted .50 caliber. Nunez is at a side portal, the barrel of a SAW sticking out, and three new guys are strapped in seats, holding M4s. All of them have that deer caught in the headlights look. Corporal Thomas is the driver. He wants to do this, but for some reason, he feels a little shaky. Maybe because he's short. Going home soon. Six days and a wake up will do that, even to the baddest of the bad.

One of the guards at the entrance steps from behind his concrete blast wall and stops the two trucks. He stands on the passenger side of the Humvee and leans into Lieutenant Jarvis's window. He's holding what looks like a small computer that an attendant might hold if you were checking in a rental car at the airport.

"I told you, sir," the big, young marine says. "I got nothin' showing on the screen. Nothin' here indicating you have permission to leave with two vehicles and eight marines."

"Y'all got to be shittin' me. We're on a quick action. Now open the gate. Now!"

"Sorry, sir. Now will you shut down the vehicle and get out of the truck?"

❦

The firing has stopped at the schoolhouse. The pickups have sped off. Mike is crouched on the floor next to the window. He takes another shirt out of his pack, covers Cody's face, and thinks again what a waste all of this is. What good comes of his dying? He won't even get a military funeral or a ten-gun salute. There won't be a story on the cover of *Time* about how he died or what his sacrifice means in this sorry-ass war. He's just another press guy stuck on the obituary page.

Mick pulls Cody across the room as Debby lets out a sound of great pain, but she too is a marine, so she eats the pain and shuts down inside.

"Goddammit! I liked that kid," Mike says. "He was a good kid." Mike's face hardens. *He'd still be alive if I'd stayed home. Shit.*

"Yeah," Mick says, pulling Cody to the middle of the room and sliding a table over him to somewhat obscure his death. Quickly, bent over, he rushes back to Griff.

Griff's at the front window opening, butt on the floor, back to the wall, facing Mike on the other side of the room. He's about to rage out. "I want to kill every one of those cocksuckers. Just shoot the fuck out of them. Every damn one of them."

"Get a grip," Mike shouts. "You'll get another chance. Those assholes will be back."

Mick pats Griff's leg, bumps fists, and says, "Lock it." This calms Griff down, and Mick makes his way to the back window.

"What do you think, Pops?"

"Mick, you're the guy. Not me. All we can do is wait. I missed everything that first round, but I'll do better." Then he reaches in a pocket on his armored vest and pulls out his pistol and four clips and sets them on the bench.

"Where did you get the piece, Pops?"

"In the rear."

Mick needs no more explanation. As his dad might say, "It is what it is."

"I'm hungry," snorts Griff. "'Bout now, I could eat a whole pumpkin pie. With whipped cream. Smothered with whipped cream."

"I'm too beat-up to be hungry," Mike laments. He rubs his knees and feels cartilage move, then he straightens his back and a streak of pain fires down his backside into the balls of his feet.

Griff shifts from the right side of the window opening to the left and glances to the courtyard. Ravens are back, pecking around the base of the well, stirring up the dirt. He ducks beneath the windowsill and slides to the other side.

"When we get back to camp, I'm going to take a dump," Griff informs the group. "Take a shower for an hour and then wolf down a large pepperoni."

"What about the pumpkin pie?"

Before Griff can answer Mick, there is movement in the courtyard.

"What the hell?" Griff snaps, peeking out the opening. "Someone's coming, pushing a bike."

At the far entrance to the courtyard, a short, heavyset Iraqi in jeans and a plain coat is pushing a bicycle. He is a boy. His head is deformed, like someone with Down syndrome. Mick scurries to the opposite side of Griff's window and briefly looks as the boy keeps coming.

"Dude, what's up with this shit?"

"I don't know. Pops, there's a kid pushing a bike with a basket on it through the courtyard."

"He's got a fat head," Griff says.

"I think it's Down syndrome, douche. Pops, what do you think?"

"He's a suicide bomber. You got to kill him."

"We can't just do that. I'll fire a shot and get him to stop."

"If he is a suicide bomber, he might not even know it," Mike barks from across the room. "Al-Qaeda might have brainwashed him and convinced him that bullets won't harm him. He might not even know he has on a suicide vest."

"Griff, shoot a couple rounds in front of this kid. See if that stops him. We can't just kill a kid, Dad."

Griff lets loose with his rifle. Ravens scatter as bullets pound the dirt in front of the boy. The boy is startled; he drops the bike and stands still in the middle of the courtyard near the well, looking confused. A moment passes, and then he walks slowly toward the schoolhouse with a dumb smile on his face. Griff fires again. The boy stops about ninety feet from the window. His smile is gone. The sun is in his eyes, and he looks frightened. He turns to run clumsily back toward the bike, nearly falling. As he reaches the bike, he picks it up, and there is a haji voice shouting from somewhere. The boy turns his bike away from the schoolhouse and explodes in a loud fusion of flesh and nails and steel ball bearings.

The shrapnel sprays the courtyard, the schoolhouse, and other buildings, shattering the few glass windows, tearing at doors and walls and slaughtering ravens perched on the edges of flat rooftops. The explosion creates a shock wave of energy toward the schoolhouse, rolling a storm of dirt and steel through the window, driving them to the floor, covering them in blankets of swirling dust and debris.

Mike is lying flat, coughing, spitting up, his ears ringing. He wipes dirt from his eyes with one of his shirts and calls out through the dust.

"Mick. Griff. Mick!"

"Pops, you OK?"

"I'm good. I can see you now."

"Whew," moans Griff, coughing, wiping at his face.

Mick has cleared the dirt from his eyes and opens his mouth as wide as possible to pop his eardrums. He blows dirt and snot from his nose and calls out to Debby.

"Lieutenant, you OK?"

Before she can answer, Mick says, "Hold on. I hear something."

"I can't hear anything," Mike says.

Mick quickly moves to a corner of the back window and sees a cloud of dust in the horizon. Back at the wall, he has a look of hope in his eyes as he turns to Mike.

"I think it's the good guys."

"Great!"

"'Bout time those suckers showed up," Griff says.

The walls are covered with dirt, but the explosion was too far away to damage the structure of the schoolhouse. Debby cleans her face with the shirt Mike gave her and is fighting her pain, breathing deeply, trying to relax.

"Lieutenant, take a sip of water," Mike says, scooting over close to her and handing her the bottle. "You hang on to it."

"Thanks."

Mike quickly crawls back to the window that is now receiving fire. Mick opens up on a group of fighters setting up a mortar as the Cougar heads straight toward the back of the school, taking machine gun and small arms fire. A half-dozen insurgents fire from behind the rock wall, rounds kicking up sand or bouncing off the armor plating. An RPG misses, and a second one hits a side panel, exploding. The up-armored truck plows on. The Cougar turns right fifty meters out, running parallel to the rock wall. Lieutenant Jarvis and his crew are in the Hummer at its rear. Hop is in the Cougar turret with his .50 busting the hell out of the rock wall and whatever's behind it. His gun's heavy spray punishes patios and pierces brick-and-mud huts like an exploding wrecking ball. Boom. Boom. Boom. At the same time, in the courtyard, four enemy in black masks rush out from a building toward the well. Griff opens up, kills one, and wounds another. AK-47s and old M16s rake the front of the schoolhouse, coming from behind the well, from inside buildings, and from rooftops.

Meanwhile, the Hummer circles and breaks off at the top of the courtyard, where two marine shooters dismount. As they do, two men on motorcycles race toward the Humvee. More fire hits the Humvee, and as it spins around, both cycles hit the Humvee. The first cycle is destroyed on impact and ruins the front of the Humvee. The rider flies over the bike's handlebars and his head smashes the windshield. A split-second later, the second bike lies down, and the bike and the rider slide under the Humvee and explode into a hell storm of broken steel, glass, body parts, and fire. The explosion kills Lieutenant Jarvis and the other marines and shakes the schoolhouse again, like it was rammed by a bus. Pieces of fenders and doors punch holes in walls and kill the three enemy hiding next to the well.

The Cougar keeps churning toward the schoolhouse, picking up rounds from buildings, windows, and behind the wall. Hop unloads. Thunk. Thunk. Thunk. And Nunez fires from his portal before they pass the back side of the school, hit the brakes, and skid to a halt, and then the Cougar turns sharply into the courtyard in front of the school. The back opens and more rounds hit it, kicking up dirt as Corporal Thomas and another marine duck out and sprint with their rifles toward the school, dodging bullets. Thomas hits the door as a round snaps from an AK and hits the other marine from behind, just above the earlobe, spinning him in a slow pirouette, tumbling him to the ground. He does not move.

Hop sees the sons of bitches, two of them ducking into a hut, and he unloads a dozen heavy shells, breaking up the building and collapsing part of the flat roof. A satellite dish crashes to the ground. The firing slows.

"Jesus," Mick says, slamming the door shut with one hand and watching the fallen marine at the same time. He turns and scans the courtyard. "The Humvee's destroyed!"

Corporal Thomas, now huddled under the front window, screams like a madman, "This is fucked. That was Jarvis. Oh Christ. Oh shit. Jarvis! This is really fucked. What were you thinking? You shouldn't o' been on that chopper."

"Fuck you," Griff yells.

"And if we weren't on that chopper," Mick roars, "My old man would be dead and Lieutenant July would have been raped and cut into pieces."

"Listen up, both of you," Mike yells. "Let's figure out how we're going to get out of here."

Another RPG explosion rocks the building, knocking everyone on their asses, splintering the door, and sending up a big plume of dirt and busted wall.

Mike pulls himself up. "Mick!" he shouts, a cloud of dirt floating in the window. Then out of the corner of his eye he looks up and sees a guy in white Nike warm-ups running, zigzagging across the soccer field toward the swing set. He places the barrel of his 14 on the windowsill, takes a deep breath, holds it, and catches him on a zag, gut shot.

Mike's face contorts, and a vein runs across his forehead.

"I got one of those assholes," he yells over his shoulder. As he sees Mick is OK, Mike feels like he's not a worthless old man anymore. He dips below the window. *They'll bring the choppers any minute now and get us out of here,* he's thinking. *And I can go home. Mick can take care of himself. He doesn't need me to watch over anything anymore.*

Mick dusts himself off and shouts out, "You OK, Pops?"

Mike cranks his head, moves his shoulder, and throws a thumbs-up. "Don't worry about me, Son. Just get us outta here."

When fighters appear, Griff and Mick spray rounds out the window and door. They walk rounds across the courtyard and fire short bursts at the rooftops when bodies appear or at figures running between buildings. Soon it's quiet. Streets and rooftops are empty.

"Where are the choppers?" Mick asks Thomas.

"There's not going to be any," Thomas says, sitting on his butt, back to the wall. "Bravo's getting hit, and Fallujah is on fire, and all the outposts are catching shit. You're lucky you got us. They even shot a fixed wing down a couple hours ago."

"Who else you got in the can?"

"Just Nunez and a couple new guys. I'm telling you, we're fucked."

Mike picks up on the conversation. "We got to get everyone out of here and do it fast. The reason we're not getting fired on now is because these fanatics are probably having a noon prayer. In about ten minutes, they'll be coming at us strong."

"Thomas, tell the new guys to get their asses in here and get Lieutenant July ready to move," Mick orders.

"Lighten up," Thomas says. "I'm calling the shots. Let me think."

"Think all you want, we need to get moving," Mike responds anxiously. "Come on, we're burning light."

Thomas acts disoriented. Unsure. "OK. All right." He gets on his headset and tells Nunez, "Get the newbies over here now!"

There is no fire, and Mike imagines the insurgents down on their knees, facing east, praying to Allah.

Two marines, baby-faced in new uniforms and clean helmets, rush out from the back of the Cougar with a folded stretcher. They run inside the ripped-open doorway, both of them tripping over the doorjamb. Griff duck walks over to July and, with his good arm and shoulder, helps her on the stretcher. Mick pulls her .38 and slides it across the room to Griff and Griff rests the gun on her belly.

Face twisted with pain, she says, "Semper Fi."

She glances at Cody, his face still covered, and back to Griff. She locks eyes with Mick. Her face is swollen and her lips are dry and cracked. One marine touches some water to her lips while the other marine hands his canteen to Griff. Then the two boys lift her, fear running through their eyes. They stumble out the door, and the world breaks loose.

A sheet of fire comes from the rooftops across the courtyard and buries the marines and Debby July. They are hit multiple times as Hop starts hammering away, trying to suppress them. Griff runs to the doorway and starts firing.

"Hop's hit," yells Mick. Heavy machine gun fire pounds the Cougar, rakes the turret, and Hop is cut to pieces.

"Those motherfuckers!" Griff screams, and he leans out the door and fires a grenade from his M4 and then empties a full clip onto the rooftop and into the windows below. At the same time, Mick unloads on black-clad insurgents storming toward the school.

Mike and Mick fire until the group is dead or wounded, sprawled across the soccer field, heads back, mumbling prayers to Allah. Suddenly, Griff runs to the Cougar, rounds ricocheting all around, and climbs inside and pulls Hop down into the truck. He sprints back to the school and is brought down in another hail of fire. Nunez fires the SAW from the side portal facing the onslaught.

"Griff!" Mick shouts. Griff lies near the boys and Debby.

"Griff," Mick shouts again. Griff starts to crawl and is hit again. Finally he is still. The firing slows.

Corporal Thomas is frozen. Mick is in shock. Something has clicked in Mike. Something has clicked in his conscience and turned his mind like it once did so many years ago. He becomes flat. Not feeling. Not afraid of death. Resolved. His thoughts race through the situation. Save my boy. Four dead outside the door. Cougar running. Nunez. Get the fuck out of the killing zone.

"Dad. Dad." Mick is near tears. No rage. Just tears and resolution.

"I know, Son."

Thomas is trembling.

"Corporal," Mike demands. "Snap out of it." Mike starts to move but his knee locks up, so he massages the front of his kneecap until the floating cartilage shifts so he can bend it.

Mike is calm. Mick is quiet, edgy. Corporal Thomas is shaking. After two tours Thomas has seen too much. There is only so much a young man's mind can stand. His face fills with the worst kind of fear. Crippling. He can barely speak into his headset.

"OK, Corporal. We're going to get out of here," Mike says. "But we have to focus. Stay calm. Get Nunez to back up closer, and we will put out suppressing fire as the dead are loaded, and then we'll get the fuck out of here. We've got moments."

Just then, there is another rush from the soccer field, and a squad of black is running toward the school firing. Mick is at the window, and together, he and Mike are firing in a controlled madness, ignoring the incoming rounds as they riddle the building. A handful of enemy is shot, and they fall, some scatter, and one blows himself up, tangled in the swing. At the window, a terrorist dives through, knocking Mike back. And before he can explode, Mike shoots him in the neck with his pistol, and Mick picks him up like he's nothing and throws him out the window.

Corporal Thomas is shouting into his headset to Nunez, telling him to back the fuck up. "There's no wounded. We'll have to leave the dead."

Mike and Mick both catch the corporal's words and look at Thomas hard, as if to say you stupid fuck, and then Mick breaks it.

"Fuck that, hillbilly!" Mick says, and Thomas looks confused.

"We staggered them. Just get Nunez to back up, and we load up, and we're outta here," Mick commands. He stands, his back to the wall, facing Mike and the other corner of his window.

"Pops, we'll lay down some suppressing fire, and if we can get the Cougar close enough, it can shield us on one side while Thomas and the other new guy move our men. What'd you think?"

"Perfect," Mike shouts. He's pleased. That's right, he's thinking. Take over, Son. Fuck the chain of command. Get us out of here, and we'll all get drunk. Then he starts thinking about Claire and Madie and how it takes this kind of thing to really make him see that home is everything. *Mick's manned up, and he can do it all. He's a better man than me. And when he comes home...*

The Cougar backs up slowly, Nunez driving, its doors open and facing the school. The dead are just outside the door, lying at the back end of the Cougar.

"Let's roll," Mick says.

Mike bends over and his back cracks as he carries the 14 and pushes past the tables and toward the door. Mick drags Cody by the back of his shirt across the floor and sets him under the window. It's quiet again. The only sounds are the hum of the engine and the flies buzzing over the schoolteachers.

"Dad, you fire at the three buildings on the left. I'll rake the roof. Thomas, that should give you time for you and Nunez to load 'em up." Mick is commanding, and Thomas is compliant as they work as a team.

Nunez shouts from inside the Cougar. "I seen about a dozen more o' them motherfuckers goin' into buildings."

Mike can see Nunez in the back of the Cougar near the ramp, with a marine next to him and Hop dead on the floor.

Mike thinks the school is being surrounded like a horseshoe. Black-clad militants, an SUV, and one pickup filled with mismatched insurgents are moving in, shrinking the horseshoe.

At the same time, Thomas and Nunez and the young marine move the dead quickly into the Cougar. Mike and Mick are still firing. Mike drops a magazine and snaps a new one in place. The bodies of Griff and Lieutenant July and the other marines are loaded on board. Mick stops firing and sets his machine gun down and bends over and throws Cody over his shoulder and dashes out the door into the Cougar. He sets Cody down as Thomas shoves Cody's body aside.

The end of the courtyard is in flames, smoke is rising, and Mick rushes back into the school, AK-47 bullets clanging off the Cougar and ripping holes in the schoolhouse wall.

Mick picks up his M240 and turns to Mike and yells, "Go, Dad! Go!" And as Mick starts firing again, Mike steps through the doorway and tries to run, and on his third step, a bullet hits him in the shoulder, spins him around, and his knee gives away, and he falls just short of the Cougar.

Mick sees Mike lying in the dirt and stops firing and runs out the door, under fire. With his left hand, he grabs Mike under one arm and lifts him to his feet and Thomas reaches out and pulls Mike inside. At the moment Thomas grabs Mike, an explosion shakes the Cougar, and Mick is hit with shrapnel and knocked back out.

Mike lands on the pile of bodies, and when he shakes his head clear, he sees Mick. He pushes himself up, steps out onto the ramp, reaches for Mick's arm, and pulls him up as if God's strength is in him. He takes a step and is hit by a burst of AK-47 rounds. He steps again and falls with Mick into the Cougar.

Nunez drives like a madman out of the courtyard, and courage has grabbed Thomas again. He fires the SAW from a portal, a steady stream. They pass what's left of the burning Hummer and torn-up huts, with Griff, Hop, Cody, Debby, Mike, Mick, and the dead marines lying in a twisted pile on the floorboards.

Nunez screams and screams and drives out of the village and onto the road.

"Oh, Jesus," Thomas says.

Mike lies on his back; Mick is draped over his chest, face down. For a moment, neither moves, and then Mick stirs and pushes himself up, grimacing from his wounded arm. He looks at his father and can see he is dying. Blood is on Mike's slack lips and there is a tear in his neck.

"Dad. Dad!" he cries under the roar of the Cougar shifting gears.

Mike's life is ending. His voice is a whisper. He looks at his son with eyes full of love and sorrow. "I'm so...proud of you. I love you...Tell Claire and Madie...tell..."

Mike's head turns slightly, and his eyes are open, but the light is gone.

Mick bows over the body of his father. He is exhausted, spent. Numb. He hears nothing. And feels nothing except the longing for his father. Grief has settled in. He gently closes Mike's eyes and places a hand on his wound. He feels the blood of his father and a closeness he has never known.

Chapter 38

It is a beautiful day in Oregon. The sky is blue, and daffodils and roses are in bloom. Portland International Airport is busy with long lines of cars loading and unloading in front of the terminal. At the far end of the tarmac, a military C-130 approaches.

It hits the tarmac, its big engines reversing and slowing down on the runway. It turns toward a huge hangar, where a modest crowd waits. There are no bands, no balloons, and just a few placards; there is only a handful of soldiers and marines in dress blues, standing at attention, and a group of nervous loved ones waiting for their heroes.

Claire stands with Madie, Little B, Cait and her baby, Glen, and Griff's parents. They all wait behind a rope, near the hangar's opening. They stand quietly as the engines shut down. The marines and soldiers cross the tarmac.

The ramp lowers, and the men walk up the ramp and disappear. For a long moment, no one in the crowd speaks. The marines and soldiers emerge from the plane and walk down the ramp, carrying stretchers with wounded soldiers or silver caskets covered with American flags.

Some of the crowd gasp or cry as the caskets come off the plane and are loaded onto carts. A marine dressed in a white cover, khaki shirt, and blue trousers with a red stripe on each leg salutes a casket and then turns and leads Griff's parents back to it.

The last casket carried from the plane has Mick in front, one arm in a sling, his other arm helping the marines carry Mike's casket. Mick is in dress uniform, his white cover pulled down across his eyes. His back is straight; his jaw is tight. There are no tears, only moist eyes, and only he knows that he is crying.

A throng of reporters and television camera crews push in and snap pictures of Mick and of Mike's casket.

Claire is holding a hankie to her mouth. Madie is wailing.

Mick helps load the casket onto the cart as Claire, Madie, and Cait, with baby Mike in her arms, run to his embrace.

Six months have passed since Mike and Griff came home. The leaves have turned and dropped in magnificent reds and yellows all over the yards or have blown into the lake. It's Veterans Day, and Mick, Cait, baby Mike, Claire, and Madie are gathered at the table for dinner. Their heads are bowed, and Claire says, "This is the gift of the whole universe. The earth, the sky, and much hard work. May we live in a way to deserve it. And dear Lord, blessings on Mike as he watches over us. Amen."

Baby Mike is smiling in his high chair and starts a run of gibberish that has the table laughing. They pass plates of mashed potatoes and peas. Mick stands up, his elbow wrapped with an elastic bandage, and starts cutting through a nice, fat chicken. He wears a black T-shirt with OSU in big orange letters on it. He looks strong and healthy and clear-eyed.

"Mick," Cait says, as they start to eat, "what do you think about your mom running for city council?"

"Maybe she can get me out of those parking tickets," he says.

Claire blushes. "I'm still just thinking about it."

"Well, I think it is tremendous!" Madie says. "Mom fought with those jokers on the school board all the time, and I think she's ready to take on the hard heads at City Hall."

"Oh, mercy." Claire sighs.

Mick turns to her and says, "Well, Mom, as you know, I was accepted at Oregon State. What you don't know is that I'm going to play baseball. Tryouts are in a couple of weeks."

"That's awesome! Dad would like that," says Madie.

Claire is fighting tears as she smiles at Mick. "Yes. Yes, he would."

Claire lifts her wineglass, and everyone follows. "To Mike," she says. They all repeat the toast.

Then she holds up a newspaper clipping covered in clear plastic. "I found this when I was going through some of your dad's things. And even though this is Veterans Day and not Memorial Day, I'd like to share what he wrote from years ago." No one moves, except little Mike, who is working on a piece of banana. Claire sips some water and reads.

"Memorial Day, by Mike Kelly. It's almost Memorial Day, and I'm in our backyard, sitting on the patio, across from our pink dogwood tree, contemplating changing my way of thinking. I'm also watching my not-yet-two-year-old boy, Mick, totter across the grass, chasing the cat. Mick likes to run. He stops at a bed of blueberries. He looks curiously at the berries, bends, and stuffs a couple in his mouth.

"As we march through spring, I find that along with this change in weather, there is a change in me. I'm forty-five years old, and the darkness of the jungle is fading. I can barely remember who I killed or what day Jesse died or Padre. Did our dog handler perish in the rice paddy or close his eyes as we lifted him into the chopper? And what happened to his German shepherd, panting next to him?

"This year, I'm questioning the sanity of war. I'm getting old, and I feel my anger and grief are dying, just as the boys did that I once carried out of the battlefield. I can barely remember why I thought fighting in Vietnam was just. I am confused and wondering if these calls to battle are worth the human sacrifice. I suppose having a son inspires this way of thinking.

"Claire and I took Madie and little Mick with us to the nursery to look for more blueberry plants. He sat in a shopping cart while Claire watched Madie and made the executive decisions. In the aisle next to the strawberries, I noticed an older man moving slowly, shoulders rolled, wearing a Korean Veterans hat. We talked and shared a war. The man told me about the horrible battle at the frozen Chosin Reservoir and how the enemy would attack at night, in waves, diving into the perimeter's concertina wire, while their Chinese comrades ran across their backs, screaming, firing rifles, driving into a hell storm. 'We killed them by the thousands,' he said, hands shaking, eyes misting. My friend Tom Paulus also fought in the Korean cold, where rivers froze and tanks rolled across them. Where our weary soldiers would fall in the snow, exhausted or wounded, and would quickly freeze solid, like the river. Over thirty-three thousand Americans died in Korea, six hundred thousand North and South Korean soldiers, maybe a million Chinese, and millions of civilians. Yet, who wonders why or knows what for?

"Does going to war to solve conflict make sense anymore? Is the human cost worth what we achieve? We fight and die and pile up our youth like human debris, and does it make sense? Steven Grant is from Eugene and graduated from Oregon State University before he became a lieutenant in the marine corps and fought in Vietnam. He was awarded a Bronze Star and was wounded. After years of working on a book, he's written what critics say is an epic novel about Vietnam, titled *War and God*. One night, he led an assault up a hill against fortified enemy bunkers and overran the North Vietnamese Army's position. 'We killed them and kept firing on the NVA as they retreated. Why did I order that? I could have stopped the killing. Then the next day, we abandoned the hill and nothing changed.' By the end of the war, over fifty-eight thousand American soldiers were dead.

"I know I couldn't charge up a hill anymore. Or even hump my machine gun and ammo across our backyard without blowing out my knee again. But Korea and Vietnam were nightmares from decades ago. What really matters now is what our marines and soldiers of today are fighting for. Is it democracy? Freedom? Will we be safer?

"Tim Sullivan is twenty-six and a sergeant in the marine corps. He's tall and sturdy, and from a distance, you'd never know he was blown up by an IED during Desert Storm a few years ago. He has a long, jagged scar running down his neck, a wrecked hand, and an arm that looks, well, like it was torn apart by an explosion. Not too long ago, his pretty wife and their baby sat at his bedside, praying for his survival. This is a guy who should be angry but isn't. Who didn't have to go to war but did. And why? 'I wanted to go to do something amazing. I wanted to help my country. I'm not political. I fought for my buddies over there. And I'd go back in a heartbeat.'

"We planted the blueberry bushes, and Mick played in the mud, quite happy. I want him to grow up clear-eyed and strong, play baseball maybe. I don't want him to end up wounded like Tim or damaged inside. It's almost Memorial Day, and I've almost changed my way of thinking. Maybe it's time to end our country's madness. I just wish I knew how."

Claire lays the story on the table.

Marines are fighting, street to street, in Fallujah. There is rifle fire rattling the buildings, and there are explosions. Insurgents dressed in black lie dead in the road or are on rooftops, firing.

Mick leads a squad up the street, hugging the building, running, firing his M240, and then he turns back and yells, "Pops!"

Mick sits up in bed, sweating. Cait is by his side. A crib is in the corner. The moon is shining through his window. The clock on his nightstand reads 5:00 a.m. He gets out of bed and pulls on a pair of sweat pants and an OSU sweatshirt. He sits on the bed and laces his tennis shoes and then grabs a baseball bat that's leaning against the crib. He reaches in the crib and smiles and touches little Mike.

In the backyard of the Kelly home on the lake, there is the sound of an aluminum bat striking baseballs. Under a spotlight attached to the back of the house, Mick is hitting balls off a batting tee into a net, again and again, until the sun rises.

ACKNOWLEDGMENTS

I want to thank the following folks for working with me to help shape A Soldier's Son. My wife Colleen O'Callaghan. She edits everything I write and provides great insight, support and encouragement. Margaret Dahl, my voice of clarity. Pam Wells. Marlene Howard. Karl Marlantes. Karen Karbo. Larry Colton, Pete Charleston and Tom McGee, a fellow marine. Thank you all, so very much.

ABOUT THE AUTHOR

Jack Estes is also the author of the critically acclaimed Vietnam memoir, A Field of Innocence. As an 18 year old Marine Mr. Estes fought in Vietnam in 1968/69 during the bloodiest years of the war, where he was wounded and decorated for heroism. When he came home he attended Portland State University and Southern Illinois University, and began writing and speaking about the plight of veterans. He became a National Collegiate Speech Champion, talking about war and the mental and physical damage it does to soldiers and their families. Over the years his articles and essays have appeared in Newsweek, the Wall Street Journal, Chicago Tribune, LA Times, Timberline Review, the Oregonian and many more. In 1993, he and his wife traveled to Vietnam to deliver medical and educational supplies and toys to schools, hospitals and orphanages. He also returned to the village where he once lived in, to what his wife Colleen calls his "original point of pain." The purpose was to carry humanitarian goods instead of a machine gun, to replace bad memories with good. He also wanted to try to find a Vietnamese soldier who once helped save his life. From that trip Jack and Colleen created the Fallen Warriors Foundation, to honor the sacrifices of American soldiers, and to help heal the pain of war. Over the years, Fallen Warriors Foundation has delivered hundreds of thousands of dollars of medical and educational goods to the poorest of the poor, in tiny Vietnam villages. Jack has taken doctors and nurses back to remote villages and primitive hospitals to give care. He led a group of disabled combat veterans to Vietnam, to their original point of pain to help them heal. In addition, the foundation has held retreats, events and theater pieces for veterans and their loved ones. In 2013 Fallen Warriors Foundation released a documentary about veterans and Post Traumatic Stress Disorder and co-produced a documentary called Mind Zone on how veterans are treated for psychological trauma in current battle zones.

Please visit:
www.jackestes.com
www.fallenwarriorsfoundation.com